Praise for
You Were Always Mine

'The work of Jo Piazza and Christine Pride sits squarely at the tender intersection of race, class, and ethics – wrapped in beautiful prose and a killer plot that keeps you turning the pages. Before you begin *You Were Always Mine,* ask yourself why you often see white foster parents with Black kids . . . but rarely the other way around. What makes a family? Who has the right to raise a child? Does race matter more than love or security? And perhaps most important of all – why don't we feel comfortable asking these questions?'
JODI PICOULT

'I picked up this book on a Sunday morning and could do nothing else until I finished it that evening. Tender, provocative, thoughtful – I was invested in this story from the very first page'
KATE BAER, *New York Times* bestselling author

'A touching, deeply thoughtful meditation on motherhood, race, chosen family and the many forms of love that make up the lives of women. Cinnamon's love for her adopted daughter and her willingness to challenge age-old structures of power in order to provide the love she so desperately craved in her own childhood is a reminder that in attempting to rescue others, we are sometimes able to save ourselves'
ASHA LEMMIE, *New York Times* bestselling author

Christine Pride worked in publishing for fifteen years. Over the course of her career, Christine worked with a variety of established and debut writers and published many *New York Times* bestsellers and critically acclaimed books including *From Scratch*, *Heaven is Here*, and *A Reason to Believe*. Christine pens a regular column, 'Race Matters', for *Cup of Jo* alongside her novel-writing.

Jo Piazza is an award-winning journalist and editor who has written for *The Wall Street Journal*, *The New York Times*, *Glamour*, *Marie Claire* and *Elle*. The bestselling author of *The Knockoff*, *How to Be Married*, *Fitness Junkie*, and *Charlotte Walsh Likes to Win*, she currently lives in Philadelphia with her husband and three children.

Their debut novel as a writing duo, *We Are Not Like Them*, was published to wide critical acclaim and was a *Good Morning America* Book Club Pick. *You Were Always Mine* is their second novel.

you were always mine

CHRISTINE PRIDE & JO PIAZZA

HQ

ONE PLACE. MANY STORIES

This novel is entirely a work of fiction. The names, characters and incidents portrayed in it are the work of the author's imagination. Any resemblance to actual persons, living or dead, events or localities is entirely coincidental.

HQ
An imprint of HarperCollins*Publishers* Ltd
1 London Bridge Street
London SE1 9GF

www.harpercollins.co.uk

HarperCollins*Publishers*
Macken House, 39/40 Mayor Street Upper,
Dublin 1, D01 C9W8, Ireland

This edition 2023

1
First published in Great Britain by
HQ, an imprint of HarperCollins*Publishers* Ltd 2023

A catalogue record for this book is available from the British Library.

ISBN: HB: 978-0-00-833598-4
TPB: 978-0-00-833599-1

FSC
www.fsc.org
MIX
Paper | Supporting responsible forestry
FSC™ C007454

This book is produced from independently certified FSC™ paper to ensure responsible forest management.

For more information visit: www.harpercollins.co.uk/green

Interior design by Erika R Genova

Printed and Bound in the UK using 100% Renewable Electricity at
CPI Group (UK) Ltd, Croydon, CR0 4YY

To our mothers, Tracey and Sallie.
To all mothers.
And to anyone who is childless by choice or circumstance.

PROLOGUE

Dear You,

I was desperate to make everything perfect when I left.

If you knew how many times I rearranged the quilt around you, tucking and untucking it over and over until I could get the little yellow duck in the corner lined up just so. Even with all my planning, it all came down to this one thing, this one stupid thing, and if I could get that right, then it would mean it would all be okay.

You were fast asleep so the duck didn't make one bit of difference to you, much less the matching yellow knit cap on your teeny head, but I pulled it down until it grazed your barely there eyebrows. One last time, I let my fingers trace their soft arcs.

I leaned down to sniff you, the delicious scent of newborn breath, brand-new skin, and life itself. If I inhaled deeply enough, I thought I might keep that magical smell stored inside me forever. But when I exhaled, it was gone, and that panicked me, that feeling like I couldn't hold on to anything. So I focused on memorizing your face, every detail, even though it was already imprinted in my brain, seared in my soul. I stared down at your translucent lids, blue veins showing through like little streams, and kept debating whether I wanted you to open your eyes or not. On the one hand, to see them just one more time. On the other hand, if you did flutter them open right then and looked at me, I knew I would never be able to leave.

Everyone thinks their baby is beautiful, even when they're not. But you truly were, especially your eyes. They were these perfectly round blue pools, clear as glaciers, impossibly wide. Striking. I knew it would be your thing. All your life people would say, "Oh but those eyes."

I squirmed down on my back next to you, ignoring the grass and dirt that wormed into my ponytail. The view above you was perfect, a hashtag of leafy branches crisscrossing a patch of fluffy clouds.

It was when I realized that the color of the sky at that very moment was the exact same color as your eyes that I truly lost it. It was then I knew I had to go, right that second before leaving became impossible. I bolted to my feet and slapped my cheek like I did when I was having a nightmare and I needed to wake myself up.

I made it two steps down the path and then two more, before I stumbled back. I tried not to beat myself up about returning to you since I'd known it would take more than one try to tear myself away. But I also knew time was running out. Like I said, I had planned everything so carefully. For weeks and weeks. And now I was risking it all by running late and lingering there, exposed. So I took off again, distracted momentarily by the damp circles on my knees where I had kneeled beside you saying "I'm sorry, I'm sorry" over and over. This time I made it a few feet farther before I remembered. The note! I wiggled it out of the pocket of my hoodie. The card I had labored over for so many nights.

Quick as I could, I tucked it under you and then darted over to the edge of the pond where I pulled out my phone and threw it as far and hard as I could into the murky water. I was gone down the path before I even heard the splash, running faster and faster, despite my sore, swollen boobs and the fire between my legs, like I was a kid again, flying top speed through the soybean fields, my long auburn hair streaking behind me like a flag. Now I was nineteen and fat and slow, but in my mind, for one split second, I was that little girl. And if I ran fast and hard enough, I could outrun my problems. Or outrun what I'd done. I was heaving by the time I made it to the bus station, sweat and tears rolling every which way. I looked almost as wrecked as I felt. I remember catching my reflection in the bathroom mirror and thinking, *This is it. This is your lowest point.* And there was something freeing about that, just letting myself sink to rock bottom, nowhere lower to go.

Or so I thought.

Turns out there's always another millimeter. As the Greyhound bus was lumbering out of the station, I realized I forgot the most important thing. I forgot to say I love you. My body jerked with a laugh and a sob, like it was all mixed up and didn't know what to do with this realization. Like my soul itself skipped and twitched. It was all I could do to stay in my seat when an invisible force was making my legs twitch to run up the aisle and beg the driver to turn around. It's the same force that haunts me to this day, the one that tugs at me to reach out to you despite my promises.

Most days, the good days at least, I can convince myself that you know this, how much I love you. Wherever you are, right now at this moment, you know deep in your bones that I loved you from the moment you came into the world. On days when I need more convincing, I say it aloud, sometimes a whisper, sometimes a scream in the wind: *She knows you love her. Of course she knows that. You're her mother.*

CHAPTER ONE

Cinnamon Haynes can't remember when she stopped wanting things in life. When she was younger, she was filled with longing for silky straight hair that would slide around her shoulders, for bright-white Rollerblades with pink wheels, for her own room where she could paint her walls neon green or orange or whatever color she wanted and have one of those beds with a canopy over it and a slew of pictures in white frames made out of seashells. She would also have photos to put in those frames, pictures of her friends and family. She had none of that.

Perhaps her strongest longing was for her mother to come back from wherever she'd disappeared to when Cinnamon was barely out of diapers, leaving her with her sixty-two-year-old grandmother who passed away three years later. No, her strongest longing was actually for Grandma Thelma to return from the dead and save Cinnamon from everything that came after.

These yearnings used to be a roaring furnace deep within her, hot and constant and consuming. But at some point along the way the fire just burned itself out, slowly, little dying embers one by one, and what was left when the smoke cleared was acceptance: this was, and would always be, the life she got. It was almost liberating because with that resignation came the freedom of surrendering, come what may. It was pointless to pretend that she had any control over her circumstances, better to abandon herself to the current and let it carry her along while maintaining an almost detached curiosity about where she would eventually wash up, which turned out to be here: a pin dot of a town spitting distance from the Atlantic Ocean in a run-down but cozy cottage, listening to her husband snoring like a lawn mower in bed next to her.

Lucky and Cinnamon aren't two words that rightfully belong in the same sentence, but some higher force had a hand somewhere along the way. Because if you'd told her twenty years ago that this future was waiting for her, she would have laughed out loud and asked what you must have been smoking to see *this* in the cards. The statistics promised a very different trajectory for a girl like her: she was supposed to be alone, homeless, dead, on drugs, or some combination of it all. But somehow—through a rare and brilliant twist of luck, or grace or fate—she'd found herself in this life and let herself settle into it like a warm bath. Granted, it's not like her present circumstances are particularly opulent by any means—it's a little gold band on her ring finger, a roof over her head, and a "real" job at the local community college, with a desk and benefits, where she gets to help kids and maybe make a difference in their lives. Wasn't it something that that could feel like hitting the lottery?

This is why she's constantly reminding herself to have the good sense to appreciate what she has and wish every day that it doesn't get snatched away. Or more specifically, that no one discovers that she doesn't deserve it after all. *Good, quiet, grateful.* That's her mantra.

So why, then, is she being tormented by the same relentless dream night after night, the one that leaves her shaken and unsettled all day? Here she is now, blinking up at the ceiling, with a hammering heart and beads of sweat frizzing her edges before it's even crossed the sun's mind to make an appearance.

In the dream—nightmare, more accurately—she's riding an elevator in some impossibly high skyscraper in a gleaming, fancy city she's never been to. People get on and off as it climbs until Cinnamon finds herself all alone on the top floor. The doors refuse to open no matter what combination of buttons she jabs. Eventually the walls start to press in on her from all sides until the elevator shrinks to the size of a closet, then a coffin. It's a good day when she wakes up before the ceiling starts pressing down on top of her thick braids. Today is not one of those days.

She knows getting back to sleep at this point is about as likely as the Mega Millions ticket on her bedside table being a winner. So she slinks out of bed and pads down the hall to the tiny spare room at the back of the house. In the corner, behind a clutter of old junk they never cleared out when they inherited the place from Jayson's grandmother, there's a saggy corduroy beanbag chair nestled under the window. A teetering pile of books flanks either side. She affectionately thinks of this little clearing she's carved out for herself as her reading nook—emphasis on *nook*. If there were a place that embodied Cinnamon's lifelong quest to feel safe, it would be this one right here. Dark, tucked away, and all hers.

The book is just where she left it—hidden under the beanbag she settles into. Old habits die hard, and hiding things is one of them. She digs out the stained, dog-eared copy of *Charlotte's Web*, one of two possessions she's had since childhood. The other, Grandma Thelma's leather-bound Bible, she keeps in her bedside drawer like they do in hotels.

Reading is supposed to calm her. Books have always been her truest salvation and most constant companion. For some people it's drugs or booze. Cinnamon has always steered clear of those, maybe out of an innate sense of self-preservation—losing herself to them would have been too easy. As far as addictions go, reading was at least one that couldn't destroy her. And she'd bet good money it was as effective at soothing her as any of the drugs she'd never tried would be. Cheaper too. For as long as she had a book open in her lap, she had a portal to escape everything going on around her and in her mind. And so reading became her respite from the very first moment she made the wild discovery that she could string letters into words, words into sentences, and sentences into ideas. Since then she's had to have a book within easy reach, like a life jacket or fire extinguisher. Every time she settles down in this beanbag chair she might as well be ten years old, tucked away in the corner of the Wooten Hills Regional Library, which is where she'd stolen the book in her hands from. After reading it through eight times crouched in the back of the stacks, she didn't see how she had much of a choice. She simply couldn't live without it, without knowing she could devour *Charlotte's Web* at least a hundred more times, its pages warping with age. And it wasn't like anyone was going to buy her a brand-new meticulously wrapped copy for her birthday. Any guilt that she'd felt slipping it into her bag was offset when Sarah the librarian smiled at her on the way out. Cinnamon swore Sarah could see the book burning a hole in her bag and knew her secret. So when Sarah nodded and let her go, she figured the librarian—her favorite—understood. There were so few mercies in Cinnamon's young life—she couldn't be shy about grabbing on to one or two.

The problem is, reading is bringing her zero comfort this morning. The words just dance around the page like waving hands, whispering, *Girl, wait—is this all there is?* What is she to make of this sudden restlessness that came on like an itch she'll never be able to reach? This growing anxiety that even a book can't quell.

Lucia has decided this is all just the birthday blues ahead of Cinnamon's thirty-fifth birthday next week. Cinnamon had no intention of mentioning to her best friend how out of sorts she was feeling lately, but when Lucia caught her zoning out while sitting in her driveway a few weeks ago, some sort of explanation was required, so she admitted she was a little off. But Lucia's theory doesn't hold much water with Cinnamon. She's never had the time or luxury for existential angst.

Lucia had hopped in the passenger seat while Cinnamon was still in Lucia's circular driveway and had an immediate solution for her woes. "You know what'll break you out of this funk? A party! I'm going to throw you a big birthday bash. I'll do it on Friday, the night before, so Jayson can still sweep you away for something on your actual birthday Saturday."

Lucia has more faith in Jayson's planning than Cinnamon does. And her friend's offer was less about Cinnamon and more about Lucia having an excuse to throw a party, but putting her hatred of being the center of attention aside, Cinnamon agreed with the hope that it would work to snap her out of these doldrums. It will also be the very first birthday party Cinnamon has ever had, and it's fitting that it's being thrown by the first real and true friend she's ever had too. She can't tell if any of that is sweet or sad, but that's the case with so much, isn't it? A murky mix of the two.

Cinnamon abandons *Charlotte's Web* and gives herself fully over to the angst—it's like trying to fight the current anyway; there's really no point and ultimately it's more exhausting than just giving in. Tracing its source is futile too, but she can identify at least one likely culprit: her husband. The anger and resentment sticks to her like the film of tomato sauce you can't quite get out of the Tupperware no matter how hard you scrub. This, despite her best efforts to get past his shocking foolery. Cinnamon's worked as hard to forgive him as she has at anything else in her life. There's a stack of books in the recesses of her closet that's a testament to that commitment. *How to Improve Your Marriage without Talking about It; Be the Spouse YOU Want to Have; Forgiveness Is for You.* The goal was to read herself to a better place. If books can save your life, maybe they can also save your marriage. It just isn't working as fast or effectively as she hoped.

Well, the forgiveness book has helped a little. It could be the author's wisdom, but it could also be because Cinnamon well knows she can't afford to let herself stay angry at Jayson for any real length of time. Which is why it makes her laugh now to think just how mad she was after he dropped his bombshell last summer—mad enough to actually have packed her bags.

She'd also contemplated setting Jayson's clothes on fire, *Waiting to Exhale* style, on her way out. But that was a bridge too far, and she only got as far as the front porch anyway. Not even to the car. Because where would she even go? Move in with Lucia and Adam and the twins? Hardly, even if they did have the space in their McMansion. Was Cinnamon going to call all the family she didn't have? Was she going to call Reverend Rick and slink back to Atlanta and her attic apartment above All Souls Heavenly Fellowship storefront church? She'd come too far for that, and besides, the Rev had already done enough for her for several lifetimes. Her lack of options made her feel the same as when the elevator wall came pressing on her head in her nightmares, and she had a mighty headache to show for it.

So she'd set about the work of forgiveness, which was a new skill to Cinnamon. Given that the trail of people who've hurt and wronged her is longer than all the rivers in the world strung together, there was no way to muster enough energy for all the forgiving she would've had to do, so she'd never even bothered. But Jayson is a different story. With Jayson she doesn't have a choice. That's marriage, right? You have to keep on keeping on somehow? Or else . . . or else what?

Sometimes she tries to think of it this way: she should actually be grateful that Jayson messed up like he did. It balances the scales between them to be reminded that he isn't Mr. Perfect, as much as he'd like everyone to believe that. He also isn't the only one to have lied. In a way, it's a silver lining that his infuriating antics soothed Cinnamon's guilt about all the secrets she's kept from her husband. Except he came clean. And that makes one of them.

A shadow passes outside the door and Jayson appears in the hallway, as if her very thoughts conjured him, as if he just knew he was winding through her brain at 6 a.m. She tries to get her mind to just hush up, a futile task if there ever was one.

Jayson stands there a moment, watching her pretend to read before he speaks. "You good? A little early to have your nose in a book. Even for you."

"Yeah, I'm okay. Just couldn't sleep." She hasn't told him about the nightmares. Or the lingering rage.

"Is it early menopause?"

"JAYSON!"

"Girl, you know I'm just messing with you. We need to get you some melatonin tonight. You've been restless for a minute now."

"Yeah, maybe that'd help. I got a lot on my mind."

"Let me guess. Thinking about some drama with one of your students again?"

"Yeah, that's it." Her students and their constant struggles are always an easy scapegoat for any stress.

He squeezes in next to her even though there isn't room for two on this chair. "Cece, you know what your problem is?" Jayson doesn't wait for her to respond before leveling his familiar accusation.

"You care too much. About those kids. About their problems. You gotta learn to let go, to leave all that at work."

She scoots away from him, tucking *Charlotte's Web* back under the beanbag. "Yeah, you're right, Jay," she agrees. Even though she's lying—there's no such thing as caring too much. And it isn't the point anyway.

She swivels her head around, taking in the piles of boxes, the old yellow phone books, VHS tapes, and the scattered Styrofoam pellets that have leaked from the beanbag chair all over the floor. "We need to do something about this room."

"Too early for that too." Jayson yawns loud enough to wake the closest neighbors a mile down the road.

He promised he'd fix this place up as soon as they'd moved in three years ago. Jayson promises a lot of things. He has more plans and promises than most people have pants. His schemes and dreams are how they'd ended up back here in Sibley Bay, the little town where he was born and raised, where he got to be a big fish in a little pond instead of the goldfish in an ocean he'd been in Atlanta. Those schemes and dreams might also destroy them both, but she can't think about it right now. She's got to get to work—to the job that currently, and barely, supports them both, even though she doesn't want to think about that either.

"Well, it may be early, but I'm going to be late if I sit here too much longer."

She lets Jayson pull her up from the beanbag chair, if not out of this dreadful mood. It is nice to pause in his arms for a minute, breathing him in. Despite herself, the urge to stay nestled in the crook of his neck all day, warm morning breath on her face, comes on strong. But work awaits. She has an appointment with one of her students at 8 a.m. sharp, and Preeti is sure to be in her office fifteen minutes early, already in a tizzy about something or other.

Back in the bedroom, she digs out a tired old black dress, which feels right on so many levels and is the only thing she can think to wear to the work party she does not want to go to tonight. She does have a brand-new dress tucked away in the back of the closet that she got on a whim for her birthday party next Friday, but every time her eye catches the price tag, she vows to return it. And anyway, she wouldn't waste it on Vera's retirement bash. The woman's pale, pinched face and her string of different yappy "therapy" Yorkies have greeted visitors to the reception desk at Sibley Bay Community College since it opened its doors forty years ago, and now her reign is done and she's moving closer to her son somewhere in Texas. To which Cinnamon thinks, *Good riddance*. This is a woman who announced out of nowhere one day, "You know, Cinnamon, you're the first colored friend I ever had," with the proudest look on her face like she'd earned the hardest Girl Scout badge tying knots or some other useless activity. Cinnamon was not the least bit surprised by this information, nor by Vera's use of the term "colored," nor by the fact that Vera obviously expected to be rewarded for this confession, judging by the eagerness with which she awaited a reply. Cinnamon's "Okay, cool," apparently fell short of whatever Vera was hoping for. She was clearly supposed to be congratulating her on her valiant open-mindedness. But it was a helluva lot nicer than what she wanted to say, which was, "What on earth makes you think we're friends?"

Cinnamon slips the dress over her head and appraises herself in the wobbly full-length mirror leaning on the wall, twisting around to decide if she needs Spanx. Not that she would suffer Spanx for Vera, and anyway, her hips and butt are as narrow as they ever were. She takes in her perky breasts, smooth dark skin, and round doll-like eyes with highly batable lashes, if Cinnamon had ever mastered the art. Even the stray tooth that refused to fall in line somehow adds to the overall effect of her shy smile, which is good because braces weren't in the cards. Cinnamon allows herself her vanity, beauty being one of those things like a trust fund or royal lineage—it doesn't matter who's deserving; it is the luck of the draw, a blessing bestowed by fate, which overall, has not been particularly kind to her. So who is she *not* to acknowledge and appreciate this one saving grace? She doesn't take for granted the times it got her an extra kindness, or how it allowed people to assume things about her and her life. She's no fool—she knows it got her her husband too. She had easily marked Jayson as the sort to want a pretty wife to show off and complete his "image." At least she had that to trade for love.

Suddenly, Jayson's voice floats over the racket he's making deep in the closet. "You know where the medium suitcase is?"

"It's nested in the larger one. Like always. Why do you need a suitcase?"

He reminds her about the deep-sea fishing trip he's going on this weekend that she'd fully blocked out after unsuccessfully trying to make the case that this was not the best use of the funds they didn't have. Jayson claimed Alex, one of his buddies who just got a big bonus, was bankrolling the whole group and renting some ridiculous yacht, a move Jayson described with equal parts bitterness and reverence. "You know how Alex loves to show off he's ballin' like that. White dudes and their boats, man. We make it far enough out there, it's going to be some middle passage shit. Can't wait to see Alex's face when I bring that shit up to mess with him."

When he emerges from the closet clutching their faded gray American Tourister, he looks confused. "Why you all dressed up? You usually wear those Oprah's Favorite Things leggings on Fridays."

It's her turn for reminders. "I'm going to be home late tonight. Remember? I have Vera's retirement thing."

"Oh man, that crusty cracker."

"Jay!"

"What? This is the woman who called you 'colored' to your face. If that doesn't qualify her as an ole crusty cracker, I don't know what does."

He gives her a playful tap on the butt. Jayson always jokes that he found the only Black girl with a flat ass in all of Atlanta.

"Well, I'm just glad you have a reason to wear something other than those tired pants. Lookin' all grown and sexy this morning. Actually, why don't you get over here and let me remind you just how fine you are." He kicks the suitcase away and makes a show of falling onto the bed and patting the mattress beside him.

His hungry eyes send a surge of love through her that scatters all the angst hovering over her this morning. It occurs to her that the key to forgiveness could be simpler than she was allowing. Maybe the path to settling herself down once and for all is to remind herself as often as necessary how much she loves her husband. She truly does. With his slow drawl and easy charm and the way he can tell the same joke a hundred times and still make it funny. Also, good Lord he has the most beautiful smile she's ever seen on a grown man, and damned if he isn't always smiling like he doesn't have a care in the world. Jayson is relentlessly upbeat, more than ought to be possible, given this world. He doesn't have the stone-faced expressions most brothers wear—either an affected swagger or an aggressive stoicism, world-weary or too cool or both. It was the first thing she noticed about him—that Labrador puppy energy—when he'd sidled up next to her five years ago during a packed book reading in a too-hot Barnes & Noble in Buckhead. All those teeth lined up like shiny piano keys when he turned to her, looking down at her sweatshirt, clearly ready to spit out his best game. "Spelman, huh? Smart and fine, I see." There was an honest-to-God actual sparkle in his eyes, along with a touch of hazel, or maybe the light was catching them just so, but Cinnamon felt that thing, a terrifying wooziness at the instant attraction and the shock that this good-looking man with his expensive-smelling cologne and Italian leather satchel was so interested in *her.* She'd looked down at the thrift store sweatshirt she'd forgotten she was wearing and nodded, only slightly, but her being a Spelman girl was still the first of many lies she'd let him believe about her life before they met.

Jayson's interest, attraction, and eventual love felt like a gift. It did then and it still does.

But as she meets his gaze again in the mirror now, a familiar question nags her: Did she fall in love with Jayson, or with the version of herself that he evidently saw—someone worthy of love and commitment? Her love is all mixed up with so many other complicated emotions—namely, a white-hot gratitude. Being loved, she fears, is something she may never get used to, even after all these years. But no one has to know that, least of all her husband.

"I don't have time for all that this morning, Jay." She eases the rejection with a smile at him in the mirror. "But how about I make you some eggs?"

She doesn't know how to account for this, but out of nowhere she wants to make her husband breakfast, even more so when he looks downright touched.

"For real? It's been a minute since you made me breakfast like you used to."

It's been more than a minute—it's been almost a whole year. Ever since the day he said those words, "Cinnamon, I have to tell you something." It was "Cinnamon" not "Cece," which stopped her cold. In the wake of his confession, she'd let up on her determined efforts to be some sort of perfect sitcom wife, television being her only real model of what marriage should look like. The desire to make her man eggs this morning is her vigilance returning to her. Swallowing her pride, being the dutiful wife, remembering to be grateful—these are the ingredients to make her feel safe. *Good, quiet, grateful.*

"Oh stop, I can make my man a couple of eggs now and then."

"Cool. I'll be down in a minute." Before she can get to the bedroom door, he calls out. "Unless . . . wanna come back and . . . ?"

The eggs are one thing, but he's pushing it. She hesitates for a minute, trying to decide if she has it in her to peel off this dress, crawl back into bed, and give herself over to her husband. She knows Jayson's invite is only half-hearted; he's like a little kid finishing dessert—you always ask for extra even when you know the answer'll be no. But she's tempted. Tempted to lose herself under Jayson's weight, have all these discomfiting feelings washed away with sweat-soaked skin, hide in her body so her mind can't reach her.

As a consolation she goes back and kisses him. Jayson grabs her arm to hold her there. When he shoots her that lopsided grin, she knows a request is coming before his lips even fix to move. "Any chance you can swing by Sandy's on the way home after Vera's thing? I've been craving creole catfish bad."

"Yeah, yeah, no problem." She lets her tone sound all begrudging, but she means it. She could use a pile of creole catfish too. And they can watch an episode or two of *Power* they've been saving.

Cinnamon leans down and nestles her face in Jayson's soft waves. He reaches for her and pulls her back to kiss her lips, mumbling, "I love you." Though love was never really the problem. It almost never is.

The bird is an omen. Cinnamon will come to see that later, but for now she's not one to believe in signs or magic, or spells, or even wishes on birthday candles. The bird though. That bird. Sitting right there in the kitchen, smack in the middle of the table, perched on the towering stack of past-due bills like it's the most natural thing in the world. It is about the teeniest thing she's ever seen, bright neon yellow as a highlighter and as still as a ceramic figurine. In fact, she assumes it's a strange little statue until it suddenly cocks its head.

Cinnamon's eyes dart around their kitchen. The bird squawks, loud and urgent.

How in the world did this creature get in here and what does it want?

One of her foster dads, Doc Parker, had been an "amateur ornithologist." That's how she learned the word "ornithologist," which she eagerly added to her mental vocabulary collection that would eventually lead her to a near perfect verbal score on the PSATs, useless as being in the 98th percentile would prove to be. That new word was the best thing about living with the Parkers. It was the first time she'd ever lived with white people—Doc and his wife and their two blond children who stared at Cinnamon like she was a rare bird in a tree—and amateur bird-watching was nothing if not peak whiteness. It seemed crazy to take long drives to the middle of nowhere and try to spot birds in trees before they flew away. Somehow Doc Parker always took her out in his wood-paneled station wagon on days that were hotter than the devil's breath. Doc delighted in "exposing" her to a new hobby. White people were always very big on "exposing" you to things, as if they held a passport to a different world, which they basically did. The bird-watching grew on her in the six months she lived with the Parkers before Doc got relocated to a job in Portland and they left her behind like an old piece of furniture too unwieldy and impractical to bother to move. But those first few times they went bird-watching, she hated it. She felt like she was going to die of heat stroke or boredom, whichever got her first. There were a thousand things she'd rather be doing (namely, reading), but whenever he looked at her expectantly and asked if she was having fun, she beamed. "I am!" The lie came easily, a reflex and a survival instinct, for Doc Parker and everyone else. The lies were second nature by then; they flew from her lips as smoothly as all those birds taking flight: where her mother was (acting in Hollywood, or sometimes dead of cancer, depending on Cinnamon's mood), vacations she had taken (Paris, twice—*as if*), and activities she excelled at (ice-skating and horseback riding).

The reality: she'd never left the city of Youngstown, let alone the state of Ohio, before she was shipped to Atlanta at fifteen, and she had no idea where her mother was since she'd walked out the door when Cinnamon was three, leaving Grandma Thelma with a confused and heartbroken toddler. She *could* have been good with skates or horses if someone had given her lessons.

Cinnamon rationalized that her lies were harmless, victimless; it was more a game, all the ways she pretended that she had a better childhood than she had—like, for example, that she did get to go to college. She was so convinced of the alternative reality she'd conjured that by the time she met Jayson at that bookstore, tales from her spruced-up past burst from her so easily it was hard to believe they weren't true. Sometimes she could swear she remembered the feeling of being in a campus bookstore, a hefty stack of textbooks making her arms quiver, and late-night study sessions with friends over greasy pizza in her dorm room. Who could blame her or begrudge her her fantasies? Jayson least of all, if he knew the truth. After all, this is the version of herself—stable, educated, well-raised—that he fell in love with, and besides, he tries to reinvent himself every other day. Anyway, the lies are just a way of sparing her husband and everyone else any need to feel sorry for her. They can save their pity for some other poor Black girl who can't catch a break. Heaven knows there's no shortage of those. In Cinnamon's alternate universe, she escaped being a stereotype. The effort and toll to maintain the web of falsehoods to everyone in the world, including her husband, are, in the end, worth it just to be relieved of that burden.

She's angry that the past is creeping up on her this morning, and she takes the blame out on the bird.

"You need to get on outta here, right now!" She's hollering at the bird, but it may as well be the memories.

She moves slowly toward the patio door on tippy-toes, as if backing away from a deranged criminal, not a parakeet-looking something or other. Hopefully this bird has two working wings. Her plans for the day do not include nursing an injured animal back to health. She has scant experience with nurturing living creatures. She always wanted a dog, but Jayson would never go for it, his allergies and all. She trips on a thought, stopping short right there with the patio door handle in her grip: how sad it was that she's never had one single living thing to take care of in her life except for her husband. Not even so much as a plant. She vows to ask Jayson for one for her birthday, a succulent with thick, spiky leaves that makes her think of the desert and survival.

Cinnamon pushes her hip against the metal bar and throws open the rusty patio door while yelling, "Shoo!" as loud as she can.

The bird looks startled and then briefly confused about why Cinnamon doesn't want the two of them to spend the morning together. It cocks its head and gives her a look that actually makes her laugh a little and take out her phone to snap a picture to send to Lucia later. By the time the phone is back in her pocket, the bird has hightailed it out of there.

She will come back to this morning, over and over, where she's making eggs, kissing her husband, salivating at the creole catfish they'll never have. Vera's dreaded party that, turns out, she'll have a great excuse to miss. The promise of sex that will go unkept. And that bird. That silly yellow bird who might as well have screamed, *Oh, you wanted something to happen to you, Cinnamon Haynes? You worried this was all there was? Well, get ready.* Not that it would have mattered if Tweety had chirped her fortune at the top of its little lungs—she wouldn't have believed it, or anything that came next.

CHAPTER TWO

People leave. It's the lesson Cinnamon learned the earliest and the most in her life, and now it taunts her again as she realizes there might be another reason for her agitation as of late: Daisy. The fact that the girl has up and disappeared. It's been three weeks since she's shown up for their regular Friday lunch—Cinnamon counts them now to be certain.

She looks around, fruitlessly searching for the girl. This rectangular patch of grass, ring of trees, sludgy puddle, and smattering of benches allow this place to conspire to be a park due to their proximity to each other. Cinnamon appreciates its aspirational qualities. She thinks of the bench she sits on now as "her bench," her ownership of it so complete that she's irritated if someone else has the nerve to plop down on it, which is mercifully a rare occasion.

Cinnamon's lunchtime ritual is sacrosanct. Everybody in the career services office knows not to mess with it. She leaves the office each day at precisely 12:15, goes to Wendy's, gets a six-piece order of nuggets, fries, and a Frosty, which Terry, the elderly vet who works the drive-through lunch shift, almost always has waiting for her, and then drives the seven minutes over here to McLaren Park, where she sits on the second bench in front of the duck pond and reads for exactly forty-five minutes. The days when it rains, she sits in the parking lot and eats her lunch, a sliver of pond in view through her windshield. Routines like this are important for her. Wherever she's been, whatever has come at her in life, she's used them to keep some order in her world.

Cinnamon had raced through her morning chasing the peace she hoped lunchtime in the fresh air would bring. She makes an effort to hold still, listening to the quiet, letting the sun settle on her face, eyes open to the sky, which is a swirl of so many shades of blue it's like Mother Nature can't make up her mind this afternoon. It's cool for late May; the heat and humidity will come for them soon though, making June, July, and August almost unbearable, but for now the temperature hovers at an ideal seventy-four degrees. It's an easy-breezy kind of late-spring day, but Cinnamon is still feeling anything but. All she can think is, *Where is Daisy?*

But who can Cinnamon even tell that her friend is gone? Is Daisy even her friend? She hadn't exactly meant to keep their relationship a secret; Cinnamon just didn't know how to explain how and why she came to sit on a park bench once a week and eat french fries with a white girl almost half her age for close to a year now.

Daisy owes Cinnamon nothing if she wants to skip town, not least a goodbye, and if she doesn't want to meet for lunch anymore, it's her prerogative. Still, her just disappearing without a word stings. It is . . . Cinnamon searches her brain for the word the kids are always using . . . triggering. That's it—triggering. Everything's triggering these days. Her student Preeti had used the word just this morning when she vented about bingeing old episodes of *Full House* where the parents are always only mad at the kids for, like, two seconds, and then everyone makes up and is back to their lighthearted sitcom antics. Family drama being easily resolved in thirty minutes "triggered" her. "Why do they let us think it's so simple?" It was a fair question.

Preeti had been waiting in Cinnamon's office this morning just as Cinnamon suspected she would be and was already sobbing up a storm.

The poor girl has been locked in a battle with her parents over two major decisions that she'd recently made: changing her major from accounting to fashion marketing and transferring to Clayton State for the upcoming semester to be closer to her girlfriend, Danya. Though the Arujas are much more concerned about the latter than the former and have threatened to cut her off financially if she continues this "stupid American fad." Last night, Preeti went to use the credit card they'd given her and discovered it was canceled, which shouldn't have come as a surprise in light of their threats, but even when you see the knife coming, it hurts just the same. Thus, this morning's waterworks. For weeks now, and again this morning, Cinnamon has been trying to assure Preeti that even if she lost her parents' financial support, she could do work-study and apply for grants and scholarships, that she has a great head on her shoulders, and she would be all right no matter what. It helps that Cinnamon really believes that. She's tried to make Preeti understand that she might never change her parents' mind, but the girl remains intent on pleading with them to "accept" her—to no avail. Cinnamon understands the desperation all too well, but it also makes her bone-tired. There are some problems you just can't solve—like bad parents. Fact is, some people should just not be allowed to have kids, period. If she had to put a number on it, it would be about 30 percent, at least. Thirty percent of people who have kids should not have had them. The Arujas included, even if they would claim all they're doing is loving their daughter and wanting the best for her. Those are the worst parents, actually—the ones that are totally oblivious to how royally they are messing up.

All Cinnamon could offer Preeti, beyond helping her get her transfer credits straight, was some tough love. She had hefty doses of that because if there's one thing she knows, the truth can save you, or at least prepare you. "You have some rough days ahead of you, but it'll make you stronger and it'll let you surprise yourself. I can promise you, though, you're going to be okay," she'd told the girl.

At that, Preeti stopped sniveling and got a tiny glint of resolve in her eye, which made Cinnamon want to cheer and give her a big hug. Supporting her students gives Cinnamon a sense of purpose and pride that's probably out of proportion to the actual impact that she has on their lives, but she can't help it. It also helps ease her imposter syndrome because the idea that Cinnamon is even working as a "career counselor" is pretty ludicrous considering how little experience she has with "careers." She'd had one job for most of her life before she met Jayson. She'd stumbled into working for Reverend Rick at the church. Gratitude, loyalty, and inertia kept her there for longer than it perhaps should have, in a "career" that was an accumulation of endless odd jobs, from scrubbing the toilets to arranging the volunteers and organizing volunteers for the soup kitchen. But it didn't amount to anything that she could put on a crisp, cream-colored resume; it didn't position her to climb any ladder but the one she used to change the lightbulbs in the ALL SOULS HEAVENLY FELLOWSHIP sign.

It was just as well because Jayson was happy for her not to work when they moved to Sibley Bay, to stay home and read books all day while he built his empire. Cinnamon knows better than to think that was an entirely selfless act. Jayson is the kind of guy who feels like a big man by being able to support his woman. But the creaky old house was too quiet and allowed too much time and room for thinking. Above all else, Cinnamon needed distraction. The question was, what? What could she do in this town to make a living other than sling drinks or check people in at one of the fancy resorts, both of which Jayson dismissed as "beneath" her? *All those white folks ordering you to get them snacks and towels, thinking they're better than us. My wife isn't the help.* He solved this problem by going to Mommy.

Abigail not only knew everyone in this town but was likely their second-grade teacher at one point. Sure enough, Cinnamon's mother-in-law soon learned of a position at Sibley Bay Community College. Cinnamon jumped at the chance with an enthusiasm that bordered on desperation. Abigail's recommendation (she and Dean Bowler went to high school together) meant Cinnamon was hired without too rigorous a background check or having to produce a copy of a bachelor's degree.

Cinnamon assumed the job at the college meant that she would be doing mock interviews and rewriting resumes, but it turned out the bachelor's in psychology she let Dean Bowler believe she had would have come in handy since she is essentially a de facto therapist. It feels good to have the students open up and trust her—better, she imagines, than any of the drugs she never tried.

And she had been happy, or at least content, for their first couple of years in Sibley Bay, settling into a groove with her husband and at work, letting herself believe all the drama in her life was behind her. She should have known better. She *did* know better. And still it caught her off guard when Jayson came to her with his confessions.

Here was the thing: people fucking up was about as surprising and unexpected as the sunrise. No, the shock of it was how she reacted to the news. Just how well and truly thrown she was to have the rug pulled out from under her, even though her entire existence until then had been an endless series of pulled rugs. She'd gone soft, she'd let her guard down and stopped bracing herself for disaster, and the price to pay was getting caught up in a whole tornado of emotions that she couldn't keep at bay.

It wasn't like she didn't know Jayson had his . . . shortcomings, or was naive enough to think that he wouldn't screw up one day. In fact, Cinnamon had prepared herself for any cheating he might do before they even walked down the aisle. Which was not so much an aisle but a small room at the courthouse with blinding fluorescent lights and the scent of a tuna fish lunch hanging in the air. Her plea to quietly tie the knot, just the two of them, was one concession Jayson, who ideally wanted a bigger wedding, made for her when she insisted she couldn't bear the fuss. As soon as they said, "I do," she could see herself some years hence, holding Jayson while he sobbed uncontrollably, begging forgiveness and assuring her it was "just one mistake." But she'd prepared for the wrong scene. In the end, she only wishes it *had* been another woman—even some skinny white chick with stringy blond hair—that had her crying that day on the bench like someone had died.

What actually died that day was their savings—and her trust when Jayson told her he'd lost most of their money, including the nest egg Cinnamon had painstakingly squirreled away before she met him. He'd also secretly taken a mortgage out and lost that too. All chasing his dream: The Ruins, which was living up to its name.

The "world-class beachfront seafood joint" he was building was why they'd uprooted from Atlanta in the first place. Not a week after they were married, Jayson announced he had a surprise. They drove to Sibley Bay, which wasn't unusual, since they came to visit Jayson's mom, Abigail, every few months. But rather than turn into the modest new condo complex she'd moved into after his dad died, they drove a long and winding road outside of town. They continued on the desolate stretch that seemed to lead nowhere and made Cinnamon think of white men on horses with torches until, finally, they pulled up to a marshy plot of land that drifted off to a shaggy span of beach and a dark cove of frothy water. Standing in the middle of it was a measly wooden shack so dilapidated that Cinnamon could blow it to the ground in one good breath.

"This is it!" Jayson clapped his hands and looked around.

Cinnamon spotted a flash of irritation on his face when she had the nerve to appear confused.

"It's . . . our future, baby!" Jayson proceeded to announce—not ask, but announce—their new master plan. He'd inherited a plot of land from a great-uncle he never even knew! They were moving to Sibley Bay! So he could build a restaurant! Right here! He described the restaurant-cum-speakeasy he planned to build with a grandiose hand wave like he was writing it in the sky.

It was as if the sheer force of his enthusiasm would distract her from the fact that she had not bought into this plan whatsoever. It was a disconcerting feeling when your husband's plans were three steps ahead of your own. He'd already made arrangements for them to move into his grandmother's place, which had sat empty since she'd died.

Jayson's plan was to have the new restaurant up and running in a year. She knew that was about as likely as a snowstorm in this Southern town before the words even left his lips that day. But she nodded along as Jayson squinted out at the tranquil ocean as if he could see their whole future in the water. Turns out that was apt, since his vision for their future ended up drowning them in debt.

Not that she was aware of this until the day last summer when her husband decided he had no choice but to come clean since he knew the creditors were about to get more aggressive and there was a chance his car would get repossessed. He decided to tell Cinnamon before she spotted two men loading his Jeep Cherokee onto a tow truck.

Two hundred and twenty thousand dollars and climbing. That was the astonishing number that fell from his lips that day, and only when she forced him to tell her by asking, "How bad is it, exactly?" His only defense for any of it: "I was doing it for us, Cece. For our dream. I made some bad calls with contractors . . . Well, they're some shady thieves; it really wasn't my bad. And I needed to grease some palms for permits . . . You know how these white folks do—you gotta give 'em something. But I can't lose it all now. I got too much invested in the Ruins. I gotta get this up and going, or . . ." He didn't finish the sentence. He just started bawling like a baby. The funny thing was, there were no actual tears, which made her think his emotional outburst was theatrical more than anything else. He knew he was wrong. Dead wrong. And what was this business about "*our* dream"?

For her, this betrayal, him draining their bank accounts, was worse than an affair. A meaningless one-night stand she could get past, but sacrificing their stability in this uncertain world when she'd worked so hard to finally feel comfortable—that was the bitterest of pills and why she'd ended up fleeing here to this park, to her happy place, after they'd had it out last summer. She thought she had the park to herself and let loose howling at the ducks like a madwoman when she looked up and noticed she wasn't alone. The sight of a girl across the way stopped Cinnamon midsob. And what a sight she was. Her size was noticeable; she was on the bigger side and enveloped in a giant cherry-red sweat suit that was way too heavy for the hot May day. Her face was bright pink—either from sunburn or exertion—and she was carrying a giant can of tomatoes in each hand as makeshift weights. When she wound around the path and closed in on the bench, the girl plopped down next to Cinnamon and asked what was wrong, point-blank, just like that, as if they already knew each other. Obviously, Cinnamon wasn't going to say a thing about what was going on behind the closed doors of her shaky marriage. She didn't need her business on the streets like that. Short of conjuring a dead relative, which may have been a bridge too far, the best story Cinnamon could come up with was that her beloved Yorkie (Vera's stupid dogs were good for one thing: creative inspiration) just died and that's why she was on this bench, losing it.

Daisy placed a sweaty palm on Cinnamon's back with genuine sympathy. Cinnamon was still too out of sorts to be concerned about a stranger's touch invading her usually well-guarded personal space. Daisy immediately started in on a story about how she grew up on a farm with a pack of dogs and every single one of them was named Star. As soon as one of them died, another puppy took its place, a new Star, a constellation of Stars. The story had zero bearing on what Cinnamon was going through—it wasn't actually a dead dog vexing her, but a deadbeat husband—but boy was it nice to be diverted by someone else's chatter.

Somehow they had gone on to talk for two full hours, about dogs and movies and the weather, about how they both were still getting used to Sibley Bay and how hard it was to get to know people in a place where they had either dropped in for a weeklong vacation or had lived here for generations and didn't exactly embrace "outsiders." Daisy had just moved to town the summer before with her childhood best friend, Caleb.

Cinnamon chalked up their lovely, if surprising, chat to a happy accident—she'd never even been to that park on a weekend before—

and a one-time interaction that turned around a dark day, or at least distracted her from it. But then Daisy showed up again the next Friday.

"You mentioned you come here for lunch during the week and I wanted to check on you and give you this." She'd thrust a metal trinket at Cinnamon. As she did, the sleeve of her shirt rode up a few inches and Cinnamon spotted a neat line of faded scars like hash marks. Daisy nudged the sleeve down quickly and kept talking, but Cinnamon knew exactly what she had seen.

"It's a personalized keychain . . . in honor of Charlie . . . your dog? I got it at one of the tourist places near the boardwalk. It's dumb . . . Sorry . . . I just thought . . ."

That's the problem with lying; it required an exhausting vigilance. She'd already forgotten what she told Daisy about the dead dog. But damned if a lump didn't rise in Cinnamon's throat at the gesture. It's these tiny kindnesses that can undo a person.

That day she and Daisy chatted again for another easy hour. When Cinnamon had to get back to work, Daisy looked up shyly. "Same time next week?"

The next Friday, Cinnamon showed up with extra fries, which she felt bad about since the girl was obviously trying to lose weight. But they scarfed them down as they dissected the latest episode of *Real Housewives of Beverly Hills*, which they'd discovered they both loved. And which Jayson refused to watch on principle. "Like I need to watch a bunch of skinny rich ladies make up drama. Like they got any real problems beyond those tarantula fake eyelashes they all wear."

And so began a weekly ritual of Friday lunch, talking about TV or books. Daisy was into fantasy and sci-fi, which weren't Cinnamon's preferred genres, but she tried and ended up actually liking a couple of Daisy's recommendations, especially *The House in the Cerulean Sea*, which had her rooting for a cast of misfit magical children and sobbing with joy by the last page.

The best moments might have been when they weren't talking at all. It was the comfortable silences that Cinnamon appreciated the most. So few people in this world can just sit in silence with another person without yammering on and on. But for all their talking and their companionable silences, what does Cinnamon know about the girl, really?

She knows Daisy was raised by her grandparents. That had come up around the time they met last year. Mother's Day had just passed.

"You got kids?" Daisy had asked Cinnamon. "I figured I should say, 'hope you had a Happy Mother's Day' if you do."

Whenever she gets asked this, Cinnamon affixes a neutral expression on her face as she shakes her head so as to avoid pity, confusion, or any nosy questions.

"None of my own, but I have a couple of godbabies—my friend Lucia's kids—who I love more than I love french fries . . . almost more than I love french fries. Maybe the same. But no—no kids for me."

"What about a mother—you got one of those? Sorry, that's a weird question. I only ask because I don't. She died when I was like two. I was raised by my grandparents. So Mother's Day is always . . . weird. Hard. You know?"

"I do know, actually. I lost my mom when I was 'bout that age too." (Like her mom was a pair of sunglasses gone missing in a taxi.)

That Daisy may have assumed Cinnamon's mother is dead was not something she went out of her way to correct. She might as well be dead, so what is the difference, really?

Their shared circumstances were one of the reasons they'd bonded quickly and intimately in those early days spent together on this bench. Cinnamon recognized a kindred spirit when she saw one. They were both members of a club no one wants to belong to: motherless daughters. And she could also sense Daisy's hidden traumas as if they emitted a dog whistle loud and clear to those who had their own. It shouldn't have come as a surprise that Daisy's history made Cinnamon feel immediately protective of her, a sentiment that was easily accompanied by affection.

And yet, she still lied to Daisy when she asked Cinnamon who raised her after her mom was gone.

"Oh, my aunt." It came out easy enough; it always did.

When Daisy then asked, "What's your aunt like?" the best response Cinnamon could come up with was, "She's a piece of work." But she said it with a beneficent smile that allowed the phrase to be interpreted in a positive light, and it was sufficient enough to move the subject along. She got away with the same breezy description with Jayson when describing Aunt Celia, the woman he believes raised her, carefully omitting all of her years in foster care *and* what went down with Aunt Celia in the end. It helped that Jayson has never been the probing type.

Nor, apparently, is Cinnamon herself given the paltry breadcrumbs she has to piece together about Daisy and where she's gone off to. She doesn't even have her phone number, or know where she lives other than in an apartment near the little airport outside of town, which isn't a big help. Daisy never mentioned a job, but Caleb, that guy she's living with, works construction, if Cinnamon remembers right. Daisy was distraught when he went off somewhere for a gig, which Cinnamon recalls must have been sometime last fall, that was around the time of Daisy's birthday. She'd turned nineteen—Cinnamon had brought her a cupcake that day.

Cinnamon had used her birthday as an excuse to ask Daisy about her dreams and plans for the upcoming year and beyond. She'd sensed potential in the girl, as wayward and lost as she appeared to be.

She wasn't prepared for Daisy's answer though. The girl's dream for her future was to be a pilot. Of all things. Cinnamon nearly fell off the bench when Daisy had offered this up like a secret confession. But she didn't. She held the muscles in her face firmly in place lest they betray her doubts. Lord knows Cinnamon had had too many teachers and people give her that look—that *Oh, you think you can do that, little poor brown girl?* patronizing look—when she dared even dip a toe beyond what they thought was appropriate for her, whether it was a harder book, an honors class, or a spot on the all-white dance team. She knows all too well how people will shit on your dreams just because they size you up and take it upon themselves to decide if you are worthy of them or not. If you are the right size or color or gender to do what you want to do. This is why she vowed early on to never talk her students down from their dreams or their goals, however high they want to aim—in Daisy's case, all the way to the literal sky. And, hell, why shouldn't she be a pilot? Cinnamon loves the idea of people living lives they aren't supposed to have, that are supposed to be out of reach. And she makes it a point to believe in people—her students and strangers alike—her theory being that maybe you can get better at believing in yourself if you practice enough on other people.

Who knows? Maybe Daisy got into some flight school in the last few weeks and that's why she had to leave in a hurry. Cinnamon is momentarily thrilled at the thought, but then an ominous feeling sets in. Daisy had been acting strange the last few months. Cinnamon can see that now. Last time they were on this bench, last time Cinnamon had laid eyes on her, she'd noticed the dark hollows under Daisy's eyes, her twitchy knee, the pounds that she'd worked hard to lose back with a vengeance. She'd seemed preoccupied, mindlessly downing the pack of Twizzlers Cinnamon brought her.

Something terrible could have happened. Daisy has only ever spoken kindly of Caleb in a way that makes Cinnamon think she's in love with the guy, even though she said they were just friends. But that doesn't mean anything—it's possible he was abusing her. Kidnapped her? Cinnamon's mind races through every *Dateline* and *SVU* episode she's ever seen—they all end badly.

Cinnamon needs to go on ahead and put Daisy out of her mind. She's no Olivia Benson, and she's devoted too much time to worrying over her anyway. She's letting her precious lunch hour pass her by, and that won't stand. She opens the greasy bag of fries that have become cold and soggy while she ignored them and digs into her bag for her book. A brand-spanking-new one. God, how Cinnamon loves a new book, the promise and anticipation. A new book makes you feel like anything is possible and that all the hard stuff is going to go away, even if it's just for thirty minutes, and that's exactly what she needs right now.

The novel she'd just finished, a silly story about a wealthy divorcée who inherits a haunted beach house and falls in love with the ghost, a Civil War vet, was a straight-up dud. No surprise since the recommendation came from Sheila, the owner of Bay Books, the one bookstore in town, and the woman had terrible taste. Each novel she suggested to Cinnamon featured a rambling beach house and a summer to remember and four blond women from Maine. Cinnamon prefers more edge to her reading, not to mention some brown people. Give her a battle with cancer or a falsely accused death row inmate or a recovery memoir any day. Who knows what this says about her? The memoir she's about to crack, *Aurora's Light*, is one Cinnamon heard about on *Good Morning America*, and she knew she wanted to read it immediately. She runs her hand over the glossy cover, embossed type and a family picture lit with flames, which is rather on the nose but arresting nonetheless. She lifts the hardcover and smells the pages. There's nothing better than the scent of new paper. Except maybe the smell of her grandmother—menthol cigarettes and cocoa butter—which comes to her sometimes like a whisper of a memory.

She pulls in another deep breath for the moment of truth, that first line of the book. She always knows whether she'll be hooked by that first line.

The way the sun glinted over the broken glass in the alley made the shards look like a field of diamonds. As I lay there on the cold asphalt next to an overflowing dumpster, eye level with a rat caked in grease, those glittering specks made me wonder if I wanted to be dead after all.

All right, then—Cinnamon's sold. She's right there, lying on the cold asphalt with the author, Kincaid Hamilton. The memoir is about her escape from sex slavery after being sold by her mom at age seven. It's one of those harrowing stories that reminds you, *Hey, it could always be worse*. A welcome perspective this afternoon.

Before she can get into the pages, a prickle crawls across her neck. That anxious feeling creeps back before it was ever really and truly gone. She can no more shake it off than her shadow. *Get a hold of yourself,*

Cinnamon. She forces her eyes back into the book and starts reading out loud. She does this sometimes when she's alone, all dramatic too, like she's entertaining the geese who glide across the water unbothered.

That's when she hears it. A muffled mewling as soft as the sound of her turning the pages. She stops reading to listen, but there's nothing but a slight ripple of the breeze blowing through tree leaves. Then, just as she's convinced herself she'd imagined the sound and starts reading again, it returns, louder this time, insistent and unmistakable.

Cinnamon stands so quickly the book tumbles out of her lap, the glossy cover scuffed by the gravel. She takes a few steps into the patch of leaves behind the bench and stops short. What's in front of her makes about as much sense as a bird in her kitchen. She closes her eyes, again convinced she must be imagining this. But when she opens them, there's no doubting what she sees, even though it's no less confusing or shocking. Her brain works overtime to make sense of the scene. Looking up, with the brightest blue eyes she's ever seen, is a newborn baby.

CHAPTER THREE

Her first inclination is to laugh. It's completely inappropriate, but then what is the right response to finding a baby tucked in some bushes like Moses floating down the Nile? The preposterous scenario has short-circuited Cinnamon's brain. But a more apt reaction kicks in in seconds: panic. She doesn't dare touch the carrier, lest someone come charging at her out of nowhere accusing her of kidnapping—or worse.

Cinnamon's head swivels, frantically scanning every inch of the park, squinting to make out the woods past the far bank of the pond. There's no one here but her, and that hasn't changed since she sat down twenty minutes ago. She'd have to be blind as a bat to miss someone walking past her and dropping off a child in the time she's been sitting here. It begs the question of how long this poor child has been tucked behind a bench. And an even more pressing one: Who would just leave a baby in a park all alone? And one this young, at that. It's just a little tiny thing. To its credit, the infant seems entirely unfazed by this predicament, or by the stranger staring down at it.

"Momma's coming back. She'll be here any minute," she says to the baby, who gazes back blankly. It's the only possibility that Cinnamon can entertain—that there's a reasonable explanation and someone will return soon to claim this child. Otherwise, what's Cinnamon going to do? She can't exactly shoo a baby away like she did the bird this morning.

Leaning over closely, she stares at the baby, entranced by its eyes. She can't even come up with the right way to describe their intense blue: Cerulean? Cornflower? Turquoise? The way they fix onto Cinnamon also makes her think of Tweety: intense, watchful, knowing. It's like this child understands something she doesn't. For example, the fact that whoever left her here may not actually be coming back. Which is starting to dawn on Cinnamon too. But it's still wholly incomprehensible. She plots what she's going to say to whoever might eventually show up to get this baby. It starts with *Have you lost your mind?* Because they must have to leave a baby like this. Clearly, this mother is one of those 30 percent of people who shouldn't be allowed to have a child. Or maybe this is the work of a hapless father. Cinnamon wouldn't put it past her own husband to leave a baby alone for a "hot second."

She scrambles for her phone and googles. *What do I do with an abandoned baby?* The answer is fairly obvious: Call the authorities right away. The state's Child Protective Services (CPS) will take custody of the child and try to find relatives. Just the mention of CPS makes her shiver. She wishes that fate on no one. Then again, a cute white baby? Someone'll come and claim this child. The entire town will be searching for the parents within the hour. And if they don't find them, then some rich family will pull all the strings to adopt her. This little thing will never have to go through what Cinnamon went through. When she turns the infant in, Cinnamon may even be hailed a hero. She sees a flash of her picture in the *Sibley Citizen* and is immediately embarrassed by the thought. She doesn't need to be anybody's hero . . . or headline.

Glancing down at the baby, Cinnamon feels a flash of irrational irritation that Daisy didn't show up here today. If Daisy were here, they'd be in this together. She'd have someone to share in this surreal situation and help her figure out what to do. What a thing to bond them: *That time we found a baby—remember that?* The silver lining of this surge of frustration is that it's fuel to get her moving; she has to do something besides sit here all day waiting for someone to appear, to save her or this baby. The two of them are on their own. And she needs to get back to work. She could call 911, but that seems a bit over-the-top—it's not like this is a fire or real emergency. The baby is no worse for the wear, it seems, jerking little limbs around as if dancing to a silent melody. It'll be easier just to take her down to the police station. It's in the opposite direction of campus, but she can still make it back for her afternoon meetings.

When the baby makes a soft little squeal like a kitten, Cinnamon takes that as agreement to the plan. She finally dares to lift the carrier; it's lighter than she'd imagine in her slick palms. Dirt and leaves shake loose and fall to the ground as Cinnamon brings her face close to the baby's. "I'm here. I'm right here," Cinnamon says, taking in the impossibly small face peeking out from under the cute cap rimmed with a line of embroidered ducks. "Who are you? What's your name, cutie?" She doesn't even know what sex the baby is. Cinnamon decides to lift the corner of the blanket draped over the baby and take a quick peek under the onesie, which reveals that it's a girl, and that she's desperately in need of a diaper change, which makes the situation more urgent. Poor thing's likely hungry too.

"Who are you, little one? What's your name? Are you hungry?" The baby launches a fist into the air in response to Cinnamon's stream of inquiries. It's no bigger than an acorn. Cinnamon reaches for it. Minuscule fingers, soft as silk, wrap around her thumb. "All right, let's get you out of here. The police will help find who you belong to. You're gonna be okay." It was exactly what she'd said to Preeti just hours earlier, but who is she really to be offering up such promises?

The entire walk to the car, she still waits for someone to come barreling toward her in a panic, screaming, "DON'T TAKE MY BABY!" But the parking lot is as quiet and empty as ever. Even Cinnamon's own shadow is nowhere to be found as a sweep of clouds passes over the sun. She feels like a criminal, a thief, a kidnapper as she unlocks the door and tries to sort out how to get the carrier situated in the back seat, a task made all the harder with her trembling hands, not to mention a complete lack of experience with such things.

There's also the fact that her beloved eighteen-year-old Chevy Malibu is a death trap—the passenger-side window hasn't rolled down in years, the back bumper hangs on for dear life, and something makes a terrible grinding sound every time she starts the engine. It's barely safe for her to drive, let alone cart a child in. Lucia would never let her drive the twins around in it on account of her strong feelings about side airbags and other "modern safety features," and Jayson is too embarrassed to be seen in it and is just waiting for the car to die. Neither of them grasps how devastating it will be to Cinnamon when that finally happens. They don't understand what this car has witnessed or seen her through. It's why she'd named her Bessie—because she'd been so much more than metal and four wheels to Cinnamon.

She opens Bessie's back door and wedges the carrier in. She has some inkling of knowledge in the recesses of her mind that infants should face backward, but she isn't positive about that and she wants to be able to keep an eye on the baby, so forward-facing wins out. She wrestles with the worn seat belt that's stretched out like rubber bands past their elastic prime. After she's fumbled around with the belt until she's sure it's secure, she tugs it at least a half dozen times for good measure, imagining the horror of the carrier toppling over at the first turn. Still, she drives at a quarter of the speed limit the few miles to downtown, her toe constantly tapping the brake, making the trip take twice as long as it should.

When her phone buzzes on the seat, she taps the brake too hard, causing the car seat to lurch against the belt. She wouldn't dare answer it while driving, even if she didn't have such fragile cargo, but she glances over to see the caller's name on the screen. Reverend Rick. It's strange for him to be calling right now since they don't usually speak outside the standing date they have the last Sunday of the month. A sacred time when Cinnamon posts up at the little wrought iron table in the backyard with a full pitcher of sweet tea and whiles away two hours with the Rev until her bladder is full and she has to pee, which announces the end of their QT. Some people have therapy; she has Reverend Rick.

She goes straight to panic that something bad has happened to Rev. There's no reason for such paranoia—the man, at seventy-five, is strong as an ox (his words) and does seventy-five push-ups every morning—but thinking the worst is something she does as naturally as she pulls air into her lungs. *If anything happened to that man . . .* She doesn't let herself finish that thought. It's the one line of thinking in her life that's truly unbearable.

"Everything's fine." She says it as much to herself as to the baby in the back. "We're almost there." Cinnamon's eyes actually hurt from glancing at the back seat so much, and she misses the turn onto Walnut because she's staring into the rearview mirror. After another trip around the block, she pulls into the police station's parking lot. She hates this building, a cinder-block eyesore at the intersection of Walnut and Main. Why don't police stations ever have real windows? The rest of Main Street has been painstakingly restored over the last decade in an effort to make it look like a movie set filled with quaint Southern charm to draw tourists and even a couple of Hallmark movie productions, which makes this structure, circa 1970, stick out that much more. Then again, there might be something wrong about spending tax dollars to try to make a police station look "charming."

What will this child's future be once Cinnamon takes her inside? She's still holding out hope that this is some misunderstanding and the mother or father will be found. They might even already be inside the police station. This will all end up a ridiculous story to tell everyone at her birthday party next week. Complete with a happy ending. Having thus reassured herself, she gets out of the car and walks around to the back seat. The baby has kicked the blanket clear to the floor. When Cinnamon leans over to pick it up and tucks it back around her, her hand catches on something sharp. It's the corner of a note card, stuck slightly under the child's little butt.

Before Cinnamon even lifts it to read, she knows this isn't a good sign. No one leaves a note with a baby they plan to come back for. Her muscles first tighten, rigid and stiff, and then just as quickly release so that her entire body is liquid. It's the shock. The shock of seeing her own name right there on the top. It makes even less sense than the words that follow it. She shuts the back door as gingerly as she can and leans against the side of the car, eyes catching on the last line over and over like a record skipping.

Please, Cinnamon, please. Love, Daisy.

Daisy, Daisy, Daisy. What is this? If Cinnamon can just slow her breaths, maybe she can slow her thoughts and make some order out of them. But they refuse to cooperate, buzzing around like bees unleashed from their hive, erratic and confused. Daisy was pregnant? This whole time? And she never even mentioned it. All those lunches, all those talks.

For a minute it stings, hard, that Daisy sat on a bench hidden behind oversize sweatshirts, just lying to her face week after week for some nine months. But then again, she can hardly judge. Pot, kettle, and all that. How many truths had she told Daisy about her own life? At least this explains why Daisy had disappeared, which is barely any solace, considering it also introduces an even more urgent and pressing mystery: What is this girl thinking?

Cinnamon grips the note and reads it again, and then again. Her eyes slowly scan the careful cursive; it hits her that nothing has changed in the last ninety seconds. The words are still the same, just as insane and audacious. This part, especially:

You're the kind of mother my daughter needs. You come from good people who raised you right, and I know you'll do the same for my little girl. You'll give her all the things I can't.

Good people who raised you right. Cinnamon's got no one but herself to blame for this. She'd let Daisy believe that she had some kind of idyllic childhood; she'd stretched a few of her rare, good stories and borrowed some memories from television shows and books when Daisy asked about her childhood, which, come to think of it, she'd been extra curious about these last few months. Cinnamon misled her for no reason other than that it has been her way for years and that it brought her comfort to bask in the childhood she'd wished she had. But the result was that Daisy was out here thinking Cinnamon was basically Rainbow Johnson in *Black-ish* and had all the makings and role models for a happy family. *Oh, Daisy, I'm not who you think I am. I'm not who anyone thinks I am.*

And now she's being asked to raise a baby she has no business being asked to raise. Raise! Not babysit, not mind for a weekend. *Raise.* Her knees falter under her. They're not up to this predicament and neither is her heart, judging by the fact that it's trying to burst out of her chest and run away from all this.

It's the complete silence that makes Cinnamon peer into the back seat to check that the baby is still there. Lo and behold she is, simply sucking on her left fist, which she's crammed into that itty-bitty mouth. Such a quiet baby, as if she craves to go unnoticed. Cinnamon can relate. She plops down on the driver's seat and reaches over it to run her fingers down the girl's smooth ivory cheek. The baby leans into it, eager for the touch. The slight weight against Cinnamon's hand, the raw need, undoes something in her. Daisy couldn't have meant to do this. She must have been panicked, and desperate people do insane things when they're in that state. If Cinnamon marches into the police station right now, Daisy could get in trouble. Just leaving a baby in the woods has to be some sort of crime, and she doesn't want the girl to be in any more of a mess than she already is.

But it takes two to tango, so where is the father? Is he even in the picture? Daisy had never mentioned any guy aside from Caleb, and she said there was nothing romantic between them. Though it wouldn't be the first time a couple of friends accidentally made a baby. Besides, if Daisy would hide her pregnancy like this, she could have been hiding anything.

Cinnamon jerks back to grab her phone off the passenger seat with a shaky hand. It takes three tries to get her fingers to cooperate, but she manages to dial Lucia. Of all people, her friend will know exactly what to do. Four rings in, she remembers that Lucia is away. She left this morning to spend the weekend with her mother-in-law, Rebecca, a Mother's Day gift from Adam. "That man actually thinks sending me away with his mother to a stuffy kosher resort in Boca Raton is a *gift,*" Lucia had vented while hiding in her closet so Adam couldn't hear her. "And I won't even be able to call you and complain since Rebecca doesn't allow cell phones in her presence and wants to spend every waking moment together as if it's going to be the very last time we see each other on this earth. It's suffocating!" But Lucia promised Adam she'd be the perfect daughter-in-law for the duration of their weekend getaway. "They're still pissed their good Jewish son married a potty-mouthed Puerto Rican, so I gotta be on my best behavior, even if all she wants to talk about is the latest additions to her miniatures collection."

The only person Lucia gripes about more than her mother-in-law is her own mother, and that's something to Cinnamon, complaining so much about the family you get to have. She only wishes her own mother-in-law wanted to spend as much time with her. She and Jayson see her together often enough, but Abigail has always maintained a chilly distance from Cinnamon. With her homemade crocheted sweaters, passion for dollhouses, and walls full of wooden signs with inspirational slogans, she exudes the warmth of the second-grade teacher she used to be, and yet Cinnamon can never shake the feeling that Abigail is skeptical of her, suspicious even. She always seems to be squinting at Cinnamon like she doesn't know quite what to make of her, fixing her with a literal and proverbial side-eye, as if to ask, *How did you land my perfect son?* Which is all to say, they aren't going on a resort weekend together anytime soon, and that could make Cinnamon wistful if she let it, which she sometimes does when Lucia complains.

The phone jolts in her hand, and she answers without even looking to see who it is. She'll take anyone right now. Even Vera. But when she hears the deep baritone, a sense of calm washes over her.

"The Lord told me to check on you, Cinnamon. And you know I always listen to the Lord."

She's long since given up on knowing how Reverend Rick knows when she needs him—she can only chalk it up to the fact that his line to God is as direct as he claims it to be. All evidence points to that fact. Despite the Rev's best efforts over the years, Cinnamon still only barely believes in God, and that's because she is too scared not to, but she believes wholeheartedly in Reverend Rick because he had saved her. He gives God the credit for that too—says it was Jesus who put him in Cinnamon's path when he walked into the Laundromat that day where she'd taken to lingering to stay warm, where she could study for the GED and make extra money doing people's wash for them. She still doesn't know how he sensed her dire circumstances—she'd gone to great lengths to stay clean, to look respectable, and had learned to hide her hunger and her fear in the six months she'd been homeless. But he wrangled the truth of her situation out of her, how she'd ended up washing strangers' underwear for cash and sleeping in her car.

"You can't be living out here," the Rev declared, outraged, fist in the air like he was having a conversation with the man upstairs. And maybe he was. "Little wisp of a thing like this out here all alone on these streets. We're not having this. No way. This will not do. Come on—get your things; you're coming with me." She wasn't sure about the wisdom of following him anywhere. With his Crayola-red oversize suits, shiny loafers, and gold-capped incisor, you'd think he was running a dice game, or peddling used cars, not salvation. But something deep within her—faith and desperation—propelled Cinnamon along behind him to a giant neon green van parked down the block, with the words ALL SOULS HEAVENLY FELLOWSHIP splashed across the side in spray paint, while he mumbled under his breath the whole time. "Can't save everyone, even with Jesus himself by my side, but I can save this one. I can do that much." Listening to her heart in that moment was the single best decision she has ever made in her life, because that's exactly what he did.

And now here he is calling again at *this* exact moment, as she stares at another "little wisp of a thing" in the back seat. The intense combination of irony and emotion is enough to make her choke up. Which is exactly what she does, as she starts to explain what just happened to Reverend Rick, who takes it, as he always does, in the manner of a man who's "seen about all the shit you can see"—in stride and with a Bible verse.

"Well, Cinnamon, 'Lean not into your own understanding; in all your ways submit to him and he will make your path straight.' You remember your Proverbs, don't you?"

Cinnamon does remember the verse. It's the Rev's go-to, along with Philippians 4:13, which he has stamped across his altar. But Cinnamon doesn't need wisdom from the good book at this very moment; she needs a plan. "Right, right. There's nothing God can't help me through. But what am I going to do with this baby, Rev?"

"Same as I did with you. You're going to do what Jesus would want you to do. You're going to look out for her."

"I'm sitting in a police station parking lot. I was about to take her inside and leave her there." Saying those words out loud makes it sound absurd when just ten minutes ago it was the most logical solution in the world.

"Cinnamon Haynes. Do not take that child inside. We do not need to be turning any more of our babies over to white folks. Especially in that cracker town you moved to against all common sense." Reverend Rick still isn't over her leaving Atlanta and moving someplace where she's "outnumbered and out of place."

"They like to think it's 1954 in those parts of the country—you know, when America was great," he'd grumbled more than once.

The Rev likes to extoll the virtues of segregation. He does it just to get a rise out of people, claiming he and George Wallace had a lot in common, but in reality, he does believe it's best to stick to your own kind. *Why you think God made Atlanta?* he would say. But Cinnamon doesn't have the energy to have the conversation about why she followed her husband to "Whitey Bay" again. So she goes straight to clarifying that said baby happens to be white.

"Well, I'll be damned. Okay, that's . . . something."

"What? Now you think I should turn the baby over because she's white?"

"No, no, it's not that. I'm just processing, girl. Calm yourself. It's a whole different ball game for you to be caught with this white baby. Stakes is a little higher, is all. Look, why don't you head home and think about what to do? That girl entrusted you with her daughter for a reason, and you'd be going against the Lord to just dismiss it straightaway. The child deserves to have you think on it a little, or better yet pray on it. No one's gonna know any different if you take a minute. It'll come to you what to do about all this."

Movement catches her eyes, and she reflexively ducks when she sees a familiar face emerge from the police station's double doors. Officer Williams squints into the distance as he lights a cigarette and takes a puff so eager you'd think he was sucking in pure oxygen. She'd rather lick the bottom of her shoe than to have to interact with this guy. Williams was two years ahead of Jayson on their high school basketball team and mercilessly hazed all the younger guys to make himself feel better about always riding the bench. He was the white dude who was always belting out rap lyrics at parties and on their way to their games, singing along with the N-word as loud as he could and staring at Jayson every time he did as if daring him to make an issue of it. Ever since they moved back to town, Officer Williams has pulled Jayson over some six times, claiming he didn't "recognize" him. It would be almost entertaining how pathetic this was—an attempt to bolster his own fragile ego with a power trip—if it weren't so infuriating. The last thing Cinnamon wants is to turn Daisy's child over to this jerk and hope for the best. Reverend Rick is right—she just needs time to regroup.

"I'm still at the police station, and I need to get out of here. I'll call you later. Thanks for the advice. You called at just the right time."

"'Course I did, girl. The Lord is never early and never late but always right on time. Love you. Call me later."

Reverend Rick is the only person in her whole life who tells her he loves her, including her husband, who once told her he didn't have to say it for her to know it. Granted the Rev says it to everyone from the woman who does his weekly manicures to the guy who shines his shoes, but it still hits Cinnamon square in the chest each and every time. One of the only voice mails on her phone was a saved message he left when she first moved from Atlanta three years ago. "Just calling to tell you I love you, little miss. And you can always come home, ya hear?"

Home. A hot studio above the church where the overpowering smell of the Subway sandwich shop next door penetrated the walls and made everything in her meager wardrobe smell like bread even though the attic didn't have any windows; the first place she ever felt truly safe, the first place that was truly hers.

By the time Cinnamon eases Bessie back onto Main Street, a plan is forming. She will track Daisy down and talk some sense into the girl. Because doing what Daisy asks in the letter, taking in this child and raising it as her own? It's just laughable. Actually and truly laughable. Which explains why Cinnamon has broken into another set of hysterical giggles by the next traffic light. Her brain has short-circuited again. She has a feeling she may have to get used to the sensation, under the circumstances.

She heads toward the Walmart out on Route 94 because she'll need baby supplies and because it's far enough outside town that she can avoid anyone she knows for the time being. At the stop sign on Sycamore, she glances around to check there's no cars behind her and pulls out her phone to call Vera.

"Hey, Vera." Cinnamon makes her voice low and sickly, already two steps ahead.

"Where are you? You got us worried when you didn't come back right after lunch." Vera doesn't sound worried at all, but rather just nosy as all get out.

"Oh man, Vera, I got hit with something." (That's for sure.)

"My lunch is tearing through me. Ugly things are happening. I had to go straight home and to the bathroom."

Vera clucks. "All that fast food is terrible for you. You're gonna die of a heart attack before you turn fifty."

This from the woman who took approximately forty-two smoke breaks a day.

"Yeah, the fries—they're dangerous but so good. Can you please cancel my afternoon meetings?"

"You're going to miss my party," Vera says with the tone of a put-upon toddler.

"I know. I'm so sorry. That's the first thing I thought of when I started throwing up. Listen, I gotta go." Cinnamon squeezes out an over-the-top moan and hangs up the phone. Viola Davis she is not, but it'll have to do.

The whole twenty-minute drive to Walmart, Cinnamon periodically presses her eyes shut at every stoplight and then opens them again and looks in the rearview mirror. Sure enough, there is a baby there every single time, blue eyes fluttering behind translucent lids.

There's a rush of pure satisfaction when Cinnamon gets the carrier easily out of the car and into the crook of her elbow more seamlessly than she would have given herself credit for. She doesn't bother to hide the baby, since she knows people will just assume she's the nanny. Which is known to happen when she's with Lucia's kids. The first time she'd picked the twins up from preschool when Lucia had a doctor's appointment, the school secretary had called out to the teacher, "Nanny's here to get the Wenger twins." Cinnamon didn't even bother to correct her.

She pushes a cart with her free hand as she slowly goes up and down the baby aisle, utterly overwhelmed by all the choices. There must be a thousand different types of pacifiers. She forces herself to focus on necessities, but she gets tripped up on the ridiculous menagerie of adorable stuffed toys. When her eyes land on a giant gray elephant with oversize floppy ears, she decides she has to buy it. It makes her think of one of her favorite books—*Modoc*, the true story of an elephant who survived a shipwreck in the Atlantic Ocean, a terrible fire, cruel owners, and all manner of suffering only to become one of the most beloved attractions at Ringling Brothers. It was something, how much she identified with that elephant . . . Life just kept coming at him, and he proved himself a survivor over and over. She throws the stuffed animal into the cart. At the checkout aisle, she grabs a one-pound bag of peanut M&M'S—she needs her own supplies too.

Modoc is the last item the clerk rings up before he turns the little digital screen to show the total, at which point Cinnamon about falls to the floor. How did she end up spending $232.97 on a few baby items? She hands over the credit card and doesn't breathe for the full thirty seconds it takes to process, already tallying the things that she'll have to put back if the card gets declined. Not Modoc though—come hell or high water, he's coming home with them. Luckily the card goes through, but she still hightails it outta there like she's getting away with something.

The trip home is slow going—her nerves about driving around with this child in the back seat don't let up until she's in her driveway, and she has to practically peel her hands off the steering wheel, as hard as she'd been gripping it. She calms herself by running through a to-do list while she carries the bags and carrier as gracefully as possible, even though both clunk against her legs on the walk to the front door. The baby's neck flops in a way that highlights how fragile she is.

Once inside, she sets the carrier on the kitchen counter and warms a bottle as fast as she can. Baby girl must be starving by this point. At the last minute Cinnamon remembers to check the milk's temperature on her inner wrist. Years ago, at one of her foster homes, a baby's mouth and throat were scalded by too-hot formula. Some things you never forget.

The baby takes to the bottle like a wild animal, making Cinnamon wonder when the last time she ate was. She hates to think how long she'd been sitting there in the park. What if Cinnamon hadn't gone to the park today? Granted, her schedule is generally as reliable as the tides. She even went there for lunch during the school's summer break, but it's possible she could have gotten into a car accident, had a doctor's appointment, or gotten food poisoning for real. Daisy risked a lot just leaving her child there like that. As Cinnamon watches the baby's lips greedily sucking down formula, all she can think yet again is, *What are you thinking, Daisy?* She already knows it's a question she'll be asking herself a lot over the next few days and that she'll never get an answer that makes any sense.

The baby is out like a light the second the last drop is gone, and Cinnamon paces the house, popping M&M'S into her mouth, as greedy for the sugar fix as the baby was for formula.

She settles onto one of the metal chairs at the vintage Formica kitchen table and pulls out her phone. She opens Facebook and tries to search for Daisy, which is pointless without a last name. And then she searches for Caleb, though it's the same problem. Next she scans a map of the state. She remembers that Daisy had once mentioned the town she grew up in that was a few hours away. But that information sits in the far reaches of Cinnamon's mind, tucked in a corner covered in cobwebs behind the full list of state capitals she'd once proudly memorized. She hopes that if she sees the name, she will recognize it. But so far all the squinting at the screen scanning dozens of names of nowhere places is just giving her a headache. She's trying to blink away the blurriness in her eyes when the baby wakes with a wail. Cinnamon practically knocks the chair over catapulting to her feet. It's the first time she's heard her actually cry. A thousand terrible thoughts send her heart racing. The formula is wrong and somehow the baby has been poisoned, or the baby is sick and that's why Daisy had left her the way she did.

She takes the stairs two at a time up to her bedroom and finds the baby in the middle of the nest of pillows on her bed where she'd left her, arms and legs jerking about as she wails. The screams grow louder as Cinnamon carefully inspects each little twiglike limb, and satisfied nothing is broken, starts rocking her up and down as she continues to cry so loudly it might break Cinnamon's ears, let alone her heart. She just keeps thinking that if she were a real mother, she would know exactly what to do. But then she remembers maybe no one knows what to do. The day after Lucia got home from the hospital with her own babies, her friend called her, frantic and sobbing. "They just let us leave the hospital, Cece! We just walked out and they assumed we knew what we were doing! And now I'm probably going to accidentally kill these innocent babies. At least one of them, if not both!"

It was the only time she'd seen Lucia rattled, and yet it only took her another day or two to get it together, to craft a system, to make it look completely effortless to raise two human beings at the same time.

Cinnamon starts shuffling back and forth across the room the way she'd done with Lucia's son Mason in the early days when she'd rush over to their house after work to see her godchildren. Sometimes she'd stay until Adam got home and watch him race to pluck one of the babies from his wife's lap. She'll never forget the look on Adam's face as his eyes wandered between the twins and Lucia. It was an expression that could only be described as true awe. *I can't believe we made these humans*. The love between Adam and Lucia in those moments was almost too much to bear, like high humidity or gale-force winds, invisible but so strong it was tangible nonetheless. That sort of intimacy was something that always felt out of reach for Cinnamon, and witnessing it could sometimes leave her unsteady and bereft.

Now here Cinnamon is in her own house, swaying and sliding with the baby like she's trying to win the Mirror Ball on *Dancing with the Stars*. Just as easily as the tiny thing slipped into a frenzy of wild rage, she stops and gazes up at Cinnamon. Her eyes, all wet and wide like this, look exactly like the sea. Cinnamon can't keep calling her "thing" or "little one." Babies need a name. Daisy didn't mention one in her note. What kind of mother doesn't name her baby? Cinnamon answers her own question. One who doesn't want to be its mother. But Cinnamon can't bring herself to name her either. That's for Daisy to do when she returns. Cinnamon is just going to keep saying that like it is a fact. *Daisy will return*. One of her self-help books told her it works, this sort of manifesting. All you have to do is believe—it's so simple. But still, she has to call the baby something. She'll give her a nickname.

Little D?

Nugget?

Baby Girl?

She's trying out temporary names to go with this temporary situation when the phone rings. She doesn't even dare to think it's Daisy before she registers Lucia's picture—a selfie her friend took eating peanut butter with a spoon out of a jar. She'd sent it to Cinnamon when their friendship was brand-new and they'd bonded over having the same favorite snack ritual, scooping Skippy directly from the container.

"Hey! I'm seeing you called me about two hundred times. Sorry; I followed through on my vow not to pick up my phone, but I had to hide it from myself in the bottom of my suitcase. Rebecca's taking a nap so I have like twenty minutes of screen time. You should see me locked away in the bathroom with the phone like a heroin addict tapping a vein. Anyway, what's the big emergency? Don't tell me you were trying to get me to bail you out of Vile Vera's thing." Lucia says all of this in place of hello.

"Um . . . I did come up with an excuse to ditch that. That's why I was blowing up your phone, actually."

Cinnamon pauses, unsure how to break the news of this bizarre development. But the improbably loud cooing near the phone speaker does the job for her.

"Is that a . . . baby?"

"It *is* a baby . . ." Cinnamon starts carefully, going over to her dresser, which has been transformed into a makeshift changing table and triage center filled with bottles, formula, wipes, and Modoc. She grabs the fuzzy elephant and wiggles it around in front of the girl's face as Cinnamon proceeds to give Lucia an update on the last few surreal hours. Saying the story out loud makes it sound all the more impossible. No wonder Lucia thinks it's a joke.

"Wait. You're kidding me, right?"

"I wish."

"So let me get this straight. This complete stranger asked you to raise her child. Seriously, Cece. Stop playing with me. Is this a belated

April Fools' prank? Because it's crazy. It's like me announcing out of the blue, 'Guess what, the twins aren't Adam's!'"

"Well, Daisy, the mother, she's not exactly a complete stranger . . . I . . . We . . ." Again, she struggles to describe their relationship. When she finally settles on "she's a friend" after many fits and starts, the description feels right and true. Daisy *is* a friend. *Was* a friend.

"You've literally never mentioned this person. Come on, Cece—we don't keep secrets. What is this? And if she's such a good friend, how did you not even know she was pregnant?"

"Well . . . she's a big girl. And she always wore baggy clothes. I didn't notice anything different." Daisy made sure she didn't notice anything different. And if she had seemed a little larger these last few months, Cinnamon was hardly going to comment.

"Okay, fine, but *someone* must have known she was pregnant. This woman doesn't have any family? Any real friends? Why you?"

Cinnamon bristles at the "why you"—she can't help it. And also at the "real friends" part. Lucia pushed at her most tender sore spot without even really knowing it. "She's not a woman, Luce. She's just a girl, not even twenty. She was probably just scared. She trusted me and looked up to me. And she felt like I could give this baby a good home." A defensive tone creeps into Cinnamon's voice even though she has her own doubts about what kind of home she could give a child.

"I can't believe she just abandoned her baby. What kind of a monster does that?"

Not that Cinnamon didn't have that exact same thought, but the question is laced with a harsh bitterness that Cinnamon's never heard from Lucia before.

Someone like Cinnamon's mother, was the answer. But Lucia doesn't know Cinnamon's mom was such a monster. Or maybe "monster" isn't the right word. Maybe Margo Haynes was just young, dumb, and desperate. The reflex to defend Daisy's actions blurs into a desire to defend her own runaway mother. What if she had "good" reasons for leaving? Who even gets to decide what are good enough reasons for making the choices that we make? It seems from what Daisy had shared with Cinnamon over the past year that the girl had worked hard to escape where she'd come from and reach for a different kind of future for herself with so much stacked against her. Daisy has dreams for herself, and apparently, they don't include a baby at nineteen. It's so easy to judge, but Cinnamon isn't ready to condemn her just yet.

It occurs to Cinnamon to wonder now: Did anyone ever try to find her mom? Did anyone ever try to convince Margo that *she* had made a mistake leaving Cinnamon? If someone had, if anyone had tried harder, or tried at all, to get her mother to come home, would Cinnamon's entire life have ended up differently? It's possible her mom lived in a sea of regret but could never find her way back. Who knows? One phone call from the right friend or relative asking Margo if she really wanted to leave her little girl could have changed everything. In that light, it's worth every effort to try to save Daisy and this child from the same fate.

"Why haven't you called the police?" Lucia asks reasonably.

The plan that felt so solid mere hours ago is crumbling fast in the face of rationality. "I was going to. I drove to the police station. But I just . . . I feel like Daisy made a mistake."

They're both quiet, and in the silence, Cinnamon can feel Lucia trying to work out what to say next. She doesn't give her the chance to say anything. "Look, I know, I know. It's a lot. But I'm going to find Daisy. She can't want this. I'll take care of the baby while I look for her, and no one will be the wiser. I'll reunite them. Get this girl some parenting classes and the support she needs, a good job. I can fix this. I know I can fix this."

"So I assume you've tried to call her?"

It's hard for Cinnamon to admit she doesn't even have Daisy's phone number or vice versa. Lucia is right to be skeptical of this "friendship," but Cinnamon's also guessing Daisy wouldn't just answer on the first ring even if she had a number to reach her. She makes a mental note to update her bio on the SBCC website to include her cell number so that Daisy can always find it.

"And you've tried to google her too, obviously?" Cinnamon decides she won't give Lucia further ammunition by admitting she doesn't have a last name.

"I need something beyond Google, I think, Luce. Sources and whatnot. I need your help."

If anyone can track someone down, it's Lucia. Before she had the twins, she'd been the editor in chief of the *Sibley Citizen*. She was unceremoniously let go by the new owners during her maternity leave. So it's a relief when she puts on her *get shit done* voice.

"Do you have any idea where Daisy might have gone? What about her family? Do you think they know?"

"I know her mother died when she was young. She was raised by her grandparents. I don't know much about them though."

"What about the baby's father?"

"No idea. She lived with a guy named Caleb, a friend from her hometown. It didn't sound romantic, but we know how that goes."

"And where do they live?"

"I'm not sure . . . out by the airport somewhere is all I know."

"I mean, we can try to find her, Cece, but this seems like it's going to be hard, futile even, with what little you have to go on. I just don't know how you call this girl a friend and you know next to nothing about her."

Lucia has a fair point, but Cinnamon bristles again. After all, Lucia would call Cinnamon her closest friend, and there's so much she doesn't know about her or her past. Their intimacy is protected by an illusion—Lucia doesn't know what she doesn't know. There have been many times that she's been tempted to tell Lucia the truth about how she was raised, the nightmares she went through, but as the years and the lies accumulated, she was terrified that she'd already done the unforgivable. If the foundation of friendship is formed by sharing histories, insecurities, confessions, secrets, and vulnerabilities, then Cinnamon fears her bricks are more wet sand than cement. Can you call someone your best friend if they don't know the full truth about you? It makes the title feel falsely earned but also impossible to risk.

"Well, even if I knew where she lived, I doubt she's just sitting somewhere across town. She'd have left by now. I just have to figure out where she could have gone. She mentioned her hometown, but I can't remember it."

Tonight, Cinnamon would go back to looking at the map to try to dislodge it from her memory.

"What's her name anyway? The baby."

"I don't know. I was just trying to figure that out, actually, when you called. Daisy didn't mention one in her note, and it doesn't feel right for me to name her."

"Well, we have to call her something. A nickname at least. What color's her hair? Worked for you!" At first, Cinnamon is confused, and then she makes the connection. The story she'd told Lucia when they first met about how she got her unusual name.

"I was born with red hair. Well, like a dark rusty color," she had explained during their very first friend date. She was used to giving out this explanation. This particular lie originated in middle school and Cinnamon had stuck with it.

"You're shitting me." Lucia had snorted her Diet Coke out of her nose. "Black babies don't have red hair."

"They do. We do. Sometimes it happens. It all falls out eventually but some of us are born with bright-red Afros." She pulled out her phone to prove her point, showing Lucia a googled gallery of brown babies with crimson curls.

The truth was Cinnamon was named after a stripper her mom lost a bet to. She'd learned this by eavesdropping on "grown folks' business." It was the same way Cinnamon learned that her mother had run off, by listening to her grandmother talk on the phone with one of her bridge friends in a hushed whisper. Cinnamon had been sent to her grandmother's for the weekend while Margo visited a friend in Columbus, and her mother had simply never returned. Apparently, Margo, who had been "boy crazy since birth," chased a "good-for-nothing low-life Negro" all the way to California, and her life—and child—in Ohio were in the rearview.

No one ever explained to Cinnamon that her mother wasn't coming back. So she gripped what little she did know—that her mother was in California—like a piece of sticky candy in a greedy palm. But those weren't the sort of sordid details you divulged to your fancy new friend prospect.

Cinnamon's fiction gave Lucia the chance to laugh and talk about how her own mother would wrap bright-pink bows around her head until she was three and finally grew hair longer than an inch. And so they could bond with ease without the complicating factor of pity or prying questions.

So Cinnamon does what she always does in these situations—she laughs easily at the memory and moves on. "What about Bluebell?"

Now Lucia laughs. "What is she? Ice cream?"

"No, but she has the bluest eyes. Wait until you see them." Cinnamon's startled by the affection and awe in her own voice.

"Wait? The baby's white? I just—"

Cinnamon cuts her off. "Assumed? Assumed the baby must be Black?"

Reverend Rick had done the same thing, so Cinnamon's not quite sure why she's so bothered when Lucia does it, but she is.

Lucia starts stuttering. "I—I—I don't know. I just . . . when I picture you with the baby, she's brown."

At this, Cinnamon takes in the baby's pale, pale face, white as chalk, against her own dark hands. "Nope, has blond fuzz and everything."

Lucia zips right on past this flash of awkwardness. "And what's Jayson say about this whole mess, by the way? About Baby Bluebell moving in."

"I don't know. I haven't talked to him. He's not home yet."

Cinnamon has practiced how she would lay this on Jayson all afternoon. But as soon as she gets past "Craziest thing happened today . . . ," her brain fills with smoke. "Hear me out here . . ." All of her attempts to explain are false starts. For a second, she entertains a wild idea that she can avoid telling her husband altogether by keeping the baby hidden in the basement until she finds Daisy.

"Oh boy. I wish I could be there to hear that convo. I also wish I could be there to help, honey. Or talk some sense into you! I'm back late Sunday and will come over first thing Monday morning. You should call the police though, right now. If you don't, I'll drag you there myself when I get home."

Cinnamon is distracted from her friend's forceful proclamations by something even more urgent—the sound of Jayson's key in the front door. "I gotta go."

She hangs up on Lucia and takes a deep breath. "Here we go, Bluebell." Saying it out loud, the name suits. She repeats it for good measure. "Bitty Baby Bluebell, aren't you cute?" Then they both wait quietly, perched on the bed in the darkening room. Somehow in all the drama, she missed the fact that the sun had checked out for the night.

Jayson strides in and flips on the light. Cinnamon tries to see the picture as he's seeing it. His wife, who is supposed to be at some godforsaken work event, sitting there blinking into the too-bright overhead light, formula staining the black dress she put on that morning in another lifetime, a newborn baby with lily-white skin in her arms, bottles and diapers and wipes strewn about their bedroom. His catfish order long forgotten.

Her husband has the only reasonable reaction a human could have. "What in all hell is going on, Cinnamon?"

Dear You,

The first time I ran away from home I was maybe five or six. I only made it about a couple hundred yards from the house, across the south pastures, as far as the rusted oil drum on the edge of the Sawyers' property line. I remember being so worried about the streaks of brown that stained my shorts as I crawled into the giant metal tube and how Gammy was going to be mad because it was a week yet before next wash. I had stashed a PB&J in my back pocket that smashed flat against my butt when I sat down. It's funny the things we remember, like that sound, a soft squish.

For thirty minutes I curled up in the drum, watching a turkey vulture trace wide, lazy circles in the sky, before it dawned on me how running away was stupid and pointless. I wasn't even gone long enough to get hungry for my sandwich before I skulked home, wordlessly slipping back on the couch next to Gammy, who was watching *Judge Judy*, none the wiser that I'd been gone. No, that's not right. She probably knew. She just didn't care. Anyway, that time didn't really count, not like this.

I kept telling myself the more distance I got from you, the easier it'd be. But I'd traveled more than a hundred miles so far on the humid Greyhound bus and could still feel the weight of you in my arms. Soon as I dared nod off, I swear I heard you cry—such a short wail but so loud and angry that I jerked awake, surprising myself and the stranger sitting six inches away from me, the guy wearing the biggest headphones I'd ever seen. It was then I decided I would never sleep again. Or at least as long as the Red Bull I got at the last rest stop could keep me up. I'd chug it like my life depended on it. It sort of felt like it did.

But it went straight through me, and I had to pee so bad. I also needed to clean myself up. I knew I was probably leaking straight through one of the massive pads and big mesh underwear they'd given me at the hospital.

I glanced at my seatmate and wondered if he could smell me. I could smell myself and it wasn't pleasant, but someone had locked themselves in the bathroom for forever, so all I could do was press my thighs close together and stare through the smudged bus window, straight down at the white strip cutting the dark stream of highway that was leading me from here to there, from my past to my future. The billboards, the rough rumble of the engine, and the light slanting through the trees lining the road made me feel like I was living in some sort of country music song, something about yearning and second chances and hope on a run-down bus like Gammy used to sway to in the kitchen. Trisha Yearwood and Faith Hill being about the only thing that could put her in a decent mood.

Maybe music could have dressed up the depressing truth of it all: that the bus smelled like feet and Cheetos, that the pain in my crotch was a fire that might never burn out, and that I felt just as lost as I did when I was curled up in that old, rusted barrel.

I squeezed my eyes shut and made myself hear a melody, faint as ever, a single sad guitar playing in my mind to try to make all this feel like an adventure, promising and romantic and not desperate and doomed. I swear I could hear it. Gammy always said I was "long on imagination," which was the nicest thing the woman ever said to me, even if she didn't mean it that way.

I was so self-conscious of my body that I tried jiggling and scooching lower and lower, as if I could slide my way to invisibility, except even my long imagination wasn't enough to wish away the reality of my flesh and bones and more flesh. How I'd tried.

Last time my seatmate glanced over, I turned all hard and fast so he couldn't see these pages. Not that he could read my chicken scratch, but I angled them away anyway, trying to send a message for him to leave me alone. I spied on him from the corner of my eye. He had this headful of braids like stubby snakes that poked out around the monstrous headphones that couldn't contain the rap song he was blasting. "That nigger music. You better never let me catch you listening to that shit again." That's what Gamps screamed at me the first time I dared play a Tupac CD a kid at school had given me. Somehow, sitting next to this guy, I felt guilty even having that memory, like he could hear Gamps yelling the N-word in my mind.

I felt bad for him. My seatmate, not my grandpa, who deserved about as much sympathy as the devil himself. When this guy boarded the bus at the last stop, I watched as this white lady two rows ahead pointedly put her purse on the open seat next to her without a word when he paused there. I recognized that look: *Don't you dare.* And he'd definitely seen the nastiness in her eyes too, because he moved on without a beat. By the time he shuffled ahead two more rows, wrestling with a giant navy duffle, glancing at the seat next to me with a question on his face, I couldn't help smiling at him and nodding aggressively, overcompensating in my welcome like I was trying to make up for that awful woman, and all my people.

I was just happy he wasn't a mother with a baby. I had to protect myself from babies above all else. And the giant headphones told me he wasn't a talker either, which was good. I had to protect myself from those too.

But he was nosier than I thought, glancing over more than I liked. At one point my hospital bracelet wiggled free from up under my sleeve where I'd tucked it, and he spotted it. I should have just cut it off, but I wasn't ready yet. I wondered what he suspected—maybe that I was running away from the crazy ward, or that I had appendicitis or something. He never would have suspected what I'd done.

To me, it was obvious, like it was written all over me. And I waited for people to see it and sneer. Like I expected they would do at Mercy Memorial. That's the speck of a hospital you were born in, in a town that barely had a name. I'd taken a bus sixty miles out of Sibley to find a random hospital in the middle of nowhere. The week before you were due, I used a good chunk of the money I'd squirreled away to get a filthy little hotel close to the hospital to give myself some wiggle room for when you were supposed to come out. I couldn't believe how nice they were to me at Mercy. From the second I got into the birthing room every person who walked into my room, from the nurses to the guy who took out the trash, made sure to say "Congratulations, Momma."

The nurse, Wanda, clucked all over me, constantly offering me shoulder rubs and sips of water. "Let me take care of you," she'd said. "You'll be the one doing all the taking care of soon when you get home with that baby." She didn't know you and I wouldn't be going home and settling into an exhausting routine. Wanda couldn't tell that I was a monster, but I guess I wasn't yet, because I hadn't left you. You were still tucked inside me, flipping around like you couldn't wait to be free and get started on life.

All the YouTube videos I'd watched about giving birth tell you that you just know when it's about to happen, but I didn't know jack. It was four days past my due date when I was jerked awake with such bad cramps in the middle of the night, I hollered so loud I worried that someone would come knock on the door. When I stood up to get my phone and see if that was a sign of labor, the real pain started. I don't know how I got dressed—I don't remember a thing, even the walk to the emergency room. I can't even describe how nervous I was. It felt like a whole bunch of angry squirrels had moved into my body and were having a field day digging tunnels. I didn't know if it was the labor pains or the fear. It didn't help that I hated hospitals more than anything—all bad news and beeping machines and broken people. But then I lucked into Wanda, my saving grace. And yours. You were the 837th baby she had delivered in her twelve years on the job. She told me she'd seen it all. I had to assume that included a terrified nineteen-year-old coming into her ER with no husband, no friends, no family. Wanda's kindness, along with the overwhelming pain, made me confess almost everything. I just spilled my guts, about how I was scared to death, that I couldn't believe I let this happen to me, that I was all alone. "No one knows about the baby, Wanda. Only you." I told her all that without meaning to. She didn't look at me with pity or ask a lot of questions I couldn't answer; she just grabbed my hand and said, "Well, you got me, hun." It was Wanda who got me an epidural just in time. It was Wanda who weighed you and told me you were a healthy and hefty nine-pound baby girl and then told me not to worry when you wouldn't latch onto my breast, who showed me how to feed you drops of formula from a bottle, which was better anyway since I knew I wouldn't be breastfeeding you. It was Wanda who showed me how to care for the parts of me that were swollen and torn, and it was she who picked you up in the middle of the night as I lay sobbing in a ball on the bed and lovingly swaddled you and asked if I'd decided on a name. I just shook my head and cried. I couldn't give you a name; it wouldn't be right. It would make it all too real. You would just be "you" to me, and that was enough. When Wanda handed you to me, she said, "Well, I know you'll pick something pretty. You do right by this child, ya hear? I know you will."

When I left the hospital and took you back to the motel, I kept saying the promise out loud: "I promise to do right by you." I've never meant my words more then or since. Holing up alone for a week in that dank room was all part of the plan. You slept most of the time, waking up every couple of hours for a bottle and a diaper change, but other than that you were quiet and easy, like you were already determined to not make too much trouble. I checked the weather report every day, waiting until I was 100 percent sure there was no chance of rain. I also needed just a little more time with you, to stare at you and soak you in and tell you all these things I wanted to tell you. I whispered so many things to you over those days, like I could fill you up with me.

On the bus I brought my hands to my cheeks to

double-check that thinking these thoughts hadn't sent me crying again after the guy next to me suddenly pulled off his headphones and looked at me. Those headphones sat on a neck so skinny it reminded me of the turkeys on the farm, heads resting on a thin red cord so easy to stretch over an old stump and snap with an ax. I was doing it by seven, but only because Gamps made me and then whooped it up when I winced at the blood sprayed across my cheek. Skinny Neck asked me if I was okay, and I just shrugged even though something in his eyes matched Wanda's and made me want to spend all the miles to Florida telling him the truth. But even that wouldn't have been enough time.

He ignored my invisible shield, leaning into me so close I could feel his breath, which wasn't altogether unpleasant.

"Jacksonville your final stop?" he asked.

I told him I was switching there for Orlando.

"Disney? I always wanted to go there."

"Yeah, happiest place on earth."

I actually always imagined it was—all the shiny families you saw on the commercials crowded around Mickey or Minnie or Belle, grinning from ear to ear like their faces were going to break from all the joy. "There's a place where nothing is as it seems, where the ordinary is extraordinary," the announcer's voice would boom as fireworks exploded over Cinderella's castle. Some days I loved those commercials. Other days I'd hate them. Thirty seconds of being pounded in the face with a reminder of what you didn't have, a wholesome happiness you'd probably never know. The kind that cost a lot of money and required a dad in khakis walking side by side with a mom in a white sundress, so much love between them it spilled over onto their two giddy kids, staining their expensive sneakers. What could an orphan know of such joy? That's the kind of self-pitying mood those commercials could put me in. Even though technically I wasn't an orphan, since my dad was alive as far as I knew, but it was the way I'd always thought of myself. Little Orphan Daisy. Which is why seeing a Khaki Dad smiling down at his skinny daughter with her long, glossy ponytail and sparkly fanny pack could ruin my whole day.

"You gonna be a princess or something?" Skinny Neck asked when I told him that I was going to Disney not as a tourist, but to work there. We both laughed because the idea of someone who looks like me being Disney-princess material was definitely hilarious, and I could tell he wasn't making fun of me, or at least if he was, it was entirely good-natured.

"I'm gonna be Ursula the sea witch from *The Little Mermaid*." I was proud that I could muster up a joke, lame as it was.

"Well, she's dope," he said, like he couldn't quite tell if I was kidding and he was hedging his bets.

It was Heather from back home who was helping me get the job (as a ticket taker or parking lot attendant or something, no ball gown needed). She actually did work as a princess, though I wasn't sure which one. Heather got hired at Disney not six days after we graduated Leesville High School and was gone three days after that—poof!—like Cinderella at midnight. Story went that she wrote the Walt Disney Company a letter explaining her dream of being a princess and included a bunch of "glamour shots" she took on her phone, and they hired her. I don't know how much of that is truth or legend. I like to believe it is true though, that Heather always dreamed of being a princess and then got to be one just by wishing it so. It had to help that she was a dead ringer for Cinderella even without a costume—white-blond hair and big blue eyes, and she'd wear this bright-pink blush on her pale skin that made her look cartoonishly flushed. Then there were her lashes . . . and her boobs. All of it probably should have made all the girls hate her, but Heather was as sweet as she was pretty—like if birthday cake were a person.

Despite being princess pretty though, Heather's life was no fairy tale growing up. Whose was, I guess, but she had it particularly bad with a mom who had a parade of druggie boyfriends prone to rageful benders where they punched walls and put cigarettes out on her mom's thighs.

There was one night in middle school I found Heather sitting in the parking lot behind Rita's where I worked part-time shampooing and sweeping hair. She was waiting out the latest screaming match at home, nursing a warm forty. She looked at me that night and said, "We're getting the fuck out of here, Daisy. You and I are gonna be the ones to leave this shit place." We all thought that—everyone in Leesville spent our lives waiting for the moment where we could be anywhere else, even if we had no idea where that would be or how to get there. But the way Heather said it, so forceful, I believed her and I was happy she'd said "we" because her conviction felt like enough for both of us. We didn't talk much at school after that, though, I think because we couldn't bear to see all the secret shames we shared that night reflected back to us. But when I saw a Facebook post where she said Disney was hiring for the summer, and I remembered that look in her eyes—wild and determined, and how she had said "we" that night—I thought I could ask her for help. Within the hour she messaged me back and said she could. I couldn't believe it, but I wasn't going to look a gift horse in the mouth. I got a bus ticket.

I had tuned out and come back to realize Skinny Neck was going on about roller coasters. "Now, the Dare Devil Dive at Six Flags? That ride is sick, man. A ninety-five-foot drop straight down. Makes you feel like you swallowed your throat. But I always wanted to go to Disney. Ride on Space Mountain, see that wizard white-boy shit. That could be pretty cool."

His chatter was good for one thing—it helped distract me from how everything in my body hurt. My swollen breasts, still full from milk, were starting to throb in rhythm with the pulsing pain in my crotch and the pressure in my bladder.

"Well, you should come. Look for me in one of those booths in the parking lot or something."

"Maybe one day . . . I'm gonna be busy the next while . . . getting my butt kicked." He let out a weak laugh, but he looked scared. Where was he going, I wondered, where he'd get his butt kicked? Prison? Which was a silly thought because they didn't just let you ride the regular bus to prison.

"I'm headed for basic training. The Marines."

"Wow."

"Yep."

"Rough."

"Yep."

It was like we were playing this private game to see how long we could continue the conversation with single syllables.

"Cool," I said. A point.

"Maybe." From his smile it was clear we were in on this joke together, and what a sweet and strange thing to have an instant inside joke with a stranger. Generally I'm wary of other humans because of their likelihood to disappoint you sooner or later. But then you'll meet one who gets you, and it's often not the one you thought it would be. It had been like that with Cinnamon too that day I met her at the park.

She had this warm voice like everything she said was sort of a lullaby, and after we'd hung out a few times it was clear she cared. A lot. Actually, she was so nice to me I thought it was creepy at first. No one is ever that nice without wanting something from you. It was also weird chatting with Cinnamon since I'd never actually sat down and talked to a Black person before, which was not all that surprising since Gamps all but forbade it and would have probably had a heart attack to imagine such a thing.

What would Gamps think now, seeing me yucking it up with Skinny Neck here on the bus?

Skinny Neck's smile grew into laughter, almost a giggle that made me think he was going to last about ten minutes in the Marines. I took in the gold cross around his neck, the ornate letters in the tattoo on his wrist that spelled out "RIP Debbie," his too-tight shirt that was the slightest bit ripe. I recognized in him something we shared—we were both running from something more than we were running toward something.

"So, why the military?" I asked the question even if I already knew the answer—no other options. Same reason why more than half the guys in our senior class enlisted. Not like they could be princesses.

"I guess I'm supposed to come up with some patriotic bullshit about how I love my country. But that would be a lie—this country hasn't done nothing but fuck with me. So it's more like . . . this is the best of a lotta bad options. Get a paycheck. See the world and whatnot. Maybe get in shape." He raises an arm as thin as a noodle to form a limp bicep.

Bingo. No other options. That's how I felt when Wanda told me to do right by you—out of options and as panicked and trapped as the rabbits we snared in our garden growing up. It was a feeling I probably should have been used to. It might seem like all of it was for me—that I wanted to be young and free and selfish. And I'll admit there's some truth there. I had dreams I wasn't ready to give up on. I was going to get into school. Learn to fly. Yeah, your mother wanted to be a pilot. How wild is that? Some days that dream felt stupid or impossible, but somehow I still didn't let that stop me. Guess that was my stubborn streak. I wasn't going to give up before I even started. But then you happened. So, yeah, I was sort of saving myself, but also saving you too. I promised Wanda (and myself) I would do right by you. And that meant giving you a better mother than I ever could be considering I was broke, alone, and could barely take care of myself, let alone a baby. A mother's only job is to protect her child, and that's exactly what I was doing. If I couldn't be the mother you deserved, I would give you one who could be. Someone who knew what to do, who came from good people, a normal kind of family, who knew how to be a good friend, who always showed up, who had a happy marriage, and nice shoes, and read books about all kinds of things, and remembered what candy you liked and brought it to you just to be nice. The type of woman you meet and think, *She was born to be a mom.* How many moments did I wish Cinnamon were my mom? I knew that couldn't happen, but I could guarantee the next best thing, or the best thing, really—she could be yours.

CHAPTER FOUR

The baby is screaming. Cinnamon can hear the wails coming from inside the house the second she pulls the car into the driveway. She covers the distance between the driver's seat and the front door in a single breath, her skin tingling with terror.

What's happening to Bluebell? Where the hell is Jayson?

The screams are coming from their bedroom, where Cinnamon put the baby down before she left barely an hour ago. She flings open the door, expecting to see Bluebell on the floor, somehow flung from the carrier Cinnamon had left her sleeping in, her little bones shattered, her skull crushed.

But Bluebell's still in the bucket seat, safely strapped in. She's hardly moved. In fact, nothing has changed except the fact that she was sound asleep when Cinnamon walked out the door and now she's wailing so hard her little face has turned purple from the exertion.

"Shhhh, shhhh, baby girl." She picks Bluebell up and walks her down to the kitchen, where she knows she left half a bottle of formula in the fridge. She doesn't even bother to heat it up, but it hardly matters because Bluebell begins furiously sucking on the nipple despite the chill. She was starving. Starving and crying and Jayson is nowhere to be found.

Cinnamon only made a quick run to the office to grab her notes for an internship reference letter she promised to have for a student by next week. She'd already emailed Dean Bowler and said she planned to take some personal days. There are only two weeks left in the semester anyway—she could work from home and do her last few student meetings on Zoom. But one step at a time—thinking about juggling work and caring for Bluebell while searching for Daisy gives her the feeling of driving off a cliff. More pressing is the rank smell emanating from the baby's behind. It's so full the poop is starting to seep onto her onesie. She'll have to deal with that before she deals with Jayson. She never should have asked him to keep an eye on the baby while she ran out, especially after all his ranting and raving last night. Granted, his shock and confusion were entirely justified, given his wife came home not with the creole catfish she'd promised but with . . . a baby.

His agitated but entirely logical line of inquiries were all a version of *What in all holy hell are you doing?*

"Why didn't you go to the police? Who up and leaves a baby, Cinnamon? Ole girl just expected you to take her kid for her? Is she on drugs? This is not our problem, Cinnamon. We don't need this right now. You've got to take that baby to the police." On and on it went, as Jayson wore out the old pine floorboards while pacing their bedroom.

Cinnamon tried her best to convince him that Daisy wasn't like that, that she was just a kid trying to figure out how to do better for herself, but it was hard to explain their strange intimacy to her husband when she didn't totally understand it herself. And so she exaggerated their relationship, if only a tad, by explaining that she'd been helping Daisy to enroll at SBCC. It's not completely untrue. She actually *had* mentioned it to her more than once, but Daisy had her sights set on flight school and was going to apply when she'd saved enough.

Making her relationship with Daisy sound more professional seemed to have the right effect, and Jayson softened his tone slightly as he watched Cinnamon feed Bluebell and put her to sleep. He breathed a further sigh of relief as she conveyed her optimism that she'd find Daisy posthaste and assured him that this state of affairs was very temporary.

Bluebell's wails for food and diaper changes last night woke them every couple of hours. Each time, Jayson grumbled a little more, but one time he actually got up and picked Bluebell out of her carrier and soothed her while Cinnamon prepared the bottle.

"I got baby cousins, you know," he had said when Cinnamon looked at him in surprise. It was that moment that made her think maybe it wasn't such a big deal for him to keep an eye on Bluebell while she popped into the office this morning.

But of course it was a big deal, and of course he had gone about his business like there wasn't a baby right here that needed actual watching. And changing. Which Cinnamon does quickly, swallowing down her nausea when warm poop smears across her palm.

As soon as she's done and Bluebell is clean and fed and swaddled, Cinnamon stomps across the tiny cottage, getting through all five rooms in less than half a minute, but her husband is nowhere to be found. Suddenly, she sees a bit of movement through the blinds covering the patio window and can't believe she had missed the unmistakable whirring of a rusty motor. She shoves them aside so hard one of the slats breaks off.

There's Jayson, as oblivious as can be, pushing their ancient red lawn mower across the patchy grass in the backyard. She takes a deep breath before she opens the screen door and shouts her husband's name. He ignores her the first three times. He ignores her until she's right behind him. That's when she sees the earbuds in his ears and can hear them turned as high as they'll go. She gives him a little shove with her elbow since both her hands are still clutching the baby.

He turns and dons a silly smile, holding up one finger for her to wait as he turns off the mower and pops the earbuds out of his ears. "Hey, wife."

"What are you doing? Didn't you hear the baby crying? I asked you to watch her."

He looks genuinely bewildered that she's upset. "She was asleep.

You've been on me to mow the lawn and I figured she'd be out for a while, and I wanted to surprise you."

Cinnamon is shaking with nerves and irritation, not just at his incompetence and lack of thought, but now at his utter nonchalance. "She was screaming when I got home. She was starving and her diaper had started leaking. And you've got your earbuds in. You can't hear anything. She could have been yelling since the moment I walked out the door and you'd have had no idea. How could you think it was okay just to walk out the door and leave a baby alone in the house?"

It is peak irony because Jayson had been the one going on and on last night about how they'd be in a whole heap of trouble if anything happened to this child while she was under their roof. How they could easily be hauled away for kidnapping or not reporting a crime. How the last thing they needed was any drama, etc., etc. And here he is now, crooning along to Anthony Hamilton without a thought to the baby's well-being. It's a lot of nerve to make her feel like the crazy one now, as if she's being some paranoid, hysterical mother. Yet she can see he's ready to double down on his defense.

Sure enough, he grabs both of her shoulders and looks into her eyes. "A sleeping baby. A sleeping baby that was barely twenty feet away from me. Come on, Cinnamon. Look at her. She's fine. She probably woke up when she heard your car in the driveway, like a puppy. And you gave her a bottle and now she's good again. Just like last night. I checked on her, like, fifteen minutes ago and she was fine."

Cinnamon knows Jayson is lying about checking in on Bluebell. He's got a pretty obvious tic when he lies. He rocks back and forth from his heels to his toes like a little kid who's got to go to the bathroom, and right now he looks like he's got to pee real bad.

"But she wasn't fine, and that's all that matters. You have to watch a baby, like actually physically watch it. You have to stay close and listen all of the time."

"Cece, calm yourself down. You're blowing this way out of proportion." He leans over to tickle Bluebell's foot, but Cinnamon pulls her away like his touch could burn her and marches into the house. She can't say she's surprised when she sees him shrug and start up the mower again to finish that last patch of grass.

When he finally saunters back into the house a half hour later, Jayson has become the aggrieved party, slamming doors and flinging the suitcase he'd dug out of the closet yesterday morning on the bed and throwing clothes in it for his fishing trip. "I just wanted to do something nice for you before I left today," he mumbles, petulant as ever. "Like I said, you've been on me about the yard. I wanted to surprise you."

She thinks about trying to catalog for him all the reasons he's wrong—wrong and immature and just plain reckless. But then again, Jayson didn't sign up to care for this baby. He hasn't signed up to care for any baby.

Since they met five years ago, he's always talked about having kids in that vague way of most men—the babies will come one day and won't take a lot of work on his part anyway. He assumes it will happen when it happens, when he's "ready," when he's "successful" and has "made it financially," and that is all constantly a work in progress. That Jayson thinks it'll be so easy for them to have their own child whenever he's good and ready says a lot about his cluelessness and hubris, especially since they've been rolling the dice, so to speak, the entire time they've been together and they've never even had a scare. That he knows about at least. But he hasn't pressed the issue at all. For her part, Cinnamon is okay with letting it ride too. She can never decide how she feels about having kids. One day she'll feel a tug in her ovaries, the next she doesn't think she has it in her to care for a completely helpless human being after using all her energy to basically raise herself. Back and forth it goes, but it's all distraction from the true heart of the matter: the entire prospect terrifies her. It didn't matter in the end, however, since her body took the decision mostly out of her hands. When she was about Daisy's age, she'd gone to a free women's health clinic offered by the church to get her very first ever gynecological exam, and the doctor announced she had "fibroids as big as tennis balls" crowding her uterus. "Some of the worst

I've ever seen," he had said. He had the nerve to sound more excited than worried when he'd said this, as if witnessing a medical marvel. She'd never heard of fibroids before, but this explained the reason she bled through an entire box of super tampons during her periods, which was stressful not just because of all that blood but because tampons were expensive and therefore hard to come by, especially when she lived on the streets. It also explained the chronic pain that felt like, well, tennis balls bouncing around her uterus. Her back was sweating into the crinkling paper as the doctor, a pinched-nosed nasally white man who looked like he'd much rather be teeing off at the ninth hole than peering into her vagina, proclaimed, "It's going to be very hard for you to have children. You may even need a hysterectomy sooner than later." He said this like it wasn't an altogether bad thing. He was doing his good deed for the day, not just offering free health care to poor brown girls but, in her case, saving the world the burden of any more of them. She agreed with him that this wasn't altogether a bad thing—albeit for different reasons. Cinnamon accepted her probable infertility like every other curveball thrown at her.

What has been hard is dealing with people being all up in her business about her procreation status. Those confused stares when strangers ask her if she has kids and she says no. It's as if she's just told them the color green doesn't exist—inconceivable and outside the natural order of things. There was the man who told her she was wasting her life, and the one who said she was defying God's will. The woman, the countless women actually, who told her she was missing out and to "just wait." The mother-in-law who somehow makes her feelings clear without saying anything at all—it's just a look Abigail throws off sometimes, like, *When already?* And all the people who think they can ask her intrusive questions. *What are you waiting for? Why not? Something wrong down there?* That's her favorite, from a cab driver in Atlanta. She'd simply said, "Yup."

That cab driver knew more than her husband—she's never told Jayson about her faulty lady parts. She isn't sure why. It might be the embarrassment of bringing it up at all, or the worry that Jayson will think she is damaged goods. It's easiest to leave it all up to fate and chance.

She's relieved when she hears the sound of Jayson zipping the suitcase. He doesn't even hide his eagerness to bound out of the house. Cinnamon had been cranky about this fishing trip, but now she sees it as a godsend. The last thing she needs is her husband huffing around all weekend looking at her like she's crazy—even if she is—and resenting the care she has to give Bluebell. She'll take the two-night reprieve.

"I hope you know what you're doing, Cece!" Jayson says as he stands at their bedroom door. "I'll see you Monday—good luck! I'll miss you."

She tells herself he means it.

Forty-eight very long hours later, she's learned that what she needs is not luck but four more pairs of hands. The whole "it takes a village" saying could really not be truer. Luckily, Lucia is back in town after her spa weekend with her mother-in-law and is coming over as soon as she drops the twins at preschool, which doesn't give Cinnamon much time to pull it together. Surveying the current scene, she can't think where to even begin.

Powdered formula covers the kitchen counter where she managed to spill an entire container trying to measure the perfect amount into the small opening at the top of the bottle. For every bottle Cinnamon gives her, Bluebell seems to produce double the poop in a vast array of colors. The trash bin is overflowing with tiny diapers, all of them smelling like raw sewage. She needs to empty it all out but hasn't found the time. The few onesies she purchased are already stained with spit-up, pee, poop, and formula. At least she got them into the washer—a small victory. To top it all off, she's splayed out on the sectional in their living room (the one they are still making payments on) completely topless with a naked baby pressed to her chest. She can't breastfeed this child, of course—she's not insane or deranged. Though she did, at midnight, read a long essay by a woman who attempted to stimulate her own milk supplies to feed the baby she was fostering. That is a line Cinnamon will not cross, but she also read in the baby-care blogs she consumed all night about how important skin-to-skin contact is for newborns. Looking down though, the baby's lily-white skin pressed against the dark expanse of Cinnamon's chest is a discomfiting juxtaposition.

Images flash through her mind: generations of beleaguered Black women, slaves and wet nurses, forced into caring for precious white babies. When Cinnamon was ten, she was in a program that gave her a Big Sister, a white woman named Leslie who was always asking Cinnamon who she had a crush on at school. Leslie also couldn't stop talking about her own boyfriend—a mortgage broker named Ted. She did both so incessantly that even as a kid, Cinnamon knew it reflected something desperate and wrong about Leslie, her relationship with Ted, or both. One day, Leslie took her to an exhibit at the local art museum—*In the Shadows*, a collection of nineteenth-century photographs of Black caretakers. Why on earth this woman thought this was appropriate for a ten-year-old, let alone a ten-year-old who shared the same haunted face with those looking down on her from two hundred years into the past, was beyond Cinnamon, who had been hoping to go ice-skating. Leslie didn't say a word, just dragged her from picture to picture, looking increasingly somber and uncomfortable. When they finally got to the end of the exhibit, Leslie mumbled something about how art can be so powerful and open up our eyes to "things" and "Did you enjoy it, Cinnamon?" *Enjoy?* No, she didn't enjoy it one bit, nor was Leslie clear about what exactly her eyes were being opened to. Cinnamon's main concern was if and how she could open the volunteer coordinator's eyes about how she didn't want to see Leslie ever again, without being made to feel ungrateful for the opportunity to spend one afternoon a month with an overeager white lady.

One photograph Cinnamon saw that day stayed with her all these years, a girl who was her age at the time, a slave, holding a white baby she was clearly in charge of keeping entertained, alive, and pampered, though she was a child herself. The girl looked as wise as an old woman but also run-down and tired. Yet somehow she still looked down at the baby with kindness, maybe even something like love.

Cinnamon's not a child and no one is forcing her to take care of this baby, so she can't quite work out why she's thinking of that particular photo and why she's so unsettled, like the degradation experienced by that girl and so many others lingers in her bones.

She looks down at Bluebell, made limp by deep sleep, her mouth forming a perfect little O shape. Cinnamon wonders if the girl is still making the transition between her old world and this one, still absorbing all its newness. No wonder babies need so much sleep.

"What am I gonna do with you, little Bluebell?"

But she knows what she's going to do. Cinnamon made the decision to give herself a deadline somewhere around 3 a.m., when she took a break from her desperate Google searches for questions like "Can a newborn cry too much?" and settled into an episode of the *Golden Girls*. Bluebell was still on her chest since she bawled every time Cinnamon put her down. That's when she decided she'll give herself until Friday. If Cinnamon doesn't find Daisy by Friday, she'll go to the police. She will steel herself to surrender Bluebell and hope for the best. When Jayson called yesterday afternoon, floating somewhere miles off the coast, she made that vow to him. "Just give me the rest of the week."

He was day drunk, with Jay-Z blasting in the background, which must have scared away the fish, though what did Cinnamon know about fishing? She was still annoyed with him for being such a thoughtless and careless jackass the other day, but she was also chastened by exhaustion and was starting to think that Jay was right. She had no business with this baby. He was relieved to hear that his days with an unexpected roommate were numbered and that made him apologize for his neglectful behavior. She was relieved to end the call on good terms. When he said, "I miss you," this time she felt it.

Cinnamon startles so badly at the knock on the front door it sends her phone straight in the air, and she grabs it just before it lands on

Bluebell's delicate head. The knock, loud as it is, is just ceremonial. Lucia's bounding through the front door with a booming "Yoo-hoo, it's me," as if it would be anybody else just barreling into the house like they own the place. Cinnamon is initially annoyed that Lucia is forty-five minutes early before she realizes that it's 10 a.m. and not 9 a.m. and she somehow lost an hour this morning. It could be the same place as Bluebell's left sock.

"Jesus, Mary, and Joseph!" Lucia doesn't make it two steps into the house before she stops short, mouth agape, two giant coffee cups in her hands. Cinnamon practically drops Bluebell on the couch in her rush to throw her shirt on—there's no time to wrestle with her bra. The baby starts to cry, a reasonable reaction to nearly tumbling to the floor, and Cinnamon can only hope it's enough to distract all of them from this awkward scene. She doesn't even hazard an explanation, and luckily, Lucia being Lucia, she recovers from the outrageous tableau quickly. Not that this does anything for Cinnamon's embarrassment.

"Well, you look like shit and you smell like a Starbucks bathroom, so it's clear you have a newborn. I'm having PTSD just looking at you."

In the blur of the past couple of days, Cinnamon has careened from feeling isolated and abandoned and being all alone with this strange creature to relieved she and the baby could just do their own thing. No one had to see her incompetence, her desperation, or her exhaustion. Until now. Until she was practically naked—literally—in front of Lucia and, apparently, utterly wrecked. So much for any illusion that she has this under control. That she's inexplicably on the brink of tears to see Lucia in her living room makes that clear—and she can't even blame actual hormones.

"For the love of God, give her to me. Don't forget to support her head." Lucia drops the coffees on the counter as she lunges toward Cinnamon.

Cinnamon has never been so excited to see her friend, to happily crawl toward a cup of hot, sweet coffee, so much so that she's willing to ignore Lucia's comment. She knows how to hold a baby, for heaven's sake.

"Like this, honey." Lucia reaches over and cups Bluebell behind her head. "Otherwise, it'll just flop all over the place."

Cinnamon laughs to mask her irritation and then pulls the baby protectively to her chest before she hands her over, which is surprisingly hard to do.

The first thing Lucia does is press her nose to Bluebell's translucent scalp and sniff her. "Oh, that smell! She probably needs a hat. Does she have a hat? Newborns lose a ton of heat through their heads."

"It's around here somewhere," Cinnamon says.

"She's so small, Cece! She's got to go to the doctor. New babies go to the doctor every week, and this one can't be more than a week old."

"She's definitely older than that. Your babies were way smaller when they were, like, a month."

"Because they were twins and they were premature. This baby is definitely brand-new. And besides, you have no idea if she's healthy or not. You don't even know how old she is. All the more reason to get this child to the police. Today. Now."

She makes it sound so simple, but to Lucia it's *Take the baby to the police station and she will be someone else's problem*. Lucia would be able to put it behind her, blissfully ignorant enough not to be haunted by what was to come for this stranger's baby, with blind faith in the invisible, distant, well-meaning collective of competent professionals who guarantee that poor, abandoned children are properly taken care of.

Lucia is glaring at her, and normally that look is enough for Cinnamon to do what her friend is asking. But not today. If anything, her resolve has strengthened over the last few days.

"I'm giving myself until Friday, Luce. If we haven't found Daisy by then, I promise I'll take her to the police."

Lucia raises an eyebrow, questioning the wisdom of this decision as much as Cinnamon's use of the word "we."

"Cinnamon. You can't just keep someone else's baby. And Friday is *four* days from now—a long time!"

"Yeah, well, it's going to take some time. Or maybe Daisy'll come back. I honestly think she's not right in the head. I mean, she asked me to raise this child! She must have postpartum depression or something. I feel like I owe it to her to try to talk some sense into her, but I know I can't look forever."

Lucia turns and surveys the cluttered kitchen like she's dying to clean it up and in her next breath announces that if Cinnamon can't be deterred from this "loco idea," she can bring some of the twins' old clothes and toys by later.

"I don't really need that much; thank you, though. And it's not like I can turn her in with a suitcase."

"Well, she can't keep sleeping in her carrier. I've got a bassinet in the car. It's small. Will fit right next to your bed. And I can always bring some other stuff tomorrow. Trust me—you need more than you think." That felt like a life lesson that went beyond babies.

Lucia thrusts Bluebell in the air *Lion King* style. "Hmm—she's not that cute, is she?"

"Hey!" Cinnamon doesn't know what to make of how defensive she feels.

"What? I'm not allowed to say that? The twins were real weird-looking for the first two months too. You expect the Gerber baby to pop out of your vagina and then you get the old man from the Smucker's commercials. Why do all white babies look like old men?"

"Who knows? Black babies *are* cuter."

"Hey!"

Cinnamon flashes a grin at Lucia. "What? I'm not allowed to say that? It's true."

Lucia brings the baby back down to the cradle of her elbow, and Cinnamon drinks her in. She is truly a beautiful child.

"How are you not freaking out more? Jesus, Cinnamon. I can't believe you've got a real live baby in your house!"

She's asked herself this question at least a dozen times. Why isn't she freaking out more? There have definitely been moments this weekend when she's screamed into a pillow, and she's eaten a year's worth of sugar in forty-eight hours. She's overwhelmed but not really freaking out. Maybe it's because she learned a long time ago to just adapt to anything—no matter how messed up it is, you just go with the flow and let go of your expectations. It's expectations that lead to disappointment. Or hope—that too.

"Yeah. I know. I can't believe it either. I *am* drowning though. Look at me!" Cinnamon stands up and surveys herself for real for the first time in days. "I haven't taken a shower all weekend. I *do* smell like a Starbucks bathroom. I don't know how you did this, Luce. And with two of them! I've never been so bone-tired, and something new and terrifying happens every couple of hours. I swear she stopped breathing at midnight. She didn't—she just had the hiccups. And then her poop turned bright yellow, but the Internet told me not to worry, it was fine. Apparently, babies poop a rainbow of colors when they first come out."

"Except for white," Lucia says.

"Exactly!" How on earth do people know how to do this? For all the blogs and books, no parent can ever know everything they need to know. You can't even begin to know what you *don't* know. Cinnamon wonders if her own mother ever read a baby book. Somehow Cinnamon doubts it, and she'd bet her last dollar that her grandmother hadn't either. She can remember Grandma Thelma saying, "Lord, there are just some things you can't learn in a book." How to be a good and competent mother seems to be one of them.

"I'm sorry I wasn't here to help. Believe me—I would have preferred that to rubbing sunscreen across the psoriasis on Rebecca Wenger's back every hour on the hour."

"Don't worry; we were fine." As Cinnamon says it, she realizes it was mostly true—as surreal as it's been, she got the hang of the basics and was prouder than she should have been the first time she pulled off a perfect swaddle. She's convinced Bluebell even smiled at her in the wee hours this morning, drunk on formula. She was not prepared for how that would make her heart lurch so hard she had to steady herself.

"Well, I'm here now. Go, go, go—up and shower. That's an order."

"I will. I will. But she needs to eat."

"You go. I'll feed her. Go upstairs. Formula in the kitchen?"

"Yeah, over there." Cinnamon points to the collection of canisters and the bottles that have amassed on the counter like occupying soldiers. "Just a spoonful. And you have to shake it hard. And make sure the bottle's tipped so she doesn't get too much air; otherwise, she'll stop feeding."

"Do you think I don't know how to feed a child?" Lucia loves bossing other people around but hates getting bossed herself. Truth be told, Cinnamon appreciates this about her friend, that she's always keen to take charge. Cinnamon has a lifetime of practice submitting to authority figures and ceding control, so it's a comfortable dynamic. It's what drew her to Lucia in the first place. The month she and Jayson moved to Sibley Bay, Abigail was organizing a Red Cross clothing drive for victims of a recent hurricane that devastated Puerto Rico. Her mother-in-law had been volunteering for the Red Cross for thirty years and the drive was a big deal for her, so Cinnamon showed up bright and early, eager to earn brownie points and goodwill. That plan fell through after Abigail had sprained her ankle in Zumba class that morning and had to bow out. The whole clothing drive was in chaos without their fearless leader. Suddenly, this massively pregnant woman wearing a skintight dress the color of Tang began clapping her hands and ordering the clueless volunteers into groups.

"You're on kids' clothes," she said, pointing to another pregnant woman. "You've got old men," she directed a young man in his twenties.

"What are old men's clothes? How are they different from other men's clothes?"

"What does your grandpa wear?" The kid gave a thumbs-up. She looked at Cinnamon. "You're with me. We'll do shoes. I'm Lucia Wenger, by the way."

Once they'd sat down to start sorting through the donations, Lucia explained to her that shoes were the hardest. "People always donate their rattiest sneakers and smelliest old loafers. Makes them feel good, but think about how you'd feel if you just lost all your Nikes and suddenly you're getting someone's stinky old shit. It's great that people want to give all this, but can you imagine having to wear someone's gross hand-me-downs? So tough."

Cinnamon could imagine it, actually. It was how she got most of her clothes for most of her childhood.

Lucia fished a pair of sparkly red sequined heels out of one of the donation bags and handed them to Cinnamon. "Well, these are actually nice but completely impractical for the hurricane victims. You should take them. You can wear them when we go out to get margaritas," she instructed, as if their future friend date were a foregone conclusion.

"I couldn't."

"Try 'em on. I bet they were some old lady's getting-divorced shoes. She wore them one time going out cougar-ing and then decided it wasn't worth the blisters and switched back to flats," Lucia said. "But now they're yours. I dare you to take them."

Over the next six hours, Cinnamon learned Lucia's entire life story, starting with her moving from Puerto Rico to suburban New Jersey when she was six through busting her butt at Rutgers and landing her dream job as a foreign correspondent for the *Chicago Tribune* covering migrant issues in Central America. That's where she met Adam.

"I thought he was this dashing world traveler when we hooked up in Guatemala. Little did I know he was volunteering with Dentists Without Borders, and before I knew it, I was engaged to a Jewish orthodontist and relocating to bumfuck so he could take over his dad's practice when his parents retired to Boca. I say that endearingly after ten years here, but not so much at first. You just moved from Atlanta with your new hubby, Beanstalk?"

Cinnamon was taken aback that this stranger knew so much—including Jayson's high school nickname—and Lucia registered as much.

"Oh, don't worry—you'll get used to everyone knowing your business. Just roll with me."

Cinnamon would never get used to that, and it made her want to hightail it back to Atlanta, but on the plus side, just like that, she slipped into an easy and happy friendship with Lucia that day without having to do very much at all. It was funny: like every woman, she'd been conditioned to think getting a man was the ultimate prize, but even though finding Jayson made her count her blessings, it was really this—this friendship—that felt like a miracle. She feels a swell of love and gratitude that whatever Lucia's faults, the universe delivered her a bona fide best friend, her first, at the ripe old age of thirty-two.

Before she goes upstairs to shower, Cinnamon throws her arms around Lucia, smushing the baby between them.

"Goodness, what was that for?"

"I can't hug my friend?"

"Not smelling like that, you can't. A toothbrush is calling your name! When you get back, we'll get to work on a plan for the week and finding Miss Daisy."

Lucia and her plans, but she's right, and now the clock is ticking.

"Otherwise, we're going to have to find a sitter for the party Friday night! Not to mention for the manis and pedis I've got lined up for us on Thursday."

It takes a beat for Cinnamon to figure out what the hell Lucia is talking about, so focused is she on her arbitrary deadline for finding Daisy. But then it clicks into place, her birthday party, the one Lucia has thrown herself into planning, the one Cinnamon had been looking forward to. If she doesn't find Daisy, is she just going to drop the baby off at the police station and drink a virgin mojito as if it were nothing? The thought of that lodges a lump in Cinnamon's throat that she pushes down with a hard swallow. "Yeah, Luce. I really need your help. Don't you have sources and whatnot to track people down? Should I try to find a PI or something?" As if she could afford that.

"Oh, I've got sources. Don't you worry. How hard can it be to find a teenager? We can do this. Go take care of that dragon breath, and we'll get it all sorted out. I'll be down here eating these toes!" Lucia dramatically gobbles at Bluebell's miniature feet. "Okay, I take it back, Cece. She actually is cute," she calls out to Cinnamon's back as she leaves the kitchen.

Cinnamon is beaming as she climbs the narrow staircase, as if she can take any of the credit.

When she passes the bed, she swears she can actually hear it calling her name. If only she could lie down for just a minute, but she knows once she gets sucked into sleep, there's no getting back up. A catnap at this point would be tortuous, and she has things to do. Starting with finding some clean clothes. She strips off her shirt, tosses it on the bed, and yanks open the closet door. The next thing she knows she's still furiously rubbing her toe when a memory crashes through the pain—the time Daisy told her about how her hometown was known as the "lost luggage capital of America" because it had a big warehouse where all the major airlines sent bags that had been misplaced or went unclaimed. After about six months, the warehouse sold whatever was sellable. Daisy worked there after school for two years and told Cinnamon about all the crazy things people packed in their luggage that other people would actually buy.

"Ten pounds of expired cat food!" Daisy laughed. "A diamond engagement ring. A pool cue signed by Charlie Sheen!"

It was the only time, apart from talking about the dogs named Star, that Daisy had lit up when talking about something from her past, from back home. It would be easy enough to figure out the town with a Google search, and she'd made it sound small enough that it likely wouldn't have that many high schools, but Cinnamon resolves to call them all if she has to, no matter how many, to see if they'd had a student named Daisy. Screaming toe be damned, Cinnamon bolts for the steps, taking them two at a time to get her phone from the living room.

"I've seen your boobs way too many times this morning!" Lucia says as she streaks past. "What on earth are you doing?"

"I think I may have a lead on Daisy. Give me a minute!" She runs back upstairs and settles on her bed to google. Her fingers can't move fast enough, her previous exhaustion forgotten. Her elation intensifies when her Google search is successful. The town comes right up. Leesville, Georgia. Population: 2,484. Given the size of the place, she's banking on there being only one public high school and a further Google search proves her right.

Cinnamon is dialing before she even thinks of a story or a plan.

A high-pitched woman's voice answers. "Leesville High. How may I direct your call?"

Cinnamon pauses. "Um . . . I'm looking for a former student. Her name is Daisy."

"Who's calling?" The woman sounds distracted by the cacophony of kids' voices and lockers slamming. It's just after 9 a.m. on Monday morning, so not the most opportune time, but Cinnamon couldn't wait.

"I'm a career counselor with Sibley Bay Community College and I was speaking with one of your former students about enrolling here, but I lost her phone number and wanted to get back in touch."

"Um, okay then . . . Well, we're right smack in the middle of starting the school day. But hold on—let me see if I can find Brenda."

Suddenly, "Somebody to Love" is blasting in her ear. Queen seems like odd hold music for a high school, or period, but she's happy for the invigorating distraction. She almost starts singing since she's on hold through two full choruses. She's about to give up when a voice finally comes on the line.

"You're looking for information about a young woman named Daisy?"

"I am. Did you have any students by that name?"

"I'm Brenda Heller, the guidance counselor here. We have a policy of not giving out student information, but I can tell you that there is no official record of a Daisy graduating from Leesville in the past five years. You don't have a last name?"

Cinnamon is too tired to make up a story right now. "I don't. I'm sorry." She slumps back on the bed, deflated. So much for not letting herself have hope. "Well, thank you anyway," she says, the defeat clear in her voice. Maybe that's why the woman takes pity on her.

"But actually . . . we did have a student who sometimes went by the name Daisy. Amanda Jacobs. She would have graduated two years ago."

"Really?"

For a split second Cinnamon trips over the revelation that she didn't even know Daisy's real name. She can't dwell on that though; what she focuses on is that she knows way more now than she did not five minutes ago. A legal name!

"I probably shouldn't have told you that. But if Amanda is trying to get into college, I wish the best for her. She deserves it. She was always a really smart kid—pleasant too. Really dealt a rough hand."

"Do you know how I can contact her?"

"I can't give you any more information. School policy. I'm sorry, but I know you understand."

"I do, yes. Thank you again."

She doesn't need any more from Brenda. Cinnamon can track down the Jacobses of Leesville easily enough, she imagines. It can't be hard to find Daisy's relatives, someone who may know where she went. It was a long shot, but maybe she even went home, though Cinnamon would bet her last dollar that wasn't the case.

Daisy girl, I'm going to find you!

It's maybe the first time Cinnamon actually believes this. That's the thing with hope—it has a mind of its own.

Dear You,

The "happiest place on earth" is less than joyous when you're trapped in a hot little box in the middle of a sea of black asphalt that stretches endlessly in every direction. The worst part wasn't the heat though, or the people who yelled at you about the parking being too expensive, as if it's your fault; it was that there was too much time to think, especially in the quiet after the morning rush.

Like that day I kept thinking about the time one of the Mexican farmhands, Rico, who had worked for Gamps for sixteen seasons, got his hand sliced clean off at the wrist by a combine harvester. I was nearby getting eggs from the coop, a job I hated because I was terrified of the chickens and their razor beaks, so I saw it all. The color of bone was the brightest white I'd ever seen. Like it glowed. Rico stayed calm even as blood poured from the mess of flesh where his hand used to be. "Go get your Gran," he said. He didn't even yell it, just said it the same as he would ask me to grab him a glass of water. I ran into the house as fast as my legs could carry me. Gammy and Gamps were calm too. Farm work was dangerous. It was just a fact, nothing to get worked up about.

Rico's cousin came to drive him to the hospital and I begged to go with them. I thought it was pretty crappy how Gammy and Gamps shrugged off his injury and grumbled that he'd better not try to bill them when he was out of earshot. Least I could do was be the nice one in our family and go with him and try to make him laugh. Besides, I adored Rico; he always called me his "gordita" and said I reminded him of his own daughter back home. We brought the hand to the emergency room tucked in an old metal tackle box filled with ice cubes. But by the time we made it to the closest hospital thirty miles away, the doctor said it was a lost cause. They just sewed a flap of skin where his forearm now ended, gave Rico a bottle of painkillers, and sent him back to work. I was fascinated by the stump, and even though Rico didn't like anyone staring, he felt sorry for me, so he let me get away with stuff. He told me that the worst part of it was that sometimes he could still feel the hand—a phantom limb, they called it. He said it was worse than the pain itself. The pain came and went, but the feeling that something was supposed to be there is what haunted him and just about drove him insane.

That's exactly how I felt after leaving you. It was like I had a phantom limb. Something, someone, was supposed to be there and wasn't. It had been a week and counting and I still kept imagining I heard you cry, or I'd wake up from a restless nap and could feel a kick in my belly or your weight against my body and swear you'd been there ten minutes before and not ten days. I kept looking around, expecting you to be in reach. And then I would panic and wonder where you were, until I remembered you were gone. Safe but gone.

I wished I could call Rico and ask him how he made himself forget about his hand, but a month or so after his accident, he just disappeared. I always wondered—hoped, really—that he went back to Mexico, back to his gordita. At the time, I could only imagine how much they missed each other. But maybe it was for the best that I couldn't reach him, because I'd be afraid of his answer: that it never goes away, that the phantom pain is forever.

It was there no matter what else I was doing. Every time a car pulled up and I leaned out the window to say, "Hello! Welcome to the Magic Kingdom! That'll be thirty dollars for the day," I really wanted to scream, "You have no idea what I'm going through!" It wasn't fair that I was so mad, since I did this to myself, but I was. Raging at the customers wouldn't fly though, because the first rule (among many) of becoming a "castmate," as Disney employees are called, was "Be chipper." That was drilled home every which way in our training by a pert woman wearing a sweatshirt with "DISNEY MAGIC" splashed across it in sequins, who made all these excited hand gestures in the air as she spoke, like she was conducting a deranged chorus. I'd had my share of crappy jobs, so I was used to being treated like I was only pursuing gainful employment because I wanted to make life difficult for the capitalist overlords, not because I needed to eat.

But sure, I could do happy, chipper, joyful, so long as it didn't have to be genuine. What I didn't anticipate was how exhausting it would be to be cheerleader peppy all day when the monotony felt like someone was whittling away at your spirit with a dull blade, but a job was a job.

At the end of training, I was assigned here to the parking lots, not the admissions booth, which was seen as a more primo posting, but I couldn't see one clear advantage of one over the other, except the ticket booths have less of a hike to the bathroom, so there was one drawback to the parking lot. The other big drawback was way too much time alone with my thoughts and worries.

Like where I would go next. Heather was being generous in letting me stay on her couch, and she was never home, but somehow I already felt I'd worn out my welcome. Not because of anything Heather said or did. She was as joyful and perky as any castmate and Disney princess could be, let alone someone hosting an old classmate in their five-hundred-square-foot one-bedroom. It was like I was a broken bird she was taking pity on. Maybe because when she laid eyes on me for the first time in ages, I hadn't showered in days and my greasy hair was slicked to my cheeks. I had massive milk stains under my boobs that I passed off as sweat. She looked me up and down like I was a stray dog and she was assessing how damaged I was and if I had fleas, which was fair. I know she was also taking in how big I'd gotten—or bigger, I should say—since she last saw me in person. I almost slipped and made a stupid joke about baby weight, I was so self-conscious. Especially taking in her flat sliver of belly exposed by a crop top and her hip bones jutting out like cliffs. Every time I was around someone thinner than me, which was all the time, I felt like they were thinking, *Thank God I don't look like that.* Probably because that's what I would be thinking despite my on-and-off-again commitment to "body positivity."

But honestly, Heather didn't look all that great either. The girl who greeted me at the door looked nothing like a Disney princess and barely anything like the prom queen I remembered or what her Facebook feed presented to me. In real life, her legs were covered in bug bite scabs all the way to the tops of her thighs, where a pair of hot-pink terry cloth shorts barely covered her butt. Her once-shiny blond mane was pulled into a messy topknot, and her skin was sallow, with a weird gray cast.

Nevertheless, we both assured each other we looked

exactly the same and then hugged for a beat longer than our flimsy friendship truly justified.

When I told her how tired I was, she did another full-body scan and offered to give me her bed for the week—I guess figuring the pink floral love seat that screamed "quaint flea market find" wouldn't hold me. But I refused to put her out despite all the pain I was still in, so I convinced her to drive me to Walmart so I could spend fifty bucks out of my remaining cash to get an air mattress that was always flat by morning.

That first night she made me dinner, setting the table and everything. Granted, it was an iceberg salad and a sad white chicken breast the size of a hockey puck, which was my first hint that Heather didn't really bother with food too much. Pathetic offerings aside, it was nice to sit down together. Heather didn't notice that I tucked one leg beneath me to keep my sore crotch from the hard wooden chair. Catching up with her was pleasant, at least at first. That is until she brought up my grandparents and how her mom told her they were selling the farm after all these years.

"You'll probably get some of the money, right? I heard they cut a deal with some developer who wants to build a bunch of condos or something. Like, they're offering serious money—like, over a million dollars."

I don't care if they'd agreed to give me half, which they never would—they didn't even want to cough up money for a softball uniform in the ninth grade—I wouldn't take a dime from them. It was hard to imagine Gamps and Gammy being rich though. It made me mad at the universe thinking of them getting anything they wanted. Even if they'd probably spend all of the money on lotto tickets and a tacky pimped-out RV.

I murmured through the soggy lettuce that I wasn't really in touch with them, and Heather was smart enough to change the subject, but not to one I was any more eager to talk about.

"So how's Caleb? What happened with you guys? You still in touch? You left Leesville together and then what?"

I almost choked on my chicken hearing his name, it was that painful.

"Yeah, we ended up in a town called Sibley Bay. It's, like, three hours from Leesville. And yeah, he's good."

I didn't know if that was true though, since I hadn't actually talked to Caleb in a while. The subject opened up a whole minefield of feelings I had no idea what to do with. When Heather left that night to go meet friends, the first thing I did was raid her cabinets. I wanted to eat so bad. Not because I was hungry—I hadn't actually been hungry in days—but because I wanted the heady rush of stuffing my face with thick slices of cheese, or of creamy soft serve sliding down my throat, of biting into a thick cheeseburger and feeling the hot grease squirt into my mouth. I wanted to eat and eat until I was so stuffed there was no room for anything else, least of all thoughts or feelings. Till I was numb and safe. All I found was a lone, dusty box of Teddy Grahams that had been in there who knows how long, and I ate the whole thing without taking a breath. It didn't help. All the salt and sugar in the world couldn't chase away my guilt from what I did to Caleb, ghosting him like that. He didn't deserve it, him being the best thing that had ever happened to me and all.

I always believed that no matter who you are, you get one truly good thing in this life. You don't have to ask for it, you don't have to do anything to deserve it, and it might come out of nowhere, so you just have to be ready. That's how it was with Caleb. He just showed up one day when we were both fourteen. His family came to town with a traveling ministry. His dad, Pastor Mike, a guy with shaggy long hair as if he were trying to impersonate Jesus himself, apparently decided for whatever reason that Leesville was a town that was especially in need of some good old-fashioned saving. I got sent to the Christian summer camp he started that summer, which I hated because I'd stopped believing in God on a hot fall night three weeks after my sixth birthday. But I was happy to pretend otherwise if it got me out of my grandparents' house for eight hours a day—especially once I met Caleb. It was because of him that I almost started believing again—just because God made him and delivered him to me.

But it was Caleb I worshiped, for a hundred reasons, not just because he was the most beautiful boy I'd ever set eyes on, even though he was. He had these bushy jet-black brows that sat above the brightest blue eyes, and a graceful lankiness like a racehorse. He styled his thick, wavy hair just like Joel Smallbone, the Christian rocker he idolized. He always wore ironic T-shirts that said things like, "Got God?" My favorite one, "Walken with Jesus," had a picture of the actor Christopher Walken next to the Lord. His Dad thought they were blasphemous, but it was his only form of rebellion (at least then), so he got away with it. Because everyone knew how devout he was—the perfect preacher's kid. Every now and then I would catch him on his knees, praying with an earnest fervor that a young boy couldn't fake.

But he was also so silly. He drew hilarious paper dolls of the two of us that I swear were our spitting image except for the fact that their heads were two sizes bigger than they should have been. He surprised me with them at the end of that first summer, a Daisy doll and a Caleb doll and a whole bunch of crazy outfits from all different time periods—big hoop skirts and formal tuxedos with tails. He was an incredible artist.

Those were mixed-up times for me. I suppose they are for any teenage girl. My body was changing in terrifying and bewildering ways, and I hated it. I didn't know if I was pretty—I suspected not, but that's mostly because I felt invisible, and how can you be pretty if no one can see you anyway?

Not that it didn't cross my mind to wonder if Caleb would ever kiss me. When I thought about that, it felt like someone was scrubbing my insides with a scouring brush. He hugged me all the time, his lips would graze the top of my head, we cuddled sometimes in the tent when we went camping, but he never touched me beneath my clothes or tried to kiss me. Sometimes I was disappointed; most of the time I was relieved.

Caleb being new to town meant he didn't already know about my mom like everyone else did. So when he asked about her, I couldn't hold it against him for not knowing how this innocent question sliced through me like a hot blade. I didn't answer; I just told him I needed to take him somewhere, and he followed me the two miles out of town silently, like he knew something important was happening. We took an overgrown trail through a thicket of trees and shrubs that abruptly opened up into a vast clearing. Caleb gasped at the gaping hole before us, straight down and deep enough to give you vertigo. All around the basin were blaring signs: STAY AWAY. NO SWIMMING. NO TRESPASSING. PROPERTY OF AIKEN MINING INTERESTS. DANGER. But you didn't notice them, because you were distracted by the giant crater in the earth, filled with inky-black water.

"My mom died in there when I was a baby," I told him, pointing at the water, so dark and still it looked like it could be solid. She was drunk and swimming with friends and drowned. Everyone knew you weren't supposed to swim there—the quarry had been abandoned since the '70s—but no one listened until five kids drowned back-to-back and the bodies were never found. Turns out it was too deep to drag. Everyone talked about how they were all still down there, and even the most reckless teenagers were too scared to go there anymore. When I looked down, I imagined the water going all the way to the center of the world. People said the dead kids haunted the place. I only wished it were true because it would have meant my mom was still there in a way. As much as I tried to believe in ghosts, she never once appeared to me, all the times I went there. I felt silly hoping for it, but that didn't mean I stopped.

Gammy and Gamps never said my mother's name. Not once. Other than two photos on the mantel of my mom trapped in time as a kid missing her two front teeth and sitting in Gamps's lap on a tractor, it was as if she never even existed. Seemed like they wanted to erase her as punishment for dying, like they couldn't forgive her for doing that to them. Or maybe it wasn't the dying itself; maybe it was that they never forgave her for leaving me with them to raise. Either way, it was a comfort to talk to Caleb about her. To remember she existed. I had a mother once, even if it was just for a hot second.

It was at least ten degrees cooler in the clearing, but that wasn't why I was shivering. Caleb passed me his hoodie and then said, "Tell me about her," and I don't think I knew how lonely I was until that moment I wrapped the warm cotton around me and began to talk.

We hadn't known each other too long at that point, but I already felt like I could confide in Caleb, tell him anything, even my darkest secret. And I almost did right then. It would have been like jumping into the water below—the exhilaration of taking flight and letting go, the breathless moment that the wind carries you. But then I remembered what happened after that—the cold slap of the surface. The dark water swallowing you. Death. So I kept my mouth shut.

I guess some kids take blood oaths or get friendship necklaces, but how I knew Caleb was going to be my best friend is when he painted the rock. He took me back to the quarry the next week to show me—draped a sheet over it and everything so there could be this big unveiling moment. Caleb loved a flourish. It was one of the giant boulders close to the edge, and with a flick of his wrist, the sheet flew up into the air to reveal that the rock was no longer gray and brown but a swirl of vivid purple and green and blue. In the middle of the abstract pattern, he'd spray-painted one word in a shimmery gold—EDEN—and below that our initials. From then on, for the next three years, we spent all of our time there. We reclaimed it from somewhere terrible and tragic to a place—maybe the only place—I ever felt safe.

We'd go to EDEN, lay on the rock, and plan our futures. Caleb wanted to leave town as bad as anyone did. If he stayed, he'd have no choice but to work in his dad's ministry, and as much as he loved Jesus Christ, that was the last thing he wanted. New York was where he needed to be—art school. He just needed money. I told him my dreams too, as crazy as they sounded, even to me. Even about me wanting to become a pilot though I'd never said it out loud before.

Caleb had been building houses with the church group since he was a kid, and he got to be really handy with a hammer. The year before we graduated, he was able to pick up part-time jobs doing carpentry until he saved enough for a car and a few months' rent. We left town right after we walked across the patchy grass of the outfield of the baseball diamond and got the flimsy diplomas Ms. Heller printed in her office the previous afternoon for the twenty seniors. We couldn't make it all the way to New York but we had enough to make it to Sibley Bay, where Caleb had a lead on a construction gig. The town felt like something out of a magazine, being next to the ocean and all, with its cute little Main Street, so I didn't care that we could only afford to live in the ugliest part of town. I liked it out there by the airport. Sibley was just a pit stop, but as far as a place to escape, it did the trick.

It was wrong of me not to tell him about you—don't think I don't know that. Caleb and I told each other everything—well, almost everything. But I just couldn't bring myself to do it. For one, shame. I couldn't believe I let this happen. And two, I couldn't bear to be an anchor weighing him down or be the reason he abandoned his dreams of one day going to New York, all because he was helping me take care of you. Maybe there was fear too—fear at the possibility that Caleb would disappoint me. For the first time ever. And that I knew I couldn't bear. So when I left town, I shut him out too. He didn't know the number to the prepaid phone and I had deactivated my Facebook account, so I had no easy way of knowing if his frantic calls and texts had stopped by now.

I missed Caleb so much it was like he was right there in that stuffy booth, whispering in my ear like he used to when we were kids. "We're two sides of the same coin, and that means I'll always have your back."

I heard him so clearly it made me jump up off my pleather stool and stand at attention. That's when I saw it—blood smeared all over the shiny white surface. It must have been seeping out of me all those hours I was sitting there. At the hospital Wanda had handed me a massive bag filled with big fat maxi pads and told me some bleeding was normal, but this . . . this. I hadn't seen so much blood since Rico's accident.

My first thought was to look around for a hoodie to tie around my waist like I was in middle school. Gammy didn't believe in tampons, so I was always leaving the few I pilfered from other girls at school in for too long, which meant I basically spent five days every month bleeding through something. It was mortifying. So was the dark-red splotch seeping through my pants. I was thinking about how I'd have to sit in the booth for two more hours in blood-soaked khakis until my bathroom break when everything went black.

CHAPTER FIVE

There are no good places to hide in Sibley Bay. With every corner packed with vacationers or someone who knows you and all your business, the town's downright claustrophobic. It can also be quaint to the point of oppressive—all that forced charm and wholesomeness, all those fresh sea breezes and visiting families making "happy memories." Say what you will about Atlanta, but the crowds and anonymity are a draw. For all those months Cinnamon had slept right here in Bessie, it was easier than she'd imagined it would be to park her car in an abandoned lot or alley where no one would bother her. Curled up in the back seat, under a pile of coats, with doors locked tight, she was always surprised at how safe she felt. What were the chances that someone would happen to amble by and want to break into her car and hurt her? She told herself they were slim, and that helped her sleep. In fact, as rough as it was to be on her own at seventeen, the irony was that she was usually met with more kindness than harm. There was the owner of the hole-in-the-wall gym who let her use the showers, the woman who started discreetly buying her a muffin at the coffee shop she went to every morning and then once, around Christmas, handed her a beautiful cashmere cardigan without a word. The mechanic who once fixed Bessie for free, after Cinnamon's face fell when she saw the bill.

For the last hour, she's made a lazy loop around Sibley, losing herself in the winding roads and her thoughts, tooling around and observing like she's an outsider in these parts. Some days she still feels like she is, even after three years.

She'd grabbed Bluebell, a handful of diapers and some formula, and hopped in the car without thinking and started driving without a destination. She hasn't left the house in four full days, since she dashed to the office Saturday morning, lest someone see her with Bluebell, and lest she try to take her fledgling parenting skills on the road, but risky as the prying eyes (and her ineptitude) may be, she simply couldn't stay cooped up another second. Both she and a restless Bluebell were desperate for fresh air and a change of scenery.

Cinnamon thought newborns were quieter, too young yet to be so fussy. But it's as if Bluebell is already frustrated with her start in life and wants everyone to know. Even in the blessed moments when she's not crying, and Cinnamon is not trying to rock, bob, and shimmy with more energy and commitment than she's ever put into any sort of exercise, the wails live on as echoes bouncing off the walls.

So she could hardly blame Jayson when he announced, not an hour after he was back from his fishing trip Monday night, that he was going to go stay at Abigail's. It didn't help that he'd come home hungover and tired and had to raise his voice over Bluebell's high-pitched wails to make himself heard.

"I just can't take all this crying, Cinnamon, and I need sleep—I can't be up around the clock right now. I have too much going on." He said it would just be for the night, but last night he claimed he was going to stay over again because his mom needed help with "some things around the house," vague as that was, and so he "might as well" just stay over there until Friday. He didn't need to add *when you finally take this loud-ass stranger's baby to the police station like you promised.*

Cinnamon watched him add some fresh underwear to the fishing trip suitcase he hadn't bothered to unpack without saying a word. She didn't have it in her to argue, and she didn't have much of a case anyway.

She told herself it wasn't a big deal. It would be better not to have him underfoot, mumbling and grumbling, but she couldn't lie: his reaction was telling. And disappointing.

When they first met, Jayson struck her as a guy who could dodge any curve ball without breaking a sweat. It was one of the qualities she most admired about him, along with how he exuded complete confidence and capability, two skills that allowed him to excel at his job shilling overpriced software subscriptions to midsize companies. Where some people might have seen an overly slick salesman, Cinnamon saw a guy determined to control everything about his life, his image, his destiny. The man knew how to package the future—and how to get Cinnamon to invest.

He laid out that vision on their very first date. He'd taken her to one of those steak houses that's so dark you can barely see in front of you. The walls were bloodred and the waitstaff wore uniforms nicer than anything in her closet. Not that her room above the church had an actual closet. Jayson was clearly trying to impress her, which worked. In order to distract herself from how out of place she'd felt at the swanky restaurant, she'd taken fast, furious sips of whatever cocktail Jayson had ordered for her even though she'd never been drunk before that day and didn't altogether like the feeling. So overwhelmed was she by the choices on the menu she brazenly ordered two appetizers and an entree. It helped that there were no prices listed to make her feel guilty. When the feast arrived, she'd devoured it ravenously. It was her first taste ever of lobster; the warm garlic butter tickled her tongue. Then she tucked into the turf portion of her surf and turf. She didn't know steak could feel like silk sliding down her throat. She cleaned her plate spotless while Jayson told stories, as long-winded as they were entertaining, about the years he played professional poker in Vegas after college, how he was teaching himself to distill whiskey after reading about Nathan Green, and how he had a side hustle being an extra in movies filmed in Atlanta. Maybe she'd spotted him in *Hidden Figures?* When Cinnamon finally put her fork down, she realized Jayson was staring at her, a look of amazement on his face.

"Wow, you downed that. Itty-bitty you just housed that steak. *Da-um.* I've only ever seen big girls eat like that."

Cinnamon would have been offended had Jayson not looked so impressed. The truth was, she was just plain starving. She was used to subsisting on ramen that she made on a hot plate in her room, or the ham sandwiches the church served to the homeless every day from twelve to two.

Jayson started to enjoy taking her on dates where he could watch her feast—they began a game to try to eat everything on the menu at the Cheesecake Factory. A few weeks into their courtship, as Cinnamon was polishing off an order of Buffalo Blasts, he launched into a monologue about how Cinnamon wasn't like other girls he'd dated and not just on account of her appetite. He told her how he appreciated that she wasn't needy or demanding. "Girls see a brotha like me that has a few dollars, and they want this and that, their hair did, their nails done. New handbags. Last girl I got with asked me for help getting a new car *and* for me to change the oil in her old one. You believe that shit? But you're independent, Cinnamon. I can tell and I like that. You can stand on your own."

He said this like it was a talent she'd intentionally cultivated, and not a survival instinct. But he could be forgiven for not seeing the difference. Being an imposter though? Now, *that* was a skill.

In his next breath he'd said, "I want you, Cinnamon, and I get what I want."

It was such a cheesy line she came close to laughing. Even with her limited experience with men, she knew this was lame game and that this probably wasn't the first time he was trotting it out. But it didn't really matter, because he had Cinnamon at "I want you"—a siren call so loud it eclipsed any doubts. Besides, her gut told her his intentions were sincere, if inexplicable. It was then she made two decisions: to never order Buffalo Blasts again and to let herself fall in love. She didn't know if she was equipped for a serious relationship, having never had one before, but Jayson made it easy—all she had to do was support all his desires and decisions, radiate admiration, and not question too much. This was a dynamic that suited Cinnamon. Making sure you stay loved is a little like earning your keep, and that pursuit was familiar to her.

It was also why she nodded along solemnly every time her mother-in-law reminded her how important it is to provide your man "a safe haven" and "soft place to land." Abigail usually followed this with a domestic humblebrag about how she ironed Jayson's dad's socks for forty years before Wallace died a few months before Cinnamon met Jayson, how she made her husband a gin and tonic just about every night, how she let him "be the man."

Abigail physically puffs up with pride every time they come for dinner and she gets to gaze lovingly at Jayson, her self-proclaimed, proud momma's boy, as he devours all his favorite foods she'd slaved over. Jayson likes to give Cinnamon a look while his mother clucks over him, practically spoon-feeding him pecan pie, that says *See this? This is how you treat a man.*

Yeah, what did Black women, or Cinnamon specifically, know about needing a soft place in a hard world? Jayson literally doesn't know the half of it. But whose fault is that? And it does her no good to be resentful of her husband. And anyway, she agrees. She wants to support him.

This line of thinking inspires her to make a U-turn at the next intersection and circle back downtown to Sugar Love and get some of those pistachio cookies Jayson loves, even though they're dry as chalk. Rather than drive aimlessly up and down the coast, she'll make use of her time and deliver the cookies to Jayson at his work site. Lay eyes on the husband she hasn't seen in two days, armed with a symbol of goodwill to make up for the fact that she's upended their lives. Two birds, one stone. It's also finally time to face the progress Jayson has—or hasn't—made at the Ruins once and for all, which is probably better than continuing to let her mind run wild, imagining their life savings in a literal money pit in the ground. When she pulls up to the bakery fifteen minutes later, she realizes the problem. How is she going to go inside with the baby, the nine-pound bundle she can't risk anyone knowing about? Susie, the owner and chief baker, who she spies through the window wrestling with a giant stand mixer, will likely have a lot of questions. Cinnamon's read all the horror stories of people leaving babies in hot cars, but it's not hot at all, and Bluebell, who's fast asleep, won't be out of her sight given the car is two feet from the window and front door of the bakery, so she decides to risk it.

In the shop, Cinnamon keeps craning her head to the left to get a glimpse of the back seat. She jumps a little when the first thing Susie asks her is, quite reasonably, "You doin' okay?"

"Yeah, I'm just in a big hurry—got some ice cream in the car to go with these cookies. A dozen pistachio, please. I'm going to take them over to Jayson at the construction site."

"Oh, that's nice. How's . . . how's all that going?"

Cinnamon doesn't have the time or energy for nosy neighbors right now. Not that she needs to give Susie an update, since she's quite sure everyone in town has gossiped enough about Jayson's fortunes and foolishness, but they're polite enough to smile to her face with genuine concern. Susie has kindly offered to help Jayson—but he refuses to take advice from "that Pioneer Woman wannabe." He's pretty petty when he gets prideful.

Cinnamon toes the company line. "It's coming along."

Susie, well aware of Cinnamon's regular order, had started packing up the cookies as soon as she saw her pull up, so she's handing over the box in under a minute and Cinnamon is thrusting a ten-dollar bill at her and dashing out the door, as much to avoid any more talk of Jayson's work as to return to the baby.

When she gets back in the car, Bluebell's eyes are wide-open, searching, as if she knew she'd been abandoned again, however briefly. She looks like she may be gearing up to fuss, and Cinnamon fumbles with the keys to get the two of them moving as fast as possible.

"I'm back, baby girl. It's okay. You're okay. I just had to get some cookies. You know Jayson likes these dry cookies—heaven knows why."

She's taken to having long one-sided conversations with Bluebell. Partly because she'd read that you should try to say at least twenty-one thousand words a day to a baby, among many other random facts about child development she consumes in the middle of the night. And partly because it's just nice to have someone to talk to. These last few days holed up with an infant have given new meaning to the concept of isolation. There were hours she felt like the last human on earth and that nothing existed beyond her living room. And Lord, the exhaustion. Before last Friday, she couldn't have told you about or imagined the exquisite torture of sleeplessness, how it feels like you're drunk and dying and wired all at the same time. Until her recent nightmares started, Cinnamon had always been a good sleeper. It was like a magical ability—she could force herself to be out like a light, whatever was happening around her. No matter who was screaming, or how loud a TV was, or who was watching her—it was one of her most beneficial talents. Now she knows there's a moment where you've slept so little you've forgotten what sleep is or how you'll manage to ever do it again.

What's surprising to her is that she doesn't actually mind the exhaustion, constant feedings, or the intensity of the routine. In fact, she and the baby have gotten into a sort of rhythm, with Cinnamon opening her eyes just seconds before Bluebell stirs. Her body knows she's needed, and that feels prehistoric, dangerous, and also entirely right. Who would have thought Cinnamon Haynes had any maternal instincts? But something is at work here; something is telling her what she needs to do to keep this little human alive. Sure, she's so tired she feels it in her bones, which she didn't even know was possible, but she's also more alert and alive than she's been in years. Maybe ever.

What she's still getting used to is the fact that passing hours with a baby involves a time loop that even the most brilliant MIT physicist cannot explain. The days are approximately 567 hours long and pass in a flash at the exact same time. Driving around the last hour was at least something to do.

Something besides obsessing over Friday's looming deadline and whether Lucia has made any progress yet. Ever since they learned Daisy's/Amanda's last name on Monday, she's been trying to track down information on any Jacobses in Leesville. There are no listed numbers for the grandparents in the county, but Lucia has other databases and connections she can access from her time as a reporter. Cinnamon has also been doing her own share of googling when she can, though the name Amanda Jacobs is too common to yield much at all, and without a last name for Caleb, any effort to find him has proven futile too. Her Caleb search did, however, send her spiraling down a rabbit hole of YouTube videos starring a Caleb who challenged himself to drink all 135 flavors of Kool-Aid in a single day, and nothing has made her feel more ancient or less optimistic about the future. She looked at Bluebell then and there and knew she was in dangerous territory thinking about Blue's future and what her dreams will be. She certainly hopes they'll reach beyond "Internet fame."

Cinnamon's next step when she gets back this afternoon is to see if Leesville High has old yearbooks online that she can search for the name Caleb. Though that feels about as practical as trying to drain the ocean, it's all she can think to do.

There is something else, actually. It occurs to her as she pulls back onto Twelfth Street. She could drive out to the airport on her way to Jayson's property and see if she can find out where Daisy and Caleb live. It's not likely that Daisy's just sitting in her apartment, not eight miles away. Though wouldn't that be something—Daisy under her nose this whole time? But maybe she could find Caleb or a neighbor who knows them. Cinnamon's not that familiar with the area, has never been out that way past the town line, but how many apartment complexes could there be? Her plan is flimsy as all get out, but it's as good as she's got, so onward. She just has to keep moving, knowing that if she does so, a way out will appear. The only way out is through.

When she spots the squat air traffic control tower jutting up in the distance like a mushroom, she starts looking around for apartment buildings. She turns onto a service road that runs parallel to the single runway and smattering of gates dotted with planes about as big as Bessie. You wouldn't ever catch Cinnamon in one of those death traps. She knows herself to be a "nervous flier" even though she's only taken one flight in her life—one of those personal facts that serves to remind her of the limits of her world.

Daisy confessed to her once that she's never been on a flight at all. Which seems odd for someone who wants to be a pilot, but Daisy said she was no less awed just watching planes than actually flying in them. "Sometimes I just spend hours watching them take off. It's crazy to me that all that metal can go so fast and lift right up into the sky as if it were light as a feather. It feels like a miracle every single time."

Cinnamon slows now as a twin-engine contraption the size of a VW van taxis down the runway and heaves into the air with a shudder. Cinnamon tries to see it as Daisy would, tries to channel the girl's wonder as it rushes past her. There *is* something sort of miraculous about it. But the real miracle would be finding Daisy. As the road curves to the south side of the airport, she spots a battered three-story building across the street from the air traffic control tower. It looks like there may have been plans to have a full complex with multiple buildings, judging from the size of the parking lot and empty stretches of swamp grass surrounding the lone structure. The off-white siding is streaked with age and probably exhaust coming from the airport. Cinnamon pulls into the lot and parks next to what looks like the main entrance.

Part of her wishes Lucia were here. Her friend would have no problem banging on every door and interrogating each neighbor about whether they've seen Daisy and what they know about her. But Cinnamon can't bring herself to do that. She risks leaving the baby in the car again to go the five feet to the stand of mailboxes. *Please, please, please let there be a Jacobs.*

This doesn't seem like the kind of place where someone sticks around for a long time. Which explains why, of the twelve mailboxes, half don't even have names. The rest are mere chicken scratch, but they definitely don't start with a *J*. Cinnamon looks around for any sign of life, but the whole area is desolate. There are only two cars parked in the lot—one is a dusty Corolla with a Confederate flag decal in the back window. She hears a man screaming at someone from an upstairs unit and then an unsettling thump. By the time she hears a woman hollering back, Cinnamon's back in Bessie, slamming the door shut. It's not like she hasn't seen her fair share of ole Dixie here and there, but the flag combined with the yelling gets her hackles up. She has no good sense being out here all alone on this dumb Hail Mary attempt to find Daisy anyway.

She peels out of the parking lot and refocuses on her cookie-delivery mission. The twenty-minute drive to the jobsite gives her some time to prepare herself for what awaits her, which she's convinced will be a pile of two-by-fours and some bricks and broken dreams.

When is enough enough? When do they just give up, declare bankruptcy if they need to, and keep it moving? She's afraid that day will never come with Jayson, that he'll throw himself off the pier before admitting defeat. Which is frustrating to be sure, but this level of bullheaded tenacity is also why she fell in love with him. That's something she's learned during these few years of marriage—sometimes the things you love about a person are the exact same ones that make you want to strangle them. She'll never be able to make that make sense.

But when she snakes through the overgrown road that cuts through a canopy of cypress trees and they give way, her breath actually catches at the sight. The dirt pit and hapless piles of lumber she'd feared would be awaiting her have been transformed into a bona fide restaurant. The sad shack that once looked like it was going to collapse into the sea has been righted to form the centerpiece of a larger structure that extends out on both sides and is wrapped around by a generous porch adorned with large ceiling fans. From there, a long deck forms a bridge to a large platform that looks like it floats in the middle of the water, endless ocean stretching in all directions. She can just imagine folks sitting there, hands around sweaty glasses, watching the sun sink into the bay on a warm summer night.

But it's when she spots the sign lying in the grass—a giant piece of metal with THE RUINS carved out—that she gets downright emotional. It's a terrible name for a restaurant, and Cinnamon bit her tongue when he'd first announced it, but then he explained the history. How the twelve swampy acres were once a settlement for freed and escaped slaves. In the Ruins, they built a little hidden utopia.

Cinnamon looks through the windshield at the clearing ringed by tall trees and imagines that community in its heyday—a haven in the woods for a group of people who were self-governing and protected by a barrier of almost impenetrable swampland and marsh away from the obscene traumas of their past or what was happening at the massive plantations mere miles up the road.

And she knows Jayson's great-uncle Londell would be proud of this legacy too, what her husband is building here. Especially since some white developers had tried to steal the land with dubious claims about the validity of the lease, and the whole mess ended up in court. Londell may have actually won the case in the end, but the stress and legal fees did him in and left him bankrupt and bereft, and eventually he dropped dead of a heart attack. That's how this land got left to Jayson, Londell's only surviving relative on Jayson's dad's side. It was Jayson's free and clear with two conditions—that he never ever sell that land to a white man and that Londell be buried on the land with four generations of his family.

There's a semicircle of grave markers on one edge of the property that contains Londell's grave right near to Jayson's dad's and beyond that generations of family members all the way back to slavery. She will never get used to the way there are ghosts everywhere in Sibley. Just a few hours away in Atlanta, all the concrete and steel paved over the history, kinda like buying your meat all sterilized and packaged in the grocery store. Here, the plain truth of it was a freshly killed deer bleeding into the red earth. No soft edges or illusions.

She lets pride chase away her cynicism. The feeling of it swells in Cinnamon's chest as she turns off the engine. It's made even sweeter given it has sprung from the depths of such great skepticism. She didn't even know how much she'd wanted her husband to prove her wrong.

And yet there are still no guarantees. This restaurant will have to be packed every day for the next five years to get out of the mountain of debt Jayson has saddled them with. And she doesn't see that happening. What she sees is a pretty, empty building way off the beaten path that's going to be run by someone with no experience. As proud as she may be of Jayson's progress, it's fleeting because somehow failure is still just as likely as it was yesterday.

She's barely opened the car door and gotten her two feet on the ground when suddenly her husband materializes in front of her, hissing like a mad rattlesnake and ruining her generous mood.

"I know you didn't bring that baby here!"

His eyes dart around like Cinnamon has a ticking bomb in the car.

His crew is a half dozen Spanish-speaking day laborers who pay her no mind whatsoever, so she can't understand why he's so rattled.

"Calm down, Jay. We just wanted to bring you something."

They both register the "we."

"Well, thank you, but you need to bounce. I can't have anyone asking questions about this random white baby."

It's not this "random white baby" Jayson has anything against. Cinnamon knows that. Jayson loves kids, crawls around on the floor with Lucia's twins, happily offers up piggyback rides, and pulls candy from his pockets for them like an old man. It's this situation that rightfully enough seems so absurd to him, the way the baby ended up in their lives and what exactly they're going to do about it. Or really, what *she's* going to do about it. He'd warned her that with each passing day, she was going to get more attached, more invested, and though Jayson is wrong about a lot of things, he got that exactly right. Like when Bluebell suddenly stops crying in Cinnamon's arms and she feels like she's just won a gold medal. Or the moment she realized the baby would only sleep when she was swaddled tighter than seemed humanly possible and Cinnamon perfected wrapping her up like a compact burrito. How heady it is when she nuzzles this vulnerable creature, so helpless but trusting, and to have the power to change Bluebell's entire outlook with the right song, hip shimmy, or tummy rub. The intoxicating rush from the sense of accomplishment Cinnamon feels in these moments was beyond anything she'd ever experienced.

Not that she would admit it to her husband or anyone else.

For now, her focus isn't the baby, but placating her husband. So she abandons getting the carrier out of the back seat and channels her attention to a tried-and-true way to soothe Jayson: flattery. "Place looks great, Jay. Amazing, really." He recognizes it's a tactic but also that she means it, and he dials his irritation back.

"Thanks. It's coming along. It's possible we could be open by the Fourth."

She knows it's critical to try to get some income this summer while it's still tourist season, but Cinnamon doesn't ratchet up the stakes by saying what she's screaming inside, which is, *God help us, it'd better be!*

Somehow along the way, her husband reached into the front seat and started eating cookies without her noticing until she registers the powdered sugar hovering over his upper lip. It makes her think of the episode of *Diff'rent Strokes* when Arnold was supposed to be off sweets and Mr. Drummond caught him with powdered sugar all over his face. There was a two-month period in her childhood when she zoned out to those old reruns and wondered what it would be like if a rich white man like Mr. Drummond took her in. She was placed with Doc Parker shortly thereafter, and even though his house was far from a Park Avenue mansion, he was still an old, rich white dude. Maybe she'd willed that development in some way.

"So . . . any news?" Jayson asks through a full mouth.

"No, not yet. Still working on it. Lucia's using some connections to try to find Daisy's family, now that we know her full name."

"Good. That baby deserves to be with her people, Cece. You and I both know that."

Jayson does want what's best for this child. He doesn't just want her gone from their house. Though Cinnamon understands both can be true.

"You know my mom's been asking me all about this baby. I'mma leave that to you to explain. I told her you would give her a call."

Abigail has rung Cinnamon a couple of times in the last few days—the rare occasion she's ever called her directly and didn't deliver a message through Jayson. Normally Cinnamon would be excited about that, would see it as progress, slow going as ever even after three years. But she generally fears Abigail's judgments and questions, so she'd rather avoid them for now, for as long as possible.

A worker comes over, and Jayson starts speaking in broken yet condescending Spanish that Cinnamon finds embarrassing. He gets louder and louder like the man is deaf. Jayson also has on his white man voice, the one he dons when he's talking to the inspector's office. He says "amigo" one too many times and then dismisses the man with an "adios, muchacho" before he turns back to her.

"Look, I gotta get back. If I don't keep pushing these dudes, nothing gets done."

From Cinnamon's view, plenty is getting done—the sound of persistent hammering has been the soundtrack to their conversation—but something about the statement seemed to make her husband feel important. She just hopes the men couldn't hear or understand him.

"Yeah, yeah, get back to it." As he turns to walk away, she calls out, "Hey, I'm proud of you, husband."

Jayson's uncharacteristic shyness is adorable as he mumbles, "Thanks." He's halfway back to the construction site when he turns around before she gets in her car. "Oh hey, I stopped by the house to grab the mail during lunch. We must have just missed each other. There's something for you on the front seat of my car.

From your aunt Celia. It's been a minute since you heard from her, huh?"

Cinnamon has kept up the charade for so long—that she and her loving aunt who had raised her were still in somewhat regular contact—that she can't give in to her shock of actually hearing from her now. She steadies herself to walk over to Jayson's Jeep and leans in like she doesn't have a care in the world. *Oh, a card from Aunt Celia; how nice. Nothing to see here.*

When she settles in her driver's seat, the envelope shakes like a leaf in her hands. She tears it open right then. She can't help it. This is a rip-the-Band-Aid-off scenario. The formal floral swirls on the front of the card are similar to the fussy wallpaper in Aunt Celia's dining room. Fitting. Even her greeting cards are stuck-up.

There are few things more familiar and more jarring to her than her aunt's handwriting. She knows it so well because of the stream of handwritten missives and passive-aggressive reminders Aunt Celia left on the shiny white desk in Cinnamon's room.

> *Please remember to bring your clothes to the laundry room by 3 p.m. on Fridays. You know I like to have the wash done before I leave for the Neighborhood Association meeting.*
>
> *I expect you to invest 100 percent while you live under my roof, and that's not only with your grades but with your chores. The floors were clean, but the baseboards were not. You might as well not do the job at all if you're not going to do it thoroughly.*
>
> *Just a reminder that a positive outlook will take you a long way. Remember, God don't like ugly, and that includes your attitude.*

And on and on went Aunt Celia's never-ending barrage of admonishments. All of which added up to one singular message:

You're not trying hard enough to make me not regret taking you in. Cinnamon tried though—boy did she ever. Celia's real daughter, Corrine, never got these kinds of notes. She got long missives of praise and encouragement signed, *I am so proud of you. —Your loving mother.*

In this case, Aunt Celia's message, written in a perfectly slanted cursive below a stiff Hallmark greeting about how every birthday is a beautiful gift from the Lord, is short, if not sweet: *Happy birthday, Cinnamon. I would like to talk if you're amenable. Call me anytime: (404) 555-8719.*

It's so typical of Aunt Celia in so many ways. The brevity, the formality. There is one way this is very different though. She's called her Cinnamon, something Aunt Celia had never once done. In fact, her aunt had gone to great pains not to address her by her proper name. On Cinnamon's first day in her new school, Aunt Celia had informed the school secretary at Larchmont Academy that her niece's name was Simone, which Celia later insisted was her middle name. Cinnamon had never seen her birth certificate to know if this was true or not, and no one else had ever mentioned her having a middle name at all. So though she had suspicions that her aunt was making this up, she had no proof and so she went along with it. It was clear from the day she arrived at Aunt Celia's doorstep that the woman wanted Cinnamon to be a different person, so she might as well have a new name too, even though she never remembered to answer to it.

What is this card about? Why does her aunt need to talk to her? And after all this time?

Cinnamon fights the urge to bang her head on the steering wheel. Jayson looks over and notices she's still sitting there in the car and starts waving her away like she's escaping out his bedroom window in high school just as his parents turn into the drive. At the same time a loud shriek starts up from the back seat. Cinnamon knew this was coming—it's past feeding time.

Cinnamon obliges both of them and pulls away from the construction site to look for a place to park on the side of the main road. She can't make it all the way home before feeding this increasingly agitated baby. She finds a patchy section of rocks and mud that melts into the marshy water. It's amazing how close they built these roads to the water like there was no risk of them just falling right in.

She makes her way over to a giant piece of driftwood on the shoulder, and she spends the next few minutes getting herself and Bluebell settled on it—a blessed distraction from that stupid card. That's the thing with babies—they're always good for a little distraction. The formula isn't warmed and Bluebell doesn't like that, but after some protestation she takes the nipple anyway, resigned that this is all that's on offer at the moment.

Cinnamon's eyes trail a slow-moving container ship crossing the horizon in the distance, bound for China or India or someplace else she'll probably never see. It makes her think of the vastness of the world, of all the different lives being lived right now, and she looks into Bluebell's eyes and it all overwhelms her.

"It's crazy how much is out there, isn't it?" she says to Bluebell.

She wonders if Blue will see those faraway places, if she'll hate spiders, become a Buddhist, or go to Mars for vacation. People are about one step from doing that now. Her eyes betray her by welling up thinking about all the possibilities for Blue's life. She hates it when this happens, when she tries not to care and her body—her heart—doesn't get the message. So much for not getting attached.

Cinnamon presses her nose to the girl's pink cheek, partly a nuzzle and partly a greedy inhale. Bluebell will likely remember nothing of this time, at least in any clear, conscious way, but Cinnamon wonders if some deeper impression is being made. Like if Bluebell saw Cinnamon on the street twenty-five years from now, would there be a tug of recognition somewhere deep in her? Maybe she would stop short and turn to whoever she was with and say, "That's so strange; I just feel like I know that woman."

Cinnamon thinks about what she must carry within her from her own mother—hazy memories of the warm spot where Cinnamon's head fit just under her chin, the faintest melody of a lullaby that comes to her as she's falling asleep, the high trill of her mother's laugh. But something else is there too—something more ephemeral but stubborn nonetheless: the feeling of being loved.

It's good that this bittersweet reverie is interrupted by the distant ring of her phone. She jumps up and awkwardly hobbles over to the car without moving the bottle from Bluebell's fierce suction. She always wondered how mothers did this, but she's come to realize you just sort of figure it out, and quickly.

Her friend's voice comes through the speakerphone triumphantly before Cinnamon even says hello. "I found them!" Then there's a sharp turn in Lucia's tone. "But you're not gonna like it."

CHAPTER SIX

"You want a shot of tequila in your coffee?" Lucia holds up an amber bottle as an offering.

"It's 9:30 a.m. on a Thursday, Luce. And you know I don't drink."

"Hasn't stopped me from trying! Besides, I was kidding, Cece."

Yeah, right. Cinnamon knows better. If she were game, Lucia would absolutely have topped off their coffees.

"Did you dress like that to drop the twins at preschool this morning?"

Lucia looks down as if she's surprised to find herself wearing a skin-tight, shiny gold jumpsuit that she ordered especially for Cinnamon's birthday party.

"I sure did! Why not? I figured this beats yoga pants. I wanted to try on my look for tomorrow night since you were coming over this morning, and I got the added bonus of showing off at drop-off. What do you think? It's a winner, right?"

Lucia struts back and forth, turning her spacious kitchen into a catwalk. The ensemble is, no question about it, flat-out gorgeous, with a level of glamour more suited to the Emmys or a wedding than a birthday gathering at Minerva's Tavern . . . let alone a coffee date in her kitchen. Cinnamon also got a new dress for the party and now would be the time to tell Lucia all about it and let her friend offer to borrow the perfect accessories but fashion is the absolute last thing on Cinnamon's mind right about now.

She pulls up the email Lucia had sent her yesterday after she called and her eyes immediately go to the mug shot. The picture gives her chills, not just because of Derek Jacobs's menacing grimace, hard stare, and severe buzz cut; it's because she can see Bluebell's eyes staring back at her, and the astonishing power of genetics is worthy of goose bumps. It leaves little doubt that he's Daisy's grandfather, the one who raised her. The kicker is he's also a convicted felon and, on top of that, apparently an avowed racist. Those facts are laid out right here in the court records Lucia tracked down.

In April 2002, Derek Jacobs of Leesville had a financial dispute with Saint Walker, a Black mechanic who'd purchased an old car from Derek. When the transmission failed two days later, Saint put a stop payment on the check. At which point Derek accused the man of stealing his "perfectly good" car and snuck into Saint's auto body shop in the dead of night and set it on fire, using a lit cigarette and a pile of bills to make the whole thing look like an accident. Saint had stayed over in the shop that night and was sleeping on a cot in the office upstairs. The man only escaped because his German shepherd barked and gave him enough time to climb out the second-story window. The hero dog wasn't as lucky, which is a detail that just kills Cinnamon. That poor man had his business burned down *and* lost his pet.

Apparently, because of Derek's well-known ties to a white supremacist group, the Order of Kings, and a witness who'd overheard him say, "You're not going to get away with this, nigger," when the two men were arguing, prosecutors had planned to try the case as both attempted murder and a hate crime. But some sort of deal was reached first. Derek pled guilty and got four years in prison for arson, not attempted murder. He was out in under two. Twenty-three measly months.

Lucia takes a break from parading around like Jennifer Lopez in a residency in Vegas and leans over her expansive marble counter to peer at Cinnamon's phone, the mug shot and the court files open on the screen.

"Rough stuff."

That was an understatement, and it irks Cinnamon that Lucia is being so glib. But how can Cinnamon expect this to hit her friend in the same way it hits her? Lucia doesn't—can't—truly get what it's like to read about a person being attacked or brutalized solely because they are Black. The way it makes these types of attacks personal because it could so easily be you who offends the wrong person at the wrong time in the wrong place. Each and every incident you hear about stokes a visceral fear, one you just have to learn to live with. For better or worse, many of the memories from Cinnamon's childhood are scattershot, and she has precious few from when her grandmother was alive. But there is one that has always stood out in Technicolor—the time this white woman flicked a burning cigarette at Grandma Thelma as she walked by on the sidewalk, casual as could be. The burning orange ember flipped in the air and then landed right on Thelma's royal-blue coat collar—just inches from her face—leaving a singed scar on her good coat. It's not the evil woman that Cinnamon remembers most—she can't conjure any details about her appearance or what prompted this seemingly random act. What Cinnamon does remember is her grandmother's reaction, or lack thereof. She gripped her granddaughter's hand and said, "Some people just born ugly. You be careful around those types, Cece. Your dignity is important, and so is your pride, but it's not worth dying over."

How she knew her grandmother meant white people without her having to say it, Cinnamon doesn't know. But it's one of the lessons that's stayed with her all these years. It's also one of the few things she and Lucia argue about. Her friend has no qualms about popping off and making a public scene when she feels even the least bit slighted. Like the time last fall when Lucia accidentally took someone's parking space at the movie theater. The guy flipped her the bird and yelled out the window. "You stupid bitch. Go back to Mexico!" When they ran into him in the lobby, Lucia went off on him and Cinnamon had to pull her back, pointing out that her kids were right there, he didn't deserve her energy, and also that people were crazy these days. Lucia finally relented but not before yelling at him across the crowded lobby, "Your car's a piece of shit, and so are you!" Then adding, "And I'm Puerto Rican, *pendejo*!" for good measure.

What the guy said was messed up, but it was also such garden-variety, unoriginal racist bullshit that it wasn't worth escalating. When Cinnamon made that case as they stood in line for popcorn, Lucia was quick to lecture her about how she couldn't be a doormat. But the memory of Grandma Thelma's voice was louder in Cinnamon's head. It may be a fine line between taking the high road and being walked all over like you were the road—but it's a line nonetheless. And Cinnamon wants to stay on the side of it that keeps her alive. That's the thing: she and Lucia can both be outraged at whatever injustices, but the danger just isn't the same. Not that Cinnamon would voice that, because "Who has it worse?" is a pointless argument if there is one. Bottom line is, you sometimes have to make the choice about what your dignity is worth. Like poor Saint Walker, having the nerve to stand up for himself to a white man, and look how that turned out. All too often self-respect comes with a price . . . and it can be steep.

When Cinnamon does the math about when Derek got out of prison and how old Daisy is, she realizes it was right around when Daisy's mom died. This gives her a terrible, grim satisfaction. That no sooner had Derek got out of prison, he lost his only child. The karma shouldn't feel as delicious as it does, especially considering a young woman died, so she immediately wishes she could take her righteous schadenfreude back. But feelings have a mind of their own.

"So, Daisy never mentioned this?"

"I think I'd remember her telling me about a grandfather who was in a neo-Nazi hate group who went to prison for trying to kill a Black man."

"Good point. And you barely know anything about her anyway, so . . ."

Cinnamon can't quite tell if Lucia means this as a dig or why she takes it as one.

It allows a feeling that's been nipping at Cinnamon's heels to finally catch up. For all Cinnamon's defensiveness about her and Daisy's friendship, learning this about her grandfather begs questions about how that affects the girl, how it informs how she feels about Black people. Cinnamon is about as wary of white people as she should be, but life has also taught her to be skeptical of everyone equally, no matter their particular hue. So it was a surprise just how quickly she'd let her guard down with Daisy, and now she thinks better of it. Perhaps she could have stood to have some healthy wariness when it came to this white stranger when she didn't know anything about how she was raised. Daisy was hardly going to tell her about the white hood in Grandpa's closet. Was Cinnamon just a curiosity to the girl? Was their relationship some sort of rebellion? Was the fact that Daisy left her baby with Cinnamon an eff-you to her people? These questions send Cinnamon's mind to some dark places, and the only thing that calms her is to remember that she's spent a lifetime honing her gut and instincts to be as sharp as the blade of the kitchen knife she'd carried in her pocket when she lived in Bessie. Now isn't the time to start doubting them.

"It's awful what some people have to deal with. It makes you realize how lucky you are, huh?"

Yeah, lucky. So very lucky.

Lucia looks past Cinnamon's shoulder to her lavish living room as if to remind herself of the safety of her cocoon. The light-filled space contains two buttery leather sofas and expensive plush rugs despite being home to two toddlers. All of the toys are carefully hidden away in cute baskets and the books on the shelves are perfectly arranged by color. These are the moments that Cinnamon has to work hard to swallow down her jealousy. Also when Lucia shows her pictures of her family's all-inclusive vacations to Mexico or the Caribbean, or when Cinnamon looks at the gallery wall marching up the grand spiral staircase featuring generations of family members, or when she sits at the custom-designed fire pit just outside the French doors, all these trappings that a thriving dental practice allows you.

Cinnamon wouldn't wish anything less for her, yet it's still easy to turn green-eyed now and then. It's especially hard when Lucia buys her extravagant gifts or always insists on paying when they go out, which makes Cinnamon feel like a charity case. Actually, it's not a feeling; it's a fact. Cinnamon *is* a charity case—always has been, always will be—and that can make her resent Lucia if she's not careful. So careful.

Yeah, lucky. So very lucky.

Cinnamon reaches over and slides the carrier closer to her on the counter, checks to see if Bluebell is still fast asleep. She's been out for a long time, a much longer stretch than usual. It's a welcome break from all the crying, but Cinnamon's not used to her napping for these long stretches. "She's been sleeping a lot today. Should I be worried?"

Lucia throws her head back, laughing. "No way! You should be grateful! We should use this time to decide what *you're* going to wear tomorrow."

Cinnamon presses a hand to the baby's forehead, worried she feels slightly warm. Bluebell also looks pale to her, but Cinnamon doesn't raise this observation, because she doesn't want Lucia to ridicule her: Cinnamon Haynes, the overprotective mother who doesn't know what she's doing. Even if it's the truth . . . Well, except for the mother part.

"That'll have to wait. We have more pressing matters, Lucia. Like what to do about these grandparents. I'm not sure how they can help us get to Daisy. I don't want to come within a ten-foot pole of these people! And if I take Bluebell to the police tomorrow, they'll look for the family just like we did. They could find them. They could give her to the Jacobses, Luce! That can't happen."

Cinnamon drives this point home again, but this time with more than a touch of hysteria in her voice. "Daisy clearly didn't want that, or she'd have done it herself." The girl made her wishes very evident. Cinnamon reads Daisy's note once a day to remind herself, or torture herself—she's not sure which. And never mind Daisy's wishes; Cinnamon's own are ringing louder in her ear, an alarm bell or a siren drowning out everything else. *Not those people. They can't have her.*

Lucia marches over to the tequila bottle, pops it open, and pours a splash into her coffee mug. "Don't look at me like that. I need this."

This week has already been so out of this world; maybe she'd allow herself a sip of tequila. Lucia is right: she could use it—just to take the edge off. "Okay, maybe just a taste."

"That's my girl." Lucia takes the liberty of tipping the bottle into Cinnamon's mug with a heavier pour than Cinnamon would have liked.

"I don't think we have much of a choice—if we want to try to get any kinda lead on Daisy's whereabouts, we have to call the grandparents. And I happen to have managed to track down their unlisted number—don't ask or I'll have to kill you. Let's see if they know something." Lucia claps her hands twice in rapid succession as if the plan of the century is snapping into place.

"It's too fast for the tequila to have kicked in, so you must have just lost your mind. How are we going to explain why we're asking about their granddaughter?"

"Just leave it to me. I better be the one to call anyway in case they can tell you're Black over the phone."

It's not funny, and the daggers Cinnamon shoots Lucia tell her so. Her grin turns sheepish.

"Um, something tells me that the traces of Puerto Rico in your voice aren't going to be much more welcomed than the dulcet tones of my Black-lady voice, mi hermana."

"Oh, please. I'm going to come at 'em with my Mary Madeline Montgomery voice, and they'll think I'm calling from a yacht in Nantucket."

She's already poking at her phone and Cinnamon isn't prepared for any part of this, but she's used to settling into the slipstream of Lucia's lead and letting it carry her along. Two sharp coughs shoot out from the baby carrier. Cinnamon looks up to see if Lucia's face registers concern, but her friend is completely focused on the speakerphone ringing. Cinnamon reaches for Bluebell's hand, limp with deep sleep, for this call. She wills her to be quiet, doesn't want Derek Jacobs to even so much as hear her whimper. As if the power of acoustics and DNA would be strong enough that he'd somehow recognize it as his secret great-granddaughter he may not even know exists over the phone. Though Cinnamon is doubtful anyone will answer a random number from a strange area code, and so apparently is Lucia, because they both jump when a gruff voice fills the kitchen. "Yeah, who's this?"

It's startling how much it aligns with his mug shot photo—with the buzz cut and leathery skin. She suspects he also has a generous assortment of faded tattoos. It's nice when racists announce themselves like this, when they're straight out of central casting. It's the camouflaged ones that are more dangerous. Though Derek is a chameleon too, and that's the most dangerous of all. She'd looked him up on the Order of Kings web page. There, he's all clean-cut, in a white button-up and a warm smile on his face like he was trying to give you and your little lady a good deal on a new car.

"Hello," Lucia says. And in just that one word, she has transformed herself into Mary Madeline Montgomery, the privilege dripping from every well-enunciated syllable. "Yes, I was trying to reach Amanda Jacobs, please."

"What do you want with Amanda?"

Smooth as cake batter, Lucia tells him that she's a former teacher at Leesville High working on a book about her time there and the students she treasured. She was having almost too much fun with this.

"A book, you say? Well, she's not here. We haven't seen hide nor hair of her in about two years now."

"Okay. Do you know where she went? It's really important that I reach her."

"Don't know, don't care, and don't call here again."

The click of the line going dead is as loud as a thunderclap.

"Well, what a pleasant gentleman."

"That was completely pointless. What am I going to do, Luce?" Cinnamon doesn't know whether to collapse on the counter, chug the spiked coffee, or both. Instead, she does nothing but grip Bluebell's hand a little tighter. Thinking about what to do next has paralyzed her. It's apparently the same with Lucia. A rare moment where she too seems at a loss and without words.

The quiet is cut through by two more coughs. Again, Cinnamon looks to Lucia, but her friend has turned her attention to pulling out piles of veggies from the fridge. The longest Lucia can sit still is 2.8 seconds.

"She keeps coughing. Do you think she's okay?"

"Oh, she's fine, Cece. But I totally get it; you worry about them so much. Remember how I totally lost it when Adam's mom convinced me that Mason was pigeon-toed and I thought I'd have to get him special shoes and braces and that he might never run? I'll never get back all those hours I lost to researching his little feet on the Internet and calling a dozen doctors, all of whom told me it was nothing. And it was—his feet were fine! They're almost always fine! No matter how much you obsess."

Lucia has grabbed a knife the size of a machete and is chopping red peppers into perfectly symmetrical cubes. She makes three full meals and two wholesome snacks a day. And organizes an elaborate art or cooking project for the twins to do when they get home from preschool at 3 p.m. That Lucia doesn't work anymore but has the twins in day care eight hours a day is something Cinnamon tries not to judge and is easier to understand in her present circumstances. She can see how an eight-hour break from motherhood every day is helpful. Not that Lucia ever takes a break. Even when the twins aren't in her presence, her days are devoted to their care with the same frantic energy she applied to being a journalist, as if she were back in the newsroom and there was always a boss watching, a deadline to meet, a promotion to chase. So far as Cinnamon can tell, there aren't many accolades involved in this whole enterprise, but that doesn't stop Lucia from throwing herself into motherhood with a vengeance that conflates hard-core parenting with self-worth, if you ask Cinnamon, but fortunately, no one asks Cinnamon.

"How do you do this, Luce? You make it all look so easy."

"All of what?" Lucia looks up, her eyes wide, even though she clearly knows what Cinnamon means. Her friend devours compliments as voraciously as she does Cool Ranch Doritos.

"Motherhood. You're amazing at it. This place is always pristine. You make pancakes with funny faces on them." Cinnamon motions to the extensive chore chart on the fridge. "They're three and they help with the laundry. How did you become this perfect mom?"

By "perfect" she really means the kind of mom Cinnamon always wishes she had. It's the same kind of mother Aunt Celia wanted people to think she was—all bougie, parading around in front of the Jack and Jill moms with poor Cinnamon in tow, the wayward niece she *so generously* took in and spit shined. *If you only knew!* Cinnamon wanted to scream through the fake smile always planted on her face.

She bemoans that her aunt has creeped into her thoughts again. All because of that stupid card arriving yesterday like a literal blast from the past blowing up what little peace she's made with their history. It torments her even though she'd promptly thrown it in the trash when she got home. It had been picked up this morning and was making its way to the putrid landfill out on Gibbon's Pike. Putrid is also how Cinnamon would describe Aunt Celia's request for a call. And also pointless. She has nothing to say to the woman. It is best to leave their relationship, such as it is, in the same condition she imagines the tossed card: buried under banana peels, chicken bones, and dirty diapers where it belongs. Cinnamon is so focused on this image she has to will herself back to the conversation, to Lucia's answer to the question she's already forgotten she asked.

"I don't know about 'perfect.' Maybe 'great' on my best day. And those best days happen one or two times a year, FYI. But it's all really trial and error. Practice. Fucking up . . . then figuring it out. You just have to do it, and you really have no idea what kind of mother you're gonna be until you're in the shit. I'm still figuring it out, and I feel like I'm failing every day. You could be good at it too, Cece. If you wanted . . ."

They've talked about this before, just a few months into their friendship when Cinnamon was still fairly new to town—and her marriage. Her erratic period was even later than usual and she had the shock of her life, which was saying something: a positive pregnancy test. She decided not to tell anyone, least of all Jayson, because she needed time to herself to adjust to the idea—nine months may not have even been enough. But she also didn't believe it could possibly be real. Not with her dysfunctional uterus. She was right—it wasn't real. A few days after the test, she'd bled through her favorite jeans. A chemical pregnancy is what the Internet called it, a short-lived union of a sperm and egg that wasn't a good genetic match. So when Cinnamon told Lucia, her voice was filled with relief. Lucia's, however, was full of sadness and devastation on her behalf. Lucia confessed then that she'd had two miscarriages of her own before the twins. Tears spilled down her cheeks as she talked about her "lost babies." In light of Lucia's reveal and the awkwardness that bloomed after, Cinnamon regretted opening up at all to her new friend, which wasn't like her anyway. Of course, given the circumstances, Lucia would judge her for feeling spared by a lost pregnancy. Lucia also couldn't abide that Cinnamon hadn't told Jayson about any of it, insisting he had the right to know. But Cinnamon felt otherwise, and it was one of the rare occasions she didn't submit to Lucia's admonishments. She'd defended herself by saying that it was a moot point anyway, since there was no baby, and assured her friend she was really and truly fine. "It's for the best. It's not a good time, and honestly, I don't think I'm cut out for it, for being a mom."

"Cinnamon, that's nonsense. Why would you even say that?"

"Because it's true. Not everyone is made for motherhood."

Lucia had mercifully let them drop the subject.

But now this question hangs in the air again along with the sharp scent of sliced peppers: Does Cinnamon want this?

"I can't even think about all that. All I'm thinking about is finding Daisy. I still have a lot to finish up before I can really go on summer break from work. If Jayson actually gets the Ruins opened by the Fourth, or sometime this summer, I'm going to need to be around to help. And this . . . all this—it's a lot. My life isn't set up for this."

"I hear you on that."

The melody of Lucia's ringing phone joins the sound of chopping; her eyes go wide when she sees the number.

"Shit, it's Derek!" She frantically wipes her hands on a tea towel and lunges for the phone, putting it on speaker.

It's not his voice on the other end of the line but a woman's hoarse whisper.

"You just called here . . . about Amanda? We have that caller ID thingamajig . . . She's my granddaughter."

"Yes, we—I—did just call. As I said, I'm trying to find your granddaughter."

"And you're a teacher?" There's the rightful amount of skepticism.

"Yes, yes—well, retired. Now I'm a writer, and I'm doing a book for Simon & Schuster about . . . kids and bullying based on my time in the classroom, and . . . well, I remembered that Daisy was nice to some kids who were being bullied . . . Anyway, I just wanted to try to find her."

"That sounds like Daisy, a soft spot for every broken bird." It didn't sound like the woman was convinced that that was altogether a good thing. "Like my husband told you, she isn't here. She disappeared on us. Just up and gone. But could be her friend Caleb knows where the heck she is, if you find him. They ran off together, those two. I take it you know him too . . . from the school?"

Lucia and Cinnamon exchange a look and wordlessly try to decide how to play this.

"Yes, yes, Caleb! Just don't remember his last name. Was it . . . Shenkenmeyer?"

Shenkenmeyer? Cinnamon mouths. Lucia shrugs.

"Nah, Lerner. He's Pastor Mike's kid. You know, he and his wife run that church camp up on Old Sawmill Road?"

"That's right, that's right. I vaguely remember that. He was a good kid too."

Lucia liked to brag about her ability to get people to open up to her. She once told Cinnamon that the secret to being a good reporter was as much about asking the right questions as it was about not talking. Let people fill in the silence for you. Most people love to hear themselves talk. Lucia goes quiet now and lets the woman go on about Caleb.

"Well, he was kinda funny, if you know what I mean. But that's who Daisy left town with. Those two were thick as thieves. Pastor Mike hasn't heard from Caleb either. I always ask when I see him at Piggly Wiggly."

Cinnamon has already zoned out of the last part of the conversation, having lunged for her phone as soon as she heard Caleb's last name. By the time Lucia's made promises to be in touch if she hears anything and hangs up, Cinnamon has found three Caleb Lerners on Facebook.

Lucia pulls them up on her own phone too, and they begin combing the photo albums for clues.

"I found him!" Cinnamon thrusts her phone inches from Lucia's nose.

"How do you know?"

"Because there's one photo with Daisy in it too. This is her—in the floral dress." Cinnamon might as well be looking at a ghost. Only a portion of Daisy's face is visible, but her smile is one of sheer delight. Her arms are wrapped around Caleb's neck as she gazes adoringly at him. His own spindly arm is outstretched as he takes a selfie of the two of them in front of a beat-up old hatchback. The caption reads "#freedom." It's a couple of years old.

"Whoa . . . okay. I kinda didn't believe she could hide a pregnancy and that maybe you were an idiot for not realizing she was knocked up—no offense. But now, looking at her, well, I can see how it makes sense. But also, Caleb's a hottie. These two were doing the nasty? I don't buy that. But good on you, Daisy."

As much as it makes Cinnamon cringe to think of some little twenty-year-old who knows nothing about nothing as a "hottie," Lucia is right. He's got these chiseled features and a scruffy goatee that make him look like he'd play you love songs on a Spanish guitar. But it's the eyes that get you. Cornflower blue and so bright they almost reflect in the camera lens.

"He's the dad. He's gotta be. I mean, those eyes, right?" Lucia reads her mind. "Derek's were blue, but these are too! Daisy probably ran away with this guy, to a beach somewhere. I want to run away with him to a beach somewhere."

"Luce! They're dumb, broke kids. No one is living on a beach. Also, we already live on a beach. This is serious. We have to find him."

"Again, easy-peasy. Here we go." Lucia starts pounding the phone screen with purposeful fingers. "I messaged him."

"What did you say?"

"'I'm looking for Daisy's baby daddy. Is that you?'"

Cinnamon slides off her barstool and spills coffee down her T-shirt.

"Oh relax, Cinnamon. I was just kidding! I just told him the truth . . . I'm looking for Daisy. His last post was from this morning. Looks like he works construction. He's in Virginia, apparently. Shit, maybe that's where Daisy went?"

Just then Bluebell wakes up by way of an insistent whimper, as though she knows her future is being decided and she's damn well going to be there when it happens.

Cinnamon practically lunges for the carrier, and Lucia starts warming a bottle from the diaper bag without being asked. It's like they feed a stranger's baby together at her kitchen island every day.

"She must be soaking wet—I'm going to change her." Cinnamon gathers Bluebell and the diaper bag and creates a makeshift changing station on the plush carpet in the sunken living room just off the kitchen. She likes to take her time with diaper changes, tickling Bluebell's feet, blowing raspberries on her soft belly, and making funny faces, but at the moment she has too much nervous energy. All she wants to do is check Lucia's phone to see if Caleb has written back. And then check again two seconds later, and then again two seconds after that.

The good news is she's getting better at wrangling the wipes with one hand from the container that never seems to close properly and then grabbing Bluebell's tiny feet with the other and doing a swift lift to slip the diaper under her little butt. She's got it down to under a minute and feels irrationally proud.

"He wrote back!" Lucia drops the bottle on the counter with a thud, sending a few droplets of precious formula into the air like a geyser.

Cinnamon picks up Bluebell and presses her close to her chest. Her skin feels a touch warmer, but it could be because she'd been swaddled so tightly. Cinnamon is sweating herself, but the anticipation mixed with tequila is probably to blame for that. "Read it, read it!"

"He says he hasn't seen Daisy since he left town for a construction gig last fall."

"Does he know she had a baby? Did he know she was pregnant?"

Lucia is furiously typing. She speaks the words out loud as she writes. "Call . . . me."

"Call me?"

"Yes, I told him to call. If this is Bluebell's father, then why beat around the bush, right? He needs to step up and he needs to help us find the mother of his child, or he needs to start being a daddy . . . like, yesterday!"

Cinnamon carries Bluebell over and settles back on the barstool at the island. She jumps a little when the phone rings, even though they're expecting the call. Bluebell is quiet, listening.

Caleb gets right into it when the women answer on speaker. "Hey. I'm so glad you called. I've been worried sick about Daisy. I haven't heard from her in over a month. We usually talked like every day, and then suddenly nada—she hasn't been on Facebook or anything. Her phone's not in service. She can't just be gone. I didn't know who to call or what to do so far away."

Cinnamon recognizes the panic and betrayal in his voice. "Did you know she was pregnant?" she blurts out.

"Huh?" The confusion seems genuine.

"Daisy had a baby."

"Wait, what? When? She's not pregnant. She wasn't pregnant.

She would have told me. Can we back up a minute? Who even are you people?" He's traded worry for frustration, rightfully so. Here are two strangers calling him out of the blue, grilling him about his missing friend. Telling him she's got a secret baby. But Lucia doesn't answer or give Cinnamon the chance before she's pounding him with another pointed question.

"So you're not the father?"

"What? No! There's no way."

Lucia turns cajoling. Her *you can tell me anything* voice. "These things happen. We're not always careful."

His voice rises an octave. "It's not about being careful. We didn't . . . We've never . . ."

"Maybe you were drinking one night and things got out of control?" Lucia keeps pressing.

"Ma'am, I don't want to be disrespectful to you, but you don't know me and I don't even know how you know Daisy, but I promise you there is no way I am that child's father. Let's just say it is one hundred percent biologically impossible." He sounds like a frightened child trying to talk his way out of being grounded. Lucia shrugs and mouths to Cinnamon, *Maybe he's telling the truth.*

"Where's the baby now?" Caleb asks, and Cinnamon's blood runs cold. He has no claim to the child—any more than she does, at least—but is he going to show up making demands? Is he going to tell someone?

"With me." Pride creeps into Cinnamon's voice.

"And who are you?"

"My name's Cinnamon, and I'm . . . a friend. Of Daisy's."

"Oh yeah, I remember her talking about you—y'all met last summer, right? I remember feeling good that Daisy had made a friend when I left town. I didn't want her to be lonely when I decided to take this job up here building a stadium. I hated leaving her for so long, but the money was too good."

"Yes, that's me!" Cinnamon leans into the validation and shoots Lucia a look.

"She loved meeting up with you. Told me you were helping her get all her things together for school. It seemed like stuff was falling into place for her, for both of us. So when she disappeared . . . This is just so crazy. But if Daisy trusted you, I trust you. And God knows Daisy wouldn't want that baby anywhere near Leesville and those monsters who raised her. That's why I haven't called them. No way Daisy would go back there."

The reassurance Cinnamon feels that everyone is on the same page about the Jacobses is only outmatched by her sadness that Daisy had such a rough home life. It affirms for her why they connected like they did—they recognized their broken selves in each other without even having to acknowledge it.

"But where the hell *did* she go? This is the longest we've gone without talking since ninth grade. I just can't imagine her out on her own. She gets anxious, depressed real easily. She shouldn't have gone through this alone."

"Maybe she isn't alone. Do you have any idea who the dad could be if not you?"

"No—no idea at all. I mean, honestly, as far as I knew, Daisy was a . . . a . . . virgin." He struggles with the word like he's never said it out loud. "I can't believe she didn't—wouldn't—tell me she met someone. I hope . . . I hope . . . something bad didn't happen."

If this kid can't bring himself to say "virgin," it's certainly going to be hard to utter "rape," but it's what comes to mind. And it ratchets up Cinnamon's desperation even more than she would have thought possible.

"Can you think of anywhere she might have gone, Caleb? Anywhere at all?"

"Believe me, I've racked my brain. I reached out to a few of our high school friends, but they either haven't responded or they haven't heard from her. I just really have no clue." He sighs like he has the weight of the world on his shoulders, which is exactly what it feels like when you have a friend in trouble. They've now talked to the only people that they know who know Daisy, and yet they're no further along in finding her.

"Look, guys, I'm on a break and gotta get back to work, but will you stay in touch? And I'll tell you if I hear anything."

"Yes, yes—of course."

"Wait—before I go. What's the baby's name? Boy or girl?"

"Little girl . . . but she doesn't exactly have a name. I've been calling her Bluebell. Kinda a nickname, I guess."

"Bluebell? That's cute. You know Daisy's a nickname too? Her real name is Amanda. But she started calling herself Daisy in middle school when she read in her dead mom's diary that daisies were her favorite flower. She just refused to answer to anything but that. Man, Bluebell's got some lungs on her."

He's right—the baby's worked herself up right and good over the last part of the call. They can barely hear one another's goodbyes.

Cinnamon rains kisses on the top of Bluebell's head and tries to shush her. But when Lucia says, "Well, now what?" Cinnamon has a good mind to give in herself and join Bluebell in wailing at the world. Because the fact of the matter is she hasn't got a clue.

The smell of butter and garlic is so strong that Cinnamon's mouth is watering before she can even wonder who could be cooking up a feast in her kitchen.

"Hello? Who's there?" she calls out as if an intruder or burglar would be at the stove sautéing and not making off with their old TV. She finds Jayson standing in a cloud of smoke in the kitchen, flipping shrimp.

"Hey, you," Jayson says as if he hadn't absconded to his mother's for the week.

"What are you doing here?" It's a strange question to ask your husband.

"I know you were trying to be thoughtful by visiting the work site yesterday and bringing me cookies and all; I just wanted to show my appreciation. Go freshen up. It's almost ready."

"Wow, okay then. Give me a sec." Cinnamon is less concerned with freshening up—though she will swipe a washcloth under her pits and swish some Scope—than she is with getting Bluebell settled upstairs so she'll sleep for a nice long while and give Cinnamon some uninterrupted time with her husband. Some time to make nice.

On her way through the dining room, she sees the table is already set. Jayson's even put out some stubby candles she'd been saving for no real good reason. She watches as he selects an album from the crate by the stereo to play on his grandmother's old record player, and she knows exactly what it will be before the first note plays. The living room fills with Marvin Gaye crooning about feeling like a stray without a home. His voice burrows right into Cinnamon's bones, like the melody is her lifeblood. Her hips sway like they have a mind of their own when they get a taste of Marvin or Luther or Smokey. She has the same taste in songs as the sixty-two-year-old woman who introduced her to music. One thing she at least has left of Thelma, besides the Bible and a predilection for Neapolitan ice cream.

As soon as Bluebell's snuggled in her makeshift bassinet upstairs, fast asleep, Cinnamon returns to the living room with a quickness and goes right up to press herself against Jayson's back. "Hi, husband."

"Ohhhhh, is that how you want it to be?" He pulls back a little bit, teasing her. "Not just yet, baby. I need to feed my woman first. Go sit."

He goes to the kitchen and returns to the table with a hot cast-iron skillet. He plucks a sizzling morsel straight out of the pan and blows on it before popping it between her lips. The shrimp melts on her tongue.

"You want more of that?" Jayson asks.

Cinnamon responds by grabbing his hand and pulling it to her mouth to lick the garlic butter off his fingers. He feeds her a second and a third, and before the last one is gone, Jayson is working her out of her formula-stained T-shirt and burying his lips deep in her neck. This is how Jayson apologizes, through sex. It's somewhat self-serving, like saying you're sorry by baking a cake for your friend and then eating the whole thing yourself, but Cinnamon doesn't mind. As Jayson leaves a trail of kisses that lead to the waistband of her jeans, she doesn't mind one bit.

She didn't lose her virginity until she was twenty-five, and there was something about starting so late that made her feel perpetually behind the curve. Her husband is only the third person she's slept with, and from their very first time, in Jayson's black silk sheets, she tried to make up for her lack of experience with enthusiasm. If she didn't have the right moves, she had the willingness, and that seemed to do the trick. Soon enough she stopped being so self-conscious and started enjoying herself, a transformation she wasn't sure Jayson noticed. In those early days, she couldn't imagine doing what she does now, slipping off her panties slowly while he watches and climbing on top of him right there on the floor. She digs her nails into the back of his neck, consumed with a desire that has all the familiarity of an old song. Even when you haven't heard it in years, you know all the words.

It's over fairly fast—both the blessing and curse of knowing each other's body parts and buttons like they do—but it's just as well. This is the part she's always liked most anyway, lying together, all entwined limbs, sated and sleepy. Her husband pulls her head onto his chest. "I know I've been all MIA and pissy this week. This stuff with the baby . . . It got me all in my head. You know, we could try, Cinnamon. Really try. We could have a baby of our own. With your Nutella skin and my silky waves? Imagine how cute. It's not too late for us. Of course, I'm not having a baby with you until you finally take my name. How'd we ever be a family with everyone having different names?"

It was no surprise he was jumping at the chance to bring up the name thing—again. He'd been hounding her forever to become Cinnamon Cochrane, and she always promised she'd get around to it. She'd lost so much though; she didn't want to lose this too. What *is* a surprise is his venturing into baby talk at all. The last couple of years they'd let the subject just float away like a lost balloon in the sky, a harmless tragedy. She doesn't quite know what to do with this development. It's as ordinary as ever, a husband and a wife discussing having a baby, and yet her throat and stomach suddenly burn like she's swallowed fire. And something tells her it's not the garlic shrimp coming back on her.

Jayson turns to stare her dead in the face. "But Cinnamon, that baby upstairs—that's not our baby. She doesn't belong with us. You get that, right?"

"Do you mean because she's not our flesh and blood or because she's white?"

"Both! I mean, surely you see that."

"No one ever second-guesses whether Black kids belong with white families."

"Well, they should. Guy I used to run with at school, Cade, he was raised by white parents, and it fucked him all the way up. They just straight pretended he wasn't Black. Never told him what to expect and then were all shocked when he was tailed by the cops or when teachers said dumb shit to him. It was funny how he knew all the words to every Journey song. Oh man, we clowned that nigga about that!"

She feels Jayson's belly shake under her as he laughs, but it's bringing back too many painful moments for her to join him. Like the time when she was living with the Parkers and she was supposed to bring a dish to school that represented her "heritage" and they suggested . . . a watermelon. They weren't even trying to be obnoxious—they didn't know better—so when the Parkers asked about her day, she didn't bother to explain how the kids laughed and how humiliated she was. There was a white foster mother who wouldn't stop commenting about how exotic-looking she was. That same foster mom bought her a rotation of hats to wear since she just couldn't figure out "how to help Cinnamon with her hair."

"So you think no one should raise a baby that's a different race from them?"

"I don't know about all that, Cece. I mean you shouldn't do it just to feel good about yourself, like I suspect some of these white folks do. All *Look at me and my brown children and our matching Christmas pajamas and I'm such a good person, aren't I?* But I also like to stay out of people's business. I can tell you this though: I sure as hell don't think *we* should be raising a white kid. Just imagine me trying to take Blondie to the playground in about three, four years. I'd end up in handcuffs every time before she even made it down the slide." He laughs again but this time with no humor whatsoever. "No one would ever believe she's mine. That I had any sort of right to be with her."

It's true. Cinnamon can't picture Jayson toting a little blond girl around to soccer practice and playdates, walking her to school drop-off in the morning. Jayson would never be able to endure the looks and the questions. All the strangers watching him, scrutinizing him, making sure he was where he belonged and that he wasn't up to no good. Lord knows living with all that is hard enough without a blue-eyed baby in tow. She could get away with it. Strangers would probably give her the benefit of the doubt, assume the baby was safe with the nanny, like they did when she was with Lucia's kids, but it would be different for him. Not just different—downright dangerous. People would think she was a paid caregiver. They'd see him as a criminal.

But even putting aside the child being white, she knows Jayson would never want to raise another man's baby. He'd want a child made in his image, someone he could look at and say things like, "I did that. Looks exactly like me, don't he? Real chip off the ole block. He gets that arm from me," all puffed with pride.

She too could see something appealing about raising your own flesh and blood—seeing the magic of genetics play out in a face that has an identical dimple to your own or a weird bowlegged gait, just like you have; to have strangers say she has your smile; to feel the legacy of your ancestors pumping through generations of shared blood.

And, not for nothing, on the rare occasions Cinnamon did have glimpses of her future child or children, they involved her massaging lotion onto ashy brown knees, putting perfect parts in thick coils and smoothing them with Pink's lotion, scouring bookstores to find books that feature plucky girls that look like the two of them, books Cinnamon never had; rubbing bony shoulders in knowing consolation the first time her kid gets called the N-word, as Cinnamon herself was in second grade.

That's not our baby.

Cinnamon tears herself away from Jayson's words and this conversation by announcing she needs to run upstairs for a minute. They both know it's to check on Bluebell, but not saying it out loud gives her plausible deniability, though it doesn't save her from Jayson's eye roll.

He grabs her hand as she's trying to slip her clothes back on. "Look, that child's gonna be okay . . . and I don't just mean right now. You can take her into the police station tomorrow and it'll be okay. You know there are plenty of parents out there dying for a baby just like that."

A baby like that, a newborn white baby, "undamaged," "unbroken," the top of the adoption pyramid, a fact she knows all too well. "Yeah. Yeah. I know. Gimme me a minute. I'll be right back."

Jayson groans but lets go of her. "I bought a peach cobbler from Susie for dessert. Get your sweet ass back here with a quickness."

Cinnamon is still on the stairs when she hears the coughs—a terrible hacking that should never come out of a human, much less an infant. She quickens her pace, then stops short when she sees Bluebell, who seems to have been drained of all color. The shock gives way to a panicked burst of action and Cinnamon closes the distance to the baby in one lunge and scoops her up. She's burning up. Not just warm—her skin is hot to the touch. Cinnamon explodes with curse words and panic. She should have trusted her instincts. She knew something was wrong all day, but she turned her back for a second—she was down there having *sex*—and Bluebell was just getting sicker and sicker. The shame is a trapdoor below her, which she falls straight through.

"Jay!" Cinnamon screams. "Jayson, get up here!"

He's standing there still butt naked and something about that feels wrong. She wants him to cover himself up.

"She's sick, Jay. Feel how hot she is."

But he doesn't touch her. Fear crosses his face in place of concern.

"Shit," he says, placing both his hands on his head. "Shit, Cece. I told you this wasn't gonna end well."

Cinnamon fumbles around with the rectal thermometer she bought with all the other baby gear at Walmart. How does it work again? It seems to have three times as many buttons as a regular thermometer.

Once she finally gets it to work, she almost screams. "Her fever is 104.5. I've gotta get her to the hospital."

"The hospital? But what if . . ." Jayson's standing at the bedroom door, the light bouncing off his still-sweaty skin.

In the span of minutes, Bluebell's now completely listless, floppy and silent except for the raspy cough.

"I don't have a choice, Jayson. She needs medical attention!" Her voice sounds unhinged, she realizes, but that's exactly what she is.

"Well, let me drive you," Jayson says.

"I don't have time for you to get dressed." She's already got Bluebell buckled in the carrier. "I have to go. Right now. I'll call you when I know more."

Jayson says something but she doesn't hear it. She's already out the door.

CHAPTER SEVEN

The scene in front of her is something Cinnamon's only witnessed in movies. A baby lying in a plastic box, tangled in a mess of tubes, her little body shuddering every so often. What makes this all too real is not just the fact that Cinnamon can reach out and touch the clammy skin on Bluebell's arm from her perch on a stiff chair, but it's the smell—antiseptic, rubber gloves, and, most potent of all, her own fear. There's also the parade of doctors and nurses coming in every so often to check one vital sign or another. Cinnamon is never truly by herself in this room, and yet she's hard-pressed to think of a time when she's ever felt more alone, which is saying something. It doesn't help that she knows nothing beyond the fact that Bluebell has something called RSV. The second the doctors uttered the diagnosis, she began frantically googling and learned respiratory syncytial virus is a fairly common virus in infants and young children. Her eyes get stuck on the words "serious" and "unpredictable," but the doctors assured her it typically runs its course without severe complications. But seeing Bluebell with an oxygen feed, an impossibly skinny cannula in her nose, it looks very serious, almost dire. The doctors said they just took extra precautions with newborns. Bluebell's fever dropped just as quickly as it had spiked with a single dose of ibuprofen. Everyone seems efficient and unbothered like this is just another day at the office, which it is for them, but Cinnamon needs her panic to be acknowledged and respected, matched even, which would make her feel considerably less insane.

Each time someone in scrubs enters the room, Cinnamon wants to grab them by the shoulders and demand more information. She wants to ask a million questions and have some assurances that Bluebell is getting the best possible care. She wants to shake every last one of them and say, *Make her okay!* But for so many reasons, she knows she doesn't have the luxury of being any sort of demanding Karen right about now. Since they rushed in twelve hours ago, she's been making herself as scarce as possible, the same unobtrusive, watchful stance she would have whenever she arrived at a new foster placement. *Stand in the corner, quiet as the paint on the walls, all but invisible until you can assess the situation.*

The nurses and staff have been content, so far, with her explanation that she's watching the baby for a friend, and let any further questioning go, so focused as they've been on the medical care. But Cinnamon knows that it's only a matter of time. Sooner rather than later she'll be asked for answers and explanations about why a baby that looks like Bluebell is in the possession of a woman who looks like her.

It's been a full twenty-four hours since Cinnamon has slept, but there's no way she could close her eyes right now even if there were a place to lie down. So her only option is a serious infusion of caffeine and sugar to somehow keep her going. If she's going to have any break at all, she should go now, while Bluebell has just settled into a fitful sleep. But it's only the reality of her bladder filled like a balloon about to burst, and the real possibility that she could pee right here on this stiff pink chair, that gets her moving. Once she is up and has relieved herself in the room's inordinately vast bathroom, she decides to duck to the cafeteria.

After winding through the mazelike hallways of the pediatric unit, walls plastered with crayon-drawn thank-you notes and finger-painted pictures of the staff, she eventually reaches the large double doors she'd torn through last night, clutching Bluebell's hot, limp little body. That was also like something out of a movie. Cinnamon rushing into the ER, hair going every which way, shoes untied because she couldn't take the time, frantically screaming, "There's something wrong with my baby," and begging the all-too-calm receptionist for help. What a sight she was. It was only when she saw the woman's confused expression as she turned from Cinnamon to the baby and back that she'd realized what she'd said. *My baby*. It only mattered for a second, as Cinnamon breathlessly stuttered through an explanation that was sufficient enough to get Bluebell processed and in a curtained cocoon where another woman introducing herself as Dr. Rae blessedly appeared within minutes. She was so tall and thin it was like her white coat was hanging on a wire hanger. After a succinct line of questioning about timing and symptoms and an exam that passed faster than a TikTok video, Dr. Rae explained about RSV and the fact that they'd better admit the baby for observation to be on the safe side. The doctor then disappeared to the other side of the curtain before Cinnamon realized the woman hadn't even said goodbye.

Now, as she stands at the hospital's exit, the pull of fresh air is so strong Cinnamon doesn't realize she's walking outside until her feet carry her through the sliding glass doors, the loud whoosh of them opening and closing almost as startling as the shock of pink creeping up on the still-inky black sky.

Cinnamon has seen more sunrises in this last week than she's seen in her whole life. Even standing in an ambulance bay, looking out on a parking lot beyond, there's something magical about watching the night sky slowly lift like a curtain. It's a peacefulness that forces itself on you, calms you almost against your will. She has to get coffee, she has to get back to Bluebell, but she'll allow herself five deep breaths of humid salt-licked air as morning and night duke it out in their daily ritual.

With each exhale, she tries to release some of the worry that's making itself known in every single one of her muscles, but it's impossible. It occurs to her to pray; if there was ever a moment that called for a chat with God, this is definitely it. But the prayers Cinnamon is used to are typically of the flippant variety—for patience in dealing with Vera, for the hot-donut light to be on at Doughboys, for Bessie's engine to keep running. When it comes to anything serious or earnest, when prayers may have really mattered, true faith has always felt just beyond her reach despite the Rev's best efforts. She loved the idea of God, but lodged deep within her was the fear that he would be on the long list of people who would forsake her, and that would be too much to bear. The only other time Cinnamon came close to praying for something that really mattered was the night she thought she was going to die, and that was a reflex more than anything else.

Her defenses are down, and the memory of that night comes for her. How she lay in a hospital, almost exactly like this one, because like grocery stores and DMVs, all hospitals are pretty much the same. She hadn't meant to put a gash that deep in her thigh. She hadn't meant to start cutting in the first place. Cutting was something angsty white girls did. That's how she discovered it, when Natalie in her freshman geometry class showed off a row of thin scars like railroad tracks across her inner arm and explained in excruciating detail how she dragged her brother's penknife along her skin. It made no kinda sense to Cinnamon that the girl said it actually felt good, and that's why she tried it. Curiosity more than anything else. Much like the way she learned how rubbing a pillow against herself in just the right place between her legs would build to a release, Cinnamon discovered the cutting was the same, just like Natalie had said, a release of a different kind. The pain was so intense, but it was also, unlike all her other hurts, entirely under her control. The neat lines of scarlet bubbling up from the soft skin of her inner thighs comforted her in a way she would never be able to explain. And so she did it again, and again. Until one night she cut too deeply. She couldn't get the bleeding to stop. When she started feeling weak and dizzy, she got scared, and eventually she couldn't avoid telling someone—the only option being her foster mom at the time. Momma Jean, as all the kids called her, was loud, angry, and always hollering at whoever was in hearing range. It was no surprise that Momma Jean's reaction to Cinnamon's blood-soaked thigh was an outraged neck roll. "You did what? On purpose? Girl, you gonna be the end of me with this BS. Get my pocketbook. Guess we got no choice but to get you to the hospital."

There, the nurses had more sympathy, which actually intensified Cinnamon's shame. When one of them offered to hold her hand while she got twelve stitches, the kindness somehow hurt more than the needle. She knew better than to let herself get used to such things. It was like her relationship with sugar—better to avoid it; otherwise, you're going to just keep on wanting.

All the while she could hear Momma Jean grumbling to the nurses, one of whom tried to explain that this type of behavior was common in teenage girls. One in four teens between the ages of twelve and seventeen harms themselves by cutting. The nurse rattled off the stat as if she were reading the side effects of a medication, and Cinnamon didn't know if she should feel comforted that this was so "common" or dumb because she was just a basic cliché.

Whatever the case, Cinnamon knew she was done for, even before she heard Momma Jean respond to the nurse with an aggrieved teeth sucking. She had made it crystal clear from the jump that the kids she took into her home had to be low-maintenance. "Don't start no trouble, won't be no trouble" was her favorite line. And now here was Cinnamon, most certainly "trouble." There was no amount of scrubbing baseboards with a toothbrush and rubbing hair grease on Momma Jean's scalp while she watched *The Shawshank Redemption* for the thousandth time that was going to redeem Cinnamon. So it was no surprise when the social worker arrived at Momma Jean's not three days later. It was a new woman, but that also wasn't a surprise. Cinnamon's social workers changed more often than Momma Jean changed her nails. This one was different though—her eyes didn't bear the familiar weariness of an underpaid and overworked state employee. She was also Black. Cinnamon had never had a Black social worker before, never mind one who actually looked like a loving grandmother; looked like Cinnamon's own loving grandmother—what she remembered of her at least. Same soft gray hair that had clearly been roller set in the last forty-eight hours, same sensible khaki slacks and liver-spotted hands that she knew if she touched them would feel like silk. In fact, the urge to reach out and touch this woman's hands hit her so hard she had to sit on her own to stop herself. Up until that point Cinnamon hadn't realized you could crave a hug as badly as you could crave food or a glass of water, like your very existence depended on it. But at that moment all she wanted to do was crawl into that woman's life. As if she could read her thoughts, Sallie—that was the woman's name—stood up and walked around the table. She leaned over Cinnamon's slumped shoulders and whispered, "Don't you worry; we're going to get you all sorted out." It was being enveloped in those eerily familiar smells—cocoa butter and menthol cigarettes, like the scent of Cinnamon's childhood itself, what brief one she was allowed—that made Cinnamon want to cry. More than even the words themselves, or the fact that she actually, despite herself, believed Sallie.

"I'm going to level with you, Cinnamon." Sallie's voice was warm grits. "It's going to be hard to find a new placement for a fifteen-year-old girl."

Cinnamon appreciated her bluntness—it was like the pain in her leg, a relief, bracing. She also appreciated that Sallie understood that Cinnamon was the sort of person you leveled with. And it wasn't like she didn't already know this. It was easy to find homes for cute chubby babies. But when they started walking and talking and having tantrums and feelings and whatnot, they became "less desirable," and by the time they got to be Cinnamon's age, forget about it. Cinnamon knew she was positively geriatric when it came to being a ward of the state. But Sallie wasn't looking at her like a lost cause—far from it.

"I did some digging since I got your case a couple of days ago. I tried to find your mother, Margo Haynes, but I'm afraid I had no luck at all. But then I thought maybe I could find your dad. I looked up your birth certificate and found his name. On a whim, I checked the VA records across Illinois, Ohio, and Indiana. Lotta Black men of a certain age were in the service, so it's always worth a shot. And what do you know? I found a file for Trevor Green. Your father."

Cinnamon's breath tripped on the way to her throat at those two words. *Your father.*

Her mother hadn't given Cinnamon her father's last name. Her grandmother had put it this way by way of explanation: "I'm a Haynes, and my daughter's a Haynes, and you're a Haynes. Don't change your name for no man when you grow up and get married, ya hear? They come and go, but your name is forever."

So Cinnamon knew that she didn't share her father's last name, but she'd also never seen her birth certificate. She couldn't believe the lengths Sallie was going to help her, as if she were a private detective on TV and not a state employee. Sallie explained how she'd gone digging through the paperwork.

"I found that your father listed a sister as an emergency contact. I saw a notice that she was alerted to his death benefits ten years ago."

Sallie seemed to assume that Cinnamon knew her dad was dead. And she had always figured that was true, but hearing it was real still hit her. Sallie stopped talking as Cinnamon's chin slumped so hard it practically smacked against her neck.

"I'm sorry; that was awful of me. Did you not know your daddy had passed? When was the last time you saw him? It wasn't in your file."

"I never met him," Cinnamon whispered. What Cinnamon knew of the man was that he and her mom had some sort of fling, and then he got deployed before she even told him she was pregnant. Cinnamon had learned this when she'd dared to turn to Grandmother Thelma one day shortly before she died and ask, "Where's my daddy?" All the other kids seemed to have one of those. If they weren't around every day, they at least came around every so often, and she wondered why she'd been forgotten. Her grandmother said he was serving overseas, somewhere called the "Middle East"—which seemed to be a made-up place out of a fairy tale, not a real one like Cleveland. Cinnamon wasn't even sure her dad ever learned she existed. She wanted to believe he did though, that he wondered about her sometimes like she had about him, maybe even, inexplicably, at the exact same time, and that connected them. She would do it with her mother too—press her eyes shut and think about her mom as hard as she could, like Cinnamon was sending a bat signal to her wherever she might be—and hope some intangible bond meant that her mother knew she was doing it. If that were the case, the headache and hollow feeling Cinnamon was left with after those moments would be worth it. Problem is, she would never know.

"Well, honey, I'm sorry I have to be the one to tell you this. From what I've gleaned, he had a heart attack at a VA hospital in Memphis."

Her father had been in Memphis when he died. Not Mecca, not Mosul. He was practically down the road.

Sallie was still staring at her, the concern plain on her face. "Did you know he had a sister or any family?"

Cinnamon swiveled her head slowly from side to side. But her placid demeanor belied the roiling storm of emotions overtaking her. *An aunt.* She had family, a real family. Blood. Alive somewhere. It was something she had dreamed of since her grandmother died and the social worker, the very first social worker, arrived and helped her pack some clothes and shoes into an old duffle. Grandma Thelma had actually been dead for nearly two days by that point. Six-year-old Cinnamon understood she was dead—she knew what dead was; that lesson came thanks to two goldfish who'd been found floating belly-up no sooner than Cinnamon had gotten them in the mayonnaise jar that served as their fishbowl. But Cinnamon thought her grandmother looked so peaceful in her armchair she let her be, only disturbing her to sit on her lap and eat cereal three times a day, the one meal she could proudly fix herself. Her one transgression was that she flipped the TV to cartoons as she ate, instead of her grandmother's beloved soaps, because Thelma didn't—couldn't—object. Then the police were knocking at the door. Then they were taking her grandmother away, draped in a sheet making her look like a ghost; then the social worker with the mole on her nose arrived; then came the same steps that would fast become familiar—the packing, the sad duffle on her slight shoulder, the long drive to another strange house. First to the Rosewoods, a quiet couple even older than her grandmother. They both had matching gray Afros against identical shades of dark skin and the same round eyes, making Cinnamon wonder if they were brother and sister instead of husband and wife. They also wore identical expressions all the time, like they were confused as to how they found themselves with a young child in their house, even though as far as Cinnamon knew, it was their choice. The social worker said they wanted to "give back to their community," though Cinnamon didn't understand what they were giving. It seemed she was the one who was up for grabs.

When she proved too much for them, it was off to the Parkers, then a few other houses and people she barely remembered or blocked out along the way before Momma Jean. And then Sallie (her fourth social worker? Her fifth?) was telling her that she could deliver her to family. Nine years too late, but she wouldn't complain.

"Your aunt Celia, she's a few years older than your dad. She said they lost touch after he joined the Marines. Apparently, they'd been estranged for a while. I know all this because I was able to track her down. She wasn't surprised to learn that he had a child, or children—she figured as much after all these years. She has a daughter of her own, Corrine, who's thirteen. So technically she's your cousin, but she could be a sister of sorts."

A sister? This was icing on the cake. Cinnamon tried not to get her hopes up imagining what it would be like to have a real sibling. They could share a room, or trade clothes, keep each other's secrets—all the things Cinnamon read about sisters doing together in her books.

She wanted to give Sallie the right reaction, tears of joy and gratitude, but she could only nod numbly. This didn't deter Sallie, but she did slow down. "Look, I know this is a lot to absorb. But it's good news. Your aunt, she's willing to take you in, Cinnamon. She lives in Atlanta—in a really nice neighborhood, with good schools. And this will be a chance for you to connect with family."

"Did she know my mother?"

Cinnamon hadn't realized she'd spoken out loud—she was sure the question was stuck in her throat forever—until Sallie answered. "No, honey. She hadn't seen your dad since he left at eighteen; she doesn't seem to know much about what happened to him after that. I'm sorry. And your grandparents, your dad's parents, they've passed on."

That expression—*passed on*. She hated it. Like people were just flying through this life as if it were a pit stop on the way to somewhere else.

"So what do you say? Shall we give Aunt Celia a call and get you on a flight to Atlanta?"

Cinnamon hadn't bothered to respond, because it may have been put to her as a question, but it wasn't a choice.

Now, standing in the ambulance bay of Sibley County Hospital, she reaches down and touches her leg, feeling the place where the scars spread across her thighs, hidden under her jeans. They've started to tingle, as they do when she's stressed, but she doesn't mind the sensation. Sometimes she thinks of it as a way for her younger self to communicate to her, like a friend silently squeezing your hand in reassurance.

The scars are mostly faded, but one of the first times Jayson saw her naked he made a joke about loving her tiger stripes, assuming they were stretch marks, as he ran his hands across her thighs and hips. It was one of those rare moments when she wanted to tell him about herself, her real self. About the time she was in so much pain that all she could do was add to it. But opening herself up to Jayson would be the same as praying to God—it would require a leap of faith that nothing in all her years on earth prepared her to believe would carry her anywhere but straight down to the cold, hard ground below.

The self-serve coffee urn leaks two sad drops into her Styrofoam cup. Of course the coffee machine is empty—of course. The lone worker at this hour, an older white woman with jet-black roots and hair bleached within an inch of its life, tells her to wait while she makes a fresh batch. Cinnamon moves to one of the tables in the empty cafeteria, pondering why white women want to be blond so bad, especially when it means turning your hair to straw.

Cinnamon's heel taps a nervous beat that's even faster than her heart, which seems unable to slow to a normal pace, even though it must be tired from keeping this up for hours. She decides to finally respond to the texts from Jayson. He's checked in on her twice and even offered to come to the hospital to be with her, but Cinnamon thought having him around would call too much attention.

Before she can decide what to type, a woman materializes in front of her.

"Cinnamon Haynes?"

She knows immediately, from her well-honed radar, that she's a social worker. She's a baby one, so young the ink on her degree probably isn't even dry yet. Cinnamon quickly sizes her up as the kind of girl whose parents had enough money that she could study whatever she wanted and take a social worker job that probably paid below the poverty line while still driving the latest Audi. She exudes an air of privileged bleeding heart before she even says a word, with the expensive flats paired with the Black Lives Matter tote bag. No one is going to second-guess that this woman is well-intentioned and in the fight . . . for everything. Becky Bright Eyes is gonna change the world. Cinnamon is tired just looking at her.

Turns out her name isn't Becky, but Taylor. Which Cinnamon learns when she introduces herself and hands Cinnamon a cup of coffee. "They just filled it."

"Thank you." *Watch and assess.*

"So, I'm a social worker." Bingo. "I'm with Child Protective Services here in the county. We received a report from a nurse in the pediatric ICU that you brought a baby in that you're watching for a friend?"

It's painful how much Taylor is going out of her way not to seem like she's accusing Cinnamon of anything. She's slipped into the chair next to her like they're old friends having a warm chat. Caring tone, open-ended question, an expression that says, *No judgment here, but I'm also not a fool.* These are the kinds of things they must teach in social work school.

Cinnamon grips her cup so hard the flimsy Styrofoam almost cracks. It's not like she's unprepared for this moment—as soon as she walked into the hospital, she understood this was inevitable. She was hardly going to waltz in and out of here without scrutiny. Someone was going to ask questions, and that someone is the too-young girl with a too-eager smile sitting next to her right now. What Cinnamon has going for her is practice: lying is like learning to walk—you get better at it over time without even trying. And she has hers prepared. If not lies, exactly, then the necessary omissions that will protect Daisy, keep social services from finding out about the Jacobses, and prevent anyone from knowing she didn't go right to the police like she probably should have. Other than that, she plans on being completely forthcoming.

"I found her—the baby." There's some consolation in confessing this plain truth.

"So this is not your friend's baby, as you told the doctors?" Taylor's asking like she's clarifying whether Cinnamon is a bold-faced liar, unhinged, or something else.

"Well, yeah. Sort of. It's a little bit . . . Well, it's a crazy story."

"I know all about crazy." Taylor chuckles like they're sharing a joke, even if Cinnamon doesn't laugh. "Lay it on me."

"I work over at SBCC—I'm the career counselor there—and I take my lunch break at the same park every single day no matter what. I'm a creature of habit, I guess you could say."

Taylor smiles, nudging her to go on, as if Cinnamon might falter at any moment.

"I sat down to read my book yesterday afternoon, and I heard a noise."

Cinnamon alters the timeline slightly. She can't have Taylor thinking she's been holding on to this baby for a week. She also makes a split-second decision not to mention the note. If she does, she'll need to explain who Daisy is, and that's a surefire way for Taylor to track down the Jacobses before Cinnamon can reach Daisy. "I turned around and there she was. Sitting in her baby carrier, all bundled up. At first, I didn't think she was abandoned. I thought the mom or dad must have gone somewhere, run off to chase a dog or pee or something. So I sat there waiting."

Taylor pulls out a packet of tissues from some invisible pocket. Cinnamon isn't aware of giving her any reason to think she's close to tears, but this must be another thing they teach you in social work school. Always have tissues ready. Cinnamon, however, is focused and composed. She also makes it a point to look Taylor straight in the eye. She'd struggled with making eye contact for most of her life. When she was little, she had this irrational fear that people could somehow see inside her, eyes being the windows to the soul and all that. When someone stared at her too long, her heart would race with panic that all her private thoughts were there, exposed. She'd had a teacher at school once, Miss Washington, an older Black woman, who spent all three months Cinnamon was in her class making it her project to get Cinnamon to look people in the eye, especially white people. "You gotta show them they need to respect you," she'd implored. But respect was so far down Cinnamon's ladder of needs. She needed it now though—she needed Taylor to respect her and find her credible and responsible.

"I waited for a while, but then the baby started getting a little fussy and I worried she was wet or hungry. I had no idea how long she'd been there. I couldn't just keep waiting forever, so I brought her home."

"You didn't call the police?"

"I didn't. I just wanted to regroup and try to look up what I should do next to make sure she was safe, that I was doing the right thing. I didn't know if I should call the police. Are they really the right people to handle an abandoned baby? I assumed it was child services, but I wanted to look it up and find the right person. But first, I wanted to make her comfortable—I fed her and changed her. Just to make sure she was okay before turning her over to someone."

"And this was yesterday afternoon?"

"Yes." It was getting easier. "Then she started getting warmer and warmer and coughing, so I brought her here."

"That sounds like a lot to handle," Taylor says. She moves her hand closer to Cinnamon's on the table like she's going to grab it before she thinks better of it. "But you know you should have gone straight to the police, right?"

Cinnamon nods, ready to take her punishment.

"The important thing is that we have to figure out what to do now.

My job is to secure a safe place for this baby and try to locate her family if we can. Have you ever seen anyone with a baby in that park, or a pregnant woman? You said you go there every day?"

"No, I never saw a pregnant woman or one with a baby. It's usually empty. That's why I like it."

"Hang on a sec." Taylor takes a beat to scroll through her phone, leaving Cinnamon with her unease about what she's looking for in there. Punishments for people who find abandoned babies and don't do the right thing? She almost blurts out about the note to bolster her legitimacy, when Taylor starts talking. "I was just looking at the database to see what families we have available. The system is so overloaded right now." She stops long enough to give Cinnamon a look that says, *Do you see how hard my job is?* "I'll need to find an emergency placement for her once she's discharged this afternoon. Those are foster parents who have signed up to take kids on at any time day or night for up to seventy-two hours while we secure a longer placement. Which I'll work on while we also try to find family—that's always our top priority. Not that any of this is your problem. You've done plenty already. Thanks for getting her to the hospital."

The nurses hadn't told Cinnamon that Bluebell was being discharged today. They hadn't told her much of anything. And they'd called a social worker behind her back. They'd been treating Cinnamon like she was invisible or suspicious or both, and she'd been too distracted to even notice.

Cinnamon is picturing what, or who, rather, Taylor sees sitting next to her—a harried Black woman with dark circles under her eyes and mysterious yellow stains across her jeans. She looks like the woman they take the baby away from in the movies. It's hard to escape stereotypes, or even casting yourself in them; the white gaze is as hard to shake as a shadow.

It's insecurity that makes her question why it didn't even occur to Taylor that Cinnamon might want to keep caring for the child, which overrides the more common-sense reasons—that Cinnamon isn't a certified foster parent, that she didn't tell Taylor about Daisy's note and therefore Taylor has no reason to think Cinnamon has any claim to this child. She's caught off guard when the words line up in her mind, not to mention when they march right on out of her mouth.

"What if I kept taking care of her? Is there any way that could happen? At least temporarily?"

That Taylor slumps back in her seat is the only sign that she's thrown off by this idea, but she regroups quickly. "Um, well . . . that's interesting. I mean, you clearly care a lot about this baby. The nurse tells me she found you half asleep gripping the baby's hand and singing Marvin Gaye at 4 a.m. And is that hers? Something you got for her?" Taylor nods toward Cinnamon's lap. She'd forgotten she'd been toting Modoc around. They wouldn't let her tuck the stuffie in next to Bluebell, so she's been clutching it like a good-luck charm.

"Yeah; he's cute, isn't he?"

"He is. I still have all my stuffed animals from growing up on my bed. Like, forty of them—there's barely enough room for me! I tell myself I'm keeping them for all the kids I'm going to have someday, but really it's just because I love them."

This is the least-surprising thing Cinnamon has heard all day.

"Do you have kids?" Taylor asks her.

Cinnamon shakes her head and doesn't know what to make of Taylor's response: "Oh, really? Just assumed you must."

Taylor then explains that Cinnamon just can't walk out with the baby, with a half laugh, half snort to underline how absurd that would be. "But if you're serious about it, there's a process. You'd need to pass a background check and home inspection. We could probably expedite that because we're so desperate for more homes. Then you'd go before a judge and we'd ask for an emergency order of custody—that's usually for thirty days. In the meantime, we'd still search for any biological family, which may be hard, considering there's not much to go on with an abandoned baby."

The mention of a judge gives Cinnamon pause. What old white man was going to go for this? In all of her years in foster care, not once did she see a Black family with a white kid. She doesn't like the idea of a background check either, though that's just paranoia—who knows what they try to dig up on you? But the cat's not only out of the bag, it's scratching all the furniture, so Cinnamon doesn't let her doubts take hold.

"How long would it take?"

"Child services isn't the only one with a backlog, but like I said, since we have a shortage of homes in this county and in the close-by ones, I bet we could get before a judge next week. If all goes well, you could have . . . Wait—what did you say her name is?"

"I've been calling her Bluebell . . . because of her eyes. They're so blue."

"Aw, I like that. So yeah, if you do all that, it's possible you could get guardianship of Bluebell. But are you really up to this? Being a foster parent is a huge deal, a lot of responsibility, Mrs. Haynes. You'd be surprised at all the people who are all gung ho to sign up and then two weeks into their first placement are calling and saying they can't handle it. And these are children; they're not like puppies you're returning to the pound. It's so brutal when that happens. I'm in tears over it even when the kids aren't. And it's especially annoying because recruiting people is a whole lot of work. We offer all the training and support, and when it doesn't work out, we're right back at square one. I mean, the stories I could tell you about what they've been through. Obviously, I won't—confidentiality and all." Taylor stops for a minute to look stricken that Cinnamon would have thought that she was capable of such a breach. "I'm just saying, the trauma is real. I bet it's even made its mark on Bluebell already . . . being abandoned and then ending up in the hospital. You can't even imagine."

"Actually, I can. I was raised in foster care." There it is, the sentence she's never actually uttered to another human being except for Reverend Rick. It erupts from her now as unpredictable and unstoppable as lava. The immediate regret she feels burns the same, but she can't abide Taylor's "expertise" about trauma and foster care when the girl probably hasn't had a true hunger pain a day in her life and her biggest trauma was probably losing one of her precious stuffies. There's also the fact that this might help her case with someone like Taylor.

Just as Cinnamon expected, Taylor reaches for her hand and gasps like she's met a superhero. "Wow, wow, wow. I had no idea."

What a stupid thing to say; of course you didn't. No one does.

"Well, then you get it," Taylor continues. "You know all about what I'm talking about. And look how you've turned out. You must have had some great foster parents. And social workers you loved too?" When Taylor winks, Cinnamon's vision of poking her with the wooden coffee stirrer is so vivid she's surprised to find her hand still enveloped by Taylor's.

"I had some good foster parents," Cinnamon says. "But also some not-so-good ones. You can understand, then, why I might have been, you know, hesitant about bringing the baby directly to the authorities. I've witnessed all of this firsthand. I was nervous for her, for Bluebell. About what comes next." Cinnamon pulls her hand away, but Taylor hardly notices because she's animated by an idea that has suddenly taken hold of her.

"I can see that. You really do care. A lot. And this . . . this is such an incredible story—former foster kid finds abandoned baby in a park and becomes foster mom! What a headline! And the race angle too? Since you're . . ."

Taylor pauses like she doesn't know if she's allowed to acknowledge Cinnamon's race, so Cinnamon does it for her.

"Black?"

"Yes, Black. And the baby's white and that's pretty cool. My friend from undergrad just got a job at WNLV News, and this is a feel-good story that could be so perfect for him. We could get you all set up to take Bluebell in. Easy enough to get you all the paperwork today to fill out to get certified ASAP and then Kirk—that's my friend—he could film me bringing the baby to you when that happens. Then you guys can sit down for an interview. How perfect, right? It would be such a great recruitment tool for other foster parents too. And God knows we need them. You'd be a hero on so many levels!"

"The last thing I want is any story about me. And I especially don't want to talk about my past on the evening news." Or ever at all.

"I get it, I get it. We can just focus on your finding the baby and taking her in. That's all. I promise."

Saying no has never been one of Cinnamon's strong suits and she's hard pressed to summon the word now. Taylor takes the silence as a yes and squeals with delight.

"I'll take care of everything! What about your husband?" She pauses and glances at the thin gold band circling Cinnamon's finger.

"He'd love to be interviewed."

She skips right over what Taylor probably intended—is your husband also on board to become a foster parent? But Cinnamon can only answer definitively about the interview, because Jayson wouldn't be one to shy away from fifteen seconds of fame. As for the other question, Cinnamon doesn't even know how on board *she* is. It was all happening so fast she could barely catch her breath.

"Are you okay, Cinnamon?"

Oh, it's suddenly "Cinnamon" now. Taylor was getting familiar fast. But it's the right question. Cinnamon just doesn't have an answer.

"I know things are moving fast. Things are moving fast. But, you don't have to commit right this second—soon but not right now, you know? You can leave it all to me for the moment and go home and get some sleep, talk to your hubby, and decide what you want to do. And in the meantime, I'll work on Bluebell's emergency placement. Does that sound okay?"

All of it sounds okay, but for the last part. She can't abide the idea that she has to leave this hospital without Bluebell. The longest they've been apart is the hour she left her with Jayson on Saturday. It's insane to think of how much she's let herself get attached to this baby in just a week, how she's gotten used to her little sighs and burbles and the way her eyes follow her every movement around a room, the gentle nuzzles into the crook of her elbow, her chest, her neck.

"I'd like to get back to Bluebell now, if that's all right."

"Of course, of course—go ahead. I'll get the paperwork together and get it to you. It's not like you're signing your life away—don't worry. It's just so we can get the home inspection and reference check and stuff set up. But if you really want Bluebell, I think this could work!" Taylor went from skeptical to giddy awfully fast. But who was Cinnamon to talk about fast, seeing as how she just decided to take in a baby?

And while she should be thinking about how her husband will react, how she'll manage child care for the next thirty days or longer, and the strain a baby will put on her bank account, all those worries fade to black, and one single image materializes. A little girl with blond pigtails, knock-knees, and the bluest eyes you've ever seen, belly forward, toddling toward Cinnamon on unsteady chubby legs, her high-pitched voice floating through the summer air like a birdsong, calling for her over and over, "Mommy, Mommy, Mommy." Somehow it's the most gorgeous sound in all the world.

Dear You,

The first thing I remember when I came to was the smell of Bath & Body Works Warm Vanilla Sugar, which arrived a few seconds before Heather's face hovered over mine. My confusion gave way to full-on panic when I realized I was at a hospital, specifically the Orlando Regional Medical Center, where a sticker affixed to the beeping monitor beside me announced, WE OFFER QUALITY HOMETOWN CARE.

Waking up in a hospital was not good for so many reasons. The first was because I wondered if it meant I was dying. It sort of felt like it. The second was how the hell I was going to pay for any of this if I did live. My Disney insurance hadn't kicked in yet. And, if this place had my ID, which was in my purse, they might look at my address, which still lists Leesville, and call my grandparents. But I couldn't think of any of that at the moment, because Heather was screeching at me.

"Jesus, you scared me! Are you okay? You had a baby?!" As usual, Heather spoke in multiple sentences at a time, as if she'd run out of words if she didn't get them all out at once. "The doctors say you had a uterus hemorrhage . . . or something like that! You almost died, Daisy!"

I would have thought she was exaggerating, except for how close I felt to death. Blinking took more energy than I seemed to be able to spare. Let alone speaking, so I didn't.

"Aren't you going to say anything? Oh man, can you even talk? Is your brain okay? DAISY?"

Heather seemed completely freaked out but also

mad at me, and I couldn't understand why. I had to think fast to work out a response, which was impossible since my mind felt like a soggy sponge. I considered pretending to faint, but that would have just prolonged the inevitable. For a split second, it actually occurred to me to say you had died. A still birth. But I realized I could never do that to you. I couldn't ever say those words while you were alive and breathing in this world. And honestly, even in my current state, I knew that answer would only lead to more, and harder, questions. I took a deep breath, lungs on fire from the dry hospital air. I couldn't manage a lie.

"Yeah. I was pregnant. I had a baby. I'm sorry I didn't tell you."

I didn't know why I was apologizing to Heather, but she seemed to need it and appreciate it.

"I can't believe you had a freakin' baby, Daisy! Where is it?"

"I . . . gave it . . . her . . . the baby . . . up for adoption. So I didn't want to talk about it. It hurt too much." There was enough truth there.

"Wow. I can't imagine what that must have been like. I can't believe you did that. I could never in a million years."

It was such a Heather thing to say, compassion laced with judgment. Or maybe not. Maybe I was just too sensitive, because I couldn't imagine it either. When I was trying to figure out my options I had seen those billboards with the pretty, wayward young women who got themselves in trouble and an 800 number that promised rescue. But I couldn't bring myself to call. I couldn't imagine just handing you over to strangers. I also thought about abortion, even though it had been drilled into me since preschool that there was no more horrible sin than murdering your unborn child. But it was too hard to get one anywhere close by. I could have gone somewhere far—like New York. I found an organization called Haven that matches a woman who needs an abortion with a kind stranger who'd let you sleep on her couch or in her guest room if you went to New York City for the procedure. They would even go with you to the appointment. I loved the idea of that, that there were women who would hold the hand of a lost, sad stranger who was all alone like me. I bet they wouldn't make you feel pathetic and stupid at all. But I never got up the courage to call them. That wasn't the way I wanted to make it up to New York, and it was just too much. It also felt like it was too late. By the time I found out, I was so far along. My periods had never been all that regular, and I hadn't bothered to think about my belly or my boobs expanding in years. I didn't know what other signs to look for beyond that. Plus, I just didn't think it would be possible to get pregnant, not after just one time. But when I realized it'd been a while since I'd had my period, I did the math—and counted backward to . . . that night. I went straight to Rite Aid and got a pack of the cheapest pregnancy tests I could find and then locked myself in the bathroom at the back of the store. They came in a box of three, and I took them all at the same time to be totally sure, and all of them were positive. I collapsed on the filthy toilet and cried so hard the people in line at the pharmacy could probably hear me. It was crowded in the store, too, because everyone was getting last-minute stuff for

New Year's Eve. As if holidays weren't already lonely enough, I was crying in a drugstore bathroom instead of buying party hats and making resolutions about all the weight I was going to lose and the hobbies I was going to take up. I shouldn't tell you how sad I was, but I want to be honest. And it wasn't about you, because you weren't even a real thing I could wrap my mind around yet. It was my own reckless stupidity that sent me spinning out.

Heather was all breathless sympathy when she asked about your father, if not at all delicate. "Shit, Daisy. Who the hell knocked you up?"

"I'll . . . I'll tell you later. I'm just too tired right now. Could you ask the nurse for something for my pain, please?" Playing for sympathy was the only way to avoid answering that question. But it was also true—I was in so much pain. I couldn't bear the additional agony of having to offer any more explanations.

"Oh, you poor, poor thing." Heather started sobbing by then. "I can't believe this happened to you. And giving up your child? It's awful."

That's when it hit me, the gravity of the mistake I had made. Not in having you. Not even in leaving you with Cinnamon. No, it was telling Heather any of this and what it would unleash. But I didn't know that yet. All I knew was that I begged Heather not to tell a single soul about you, and she promised she wouldn't. Solemnly crossed her heart like we were kids again. I can't believe I was dumb enough to believe her.

Collapsing at your brand-new job is not a good look. They sent me an email saying they had to backfill my position immediately and I was welcome to reapply. Guess they couldn't have that little booth empty.

I was panicked about money and how long it would take me to find another job, but Heather took pity on me and my clearly desperate condition. Her exact words when she picked me up when I was discharged from the hospital after two days were "You look pasty like I've never seen. I'm not gonna lie." Maybe it's because my body lost so much blood and I had to wait for it to fill back up and send some color to my cheeks. In the meantime, I still looked like death. The good news: the doctors said I was lucky. In most cases like mine they have to do an emergency hysterectomy.

"You can have another baby!" Heather said, beaming, as if that was helpful at all.

She insisted I stay with her as long as I needed and offered her bed up again. This time I accepted the generosity. She seemed happy to have something or someone to dote on. Her constant, mindless chatter distracted me, but whenever she left the house, the silence closed in fast. I'd blast *Doctor Phil*, but even his relentless bluster was pointless white noise and no match for drowning out the pain I was still in from the surgery and my constant panic attacks about how you were doing and whether I should reach out to Caleb and if my grandparents would somehow get a hospital bill and try to find me. Or worse, find you.

I would wander around the apartment aimlessly from corner to corner and then fall back onto the couch, spent and restless. Sometimes, I would get out Momma's journals. They're one of the few possessions I stuffed in my backpack when I left town. Reading them was a habit when I was feeling out of sorts. I was never quite sure how they would make me feel. Sometimes it comforted me to read her words; sometimes it shattered me with loss. A hug or a knife, and I never knew which until I was done. Emotional Russian roulette. Today was one of the good days.

There was the whole section, always my favorite, that I read over and over about how excited my mom was to be pregnant with me, how much she loved watching her belly grow, how she rubbed it each night when she went to bed and made wishes like it was a magic lamp. She put a list of those wishes in the journal. She was big on lists—her journals are filled with them. Like all the places she wanted to go: Alaska, Bali, California. It took me a minute to work out that the list was alphabetic. She wanted me to travel too, to see other places like London (the home of Harry Potter, who she loved), and to go to college, to have a job where I got to do something important like save lives or make laws or create cool products that people couldn't live without. Mainly her wish, which she said more than once, was that she didn't want my life to be anything like hers. Not that she was going to let me ruin her life. She was very clear about that. The "ruin" part stung, I'll admit, but I understood. She was just a baby when she had me, just sixteen, so much in front of her. She loved me from the very start, but she loved herself too, and she wanted things for herself. She and I weren't really so different that way.

My other favorite part of her journals is when she talked about my dad, Tyler. Such a short, sad story. Tyler's family was stupid rich, as my mom described them. His dad was an executive at the Mercedes-Benz plant, and his mom was a writer—an actual writer. I googled her books once—a series of "literary" thrillers, whatever that means, about pretty, promising young girls who were murdered in quaint towns. Tyler's parents weren't happy about their son dating someone who was a "trash townie"—Momma wrote about how she'd overheard Tyler's mother actually call her that. She never told Tyler what his mom said, but she wrote how she'd wanted to be all righteous and mad about it but in the end she just felt shame—deep shame. The insult hit its mark and pierced her through and through. Tyler's mother was right: she really was nothing and going nowhere.

When Tyler's parents learned Mom was pregnant, they moved their entire family across the country and offered to pay $40,000 to Gammy and Gamps to sign a legal agreement that they would make sure their daughter never tried to contact Tyler again, and that they would never ask for any further financial support. Momma only found out about this a week after Tyler had left without even saying goodbye. By that time Gamps had already used the money for a brand-new Ford F-150 pickup and bragged for days how he looked the salesman in the eye and told him he'd be paying cold, hard cash, in full, and how did he like that.

Momma wrote long passages about how much she missed Tyler, how she couldn't believe he just left her. Over and over she wondered if their love was even real. She felt so dumb and heartbroken. There were even wrinkles on those pages that I bet were tear marks. Then Tyler called—exactly once. That's how she found out about the agreement. That he hadn't just left her—well, he had, but only because his parents had made him. Momma liked knowing that Tyler, almost three thousand miles away in Stockton, California, was at least as heartbroken as she was. His sobs scared her a little though. There was something unsettling about boys crying, but it did prove that he actually loved her.

She loved him too—intensely, dramatically, tragically. Pages and pages were devoted to all of the random things she loved about him—how he had the longest, most delicate fingers, how he wore these jeans with random-colored patches and somehow made them cool, how he made this concoction of strawberry ice cream, marshmallows, and potato chips and would chase her around trying to feed it to her, and she would let him even though it was so gross. The list went on and on, and it helped me form a mental image of who my dad was. And thank God, because the version in my head was all I had.

Once a year or so I was tempted to try to find him, but then I pictured him as a thirty-five-year-old man with a paunchy belly and two kids who may share half my DNA but would be prettier and more successful, and I didn't want to blow up my fantasy. I liked to keep him young and in love and frozen in time.

It makes me happy, how much they loved each other. It means something for a new life to be created in love. I like to think that stays with you, becomes a part of your DNA.

The good thing about my momma's journals is that I get to have this little piece of her forever and ever. The bad thing is they're so short. Sixty pages total is all I have of her eighteen years on this earth. It is never enough.

I'd always wanted to journal like my mom. I thought it would be cool to get my thoughts on paper and see them years later and think about who I used to be. But every time I tried, I felt too exposed having my secrets all laid out like that, so I ripped up my very first entry. I wanted my thoughts to stay locked up safe and private and just for me. But they were there, swooping around like bats at night. Even though my teachers always called me distant and acted like I was slow just because I kept to myself, long as I got good grades (which always seemed to surprise them) and didn't cause trouble, they were satisfied for me to sit in the corner, quiet and invisible. No one knew about my rich interior life. I learned that term from Cinnamon. She said a character in one of the books she was always reading had one of those—a rich interior life. That sounded so nice, like my brain was an apartment with beautiful paintings and a bloodred velvet couch and wall-to-wall bookshelves with one of those ladders to get to the highest shelf. And it was all mine—no one could ever go there but me. My ideas, my dreams, my secrets; no one could have them unless I said so. It was about the only thing that made me feel powerful. People could take so much from you, but they couldn't take that.

I've been trying again to get my thoughts down since I left for Florida, because as much as I want to forget, I want to remember too. It's confusing.

My mom's journals were also how I learned that my grandfather went to prison right before I was born. He'd never mentioned it once. Momma didn't really say all the details, just that she was glad he was gone for a while even though all Gammy did was complain and even if she had more chores with the two of them having to run the farm alone.

She wondered why Gamps hated Black people so much. I guess his hating Black people had something to do with his going to prison. It's not like I could ever ask about it, what he did exactly, or even that I wanted to know, but I already knew about Gamps's general feelings because he went on about nigger this, nigger that all the time.

This one time, when Gam started cleaning houses when times were extra bad, she came home barely after she had left the house for a job with a new client. It had been a referral from her friend Frieda, and Gam was all agitated that Frieda hadn't warned her that the woman was Black. Gamps was outraged. "I can't believe that woman thought you'd come to clean her house. We don't need the money that bad."

"Well, I came right on home. I think she's a doctor," Gammy muttered.

"Who's gonna go to a nigger doctor? That's crazy."

Same as my mom, I never did understand why my grandparents hated Blacks or Mexicans or anyone who wasn't white, for that matter. It wasn't even so much that I was embarrassed by their views. I knew people didn't like Black people, and I never had reason to form an opinion one way or another, considering I didn't even know any. What bothered me was how obvious Gamps was about it as if he were playing a racist redneck in a movie. Did he have to be so over-the-top? So theatrical? I also had far more reason to hate him beyond that he was a bigot. But then after I met Cinnamon, who was probably the least hateable adult I'd ever met, I really didn't get it.

Here's a secret, because I said I'd be honest even though it's something I'm not very proud of. Part of what drew me into a friendship with Cinnamon in the first place is thinking about how much Gamps would hate it. I felt a strange kind of satisfaction sometimes when I'd be sitting with her, sharing fries, knowing all Gamps would see was yet another uppity Black woman who didn't know her place.

Sometimes I worried the racism and hate seeped into me and marked me and Cinnamon would know. Maybe that's why I didn't tell her much about my grandparents. I only ever mentioned my mom and how she'd passed when I was real young. Cinnamon put her hand on my back when I told her—it was the first time she'd touched me, the first time a Black person had touched me, and it made me sick that I even registered that. More so that my first thought was to flinch. My grandparents always said you had to wash yourself if you ever touched a Black person, because you'd be dirty. I knew that was ignorant bullshit, but I flinched anyway. Not that she noticed.

"You've had more than your share of shit, Daisy. It isn't right . . . someone so young, so much loss." She didn't say it like she was pitying me though. Her tone was matter-of-fact, like she understood, maybe even admired me a little, if I wasn't imagining that. At first, I was confused by the lump that appeared in my throat, the stinging in my eyes, but I just hadn't realized how much I needed someone to acknowledge this until that moment. I had had a hard time of it.

It was this moment that I thought about later on when I decided that Cinnamon should be the one to raise you. The day it came to me that I could leave you with her, Cinnamon had been telling me a story about how she was watching her godkids the next day and how she had planned a whole scavenger hunt even though they were only three. She was hiding all their favorite snacks and candy. She knew her friend would be horrified at all the sugar, but Cinnamon said making the twins happy would be worth it. She didn't have the slightest clue I was seven months pregnant, but I took it as a sign from the universe—Cinnamon might as well have been screaming, "I'd be such a good mother." I could have told her I was having a baby then, but I knew she would be full of questions.

But that night a plan formed. It came to me like a voice from beyond, like the kind Pastor Mike always said came to him: *Cinnamon could raise your baby.* It was completely crazy, and it made all the sense in the world. The way Cinnamon talked about her friend's kids all the time, I knew she wanted one of her own.

Yes, I know I should have talked to her about it. But as every week went by and I got closer and closer to the inevitable, I was too scared. If she freaked, or if she said no, then what was I going to do to ensure you had a loving home?

I convinced myself this is what Cinnamon would want for me since she was always invested in my dreams, always asking me about my future. She didn't laugh when I admitted I wanted to become a pilot on big commercial airplanes, flying across the country at a moment's notice, being able to up and escape anytime I needed to. She didn't look at me and think, How is this girl gonna fit in a teeny-tiny cockpit? which is what I thought about whenever I researched flight schools and training programs that taught you to fly in those little planes. Problem was those programs cost approximately a gazillion dollars. But there was another way, according to Cinnamon. I could also get an aviation degree at a regular college. That way I could get scholarships or aid. It all felt almost possible, within reach, when Cinnamon said it. And then it had all gone to shit. Ruined. That's a bad choice of words—"ruined," especially, given what I said earlier about my own mom, her determination not to be ruined. You didn't ruin anything for me. "Upended" is maybe a word to use. "Changed," for sure. I was like a plane in a spiral of turbulence inside a cloud. You can't tell which way is up or down. But you have time, more time than you think, to get yourself level again if you stay calm and let your instincts override your fear. It's the panic that kills you. If you want to survive, you have to stay calm. I'd been calm. I'd made and executed plans. I'd found you a home with someone caring and capable. I needed to make a little more money, but I would be able to start a real college with a real flight program next year. I was going to make something of myself and had to believe you would want that for me too.

My plan to stay calm was all but impossible when Heather came home completely hammered about a week after I collapsed at Disney. A bunch of the princesses had hit up happy hour—they weren't allowed to be in their costumes when they were out at bars, but they liked making guys guess which princesses they were and then the girls had to do a shot if they got it right. Guess Dale and Greg and whoever else had a hot streak that night, because Heather seemed to have consumed enough shots to drain an entire bottle.

She ran through the door and beelined for the bathroom. I hardly made it in there in time to hold her hair while she puked. She looked so young then, younger even than the time I found her in the parking lot behind Rita's.

"Oh, Daisy. I'm so, so sorry," she slurred.

I couldn't imagine what Heather was apologizing for—she'd opened her home, she'd taken care of me, she'd helped me find a job. I would never be able to pay back my debt to her.

"Heather, you're just drunk. Let's get you to bed."

"No, Daisy, listen. I told my mom. About the baby, the adoption. It just slipped."

She started crying, the messy, sloppy sobs of drunk girls. "Don't worry—I told her she could not tell a soul." She dragged out the *s* in "soul" so long it sounded like she was doing an impression of a snake.

I knew better. That's what caused the bile to leap right up my throat and shoot into the toilet that I hadn't even had time to flush. My vomit mixed with Heather's, which was tinted pink from whatever sweet drink she'd been downing. Seeing that noxious mix sent me heaving again.

"Did you tell her I'm living here?" I sputtered. Heather shook her head. "Don't, okay? Please, please, please don't."

Heather, limp on the floor, mustered up enough wherewithal to promise she wouldn't and then asked me if I was okay. Well, duh—I was NOT okay. Heather's mom was the biggest gossip in our town, and she loved bad news above all else. So it was only a matter of time before my worst fear came true: they would know about you.

CHAPTER EIGHT

She should be getting ready for the birthday party in her honor. She has a few hours to get in a power nap, a long shower, and dig the new dress out of the back of her closet and iron it. But given that she hasn't slept in days, currently has the emotional stamina of a slug, and is preoccupied with the thought that Bluebell is miles and miles away feeling she's been abandoned again, the idea of eating sliders and making small talk feels about as manageable as lacing up her tennis shoes and jetting out for a 10K.

Instead of primping, Cinnamon's eyes bore into the bathroom mirror because sometimes you have to give yourself a cold, hard look. There's a type of conversation you just can't have in your mind. You have to face yourself down. This is one of those moments, and Cinnamon has been staring so long and hard at her reflection in the bathroom mirror her features have become a blur.

She used to do this all the time. It was a refuge, to find a bathroom, lock the door, and study herself in the mirror, usually alongside a picture of her mother. That one tattered Polaroid, the only image she ever had or saw of her mother, was her most prized possession. The biggest mistake she'd ever made was letting anyone know that.

For years, Cinnamon kept it tucked in her other prized possession, her grandmother's Bible—the one in her bedside drawer. Starting when she was ten or eleven, she got into the habit of carefully pulling the photo out and staring at herself in the mirror so she could scrutinize her face and her mother's side by side. Sometimes she would try to match her mother's expression in the photo. It helped that Margo was looking straight into the camera, bright-eyed and defiant, her mouth opened in a half grin, half smirk that said, *Chile, try me—I dare you.* Her skin was clear and pulled taut across her face, exposing the sharp cheekbones they shared, along with the almond eyes, the straight nose, the full lips. By twelve or thirteen, Cinnamon was used to people telling her she was beautiful—they often said it with a note of surprise, like they were shocked that such a fine specimen of a child had been abandoned so many times. Pretty girls like her weren't supposed to be poor, in sad hand-me-downs, with no family. Pretty girls like her were supposed to be cherished, adopted, or better yet, never abandoned in the first place. Even the Black ones. She'd overheard one social worker lament how it didn't make sense that Cinnamon couldn't find a more permanent home. "She's so cute, and an easy child too, if sort of withdrawn. But that's not a bad thing. I really can't understand it."

Cinnamon didn't so much appreciate the fact that she was attractive as she did that she looked so much like her mother. Margo's cheekbones and curves and curl pattern were a legacy of sorts, and if this was her inheritance, Cinnamon would cherish it. If there was strength to be had in looking at her mother frozen in time, she would hold on to it for dear life.

Then one day Cinnamon went to reach for the picture—always between the first pages of Ecclesiastes because that chapter contained her grandmother's favorite verse—and it was gone. She didn't even have time to feel panic about trying to find it because it wasn't missing for long. It was right there on the floor by the twin bed on her side of the room at Momma Jean's, cut into four pieces.

The culprit was obvious: Ashley, the new occupant of the twin bed opposite her, who was pretending to be asleep, even though Cinnamon knew she was waiting for a reaction, for the satisfaction of witnessing the agony she had caused. She took a dislike to Cinnamon from day one, even taking issue with her breathing, which Ashley claimed was

"All loud and heavy. You got asthma?" She also constantly accused Cinnamon of thinking she was "cute."

Cinnamon had never been one to go head-to-head with anyone, but Ashley was one of those kids that pushed and pushed until they provoked and you just had to give in to it to get it over with. This was how Ashley dealt with her pain, by passing it along, and she was just the first of many that Cinnamon encountered who had that habit. Cinnamon couldn't really blame her. Cinnamon's approach, to swallow it down until the balloon in your stomach threatened to burst, wasn't much better. Ashley had been abused by her uncle for years, and her mom wouldn't believe her. Cinnamon wasn't supposed to know all this, but their stories always seeped out, the whisper mill strong as the thick black coffee Momma Jean let them drink.

So it was sympathy that had allowed Cinnamon to take a deep breath in that moment holding the Polaroid shards in her hand and pretend she wasn't utterly shattered. That and survival. It wasn't to keep Ashley from the satisfaction of seeing how devastated she was, and it wasn't just to avoid the hurt itself, though numbness was a well-honed coping skill by that point. It was because she already knew she would lose her mother again one day. And there was some liberation in the worst happening. She hadn't held on to much, so why this?

Cinnamon had put that lost picture and that day out of her mind for twentysomething years, but leaving Bluebell in the hospital undid something in her. The emptiness she feels in the house, in her arms, in her heart, reminds her of the ache for her lost mother. Facing herself in this mirror at this moment is one of those times when Cinnamon misses Margo with a confusing desperation, considering she has no real memories of the woman. Or maybe it's actually the picture she misses—that's more tangible. Either way, here she is, nerves completely frayed, chest heaving, legs unsteady, staring at herself in the dusty bathroom mirror.

She tries to muster up a pep talk or a lecture, or both, until she figures out which will do the trick. *Cinnamon Haynes, you are not crazy.* These are the words she needs to hear, so she says them out loud. "This child needs someone to care for her, and you've stepped up. How could that be a bad thing? When Taylor calls, you will tell her yes—yes, you want Bluebell back, and you will take care of her. Officially. For however long is needed. You can do this."

This, though, and all that it entails, is overwhelming. The key is to stop this overthinking nonsense—too much of that won't do her any good. It'll crack the door and then doubt will come kick it in. Momentum is her friend. And if she just keeps moving, maybe she'll stop looking around for Bluebell like she's lost her keys.

It should help knowing the baby is safe. Taylor had called Cinnamon not an hour after she left the hospital to tell her she'd found a "great" emergency placement for Bluebell with a woman with "tons of newborn experience" who will take "excellent care" of her. Cinnamon hates that term—"placed"—like Bluebell is a knickknack. She also hates that Bluebell is anywhere else at all.

Cinnamon's empty house isn't doing her any favors right now. Jayson has been preoccupied all day with the HVAC install at the Ruins. Hank Rowe has a monopoly on all the HVAC work in town and has to be booked months and months in advance. The crew was scheduled for exactly one twelve-hour shift (at a whopping twenty grand), so she knew better than to bother her husband—especially with this news. *I've decided to become a foster parent in order to keep Bluebell . . . for a while longer, at least.* Every time she thinks about saying those words, she slams straight into a mental brick wall so hard it gives her an actual headache. So when she decides that this is best dealt with face-to-face, she's relieved to let herself off the hook and easily convinces herself it's not a cop-out but the right thing to do. She'll wait to tell him in person. He's due home around 5 p.m. to change and get ready for the party, the very one that she's about to bail on.

Cinnamon knows this makes her a terrible friend, canceling on Lucia and the party she's been planning these weeks. If she thinks too much about Lucia's thoughtfulness, she'll fall into the usual spiral of guilt, thinking that she doesn't deserve this kind of friendship, or happiness, or life. She tries her best to be there for Lucia—pinch-hitting with child care when her friend is in a bind or ordering a special lotion or funny T-shirt that Lucia would like, just because—but it's hard to have a bestie who is so capable and independent and, well, frankly, rich. There's not much Cinnamon can do to make herself indispensable. And yet it gnaws at her because thinking of her relationships as transactional is a habit that dies hard. The saving grace is Lucia doesn't seem to think about it at all—she's happy to give and give and get nothing in return.

But it's also true that Lucia's going to be furious. Cinnamon realizes just how spent she is that she's willing to risk that wrath and say the word "no" to someone. There is no truer sign that she's really and truly at the end of the rope. It doesn't make her dread the call any less. Her heart beats faster and faster between each ring of the phone like it's in a race with itself.

"Well, hey there, stranger." Lucia can be passive-aggressive like this. Just four words and Cinnamon is already on the defensive. But it's valid, given Cinnamon's radio silence the last twenty-four hours apart from the two brief texts she'd sent from the hospital.

"Hey—sorry. I know I've been MIA. It's been crazy with the baby. She's okay; she's okay. The virus is passing . . . but I talked to a social worker at the hospital and—"

"Oh, honey." Lucia cuts her off with a voice that has softened like candle wax. "That must have been so hard. But this is good. I know the social worker will find Bluebell a good home. I'll have a big hug waiting for you at the party, not to mention a tower of sliders. That should help too."

Cinnamon is silent long enough that Lucia has to prompt her to speak.

"You there?"

Cinnamon holds on one more beat before the moment of truth. "Actually . . . I . . . I decided to keep Bluebell. Temporarily. The social worker . . . she's helping me with this. I have to do a bunch of stuff like get fingerprinted and whatnot, and Bluebell is with someone else—an emergency foster home—until then, but I can get her back soon. It's still a process from there, but . . ."

She leaves the rest unsaid not so much because she's being circumspect but because she has no idea what happens from there. And she can't let herself get that far ahead, especially as the silence on the line grows louder. This is why Cinnamon breaks it—it's too unbearable.

"I mean, it doesn't mean it's forever. I'm still going to try to find Daisy. I just decided to keep Bluebell . . . for now. I can't imagine her getting bounced around, and she's really starting to know me, and I know her. It . . . I don't know. It makes sense in a weird way to keep her."

"Keep her? Cinnamon! A baby's not an impulsive decision. This isn't a splurge purse that you can just debate whether to return or not." Lucia stops as if gathering herself. "You can't do this. It's crazy. Do you understand how hard motherhood is? You've just gotten a taste, Cinnamon, just a taste. You did six days—try weeks, months, *years* of it. It's exhausting. It's impossible."

What happened to you figure it out, it's all trial and error?

It's Cinnamon's turn to gather herself. "I can't explain it, Luce. I just . . . I just feel like I have to do this."

"You don't have to do anything. This is not your responsibility! And dare I remind you you have a full-time job and no child care! I can't imagine Jayson, your husband—remember him?—is on board with this. And babies are expensive! You don't have the money for this!"

She can't believe Lucia is throwing money in her face. Her finances are none of Lucia's business. You have to be rich to get a lot of things, but a baby isn't one of them. You don't lose your right to be a parent because you don't have an Instagram-perfect "sitting room," a vacation house, or a fat savings account. And having more money doesn't make anyone a better mother, even if some folks like to believe that, particularly the ones with money. Not that Cinnamon can get a word in edgewise to say any of this—Lucia clearly isn't done.

"I'm just going to say it, because friends say the hard things, right?"

Oh, to think she was holding back to this point. Cinnamon realizes her knuckles are strained from her grip on the phone.

"You said yourself when you had that scare that you're not meant for motherhood. You straight up told me you weren't cut out for being a mom. You said, and I quote, 'not everyone is made for motherhood.'

Remember that? That's something to think long and hard about, Cece. What's changed?"

Talk about your words coming back to slap you in the face. This is infinitely worse than bringing Cinnamon's finances into it. That Lucia even remembered Cinnamon saying this, let alone filed it away to fling on her at this moment, causes the kind of wretched emotional pain she's always bracing herself for, but somehow it doesn't hurt any less. Cinnamon can only conclude that Lucia agrees with her most vulnerable confession; otherwise, why would she throw it in her face? It's one thing for Cinnamon to find herself lacking, but it's another for her very best friend to think she'd be a shit mother to Bluebell or, presumably, even her own kid. She's so overcome she sure as hell can't make her lips move to answer Lucia's question: *What's changed?* Nothing, but also everything. Including, in this moment, their friendship. And so all Cinnamon can think to do is end the call and drop the phone. She's never hung up on Lucia before, but she isn't so much making a point or punishing her friend as she is simply and utterly unable to finish the conversation.

With shaking hands, she starts to send a text saying she's not coming to her birthday party tonight, but then she decides not to bother—it should be obvious right about now.

Her hands are still shaking as she goes to the junk drawer in the kitchen and gets out paper and a pen to leave Jayson a note that she isn't feeling well and she isn't going to the party and to please let her sleep. She wedges it under the stack of bills splashed with ominous red print that have become a mainstay on the kitchen table. Then she trudges up the narrow wooden staircase to the bedroom and slips into bed to escape it all with a few hours' sleep.

When she pats the night table for her cell phone, eyes barely open into slits, she thinks she must still be dreaming when she sees the time. It couldn't be 11:45 p.m. on Saturday night. She couldn't have slept for more than thirty hours straight through—she didn't think that was even physically possible. But she had—a blessed void. There was no restless tossing and turning, no being alert for the slightest cry from

Bluebell. This was the sleep of the dead. She must have gone to the bathroom at some point, but she has no memory of it. She doesn't remember eating either, but a fully sealed packet of crackers that was on her bedside table Friday afternoon is now a pile of ripped plastic and crumbs. She focuses on the phone screen to read two texts from Taylor. The first one reminds her of her appointment to be fingerprinted at the police station on Monday morning for the background check.

She moves on to the next text that came hours after the first, in which Taylor announces she has "great news"—she'd already managed to secure both the home inspection and get on the judge's calendar for a hearing this coming Friday. He happened to have an opening sooner than she would have thought. She'd added, *That doesn't mean you can't have a change of heart, Cinnamon. Things are moving fast, but you still have time to make a decision. It's a big one. So let me know if this is what you really want.*

Cinnamon's not used to people asking her what she wants. The majority of the things that have happened to Cinnamon have not involved her having a choice. For so long she's felt largely out of control of her destiny. Being presented with such a choice is both terrifying and exhilarating. But the exhilaration is winning out. Right now, today, she can reach out and choose something for what might be the first time in her life, and she's not going to let that opportunity go.

But it's also not a choice at all.

The idea of giving Bluebell fully over to the system is no more a possibility than it was when she sat in the police station parking lot eight days ago. And if she's being honest with herself, it's no longer just because she feels the need to find Daisy, though she still believes she should. She wants to foster because she's grown attached to this baby in a way she hadn't thought possible, and more than that, she's proven to herself that she's capable of this. She's also enjoyed it so much more than she ever could have imagined. It's hard, but hard in the way that makes her feel as though she's accomplishing something. It's not like she's unearthed some long-dormant desire to be a mother or awakened her maternal instincts with the sickly sweet smell of a baby. It's something else. She wants to love *this* child, serve *this* child, care for *this* child. This little baby girl who she's watched grow and change every second of every day like a spring flower that goes from sprout to bloom in just a week. When she thinks back over the last week, her limits have stretched and grown like the elastic on her well-worn, stained sweats. Her old life, like those pants, may never fit again.

Her conviction falters when she hears footsteps on the stairs.

Within minutes, Jayson is staring down at her. "You're awake. Finally. I thought I was going to have to eventually throw a bucket of cold water on you!" He plops down on the bed and gives her leg an affectionate little shake. Cinnamon wants to dive back under the covers to avoid facing her husband and this conversation.

"I was so tired."

"'Course you were—all that's going on. Lucia's been texting me."

She swallows the flash of rage that Lucia would go behind her back like that. She doesn't need Lucia in her marriage any more than she needs her commentary about her suitability for motherhood. The betrayals pile up. "What did she say?"

"Ole girl was chilly as a blizzard. What's up with you two? All she said was I need to talk to you right away. Is this about the baby? She still at the hospital?"

Cinnamon sits up straight against the pillows as if good posture will give her strength for this conversation.

"No, she's actually with a foster parent."

His shoulders go slack with relief. "Oh, okay; that's good. That's good. Things can get back to normal 'round here."

She reaches for Jayson's hand. "Look . . . I—" Cinnamon attempts to start this next sentence three times.

"Damn, girl. You're making me all nervous. Just spit it out."

So she does. "I'm going to keep the baby, Jay." She realizes her mistake and quickly revises her use of pronouns. "I want *us* to keep the baby. To be her foster parents."

Jayson's reaction to this is to shake loose from her hand and spring to his feet.

"You just said she was with a foster parent? What the hell do you mean you want us to be her foster parents? Like we're gonna get her next or something? I was afraid of this! And what are you saying, '*I'm* going to,' like this shit is already decided? What are you thinking, Cinnamon?"

It's a fair question, but she's getting downright tired of people asking her. Maybe because she doesn't have an answer that involves "thinking" whatsoever but more a feeling deep within her truest self, a place where she still feels like a tourist most days.

When she doesn't answer, Jayson starts pacing the room.

"Remember that time when we were first married and you got all mad that I surprised you with a lease on a brand-new car because I was worried about you riding around in that junker you refuse to part with and you were all, 'I hate surprises' and 'You shouldn't have done this' and made me return it?" Jayson takes a minute to leave her enough time to nod. "And then you're going to do something like this? Decide to become a foster parent? While I was at work?" He shakes his head with the weariness of a man who's never been more disappointed in someone he loves, and that is worse than anything he could have screamed at her.

"Jayson, what can I say? I just feel like this baby needs me."

"The people this baby needs ain't us—they need to be blond and blue-eyed and have a Subaru in the suburbs and whatnot. I'm telling you, if you flat-out think that I'm going to raise this white child, and if you can't understand why this is problematic on every single fucking level, then we have a bigger problem. And I can't believe you're doing this now too. When I got all this shit going on with the Ruins. I'm opening in just over a month and you want to become foster parents? I don't even know what to say. Last week you wanted me to mow the lawn, and now you want me to *raise* some child you found in the woods, like they're the same thing! I got whiplash over here. There are two people in this marriage, Cinnamon."

Are there? She's realizing it hasn't felt like it, not in a long time, maybe not ever.

She summons a quiet conviction and looks him right in the eye.

"I'm doing this, Jayson. I don't know if it'll be for a week or a month, but I'm keeping Bluebell."

It's power—that's the feeling that sneaks up on her when she's the one to make a decision for once and not just follow every one of Jayson's whims and declarations—and it's like turning her face to the sun.

"Oh, you're keeping the baby. Oh, you've DECIDED? I don't know how you're gonna do me like this, Cinnamon. But I can't do this with you right now. I got too much going on. I'm sorry, but you call me when you've come to your senses and you're thinking like a rational person. I'm going back to my mom's."

With that, Jayson strides toward the bedroom door in three quick paces. He stops and turns. "Happy birthday, by the way."

Today is her birthday and Cinnamon didn't even realize it, having slept through all but the last few minutes of it.

"Thank you," she says, a whisper that floats toward his back, but he doesn't hear, because he's already gone. In so many senses of the word.

Pulling up to the police station is déjà vu. It slingshots Cinnamon right back to the day she found Bluebell. As she parks Bessie in the exact same space, she indulges a game of what-if. A dangerous diversion if ever there was one. What if she had ripped up Daisy's note and walked right into this police station and left the baby? But she didn't. Not because she was making a clearheaded and rational choice, but because she was running on shock and adrenaline, reacting the best way she could. It's different now, just ten days later, standing in the same spot. Her every action from this point on is a choice and a weighty step into the unknowable. Ascending the five concrete stairs to the station's entrance makes that feel quite literal. Cinnamon vaguely recognizes the officer at the front desk who's intently focused on a sudoku puzzle. She vaguely recognizes just about everyone who lives in this town from the Kroger aisles and Albie's Hardware.

When the officer finally looks up, it's clear she recognizes Cinnamon too, or could be she's just expecting her because Taylor had called ahead.

"You must be Cinnamon Haynes?"

"Yes. I'm here for fingerprinting."

"Yep. Taylor said you'd be coming in this morning. Just you? I have an appointment for two."

Jayson was supposed to be fingerprinted too. Taylor had made it clear that she'd have to submit the records of anyone living in the house with Bluebell to the judge. Technically, then, Jayson is exempt because he's run back off to Abigail's and isn't going to be living in the house at the moment, or anytime soon. This was the part of her future that felt most unknowable at the moment.

Cinnamon has no good spin for explaining her husband's absence to Taylor or the judge. The best she can come up with is that Jayson's just too busy with his imminent grand opening and doesn't have time to get fingerprinted, so he'll stay at his mother's for the time being until he can complete his own background check. She can't tell how credible this is, but it'll have to do. She could hardly admit that her husband is not on board with any of this and that her only plan is to wait and see if he'll come around, which is no plan at all.

"Nope, just me." That sentence contained a whole memoir.

"Okay then, follow me." The officer jumps up, revealing the skin-tight pants that make up the bottom half of her uniform. There's no way she could chase a suspect in those pants. Cinnamon can't help but stare at her butt as she follows her a few feet to a tall counter right next to the holding cell, close enough to smell a hint of urine.

Another officer who's a dead ringer for Liam Neeson stands at the counter. "You finally caught yourself a perp, Maddy? Serial killer from the looks of her?" He leans into Maddy as he makes this lame joke. The look on her face tells Cinnamon she's been on the receiving end of these sorts of jokes and this too-personal touching more than she would like.

"This is Cinnamon Haynes. Taylor sent her over to be fingerprinted for a background check. She found a baby in McLaren Park last week and is going to be a foster parent—that's nice, huh?"

"I'm more concerned about the baby left in the park. We're going to find that woman and bring charges. Can't let people out here think you can just leave a baby like an old pair of shoes."

Cinnamon looks over at the sad cell with its pee-stained floor. Daisy could have and should have made better decisions, but she doesn't belong behind those bars. Women shouldn't be locked up because they can't take care of their kids, and they shouldn't have to raise a child if they're not able. Heaven knows a young, poor mother in this country doesn't stand a chance. It is this line of thinking—objective, rational, and reasonable—that allows Cinnamon to accept that her mother did the exact same thing. Does she want the woman who gave birth to her locked up? Does she want her punished? No. What good would that do?

But at the same time Cinnamon can't stop the condemnation gathering like storm clouds when she considers how hard she's trying to do right by the child, how badly she would feel if she just left her at this station and walked out. If she's having this much trouble letting go of Bluebell after just over a week, how did Daisy walk away from a child she carried for nine months, a child of her own flesh and blood? Cinnamon, who's experienced just about every range of emotion that she could have imagined over the last week, makes room for another one: anger. She's mad at Daisy and that's okay—not just okay, but justifiable, understandable, reasonable. That Daisy could abandon her baby, leaving Cinnamon with the consequences—without so much as having a conversation with her first, without even telling her that she was pregnant even—was problematic to say the least. Maybe even unforgivable. It's dizzying to decide who should be forgiven for what and what can be justified—a knot that can never be untied no matter how patient you are. But she also realizes she's already started the work on letting her anger toward Daisy go, almost before she'd been aware it existed.

"Sure, Sarge. I'll get some details from Mrs. Haynes after the fingerprinting. Taylor asked me about helping with the family search anyway. Checking local hospitals and such."

"I'm confused, Maddy. Is Taylor your boss? Neither she nor CPS makes the assignments around here. I do."

"Got it, Sarge."

"We'll discuss the investigation after we get Mrs. Haynes here sorted." He steps toward Cinnamon and she's suffocated by the smell of his aftershave, so overbearing and musky it should be a crime. "Step right over here. Ever been fingerprinted before?"

The sergeant doesn't seem to register Cinnamon's answer, so transfixed is he on leering at Maddy as she walks back to her desk.

When the spell is broken, he pulls out a stack of thick cards with ten finger outlines on them and a rectangular ink blotter.

"Let's go. You nervous? You seem nervous. Nothing to worry about . . . unless you have some skeletons in your past?"

His tone is ominous, until he breaks into laughter like he's used to cracking himself up. Here's a man who dreams of open-mic nights.

One by one, he takes each of her individual fingers and presses them firmly into the ink—firmly enough it borders on uncomfortable—and then onto a small piece of cardboard with a designated outline for each digit. When he's done, she holds up her hands like a surgeon headed into an operating room, wet, jet-black smudges on the tip of each finger.

Her whole purse shakes when her phone inside starts vibrating.

"Don't reach for that!" Sarge yells so loud Cinnamon shakes like the purse.

"Sorry, didn't mean to holler at ya—just don't want you to get that nice bag dirty. You'd be surprised at the number of people who are so obsessed with getting to their phones they reach into their bags forgetting about the ink. One lady wanted us to buy her a new one. The nerve. Anyway, here's a wipe, and then you wash up properly in the bathroom down the hall."

She feels it's safe to leave her handbag with the officer while she goes to wash the ink off her hands. It would be something to be robbed at the police station. So it isn't until she's back that she sees the number of the missed call. She had wondered if it was Lucia or Jayson—they are the only people who ever regularly call her, but they are also both avoiding her. Or is it the other way around? She can't be sure.

She doesn't recognize the number, but the area code is very familiar—

Atlanta. And so is the voice when she listens to the voice mail, sending Cinnamon grasping for the countertop to steady herself. Aunt Celia sounds as imperious as she remembers. Snooty might be a better description, all nasal formality, like you can just picture her literally looking down her nose at you. It calls to mind all of her aunt's endless lectures about diction. Her insistence on crisp consonants and "yes ma'ams." *You need to talk like an educated young lady. We can't have people thinking you don't know any better.* Her aunt even had this ancient videotape she'd made Cinnamon watch—*Elocution by Eloise*—which featured some prim gray-haired woman enunciating words ("halcyon," "detritus," "zaftig") that no one, not even people obsessed with vocab words like Cinnamon, ever said out loud, and doing it so stiffly and slowly Cinnamon wanted to watch on fast-forward. Why on earth she would ever want to talk like an old white lady from some place called Sausalito was something Cinnamon never got an answer for.

First a card and now a voice mail. These two overtures are fairly tame—some birthday wishes and a phone call from your flesh and blood shouldn't be a big deal, and yet they are. Mostly because there's no reason Cinnamon and Celia ever need to speak again. Not to mention it has been nearly two decades since they had last spoken. She's struggling to work out how Celia even got her number until she remembers that she'd added her cell to her bio on the SBCC website the very same day she found Bluebell. She'd done it as soon as she realized that Daisy didn't have her cell phone number and she wanted to be reachable. By Daisy though. Not Celia. Never Celia. Cinnamon has brought this on herself without even meaning to—isn't that so much of life?

She wishes she were back in the car to listen to this message, but as usual when it comes to her aunt, she feels a certain powerlessness, even to cut off the voice mail that continues to play. "Cinnamon, it's Celia Freeman." No surprise there was no "your aunt Celia"—she was always trying to distance herself from their connection. "I'm hoping you can call me. There's a matter I'd like to discuss with you. I also wanted to wish you a very happy birthday. I trust you received the greeting card I sent to you."

Just like that Cinnamon is back in Celia's immaculate kitchen celebrating her sixteenth birthday. Her first at her aunt's house. It wasn't a party. Aunt Celia had a way of turning anything that was supposed to be fun into a lesson or an exercise in self-improvement—even birthdays. Which was why they were using the occasion to bake French macarons. Cinnamon wasn't a niece; she was a project. A not entirely welcome one at that. The only thing she had going for her was "good hair" and skin and a figure. Her aunt dressed her like a doll. The other kids at school were wearing Nikes and Abercrombie & Fitch, while Cinnamon and Corrine were among a handful of Black kids sprinkled at the school and the only kids—period—in Lilly Pulitzer. That was her birthday present that year—a ridiculous floral sheath dress. She didn't want to be rude and not wear it, and besides, she knew Aunt Celia would insist on it anyway—so she just had to brace herself for the looks at school and the clowning that came behind her back. She wasn't cool or confident enough to turn the outfit into anything interesting or ironic—only mortifying. She would always be a poor foster kid anyway, no matter where she was or what she wore.

Her curiosity threatens to get the better of her, and Cinnamon considers calling Celia back right now. *I know we haven't spoken since you kicked me out of your house, under the most messed-up circumstances possible, but what's up? Oh, me? Not much—I'm just at the police station. Probably what you expected of me, huh?*

But the temptation passes so fast she wonders if she had the thought at all. Dealing with her aunt would require a lot of stamina on her best day, let alone right now. Cinnamon would have to be crazy to engage. But here she is, about to take in the white baby of a woman she barely knows, and she realizes that train—the crazy train—may have already left the station. She thinks back to Friday afternoon, staring hard at herself in the bathroom mirror, wondering if she was crazy for wanting what she wanted, for craving a little support, for letting herself fall for that little bitty thing who needed her. But suddenly, standing here in the police station of all places, with Aunt Celia coming back like a ghost and her husband disappearing on her like one, Cinnamon thinks of it another way. Maybe, just maybe, if she has lost her mind, it's about damn time.

CHAPTER NINE

Who knew there were so many shades of yellow? Cinnamon thought she would just waltz into Albie's Hardware, ask for a gallon of paint, and be on her way, but now she's torn between Buttercup, Tuscan Sun, or Eye of the Tiger. They all look the same but also completely different depending on how she squints and how the light hits the row of samples. In the middle of the night she came to the conclusion that yellow is the right color for Bluebell's makeshift nursery. Definitely not pink. Who wants to spend any amount of time in a room that reminds you of the medicine you take for tummy troubles?

Her chapped and ashy hands are at odds with the sunshine-colored swatches. When Taylor, whom Cinnamon has started thinking of as Tenacious Taylor, announced yesterday that she secured a home visit for tomorrow, Cinnamon went on a tear to get the house ready—and she has the dry, cracked skin to show for her efforts, along with the lingering smell of bleach in her nose. Also, a very sore back from cleaning out the junk room, even letting go of her reading nook and trashing the beanbag chair that leaked hazardous little Styrofoam balls of stuffing. As it stands she has an empty room with a floor you could eat off and a mess of aches and pains, but she's determined to finish up today. Paint the walls, hang some curtains on the one window, wash and fold the clothes she'd ordered. She'd be ready by the time of the inspection at 2 p.m. tomorrow—or at least the nursery would. Even if it took her all night.

Taylor had seemed as laissez-faire about the home inspection as Cinnamon was anxious. "Don't have a gun in the house—that's a big no-no. Lock up all the cleaning supplies and medicines. No one's going to take a white glove to your baseboards; they're just checking to make sure that it's a safe place for kids."

How Momma Jean ever passed a home inspection is beyond Cinnamon. There wasn't a single night when Cinnamon didn't hear an army of critters scurrying across the floor of her bedroom. Their fridge was only ever full of Lean Cuisines and orange juice from a can. And Momma Jean *did* have a gun in the house, an ancient revolver she'd inherited from her own mother that she showed off to the kids as a way of saying, *Don't you worry—it's to keep you all safe.*

But it's not just to pass muster with some CPS authority that Cinnamon is breaking her neck and obsessing over 245 shades of yellow at Albie's Hardware at 9 a.m.; it's because she wants so badly to create a happy place for Bluebell.

If she's going to become an honest-to-goodness foster parent, she's going to do it right, even if that forces her to remember all the things that were wrong with all of her placements—all the hurts and slights and unkept promises—so she can avoid the same pitfalls. The bedrooms are what keep coming back to her: the sheets with stains made by other kids, the drawers filled with clothes worn by someone else. All of it used and impersonal. Bluebell will get the exact opposite. Her room will be filled with love and intention, no matter how long it's hers. All of this probably matters to Cinnamon more than the baby, but nonetheless, she's determined. And thus, she's been obsessing over paint colors for almost thirty minutes.

Buttercup. That's definitely the color. Not too bright, not too dark. Simple and yet cheery. Just as she tells Albie her order, the bell above the shop's door rings and Cinnamon hears a woman calling out loudly, "Allbieeeee!"

Lucia.

What are the chances of running into your best friend whom you haven't spoken to for five days at 9 a.m. in a hardware store? In Sibley, those odds are not in her favor, and Cinnamon curses the fact that there aren't a few thousand more people and a few more stores in this town.

The greeting was directed at Albie, not Cinnamon, who faces away from the door toward the counter, which she considers throwing herself behind. Even if that plan weren't absurd, it's too late. Lucia has already spotted her, and it's time to just get this over with anyway.

Lucia is the first to blink—or nod, rather. That's how she acknowledges Cinnamon before she turns to Albie and asks him for four wooden rods to build the twins an indoor tent fort.

"Gotcha. Some wooden dowels and I'll go mix up your paint, Cinnamon. Back in a jiffy."

It won't be a jiffy. They both know Albie's jiffies inevitably include a smoke and bathroom break on account of his prostate, which was forever "acting up" and which he was all too happy to tell you about in stunning detail.

They're alone in front of the counter, and the tension spreads like an infection, invisible and unstoppable. Cinnamon braces herself to hear what Lucia has to say; she has no idea if it will be another lecture or an apology. With Lucia, it could go either way.

In the blooming silence, Lucia's accusation rings in her ears: *You're not motherhood material.* That's what she meant, even if those weren't the exact words. Even if such a withering asessement were true, is there no hope that she could rise to the occasion? It strikes her that being a mom is the sort of thing that no one knows if they'd be good at . . . until it's too late.

A part of her, deep and tender as her heart itself, is desperate to prove Lucia wrong, even if that's a terrible reason to raise a whole child—to spite someone, let alone your best friend. If there's one thing Cinnamon can't stand, though, it's being underestimated. After all, look at her—she's a survivor. There are days that she wishes she got more credit for this. When Lucia complains about having to wait too long at the nail salon, she wants to tell her a real problem is waiting in endlessly long lines to donate your plasma for fifteen dollars, which Momma Jean made her do up to three times a month—at a sixty-forty split. Or when Jayson jokes about how "high-maintenance" she is when she drives all the way back to Pizza Hut if they get her order wrong. She wants to remind him of all the times she went hungry or snuck other people's leftovers from their dirty plates in a coffee shop, when she had no choice or agency over what went into her mouth. So today, if she explicitly says no onions, well, then she's going to get the pizza she's paying for to her exact liking.

Jayson would have fallen apart dealing with an iota of what Cinnamon had gone through, and Lucia would have straight up vaporized. They have a softness born of regular meals and parents who loved them and knowing where they would lay their heads year after year—but it isn't their fault, and she doesn't begrudge them, at least not entirely. Besides, you don't get a medal for surviving bad shit—if you are lucky, your reward is that the scales right themselves, and for each dark day, you get a bit of joy, too, which you can claim as your own. The reward is that you appreciate those slivers and scraps all the more. The reward is perspective, and that isn't nothing.

"What's the paint for?" Lucia finally asks.

"Bluebell's bedroom."

"She's getting a bedroom?"

"Well, babies need somewhere to sleep. Your children each have their own rooms," Cinnamon says pointedly.

"But how long is she even going to be with you?"

Cinnamon sighs. "I don't know. But . . . but Luce. Why does it matter? She's gonna be with me until there's a better place for her. Why are you being like this? Why did you say what you did to me?"

"What?"

"Give me a break. Like you don't remember?"

They both know she remembers—the words are practically there between them, floating in the air along with the sharp smell of turpentine. Luce is just stalling, and Albie's reappearance helps.

He lumbers over with a gallon of paint dangling from one hand and four tent poles gripped in the other. He's clearly oblivious to the showdown he's walked into, or he'd likely flee right outside for a Marlboro Red. Cinnamon has never smoked a day in her life, but she might have a good mind to go with him if she had.

"I forget who was here first," he says, huffing and puffing as he rids his hands of the cumbersome items.

Lucia makes a big show of stepping back. "She can go first. She's real busy these days; couldn't even make her own birthday party."

Cinnamon's righteous indignation, so electric just seconds ago, falters. Guilt always wins the emotional tug-of-war. Cinnamon had felt bad—still feels bad—about ruining the birthday celebration Lucia had worked so hard on. And as she hands Albie her credit card, she's working up to apologize. Despite how hurt she still is by Lucia's words, all she wants is to make this right. If they both can apologize as quickly as possible, they can skip to the part where they're hugging and laughing, and Cinnamon can be rescued from this lurching in her stomach, this sensation that she's being thrown around an angry ocean, which she recognizes as the sick anticipation of something or someone being torn away. It was only the intense distractions of the past few days that had kept it from consuming her . . . until now. But when she looks up and sees Lucia's expression, all entitled and expecting Cinnamon to be the one to apologize, because it's always all about Lucia, she just grabs the gallon of paint, her credit card, and the receipt and storms out, letting the clanging bell of the door and the soft slam be her voice on the matter.

She's nearly in the car when she hears Lucia's heels clicking on the sidewalk behind her.

"Wait up a sec. Cinnamon. Okay, okay, I shouldn't have said that about your birthday party. It was petty."

"*That* was petty? That's nothing compared to telling me I'd be a bad mother."

"I didn't say that."

"Yes, Lucia, you did."

"Well . . . that's not what I meant."

"Then what did you mean?"

"Look, Cinnamon. I was just worried. And caught off guard. And frankly, I was pissed too, okay? You don't bother returning my phone calls and then suddenly you're telling me you're going to be a foster parent? It was a lot. And maybe I didn't deliver the message the right way but . . . taking in a child *is* a big decision. You've always said you didn't want to be a mother, and YOU said you wouldn't be good at it. *You* said that. So I wasn't so much accusing you as reminding you, so you could make sure you weren't getting in over your head here."

"I *am* over my head, Luce! I found a baby in a park. A girl I barely know asked me to *raise* her child, and that baby got sick and went to the hospital and I worried she might die. Barely two weeks ago I didn't own so much as a plant, and now I'm going to be a foster mom. You don't think I know I'm in over my head?"

"Well, when you put it like that. You're basically living in a Lifetime movie! And that's my point." Lucia reaches for humor, and she's not wrong—all of this is so dramatic and improbable it does feel like a movie—but Cinnamon's also not ready to let this go. Now that she's on it, she's going to ride this wave of her anger all the way to the shore like the surfers she sometimes watches on Bailey Beach. She finds what their bodies can do—stay upright—impossibly hard, but it occurs to her that so is this. So is allowing herself to be angry when it was never an option for her—the stakes were too high and the costs too great to have the luxury of this emotion. Which explains why she feels as unsteady as she would trying to get herself upright on a longboard.

"What you said really hurt me, and I think you knew it would hurt me, and *that's* what makes me so angry."

She hugs the paint can tighter, waiting to see how Lucia will respond. Defensiveness or understanding—it'll make all the difference.

"I didn't mean to hurt you." Lucia's tone eases up even more. "It was an awful thing to say. I shouldn't have said any of that, Cece. I'm the worst. I know I'm the worst."

Cinnamon lets her friend's words wash over her. And is eager to reciprocate. Eager to balance the seesaw of blame and forgiveness. But she holds out a little longer.

"And you shouldn't have texted my husband."

"I was worried about you."

"Then you should have worried about what you said to me instead of getting Jayson involved. That wasn't your place."

Lucia clearly isn't used to Cinnamon having this kind of tone with her, or this level of confidence, but she doesn't balk at it the way that Jayson had. She takes it in, almost as if she's admiring her.

"It wasn't my place. You're right about that, and I'm sorry."

All Cinnamon wanted was an apology and some acknowledgment, and once it's out there, she's willing to give one right back.

"And I shouldn't have bailed on the party. I know how hard you worked. I was just exhausted . . . with Bluebell being in the hospital and I hadn't slept in a week and having to make a decision about her so fast or she'd be gone. And don't get me started on Jayson. I wasn't up for it. But you did so much and spent so much money, and I feel terrible. I do."

"It's not the money! Don't be silly—that's nothing. I just wanted to do something special for you. You're always there for me, listening to my whining and helping with the babies and talking me off the ledge when I worry I've married the most boring man on earth. I wanted you to be the star of the show for one night."

"Well, I *am* in my own Lifetime movie, so there's that. A dark-skinned Kellie Martin."

"Oh God, remember when we watched that twelve-hour *Stranger Danger* marathon and didn't leave the couch? I swear we didn't even pee. How's that possible? We were drinking Big Gulps, for heaven's sake." Lucia's laugh bursts from her like fireworks.

Cinnamon does remember this particular afternoon; it's one of her favorite memories with Lucia, in fact—snuggled on the couch, buttery fingers plunging into bag after bag of microwave popcorn. She's so relieved by the warmth of the memory and the tension melting between them that she sets the paint can down and pulls Lucia toward her.

She loves the feeling of Lucia's warm breath in her ear. "Can I come over and help you paint?"

"Yes, yes—please! I have to get it all done tonight. The social workers are doing a home visit tomorrow."

"That girl Taylor? She called me. To be a reference for you. She's chatty, that one. She also asked me if I wanted to be a foster parent one day, like she was an army recruiter or something. I was like, 'Can you hear these two kids I already have screaming?' Taylor seems like a lot. Did we have that energy when we were her age? She sounds about twelve. Like, is she old enough to babysit, let alone be in charge of the fate of kids all over the county?"

Cinnamon had almost forgotten she'd needed to put down both a personal and a professional reference on the paperwork Taylor had given her to fill out before she left the hospital. She'd considered putting Dean Bowler down as her professional reference, but there was the fact that she wasn't ready to tell him and everyone at the office about what was going on just yet. She'd missed a week of work using the vacation days she'd accumulated and then was able to be around and available just enough to finish up the semester with no one the wiser. She imagined she was still in the dean's good graces, but she listed the Rev as her reference instead. She could count on him to sing her praises and invoke God along the way. She can only hope Lucia did the same—the singing-her-praises part, at least.

"What did you tell her?" Cinnamon keeps her expression neutral.

"That you keep a man in a cage in the basement. But only one, and he deserves it."

"Lucia."

"Just kidding. Too soon? Yes. Too soon. No more jokes. Honey, I told them the truth."

Lucia grabs her by both shoulders and digs her hands in so hard it hurts so good. "That you're the most competent and caring human being that I know."

"Thank you." Sometimes you say thank you and it's just to be polite, almost a meaningless reflex, and sometimes, like in this moment, there's so much behind the sentiment you almost choke on it.

"Oh, and guess who else called me! Caleb. I think he was a little drunk—it was after midnight—but he wanted to know if we've heard anything, so I told him about how you were going to foster the baby. It was cute—he seemed excited about that."

"Really? He should come see her if he ever comes back to town. I have a feeling Daisy would like that."

"Yeah, and *I'd* like that too. To see those cheekbones in person! Now, can I come over and spruce up that nursery with you?"

"Yeah. Of course you can."

"Well then, let's go, Joanna Gaines . . . I've got you."

A whole friendship in just three words.

"This door can't lock from the outside. You'll need to remove the doorknob." Jessica, the home inspector from CPS, jiggles the antique brass knob to Bluebell's bedroom that happens to have a locking mechanism on the outside of the door. "You can't lock the child in their room as punishment."

It's already bad enough that Cinnamon has to open her home to this white woman to be scrutinized and judged, but it doesn't help that she seems to have missed her true calling as a prison warden. Every single thing about Jessica (her clothes, her expression, her vibe) is dark and dour. She acts as if smiles and chitchat cost money. Cinnamon had planned to ingratiate herself using both, but one look at her severe face and the clipboard she wielded like a weapon told her not to bother. Jessica's officiousness even quiets Taylor; they both follow her through the house like obedient ducks. They speak only when spoken to.

"I wouldn't do that. I wouldn't lock a child in a room," Cinnamon says as she stands behind Jessica and her clipboard, squinting at the pages and trying to figure out what the woman is going to check for next.

"But you could," Jessica insists. "And we can't allow that."

"Bluebell's a baby. Why would I punish her by locking her in a room in a bed she can't get out of, much less a door?"

"This isn't just for Bluebell, but for any child that might end up in your care."

"But I'm getting certified for Bluebell." Cinnamon tries to keep her voice even and calm, but since entering her home an hour ago, Jessica has only spoken in sound bites about catchall safety and protocols that seem directly lifted from some bureaucratic handbook.

"Home certification prepares the home for a child of all ages, potential disabilities, and traumas," Jessica continues in her deadly monotone. "You'll have to remove the knob."

Cinnamon relents. You can't fight bureaucracy. She knows this too well. Jessica has already inspected her fire extinguishers and carbon monoxide detectors. Cinnamon has sworn both verbally and in writing that she doesn't have a gun in her home. Jessica has checked the heating system even though the temperature is expected to creep up to ninety degrees today. Cinnamon's shown her the fire ladders she'd run out to purchase at 11 p.m. yesterday, and she'd drawn up an escape route in case of a fire for every room. Cinnamon had also thrown out all the beer in the fridge and stocked it with all manner of fresh fruits and vegetables, which was a waste because that's the one door Jessica didn't peek behind and because Bluebell can't eat real food.

By the time they open the door to the actual nursery, Taylor breaks her silence with a satisfying squeal. "OMG, this room is so cute!" The décor and the cheery yellow on the walls even seem to have an effect on Jessica. There's the slightest hint of a smile. Blink and you miss it.

Cinnamon and Lucia had been up all night and barely had time to put the brand-new sheets, still warm from the dryer, in the bassinet when Jessica and Taylor were knocking at the door. This is the first time

Cinnamon really takes a moment to soak in her handiwork. She loves the curtains with yellow birds. But what she loves most is the little silver-framed photograph she'd placed on top of the dresser. When she was at Walmart last night getting the fire ladders, she'd also gotten a photo printed from her phone—the one she took of Tweety. She'd stumbled on it the other night as she was looking back through her camera roll filled with photos of the baby, which was the next best thing to actually being with her, if still a very poor substitute. She'd thought the bird was unsettling at the time, but now she can't help but think of Tweety as some kind of good omen. Especially after she channeled Doc Parker and did some research on the creature. Tweety was an American goldfinch, a male, given its bright yellow feathers relative to the duller versions female birds have. (Nature can always be counted on to let men shine.) Sighting one is rare, let alone finding one hanging out in your kitchen, because they're almost always on the go, migrating constantly between Canada and Mexico. Cinnamon likes thinking about the lengths Tweety traveled just to survive, how it kept going and going to find food and shelter. She learned that they're also one of the few birds that fully molts all their feathers every year in order to grow back new and stronger ones for the next migration. That's a lesson Cinnamon can get behind—letting go of what doesn't serve you in order to take on the next long and arduous journey.

It is fitting in so many ways that Tweety would be right here, watching over Bluebell from the dresser. Maybe he'll even come back again. Cinnamon almost holds up the framed picture and tells the story, but she decides she'll save it—it'll be between her and Bluebell, and that'll be just fine.

Taylor strokes Modoc's soft back and compliments Cinnamon on the selection of children's books that Bluebell wouldn't be able to read for years. Jessica's flimsy smile fades fast and she's back to wordlessly checking things off her list. When everyone finally settles at the kitchen table, her expression changes from stoic to concerned.

"Your husband. Why isn't he here today?"

Cinnamon had rehearsed her answer. "Well, because of work. And also, he'll be staying with his mother during the next thirty days. He won't be getting certified. He's completely consumed with his business right now. He's building a restaurant. We thought it would be easier if I got certified on my own and if I was the only caregiver for the moment."

"So he won't be around the child?"

"He won't." This simple statement is a dagger she can't dodge.

Jessica goes about scribbling a long note. "We'll still need to talk to him eventually."

"I know." Cinnamon swallows hard, reminding herself to take this one step at a time, one day at a time.

"Once I certify your home as a safe place for a foster child to live, you'll receive a call letting you know when a child is available for placement. This call could come at any hour of the day or night, and we need to be able to reach you."

Taylor jumps in. "Actually, Jessica, these are somewhat special circumstances. I've been working to get Cinnamon fast-tracked, and we're already planning to relinquish custody of the child to Cinnamon immediately after tomorrow's hearing, pending the judge's approval of emergency certification."

Jessica is not a woman who enjoys the words "special circumstances."

"This is why we're asking if you can approve certification in the next twenty-four hours so that it doesn't get delayed. Otherwise, we'll have to postpone the hearing, and I had to call in a lot of chits to make this happen."

It has already been almost a full week since Cinnamon has smelled the baby's hot, sweet breath in her face. She still has the last image she'd seen of Bluebell frozen in her mind—her little body flush and twisted among the cords. It's only when Cinnamon finally sees the baby, touches the baby, that she will have the reassurance she craves. Two magnets pulled together locking in place—that's what it will be like, their reunion. And she's banked on that happening by this time tomorrow—not a second later. So the mention of any delay makes her want to pull her own hair. It makes her want to pull Jessica's hair, her blunt shoulder-length bob.

Jessica clearly doesn't enjoy commands or the words "fast-tracked" either. The look she gives Taylor could turn a statue to stone.

"Including one with your boss," Taylor says, her tone flipping from sweet tea to vinegar on a dime. Cinnamon wouldn't have thought she had it in her.

"Okay, then." Jessica's voice is as blunt as her haircut. "I'll have it to you first thing." She stands up and shuffles her papers and folders into a boxy leather briefcase. "I think I have what I need. Thank you for your time, Ms. Haynes. And please remember to remove or replace that doorknob."

Cinnamon shows Jessica to the door and doesn't take her first deep breath in two hours until she slams it shut behind her. It's a relief that it's just her and Taylor in the house, even though Taylor is far from a confidante and still puts her on edge with her exuberance.

She turns to find the social worker has snuck up behind her in the hallway. "That went well!"

Cinnamon wouldn't have been able to tell by Jessica's icy demeanor, so she'll have to take Taylor's word for it.

"Everything's going according to plan!" The look of satisfaction on Taylor's face is the same one she no doubt had when she saw the As marked in red across her papers and quizzes back in high school. "I'll be handing you Bluebell in just twenty-four hours! And my reporter friend is all lined up too. Kirk will come a little bit early to get set up for the big moment if that's okay?"

"I don't know, Taylor. I appreciate all your help, but I don't love the idea of being in the spotlight."

"Oh, everyone says that! That's just nerves. But it'll be fine. Kirk's really good at this and will make you feel so comfortable. This'll be a great way to maybe find Bluebell's mother or family and also a nice story for the foster system. It might even help us recruit new parents.

We desperately need people. And it's a nice thing for you, to honor you, too, and what you've done for this baby. You saved her, really."

"Save" is such a particular word—to preserve someone or something from harm. That's what she had done by picking up Bluebell in the park, by bringing her into her home, by feeding her and clothing her and keeping her clean and warm. She'd provided for Bluebell's physical safety. But it is so much more than that, more than the word "save" can fully encompass. Yet Cinnamon's still not convinced of her own heroics.

"Did I?"

"Are you kidding, Cinnamon? You most certainly did. Don't be so modest! Look, I gotta go. I have a five o'clock that is gonna take, like, forever to get there. We're so short-staffed they couldn't find anyone closer, but I'll be in touch once the inspection order comes through. You definitely passed. Great job. Remove that doorknob. I'll call you later to prep more for the hearing."

Taylor is nearly out the door before Cinnamon can ask the question that has been nagging at her. "Kirk won't ask about my past, will he? About how I grew up in foster care? Like I said, I like to keep certain things private."

The girl shifts from foot to foot. "It's nothing to be ashamed about Cinnamon. Look at you. Look how you turned out! Your story proves that the foster system works."

"Right, but that's not it. I can't . . . there are people in my life who I haven't shared this with . . . people I work with. Can you please make sure that he doesn't mention it?"

"Yes, yes—no problem. Don't worry."

In the history of the world, have the words "don't worry" ever actually stopped someone from worrying?

Not Cinnamon Haynes.

CHAPTER TEN

Cinnamon can't stop staring out the large bay window at the front of their house, craning her neck to see down the long driveway lined with old live oaks that drape moss all over their lawn. She was enchanted by that moss when they first moved into this house, but when she reached out to touch it, Jayson had nearly slapped her hand. "Don't get too close. It's full of chiggers. You'll get some nasty bites." It almost made her love the moss more, something that seems perfect and beautiful until you get too close. She presses her forehead against the warm glass and squints past the trees to look for a car coming down the road.

Bluebell's on her way. The excitement coursing through Cinnamon's body is eerily similar to what she'd felt on her first dates with Jayson, a tingling anticipation laced with nerves and joy.

"A watched pot never boils," Kirk pronounces. "My grandmother always used to tell me that when I got impatient. Which was all the time. Taylor's still five minutes away. She just texted me."

Cinnamon spins around to face the intruder—that's how she thinks of the tall, lanky reporter with the shellacked Ken doll hair who barged into her home an hour ago and took over the living room like he owned the place. A cameraman, who introduced himself as "Rod, as in a fishing pole," has busied himself picking up chairs and lamps and moving them around like puzzle pieces to create a makeshift studio set, the large badger tattooed on his bicep bulging with every exertion. Now he stands near a footstool, ready to jump up on it and start filming, capturing the dramatic moment when Taylor arrives and reunites Cinnamon and Bluebell. After overhearing Kirk murmur to Rod about the odds that there will be actual tears to film and to be prepared to split the shot if there are, Cinnamon feels pressure to cry on cue and to fake it if her tears don't come. God forbid she doesn't seem as emotional about all this as she is.

When Cinnamon goes to take another peek out the window, Kirk doesn't even try to hide rolling his eyes.

"She's coming—I promise. Is it just you today? No husband?"

"He has to work. I'm afraid you're stuck with me." That was true. But what she doesn't say is that she hasn't asked him, that he hasn't been back from Abigail's all week, at least not while she's been at home. She sent him a text telling him this interview was happening, if only so he wouldn't show up to get some more socks or underwear in the middle of it. But as far as she's concerned, Jayson is the one who chose to leave their house, to leave her, and she has no intention of begging him to come back.

Cinnamon attempts to shift Kirk's focus away from her husband by way of inane chitchat.

"Taylor says you two went to college together? Where'd you guys go?"

Kirk snorts. "Seriously? She said we just went to college together? We've been dating, like, two years. That's funny. Guess we're secret lovers." Kirk seems genuinely tickled by the whole idea. Cinnamon, however, is not. It was borderline unprofessional for Taylor to have tipped her *boyfriend* off to this story. Not that she has time to wrestle with the implications of this, because finally, Taylor's pulling up in their drive and Kirk is yelling at Rod to get his fat ass up on his stool.

"Let's roll!"

They take their places like actors on a stage. Cinnamon quickly smooths her silk wrap dress with damp palms. She finally pulled off the tags of the dress for the birthday party that never was. It was painful to look at the price again—$170. An epically foolish expenditure, especially for a dress she'd probably only have reason to wear once. She shouldn't even have let herself be tempted when she spotted it in the window of that high-end boutique on Main Street. She hates going into stores like that anyway; the shopkeepers make her nervous—like she has to prove a point or justify her presence in the store by buying whatever they thrust at her. But she had to see what that dress would look like on her body and how it would make her feel to wear something so beautiful, and when she did, it looked like every stitch was sewn with her specific curves in mind, and it made her feel like the type of person who drank cocktails on rooftops, listened to vintage jazz albums, and possessed a passport filled with stamps. It was the nicest and by far the most expensive article of clothing she'd ever bought herself, fancier even than her wedding "dress," which was a linen jumpsuit she found at Marshalls. The guilt she felt at the purchase was outmatched by the intoxication of doing one impulsive thing just because you want to and even if it's impractical. You'd get yourself in trouble if you gave in to that desire every day, or even often, but a sprinkling here and there, she reasoned, was not so much an indulgence as much as a vital infusion of delight that can keep you going.

The luxurious fabric is a cool caress against her skin, and she donned it this morning with the hope that it would have the magical effect of making her feel like the woman she'd imagined staring at herself in the dressing room—someone respectable and confident and worthy. That was the superpower she had needed when she stood before the judge at the hearing this morning. The dress was her cape.

In hindsight, it didn't matter at all; the judge barely looked at her. Or if he did, it wasn't the dress he was registering. Just as she expected, the stodgy good old boy seemed to have his mind made up from the second she and Taylor stood up before him to make their case for the foster placement of the abandoned infant the court was referring to as Baby 5370, after the case docket number.

He peppered Taylor with curt questions. *Why give the baby to Ms. Haynes? Why not place her with an experienced foster family who is already in the system? What makes Ms. Haynes a special case for emergency certification?*

Taylor laid out the circumstances of Cinnamon finding Bluebell, her commitment to the baby, her availability, and her standing in the community as the career services officer at the local community college. He was unconvinced, and the too-hot, too-stuffy courtroom spun with each furrow of the bushy eyebrows that sat above his eyes like furry caterpillars. Taylor had made the hearing sound like a mere formality, so Cinnamon hadn't steeled herself for any outcome other than Bluebell coming back to her.

"I can't help but think a baby like this will have many potential families stepping forward to care for her and adopt her in the event we cannot locate the biological relatives, which I very much hope the local police are working to do as we speak."

A baby like this. He didn't need to say any more.

But Taylor, Tenacious Taylor, didn't let up. She shot back about how Cinnamon had already prepared her home and purchased all the necessary supplies, about the current shortage of foster homes in the county. She talked about the intense needs of a newborn and how Cinnamon currently had the time to devote to her since she had no children of her own and a flexible schedule during the summer months. "It's the strong recommendation of our office that the best placement for this baby is with Cinnamon Haynes."

Cinnamon wanted to jump up and cheer.

Judge Harlow finally agreed to grant the emergency order of thirty days' guardianship, but for good measure, he mumbled, "I don't feel good about this," seconds after striking his gavel. The vagueness was intentional, yet the message got through anyway: *That baby doesn't belong with someone like you.*

But when Taylor had turned and beamed at her, and Cinnamon beamed right back, the judge's stupid comment faded in the face of the silent victory they'd shared.

It's the same wide grin Taylor has plastered on her face now as she walks the baby slowly up the front walk, like she's in a wedding procession. Bluebell is perfectly swaddled in a pale-yellow blanket, and Cinnamon clocks that Taylor has an obviously fresh blowout for this occasion. Cinnamon turns to Kirk, who makes a little shooting gun with his thumb and index finger—her cue. She bounds down the porch steps to close the distance as fast as she can.

Any self-consciousness she'd had at the camera lens bearing down on her fades the moment Taylor passes her the baby, and Cinnamon is doing all the things she'd spent the week missing—kissing Bluebell's downy head, inhaling the baby scent of her, running her finger across her silky cheek. She looks different, older; a week in infant years is an eternity. The baby is more alert and aware, and when her eyes move around searching and land on Cinnamon's, something happens. Something Cinnamon could never explain and that the child development blogs would say isn't possible. But she swears—swears—the baby recognizes her. So when the tears come, and they do, they're real.

"Hiya, baby girl," Cinnamon whispers over and over.

Rod is close now, closer than is comfortable, zooming in on her cheek, which is inches from Bluebell's as the baby yawns like a drunk kitten.

"That's perfect!" Kirk claps his hands and signals for the camera to cut. "Well done, you guys."

Taylor gives her "secret lover" a wave, and Kirk leans over and plants a kiss right on her mouth. Her flinch is fast and furious, which makes it easy for everyone to pretend it didn't happen, especially Taylor herself. She needn't have bothered warding him off since the jig is up.

He just shrugs and is all business when he turns to Cinnamon, like someone flipped a switch on his "newscaster" shine.

"Are you ready? Let's go in and get this interview started. This will be a piece of cake. No gotcha questions—I promise."

The way he says this makes Cinnamon feel like Kirk is dying to ask gotcha questions, one of those reporters who's waiting with a camera to ambush a white-collar criminal outside his office. He doesn't seem built for the "feel-good" stories, as Taylor billed, but here they are.

Cinnamon's so busy nervously puttering around the living room, fussing with the baby, rewrapping the blanket around her, fixing a sock that's about to fall to the floor, that she doesn't even notice her husband standing in the doorway until he clears his throat.

"Oh." Taylor is startled too but recovers quickly. "You must be Jayson. We didn't think you'd make it, but it's nice you're here for this."

He's all dressed up in his best pair of jeans, so smooth Cinnamon suspects Abigail must have ironed them, a crisp white button-down shirt, and his favorite blue pin-striped blazer. His outfit is met with Taylor's approving once-over.

"Wouldn't miss it."

Cinnamon has no idea how to decipher the layers and layers of subtext in that one sentence. Or what to make of the fact that he's shown up at all, given how sour he is on the whole matter. There's only one reason she can think of—her husband loves him some attention.

But she has no time to probe his intentions, or to even say a proper hello, before Kirk shuttles the two of them over to the couch and double-checks their mics. "I thought I was going to have time to go to the bathroom," Jayson says, raking a hand over a fresh fade that's clearly straight from the barber shop. "I look okay?"

Cinnamon picks a piece of nonexistent lint from his lapel just to have a reason to touch him. Maybe it's better they won't have time to chat. She can nurture a fantasy that he's had a change of heart, that his being by her side today means something. She scoots over close enough that her hip touches his on the sofa and smiles at him, hopeful as a baby's first breath.

"You look good," Cinnamon says right before Kurt gives the signal to Rod to start rolling.

It crystalizes that there's no turning back now. Any and all reservations she had about this interview are a moot point. Taylor comes and lifts Bluebell from Cinnamon's lap. "We'll be right over there watching!"

She knew this moment was coming—Bluebell being plucked from her hands. They won't have the baby in the interview itself, but Kirk will cut to a few of the 347 pictures Cinnamon has collected on her phone.

She's still staring over at Bluebell and Taylor, who's shooting her a big thumbs-up, when Rod starts counting down and then points at Kirk, who leans in, donning a mask of affected empathy and interest.

"You found an abandoned baby in the park, a newborn baby. Tell us how it happened."

You got this, Cinnamon. Enough detail but not too much.

"There's this park I like to go to—McLaren Park. I like to read there and watch the ducks. Which is what I was doing when I heard a noise behind me. When I turned around, there she was in her baby seat."

"I can't imagine what a surprise that must have been. What did you do?"

"It was definitely a shock. I was expecting to find a momma goose behind me. Not a newborn human!"

Kirk interjects with a rehearsed-sounding chuckle.

"I tried to look for the mother. Or caretaker or whoever was with the baby. I figured she had to be close. Maybe she had gone to the bathroom or chased after a dog that had gotten off the leash, but when I realized that no one was around, I picked the baby up to check and make sure she was okay."

"And then?"

"She had a cough, and she's so little. I was worried, so I took her to the hospital and that's where I met the social workers and we started the process of me keeping her in emergency foster care."

Jayson shifts his weight on the couch cushion like he's trying to make sense of her story. He knows her timeline is off, but he also knows enough to keep quiet.

"And have you given her a name?"

"I've been calling her Bluebell, on account of her eyes. They're the brightest blue."

This is the part of the broadcast where they will show a picture of Bluebell on the screen. It's the first moment where the audience will see an ivory-white baby with cerulean blue eyes before they cut to the footage of their earlier reunion and the camera flashes back to Cinnamon and Jayson. Cinnamon knows perfectly well that this isn't going to sit well with folks, but she tries not to think about it.

Kirk looks to Jayson.

"And how do you feel about all this, Jayson? People could say that you and your wife are heroes for taking this baby in. How's foster fatherhood treating you?"

"I'm here to support Cinnamon today, but I've been working around the clock . . . I'm opening a restaurant out by Bailey Bay. It's called the Ruins. I'm there day and night to get it up and running for our big Fourth of July grand opening."

Her earlier suspicion is confirmed. Jayson is here for Jayson. He loves the spotlight, and he'll do anything to bring people to his restaurant. Her jaws ache from the strain of trying to keep her face neutral as he continues.

"But I'm not surprised my wife here brought home a stray. She's the kindest person I know," Jayson says, turning to Cinnamon and looking at her for the first time all day. "She'd give you the coat off her back and her last morsel of food. She's the real deal. We just want to help find this baby's people so she can get settled safe and sound with family."

"Well, congrats on the restaurant. That's amazing. I'll have to come by."

How she wants to wipe the aw-shucks smirk from off her husband's face.

"I promise some fried clams on the house, best you've had. Right,

Cinnamon?" Now it's Jayson grabbing her hand and smiling like he's in a toothpaste commercial.

"The clams are very tasty. I'm very proud of him." The words are thick in her throat, but they make it out.

"Well, y'all seem like a real stand-up couple. This little abandoned baby was lucky to have the right people find her. She had an angel watching out for her that day."

Cinnamon has thought about that too, many times, how badly Daisy's plan could have backfired or gone wrong in a hundred ways and it didn't. Though to describe an abandoned baby as "lucky" is a juxtaposition that trips her up, but not more than the next question, which sends her full-on tumbling.

"And what makes this story even more special is that you, Cinnamon, were raised in foster care yourself. That must feel good to pay it forward like this?" The question is a fat fist slamming down on the soft and carefully molded clay of her life. Taylor had promised, but Cinnamon should have known better. Though when she looks over in Taylor's direction, the girl at least looks properly chagrined and surprised, allowing Cinnamon to believe that she didn't know Kirk would go rogue. It's Jayson's reaction Cinnamon is more worried about. She can see his reflection in the massive camera lens in front of her, and Taylor's not the only one looking surprised. And confused, so very confused.

But what can she do? She can't exactly lie with these cameras rolling. Jay clears his throat. Maybe he's about to refute Kirk's statement. Tell him he must be mistaken. No matter how she's feeling about him and their marriage right now, Cinnamon can't let her husband be made to look the fool.

"Um . . . we're done here," she says, furiously tugging at the microphone on her shirt.

"But—" Kirk begins.

"No 'buts.' You guys need to leave, please. You got what you need."

Kirk shifts forward in his seat, undeterred. "Taylor told me this story was about a former foster kid finding an abandoned baby and fostering her. I can't exactly tell that story without talking about your time in foster care, can I, Ms. Haynes?" He hasn't stopped glaring at both her and Taylor since she took off her mic, like he's been hoodwinked but can't quite pinpoint where to focus his ire.

"Then I guess you don't have a story." Cinnamon is on her feet, snatching Bluebell back from Taylor.

Jayson chooses that moment to have her back, despite what questions must be roiling in his brain. "I think you had better leave our house, son."

It's Taylor who pushes Kirk toward the door, all while avoiding Cinnamon's glare.

The crew isn't even out of their driveway when Jayson is on her like white on rice.

"What was that all about? A foster kid? What's that dude talking about?"

She holds up her hand to stop him. "Look, let me just get Bluebell settled." She needs to be able to focus on this conversation and it buys her some time to try to settle herself. Once she gets the baby situated and has hummed a quick lullaby to soothe, she turns to face the music.

"Listen, Jayson, I did . . . I did spend some time in foster care when I was kid."

"Wait, what? You never told me that. How long?"

"What?"

"What do you mean 'what?' How long were you in foster care?"

"From when I was about six to about fifteen."

"That's, like, full-on nine years!"

"Yeah . . . I didn't think it was a big deal and—"

"Not a big deal? Have you lost your mind? You've been lying to me like that and it's no big deal."

"I didn't lie. Not exactly," Cinnamon insists. "Jay . . . can we sit?" She reaches for him, but he flicks her away.

"No, we can't sit!" He starts pacing the room as if determined to do the very opposite of sitting. "I don't want to sit down with a stranger . . . in my own house . . . in my grandmother's house."

"Jay. I'm not a stranger. I'm your wife. What he said in there . . ."

Jayson doesn't let her finish. "What about your aunt . . . Celia . . . I thought she raised you?"

"She did, from when I was a teenager." It's not lost on Cinnamon that she's correcting lies with more half-truths, but she can't seem to stop.

"No, not when you were a teenager. I thought she raised you since you were little. That's what you told me."

"I never told you that. You assumed."

"And you let me believe it. You have me out here like a damn fool."

When he says the last word, an arc of spittle flies through the air and lands on the kitchen table between them. She wishes they could just sit down; the fact that they're standing across from each other, literally squaring off, is making this all feel more combative than it needs to. She hates the idea of Jayson towering over, but she takes a seat and lowers her voice with the hope of de-escalating.

"I did, Jay. That's my fault. I'm sorry." It's her hope she can accept her punishment and they can move on. She's been so focused on the future and its complications; it wasn't the past that she'd thought she'd be fighting with Jayson about today.

He suddenly makes a beeline to the fridge and throws open the door. A blast of chilly air leaks into the kitchen, but it still isn't as cold as Jayson is right now. Cinnamon shivers and sweats at the same time, a disconcerting combination.

"Where's the six-pack of Dogfish Head IPA I bought?"

"I tossed the beer when the social worker came to inspect the house for Bluebell's home visit."

"Of course you did." The way he sighs you'd think she'd tossed out all of his high school trophies just to spite him. "So, what else?"

"What do you mean? What else did I throw away?"

"No, Cinnamon." He says every word slowly like he's talking to a toddler who refused to listen. "What else don't I know about your past?"

"That's it—I spent some time in foster care. It's not a big deal. Then my aunt took me in for a few years, but that didn't work out and I didn't have a place to live for a minute, but then I met the Rev and . . ."

He cuts her off. "Didn't have a place to live, like you were *homeless?* I can't believe you didn't bother to mention that to me."

Only Jayson could make this about him. Not her trauma, not her pain—all he can see is himself, and she wishes she were more shocked. A tiny ember inside her starts to burn, heating up her belly, which is a feeling like indigestion, but she also recognizes it as anger—anger that she never felt like she could share her past with her husband, anger that she felt like she had to hide so much in order for him to love her. The burning is fuel to keep going.

"Yes, I was homeless. And you know why I ate so much when you first started taking me out, Jayson? I was hungry. Actually hungry. I existed on ham sandwiches and ramen because it was all I could afford. And you know why I was wearing a Spelman sweatshirt when we met? Because all my clothes came from Goodwill. I didn't have Mommy buying them for me."

"Hold up a minute—you didn't even go to Spelman?"

She got so caught up she didn't even realize she'd revealed yet another lie, but again, Jayson misses the whole entire point. She simply shakes her head.

"Jesus Christ, man, I'm living with a con artist. Did you even graduate from college?"

She shakes her head again.

"My mom got you that job at the college and you don't have a degree? You could get fired! Then what?"

"'Then what' is right. Then you'd have to pay some bills around here? It could be a problem for *you,* since I'm the one who supports us both." Delivering this barb is as refreshing as that blast of cold air from the refrigerator.

"That's low, Cinnamon. Real low. And I don't think you wanna go there right now, not right after some stranger tells me my wife's been lying to my face since the day we met. I don't even know you at all!"

"You do know me, Jay. I'm still the same person I was an hour ago. It's me. I just kept parts, *parts*, of my past from you because I didn't want to burden you. And it was hard, because you had this perfect childhood with wonderful parents and mine was nothing like that. I didn't want you to think less of me. Tell me honestly. If I had told you the truth about how I grew up, all the terrible shit, would you still have swept me off my feet and treated me like I was some prize that you'd won?"

"You didn't give me a chance for that, did you? So I guess we'll never know, will we?"

He glares at her for a beat and she bears the strained silence since he's not expecting an actual answer anyway. Nor would he like the one she'd have for him, which is *actually, I do know*. That truth is as obvious to her as the ache in her chest it's caused.

"Is that what this baby stuff is all about, Cinnamon? Why we have some stranger's baby sleeping over there? Like some pay-it-forward type stuff? A chance to do something over? Is this some sort of PTSD you're dealing with? Because then you need therapy, not a baby. And I don't mean that in a bad way. Just real talk."

There it is. The look in his eyes—the one she'd always dreaded. *You poor thing.*

"See? This is what I was afraid of—you feeling sorry for me."

"Well, shit, Cinnamon; yeah, I feel sorry for you. How could I not?"

"I don't want that."

"But I also got mad respect for you too. You went through all of that and you wouldn't even know it. But that don't change that you lied to me. And that's fucked up, Cinnamon!"

He stands there shaking his head at it all and then stops and lets his eyes bore into hers. "How can I ever forgive you for this?" He starts shaking his head again at the utter futility of that mission.

Before she knows it, she's on her feet, the chair screeching across the tile as she jumps up. It's the hypocrisy she can't abide. *He can't forgive me?* After what he'd done, here he is down in the swamp, trying to claim it as higher ground? Cinnamon can count the number of times she's raised her voice at someone in her life on one hand—make that one finger—so she's not even sure her throat muscles and lungs are up for any actual yelling, but she needn't have worried: they are.

"You can't forgive *me*? You stole our money, Jayson! Yes, that's what it amounts to when you take money from people—your *wife*—without them knowing! And you committed fraud by forging my name on the mortgage application. You completely wiped out pretty much any chance we had for any financial stability and made it so we have creditors ringing our phone off the hook and I can't so much as afford a new pair of underwear. But *I'm* the bad guy here?

"Yes, I lied about my past, but it was to protect myself from shame and trauma, and it was wrong, but it didn't hurt anybody. You not knowing my past never hurt you. Not once. But what *you* did? Going behind my back, lying to me—it crushed me. And yet I never, not once, raised my voice or made you feel bad. I just kept paying our bills and going to work every day and doing what needed to be done even though I was so mad at you. I hated you in those first few weeks after I found out what you did. But you never even knew that, did you?"

"Oh, I knew it."

She stops and looks at him like he's a stranger in their kitchen, which is exactly what it feels like. The fury fades to defeat, and so does her voice.

"Well, Jayson. That's worse. That you knew how upset I was and you just didn't care."

"Kinda like you don't care that I don't want anything to do with that baby?" He crosses his arms and glares at her with a triumphant look on his face, like he's trying to win something. Even though the prize clearly isn't their marriage.

She doesn't respond, because she's too overwhelmed by all the terrible realizations that hit her in no particular order. That she never forgave Jayson and maybe never can. All of her efforts and focus and intention—they've done nothing to excise the demon of her resentment. She's ignored it, she's tried to talk herself out of it and chastised herself, she's told herself this is how marriage is and how lucky she is to be married at all, to have a partner, and all it's gotten her are a string of nightmares, an empty pit in her belly, and a quiet sense of despair.

The other realization is worse: Jayson isn't all to blame for this feeling. She's allowed it, all the things she's stomached and swallowed, all the lies she told herself about her marriage.

There is this too: she was maybe wrong for pushing so hard about Bluebell, for steamrolling Jayson into going along with something she wanted for once, but even though Jayson would go to his grave telling himself the story that Cinnamon chose a baby over him, he's wrong. She's choosing herself. And for all his bluster about how mad he is that she wasn't fully forthcoming about her past, she understands on some deep and primal level that *that's* the real reason for all his anger. And because of that, she knows he's also right about at least one thing: he'll probably never be able to forgive her. Not for lying, but for that.

A deep exhale escapes her, a release and a peace that come with finally understanding yourself. All this time she'd been asking herself how she could save her marriage. But that had been the wrong question. She sees that now as an even more punishing one emerges, one that sends her collapsing onto a kitchen chair: Was it even worth saving?

CHAPTER ELEVEN

A steady thump echoes off the walls of the empty room deep in the bowels of the municipal building, and Cinnamon doesn't even realize it's coming from her. Her left leg beats a nervous rhythm until she presses her hand to the knee that seems to have a mind of its own.

She's antsy and restless after leaving Bluebell again so soon after she got her back. It had been a scramble to find child care for the four hours she needed to be away to take this foster-certification class. Lucia's twins had colds and she didn't want them to infect the baby, and the few students who Cinnamon knew would love to make extra cash babysitting were already busy with summer jobs. Her only real option was to call her mother-in-law. Before she did, by way of preparation, she'd texted Jayson to see what he'd told Abigail—if, for example, he'd mentioned that she didn't have a degree. She waited for his response for two agonizing hours imagining how furious and disappointed Abigail would be with her that she'd recommended her for a job, imagining the dean calling her, imagining packing up her office into a sad brown box and having no other employment prospects. It was no wonder she'd worked herself into such a tizzy by the time Jayson wrote back that even his response—*I'm not going to say anything, because I don't want to drag my mom into your drama*—didn't allow much respite from the adrenaline.

Even though her secret was safe—that one, at least, and for now—Cinnamon braced herself for a lecture from her mother-in-law about how she'd wronged Abigail's precious little boy, but all Abigail wanted to know was how Cinnamon was doing and how she could help. That made it easier to ask Abigail to watch Bluebell while she went to the fostering class. She didn't pause for one second before saying, "I'll be there in the morning. I'm always happy to get my hands on a baby. I'll see you then." And she left it at that. If there's one thing you can count on with Abigail, she needs to be needed.

Cinnamon was hungry for information about Jayson when Abigail showed up this morning, but Abigail cut her right off. "What is going on right now is between you and my son. You two are grown-ups who will figure out a way to sort yourselves out. Now, give me this baby."

Cinnamon knew that there'd be more to it than that. She and Abigail would be due for a talk when they had more than ten minutes, which was all the window available to them when Abigail reported for babysitting duties this morning before Cinnamon had to dash to class. She decided she wouldn't waste energy dreading it.

It was Cinnamon's luck, according to Taylor, that the next cycle of the mandatory five-week foster certification classes was starting so soon. She'd called to say she'd enrolled Cinnamon in the class in the same conversation in which she'd apologized over and over for "Kirk going rogue." Only one of those items was the least bit helpful.

Cinnamon's opted to sit smack on the end of the semicircle of empty chairs set up like some kind of support group. The cinder block walls are bare but for a rainbow-colored sign announcing that June is national foster-care month, which makes Cinnamon crack a smile. Lucia always jokes about how there's now a month or a day for awareness of everything from cupcakes to vaginal health.

Cinnamon holds her phone up to snap a picture and sends it to Lucia. She writes back immediately, a welcome distraction. *We need a month for lost things. I'm folding clothes and can't find any of the twins' fucking socks. Where do they go? I'm just going to start sending them to school with mismatched socks.*

Like Lucia would ever do that. Three dots below the last text. They appear and disappear. Lucia is clearly trying to find a way to check on her yet again as she's been doing constantly since the news story aired, ever since Cinnamon became a "local celebrity," as Lucia called it, when it was more like a D-list spectacle.

Mercifully, Kirk kept Cinnamon's own story about being in foster care out of his voice-overs. He certainly didn't have any interview footage from her to back it up. She wasn't even sure if he was going to run the story at all, but he'd already put in some effort and it was still something—Black woman finds white baby. Not that they used those words, but no question that was the gist.

And naturally people had thoughts about the story. So many thoughts. The comments on the station's website were relentless—and she didn't know why she didn't avoid them other than sometimes she was in the mood to torture herself.

Why is a woman like her taking care of this precious angel?

Who decided to let this nigger keep this child?

This baby deserves to be with a Christian family who will raise her right.

She probably stole that baby? How do we know she found it?

Why hasn't the state found a good home for this child?

Lucia keeps telling her to stop looking at them, but Cinnamon can't help herself.

Of the few kind words she'd received, one was an email from, shockingly, her favorite CNN anchor, Riley Wilson. The reporter wrote Cinnamon to say she was touched by her story and that she's reporting features about race in America through the lens of personal relationships, and this caught her eye as worthy of more exploration ("We've told the story of the white adoptive parents way too many times; it's time for a different take"). She asked if she could follow Cinnamon for a few months and added for good measure that there could be a generous outpouring of "material support" for Cinnamon after the story airs. But it didn't matter if she got plied with an endless supply of free diapers—Cinnamon wasn't interested in a speck more media attention and not just because of the terrible comments, but because seeing herself on that screen, dissecting her every movement and word, had made her feel defenseless and exposed.

The only way she could bear to watch the piece the first time was with Lucia, and even then, she hid her face in one of Lucia's lush throw pillows the whole time. It was too disorienting to see herself bigger than life on the sixty-five-inch screen—all those bald emotions on her face for three minutes for all of Sibley to see made her want to be swallowed up by the couch.

She held her breath for the whole segment, convinced that Kirk would work in her time in foster care. And when that happened, Cinnamon would have no choice but to admit all of her previous omissions about her life to the friend sitting next to her. But when the segment was over, and Cinnamon's carefully constructed past remained intact, she didn't feel relieved as she thought she would, but even more burdened. She just wanted to put down the lies she'd been carrying around all these years, like bricks on her back, and rest her weary shoulders. So without thinking too hard, she spilled everything, looking straight ahead at the TV because she couldn't meet Lucia's eyes until it was all out: how her mother had left, all the foster homes, the moves, the poverty, even what Aunt Celia did—it all gushed out through the broken dam of her defenses.

It took forty minutes to sum up her whole sorry story, and by the end Cinnamon was depleted and hoarse but also lighter. There was air inside her where there was only tightness before, like her lungs could expand to allow more in, like her heart had room to beat more fully. There was an expansiveness to all this opening up. And in the seconds she waited for Lucia's reaction, she decided that it was worth whatever came next, just to take what could be the first deep breath of her life.

Lucia grabbed her hand and held her close. "Oh, honey, I'm sorry you had to go through all that, but why didn't you just tell me?"

"I don't know if you'll get this, but I wanted you to like me, and I didn't want to start a friendship with the same pity that I've gotten from social workers and teachers for most of my life. I hated the idea that you would be friends with me because you felt sorry for me. But I also didn't want you not to be friends with me because I wasn't 'your' type of person or whatever."

"I wouldn't have pitied you. But I would have had empathy for you, Cece. I do have empathy for you. That's a lot to go through and to feel you had to also keep it a secret? That's really hard."

"I was just so ashamed. Of it all. When you grow up like I did, all you want is a 'normal' childhood, like you want a 'normal' everything."

"I get that. But at the same time, this wasn't your shame to carry. In fact, you should be proud. All you went through and you're still this amazing person—so open and joyful. All that would have broken most people, but not you. You're so strong, Cinnamon—a warrior, really."

Cinnamon realized something in that moment. For as much as she was pathologically scared of people feeling sorry for her, it actually felt good to be a little pitied, even though she was realizing that pity was the wrong word. To be cared for, to be seen for her full self, to have someone acknowledge how hard she'd had it—that wasn't pity. That was love.

She understood the expression "tears springing" in a new way because there they were, as if they'd been launched into her eyes. Lucia's were glassy as well.

"And for the record, you're exactly my type, Cinnamon Haynes. I've been in this town more than ten years, and you're my first real friend."

"Well, you're my first real friend too—not just in town. Ever."

"What? Not just your first Puerto Rican friend?"

"No, my first friend ever." Lucia's laugh faded as Cinnamon made this clear, and she grabbed Cinnamon's hand. "Well, I'm honored. We should have a party to celebrate. Maybe you'll show up this time."

She had been prepared to lose Lucia. After all, she'd spent years carrying around her loneliness and isolation like an invisible cape, half nuisance, half shield. There was a silver lining to it—if you didn't get attached to people, they couldn't hurt you. It was a simple, perfect formula, and it had guided Cinnamon for years. Until she made a true friend. How to behave like people wouldn't leave you and at the exact time prepare for them to do so was a conundrum Cinnamon hadn't sorted. But maybe she wouldn't have to. At least with Lucia. Because in the wake of Cinnamon's revelations and their long talks, Lucia's many questions—thoughtful but not invasive—their friendship has only been strengthened. Being vulnerable in front of Lucia allowed Cinnamon to experience a raw intimacy that she has never had with another person, not even, she realizes, her husband, who was all too happy to let her keep all her barriers and defenses up, while he, too, hid behind smooth talk and veneer. She and Jayson both had their reasons to let the distance grow between them like a boat slowly drifting away from shore. Soon you can't even see if the person is waving at you.

Finally, she hears footsteps coming down the long hall. They get louder and louder until a couple bursts into the room, jaunty-looking thirtysomethings straight out of a Sandals commercial. The woman, who's wearing an honest to God sweater set, awkwardly waves at Cinnamon as she follows her husband to two seats on the opposite end of the row of chairs without a word to her or each other. Cinnamon does what people do in uncomfortable situations the world over: she says hello and then stares at her phone like it holds the secrets of the universe. In actuality, it's just Instagram and a search of the foster-care hashtag, a new obsession she's developed during late-night feedings, which delivers a stream of pictures of hundreds of perfectly filtered couples holding their own little signs declaring things like, we are going to be foster parents! and we are officially licensed! and our family is growing. we're fostering!!!!! So many exclamation points, so many bright smiles. So many white couples. In fact, Cinnamon only saw one Black foster couple or mother for every dozen white folks. She also sees a disproportionate number of Black children with these white families, even though she knows from other Internet searches about foster care that most foster children are actually white—43 percent—compared to 20 percent being Black kids, not that that's what the world would have you believe. She also knows this to be true from her time in the system—there were plenty of white kids—but some folks always seemed surprised at that fact.

She looks up as the next pair walks in. An older white couple wearing matching Patagonia vests and khakis. He's carrying one of those marble composition books that Cinnamon used to use to write down new words that she loved and their definitions—her own personalized dictionary. They make a point to introduce themselves with an over-the-top joviality. This is when the sinking feeling hits: she's probably going to be the only single woman here today. She's hyper-conscious of the empty chair next to her, where a dutiful, happy husband should be. Her isolation will be on full display.

Then an Asian woman walks through the door—alone. She's about Cinnamon's age with pin-straight black hair tied back in a ponytail that runs the length of her back. She's got on a bright-yellow cardigan and linen pants that stop slightly too far above her ankle, and Cinnamon gets it in her head that maybe they can be alone here together today. But the woman doesn't come over and sit in the semicircle; she strides to the massive whiteboard on wheels at the front of the room and writes her name: Tammy Thompson, LSW.

As she turns to introduce herself, one last couple rushes in. They're Latino and also quite young—too young. Babies taking in babies.

Tammy claps her hands twice and smiles out at the group, revealing a tiny smudge of lipstick on her two top teeth. Cinnamon finds camaraderie with that smudge.

"Welcome, welcome to your first certification class for potential foster parents. As you know, we'll be meeting every Saturday for the next five weeks, so we'll be getting to know each other pretty well! Let's just start with taking attendance real quick. My, this is a diverse group—I love it!"

Looking quite satisfied, Tammy squints to look at the paper in front of her, pausing a beat too long at the very first name. "Cinnamon?"

"That's me."

"Hmm. What an unusual name."

"Thank you," Cinnamon says, for lack of anything more appropriate.

"Wait, Cinnamon. Cinnamon Haynes, right? You're the woman who's taken custody of the baby you found in the park."

The eager woman in the pink sweater set leans forward. "You found a baby? Wow! How old?"

"She's almost a month old now." Cinnamon shrinks from the feeling of all eyes on her.

"Oh my God. A newborn!" The woman raises a hand to her mouth in shock. "Unbelievable!"

Cinnamon's taken aback at the woman's naked hunger when she says "newborn," how fixed she is now on Cinnamon. Taylor had told her that in the days since the interview aired in Sibley and on other local affiliates, dozens of folks had come forward offering their homes to Bluebell. It was just like Cinnamon had expected the day she found the baby—there'd be no shortage of people clamoring to take her in. It made her mourn for her younger self and all those kids who look like her, the ones who aren't a brand-new white baby, precious and in demand. All the kids who needed homes but who'd be second choices if they got picked at all.

Thankfully Tammy moves things along, checking Cinnamon's name off the attendance sheet and going to the next name. "Piper Manning?"

"Yes, and this is my husband, Reed." The woman desperate for a newborn grabs her husband's hand and holds it up with a shake like they're celebrating a victory.

Piper? No unusual-name comment for them, Cinnamon notices.

After all seven of them are accounted for, Tammy spins on her heel and starts dragging a dry-erase marker across the whiteboard. When she's done, she turns around and points at the words she's written.

ALL YOU NEED IS LOVE.

"True or false?" she asks.

Piper shoots her hands in the air like an eager second grader, but Tammy makes a shooing gesture and answers the question herself.

"False! Love is great, but it's not enough. If all of you are here today, taking twenty hours of classes, going through all the inspections and checks and hearings, then I'm sure you have a lot of love in your heart for the children you want to be fostering."

Looking around at the eager faces, Cinnamon believes this is probably true and tries to tamp down her cynical side, which is convinced a lot of people do this for the money. Maybe that's unfair, given the monthly stipend is so low compared to all the things you need to keep a child alive, but Cinnamon can't help thinking about all the things she often went without—new clothes, food that didn't come out of a microwave, shoes that fit—when she knows her foster parents got a check every month that could have paid for those things.

Tammy keeps going. "Fostering isn't easy. After this class is over, you might decide it isn't for you. I've seen it before and that is a-okay. The concept of caring for and nurturing a child who does not belong to you is beautiful, but the work is hard. And unlike parenting your own child, you don't ease into it, getting a newborn and then a toddler, then a school-aged child, going through all the stages, getting ready for the next one. As foster parents, you could very well get a call at eleven at night saying, 'We've got two kids we removed from a bad scene,' and if you say yes, those kids are getting dropped off at your house by midnight with whatever they can carry. And with fostering, you get what you get, who you get, and you get all the baggage that comes with that, and let me tell you, it can be a real shock to a lot of people. These kids, so many of them, are damaged, broken."

Damaged. Broken. Cinnamon looks up from her notebook expecting Tammy to be looking right at her. Right through her. But Tammy has turned her attention to settling into a chair facing them, leaning in now and lowering her voice as if to let them in on a secret. "So what I want to make clear today is that love is maybe the last thing you need."

That's also not true. Cinnamon could have done with a lot more love in her life, but now isn't the time to bring that up.

Tammy continues to list the various kinds of children that come through the foster system. Neglected kids, drug-addicted babies, sexually trafficked and abused children. "We see it all, and so will you if you commit to this," Tammy says.

She pauses to let that sink in before she moves on. "There are nearly a half million kids in the foster system in this country and not nearly enough foster parents to take them in. You might think you have some idea of what you're gonna get, but the truth is that if you really want to do this, you shouldn't have any expectations. You might think you only want to get a baby. Well, the median age for kids in foster care is about six and a half, so you probably won't. Your child might be a different race from you. In fact, they probably will be. The reality is we have a lot more white families looking to foster than Black and brown families. For the past twenty years the system has been making an effort to place foster children with families from similar backgrounds. The basic argument for this is that it enhances the development of positive racial identity and coping skills to deal with racism in society. The National Association of Black Social Workers has been central to changing this policy," Tammy says, her eyes scanning her notes even though she's probably delivered this speech hundreds of times. "They argue that white parents are ill-equipped to teach children of color—especially Black children—how to navigate discrimination, create coping strategies for racism, and promote a healthy racial identity. I don't necessarily subscribe to that notion, but I see their points. I actually have some experience with this myself. I was adopted from Korea when I was six months old by John and Kathy Thompson from Sumter, South Carolina, third-generation South Carolinians, white as they come. That was a different time back then, but God help them, they tried. They learned about every Korean holiday and how to cook bulgogi, took me to the one Asian restaurant in town once a month—it wasn't actually Korean, but Vietnamese, but it was the closest we had. And delicious, by the way. Best banh mi you've ever had. All to say, I tend to think when parents' hearts are in the right place and they have the right training and support, multicultural pairings can work out a-okay. The key, I think, is really being open to listening and learning."

Cinnamon looks up just as Reed rolls his eyes toward her, like they're sharing a joke. Meanwhile, Piper has a determined smile on her face. Yet again, her hand shoots in the air. "I've read *White Fragility* twice, and the author says we need to be very careful about being defensive."

"Well, yes, exactly," Tammy says, delivering the validation Piper is so desperately craving. You can tell she's seen the likes of the Pipers of the world before and is steeling herself to deal with the woman for the next few hours, let alone five weeks. "We're going to talk a lot more about cross-racial placements in a later session. The overall goal, though, is just to create a home environment that respects and nourishes the child's culture and heritage."

Cinnamon can't help but to wonder, *What on earth does that mean for a white baby?* White culture, such as it is, is already everywhere. How should Cinnamon reflect even more of it in her home? Should she invest in some posters of Bruce Springsteen? Take Bluebell to a Cracker Barrel once a month?

"Does anyone have any questions for now before we move on?" Tammy asks.

About a thousand, Cinnamon thinks, but says nothing.

After an hour of instruction about behavior-management skills for children who have been through trauma, Tammy finally grants them a bathroom break, but before Cinnamon can escape, Piper and Reed come sauntering over.

"So what's the baby's name?" Piper's whole vibe is breathless whisper.

"I've been calling her Bluebell for now. It's sort of a nickname."

"Oh, but she'll need a real name! I've been thinking about baby names since I was a kid . . . like I really like Olivia and—" Piper immediately draws silent as her husband moves to speak.

"Bluebell's about as unusual as Cinnamon. How'd you come up with that?" Reed has a unique way of asking a question while making it clear that he doesn't care about the answer.

"Oh, on account of her eyes."

"They're blue?" Piper asks. It's an odd question, but Cinnamon knows what Piper really means is *She's white?* And the surprised silent exchange Piper and Reed have when she confirms it speaks volumes.

"Well, we actually want a brown child, right, honey?" Piper stares her husband down. "Like Tammy was just saying . . . It doesn't matter to us. Kids are kids? And so many need a good home."

"A blue-eyed white baby left in the bushes somewhere? People would pay good money for that." Reed laughs too hard, and Cinnamon imagines Piper's horrified face matches her own.

"Oh, Jesus, come on. I'm kidding."

"You can't joke like that. I'm serious. That could ruin our chances, you know, if the wrong person were to hear you." Piper looks around to see who's listening, but it's her own shrill voice that's getting attention.

"You need to lighten up, Piper. Seriously." His tone has the edge of a crisp sheet of paper slicing across a finger. The way the tension bubbles up between them leads Cinnamon to believe that it's always lurking right below the surface, ready to spring forth. She flees to the bathroom as fast as she can and sits in the toilet stall until she's sure Tammy has started class again before she slinks back to her seat.

For the rest of the class Cinnamon's thinking that maybe Piper is right about one thing. Bluebell needs a real name. When she brainstorms lists of names she loves, though, she can't help but to think she'd be stealing something from Daisy. Despite the fact that a judge has declared her Bluebell's temporary guardian, despite the fact that she's created a nursery, despite the fact that she's spending twenty hours over the next month learning how to be a parent, she still believes she can find Daisy. Or at least she hasn't given up yet. She just has no leads. If Daisy saw the television segment, she still hasn't made herself known.

By the time Tammy excuses them for the day, Cinnamon can't get to the car and back to the baby fast enough. That's the funny thing about newborns. When you're with them every minute, every hour can feel repetitive and tedious, but in hindsight those moments are elevated to the glorious. Lucia once told her this has to be some trick of evolution in our brains in order to keep small children alive.

When her phone rings, she lunges for it in case it's Abigail. Tammy said they're going to cover basic parenting tips and strategies next week, and Cinnamon is hungry for some tips for how you can force yourself to get used to the blistering unease that comes every time your child—or at least the one you're legally responsible for—is out of sight. There's got to be a trick to stopping your mind from racing with all manner of disastrous scenarios. Otherwise, how do all parents not just drop dead from dread?

When she sees it's Taylor, the unease doesn't budge. In fact, it ratchets up as soon as she hears Taylor's voice. "Can you talk?"

A lifetime of experience has made Cinnamon hyperaware of the ominous sensation—like the sky holding its breath seconds before a torrential rain—that signals the other shoe is about to drop. If only she could have made money from this talent.

"Sure; I just left the class. What's up?"

"So, we have a credible lead on Bluebell's family. A couple's come forward. They saw you and Bluebell on the news . . . and they have reason to believe that the baby's mother is a woman named Amanda Jacobs. Their granddaughter. They raised her, apparently. Which makes the baby their great-granddaughter. And they want her; they want the baby . . . Cinnamon, are you there?"

Dear You,

It was a mistake to reactivate my Facebook account. When I pulled up my profile for the first time since I'd left Sibley Bay, I was just going to take a quick peek, like looking under a rock to see what was there. Well, Caleb was there. Or rather his words. A lot of them that I couldn't take in all at once except this line jumped out above all the others: *I know you had a baby, Daisy. Call me.* There were all my secrets, all gross and exposed, splayed out like period panties hanging on the line.

He wrote about how Cinnamon had reached out to him. But how did Cinnamon even find Caleb? Who was she, Sherlock Holmes? But it actually made me feel better the more I thought about it. To know Caleb had talked to Cinnamon. This way I knew that it had all played out just as I planned. It meant Cinnamon had found you, that she still had you, that she didn't walk straight into the Sibley police station. Why did she want to find me though? That was the unsettling part, but who was I kidding? To think that she was just going to take in my baby without a beat and never think of me again. I'd allowed for the possibility, even if I never wanted to fully let it take hold. That's why I was careful—careful as I could be, at least—throwing away my phone, deactivating Facebook, not telling anyone where I was going. I even moved out of Heather's soon after the night we both spent puking our guts out in her toilet, albeit for different reasons. I didn't tell her where I was going next since I knew it was just a matter of time before she ran her mouth and broke my trust again. Granted, I didn't go far, just to another cookie-cutter suburb of Orlando, to a sublet in yet another run-down condo complex—Beauty of the Bay, despite there being no bay within an hour's drive. It was sad that I didn't even have one friend in town anymore, but it was for the best too.

I'd gotten a job as a waitress at Mezcal Maria's, one of the zillion kitschy Mexican restaurants in one of the zillion interchangeable Orlando-area strip malls. (They made us wear an actual sombrero and peasant skirt, which was hot, humiliating, and maybe even a little offensive.) After I got home from my ten-hour shift smelling like grease and cilantro, I was hit with such a flood of loneliness looking around my sad studio and realizing that it had been too long since I spoke to a single person who cared about me. That's when I grabbed for the prepaid phone I'd bought that first night I arrived in town, when I got the air mattress at Walmart. The same way it is when you're real thirsty and your body will go get you a drink of water without you even realizing it, that's how it was when I went on FB. I wasn't going to reach out to anyone, but I thought it might help just to look at Caleb's face. See what he was up to. I didn't even know if he was still in Virginia—and that thought made me shaky. Not having any idea where Caleb was in the world. I needed to know.

In his message he made it clear there were things he needed to know too. Like, *What are you doing, Daisy? Where are you? And who is the father of this baby you had?* Seems he was most curious about that. And who could blame him? It could have been an immaculate conception for all the prospects I'd ever had. But it wasn't. And Caleb might not have had any right to pry—other than the fact that he cared about me and didn't want anyone to hurt me, and that gave a person certain entitlements—but you have a right to know who your daddy is.

The only reason I've been avoiding it is because it's so boring. "Boring" isn't the right word, but I don't know how else to describe it. "Anticlimactic" is more like it. I would have loved it to be a better story, a romance, at least, like my mom and Tyler or like Ross and Rachel on *Friends*. But it wasn't like that at all, and I can't do it over. That's the worst part of this life—no rewind, no second chances, no never minds.

The night Caleb left for Virginia, I was so distraught. And angry. I know it was a great gig and we needed the money, and it didn't make sense for me to go since we had already paid our rent in Sibley for six months and I had a good cleaning job, but I still felt betrayed that he was leaving me all alone for practically a year to build some dumb stadium. Granted, the money was too good to pass up, and he was sending some back to me too, but still, I didn't like being left—who does, I suppose? Soon as he drove away all I kept thinking was, *What if Caleb never comes back? What if I never see him again?* It was irrational—Caleb loved me, and I knew being apart was temporary—but sometimes you can't tell your brain what it's supposed to do or not supposed to do.

I couldn't just sit with my runaway negative thoughts, so I went to this bar I passed when I commuted between the motels where I cleaned rooms. A roadhouse dive with a dirt parking lot. Believe it or not, I'd never been to a bar before, not just because I was underage, but because I didn't really take to drinking too much. Caleb and I drank beer and cheap wine sometimes when we were feeling fancy. Even had a joint once or twice. But I'd never had hard liquor. That'll happen when your mom drowns drunk. It makes you terrified of touching the stuff. Like, if I took two sips too many I'd be smashed on the front of a windshield or find myself at the bottom of a lake.

But my mood was to do something reckless. I felt so out of place at the bar. I'm sure the bartender took one look at me and could tell I had no business being there, not just because I was too young (though no one seemed to care about that) but because I was dead broke. It's probably why he took pity on me and told me the first drink was on him. Which was good because I didn't even know what the fifteen dollars in my pocket could get me. I still don't know what he poured me. Whiskey maybe? But I prayed that each bitter and burning sip would help me feel less lost and mad. I got to thinking about how Caleb had not just left that day, but he'd been leaving me for a while. Ever since he'd gotten a boyfriend about six months after we got to Sibley—someone he met online. He didn't know that I knew. Well, he knew that I knew he was gay. He'd told me that secret the night before graduation, blurting it out of nowhere like he didn't know how else to get himself to say the words. His whole body was shaking like a fever was breaking. "God's gonna kill me," he said. But it was really his father he should have been worried about. Barely a single Sunday went by without Pastor Mike declaring that sodomy was a sin and that gays should burn in hell, all of the fire-and-brimstone ranting. Turned all beet red and sweaty like the pressure of saving all of humanity from homosexuality was on his shoulders.

Caleb looked so tortured and tormented when he coughed up his confession to me, and who could blame him, given that he was basically admitting to being an abomination based on what we'd heard since we could walk? I didn't even bother with any empty words like *It's going to be okay* and *Live your truth* and all that. Instead, I finally told Caleb the secret I'd been keeping for the whole of our friendship too. I figured that would maybe be the most helpful thing of all—it's always better when you know you aren't alone in your misery. And it's sure as hell preferable over some dumb BS about God loving us all just as we are.

So I just said it, quick as I could, like pulling off a Band-Aid, how my grandfather had been coming into my room since I was six years old and touching me, anytime he wanted, usually when he was drunk, and there was nothing I could do to stop him and I had nowhere else to go. Seems like it should have taken me longer to explain the horror, but it was just that one sentence.

When I saw the look on his face, I was worried that Caleb was mad at me, like I'd stolen his thunder, like I was overshadowing him, trying to one-up him in the who-has-a-bigger-secret game. I was about to apologize, when Caleb screamed, "Fucking monster!" And I realized he wasn't mad at me; he was mad at Gamps. I actually laughed a little bit because I had never heard him use a cussword before, and he just stared at me and then hugged me as tightly as anyone ever had.

That's when Caleb said, "We're leaving here tomorrow, Daisy." We had planned to save up more money by working until the end of the summer, but he was right. We had to go. The way he saw it, we didn't have a choice. It was life or death. I thought that sounded awfully dramatic till I realized he was right.

Caleb started transforming into a different person practically by the time we stopped for gas barely a few miles outside of Leesville—or maybe he was just becoming himself. Shortly after we arrived in Sibley is when I noticed that Caleb was always on his phone texting. I looked at his phone once when he wasn't around, and that's how I saw he was on websites for gay men to meet. First time I saw two men kissing. First time I saw a picture of a penis. I probably should have been more shocked on both counts, but I was hung up on trying to imagine Caleb actually kissing a guy, or taking a picture of his man parts. I wished I could ask him about it, but the fact that he was keeping it all secret made that door feel closed. I was so mad he had this secret—and here look at me now.

He had a slew of messages back and forth with some guy named Murphy—I didn't read them. Curious as I was, that didn't seem right. I was trying to give Caleb space to tell me about Murphy; I respected that it had to be hard. But him being all secretive, that's what I mean by it was like he left before he even drove away.

Anyway, all that's why I had double-downed on drinking that night. That and because some guy started buying them for me and I didn't know a polite way to say no so he wouldn't get hurt or mad. Zach was his name, the name a nice guy would have, and he did seem nice, so that's also why I said yes to the drinks and because he told me a string of dumb jokes that made me laugh. He was wearing Dockers—like Caleb's dad wore when he preached. He always paired them with a collared shirt so he could be "down to earth." This guy, Zach, was also closer to Pastor Mike's age than mine, but somehow that made him seem safer. And he had a boring, solid job: he sold tractor equipment. That's why he was in town, from somewhere I never knew and never counted on mattering anyhow.

We were in the middle of playing game after game of tic-tac-toe on bar napkins when Zach told me his company had sprung for a room at the Coastal Palace, and it was so nice and did I want to check it out? I did. I wanted to see inside the place—the grand old hotel was a converted massive Victorian mansion, painted the color of Bazooka gum and perched so close to the edge of the ocean it looked like it might as well have been a boat.

But I wasn't stupid; I also knew what that meant. When a man invites you back to his hotel room, it's not to check out the ocean views.

I wasn't raped or anything. It's hard to write that word, but I want to be crystal clear. What happened that night was all of my own free will. It was like I was living someone else's life for the night—and it was nice to be someone else. To be someone who let someone touch her willingly, who even mostly enjoyed it. But it didn't stop my regret or disappointment in the morning. I wasn't ashamed, exactly, even though I knew I had committed about a million sins, but it was more that the encounter was . . . like I said, boring. A letdown is maybe the best way to say it. I thought doing something like that would change me, but I woke up the same old Daisy but with dull pain in my head and between my legs.

Zach offered to take me to the free Continental breakfast. That was somehow the saddest part. How polite he was trying to be. How he didn't know what to say or do either. When he asked me how old I was, I lied to save us both. I could just see him rubbing his stressed temples and saying something like, "You're young enough to be my kid." It was awkward—and cliché enough—without all that. I had to spare us both.

I was just glad that Zach and I didn't get intimate enough to get to details like last names and hometowns. I couldn't have called him if I'd wanted to when I realized I was knocked up, and that made the decision for me.

Zach was a good person—I'd bet my life on that. In a way, I sort of did. It helps me sleep at night when I remember the way he rubbed my head in the morning and said, "That was nice, right?" Like he cared. And then, "I really enjoyed your company." He seemed sincere about that too, even though I was tipsy and blabbed a lot about stupid stuff like how much I love the ocean, which is what happens when I'm nervous, so I don't know why he found it so enjoyable.

I wish I had more to tell you, but sadly, that's all I know about your dad.

I debated whether to write back to Caleb's Facebook message for a long time. Finally, I decided I couldn't just ignore him. He felt the same as I did—shut out. Our secrets had become a wedge between us, and what kind of friendship is that? Caleb deserved an answer. So I got to typing a reply before I could talk myself out of it. I didn't tell him where I was though, even though he had asked twice. But I told him I was safe. I told him I missed him. I told him I was going to try to build a life for myself, or if not a whole life, then something resembling one that would carry me through the next few months until I could think bigger. I told him

I would see him again soon. I didn't just write it; I also whispered it into the air like a wish, the same way I did when I pressed my eyes shut and blew on a birthday candle or a wayward eyelash. With the fervor of begging.

As soon as I pressed Send, I came so close to calling Cinnamon. Her cell was easy to find, right there under her pretty picture on the SBCC website, after her bio that quotes someone named Maya Angelou. I almost dialed it, then stopped before I entered the last number. Because what would that do? What would I say if she answered? And how would I stop myself from calling the next day and the day after that and the day after that, just to see if Cinnamon would let me listen to you breathe on the other end? I just had to put it all out of my mind.

Before I deleted Facebook again, I checked if there was a response from Caleb. It had only been, like, three whole minutes since I sent the message, but it didn't stop me from feeling hollowed out to look at that empty in-box. I just kept thinking my whole life at the moment felt like one giant ache of missing. I understood the feeling wouldn't kill me, but boy, it felt like it could. It honestly did.

If I could have afforded it, I would have gotten on a bus or plane or train right then, straight to Virginia, to see Caleb, to cry while he held me. He'd tell me I wasn't a bad person, and he would mean it. He'd tell me that I would be okay. And he would mean that too. And he's maybe the only person in the world I'd actually believe. We could sit in an empty tobacco field or his construction sites, in the shadow of a half-built football stadium, all lumber and promise, and we'd try to make it feel like we were back at EDEN. Like when we used to hold hands and look up at the sky, watching planes trace across it, jealous that they were up there and we were down here. And he'd do the thing where he'd trace letters on my back with his forefinger. It's a game we'd play for hours—Caleb writing on my back and me trying to guess what he was trying to spell. He liked to write long messages—it would take forever, but those were the afternoons that we felt like we had nothing but time. That's what I picture when I imagine seeing him again. His finger tracking dirt up my back, making it hard to slide against my T-shirt, but I would always still be able to make out each letter he'd carve firmly with his long finger. I M-I-S-S-E-D U.

I was so lost in this fantasy that when I broke free of it, I realized I'd left all my laundry in the ancient machines in the shed at the back of the complex, and no doubt someone had already taken it all out and dumped it on the floor, which had happened the last time and was more demoralizing than it ought to be. Something about wasting all those quarters and all that time and having to start over, and the fact that someone's dirty hands were on your wash and they didn't give you the grace of a few extra minutes, just dropped your clothes on the filthy floor like they—or you—didn't matter, could make me sad for hours. So I dashed out. Then I ran into Ms. Jenkins, who maybe was the only person in the whole complex lonelier than I was. She was about two hundred years old and sat all day on an old folding chair outside the laundry just to make people stop and talk with her. Which was pleasant enough, and anyway, beggars can't be choosers when it comes to friends, I've learned, but she talked so slow you had time to boil an egg between each and every sentence. Tonight she caught me with a long tale about when she was a flight attendant at TWA in the '50s and all the diet pills she popped to stay under the weight limit of 125 pounds, and how she had to kiss each man as he disembarked from the plane. There was nothing to do but stand there captive for twenty minutes and pretend not to be outraged when Ms. Jenkins described those as "the good old days."

It was when I got back to my place, lugging my pile of clean-but-still-damp clothes since I didn't have another quarter for the dryer, that I realized I forgot to delete FB. And I could have right then, but the envelope icon shone bright—a new message. There's no way I could not read it. I figured it would be a long, emotional reply from Caleb. But it wasn't. Well, it was from Caleb. But all it said was *YOU NEED TO WATCH THIS*. I zoomed in on the thumbnail of the video he sent—and clicked the link. Then, right on the screen, so close I could reach out and trace those soft eyebrows, was you.

CHAPTER TWELVE

Cinnamon sits in her car reading a poem about death, or life depending on how you look at it, but either way it feels exactly right. Just the act of reading itself is a godsend. When it hit Cinnamon that she hadn't read a single line in a single book since the day she found Bluebell in the park—the longest she'd gone without reading since she first discovered books—she was struck with an intense longing, like missing an old friend or a former version of yourself. The book she started at lunch that fateful day three weeks ago—the memoir about the sex slave—slides around the back seat, all but forgotten. How do parents ever find time for books? Her lunch hour, sacred as it was, is a distant memory, and when else is there a spare hour in the day? Before bedtime was when she used to do a ton of reading, but these days she falls into a deep sleep midair, inches before her head bothers to make contact with any pillow. The silver lining is that her recurring nightmare is finally gone.

She seizes this stolen moment to calm herself the best way she knows how. She'd grabbed this book of poetry from the little stack in the bathroom as she left the house. She keeps a rotating collection of poetry books there because sometimes a trip to the bathroom is just enough time for the one poem that will completely change your day.

As she says the first lines of the stanza slowly out loud over and over, almost like a chant, her heart rate slows. It's a comfort to know the words have worked their magic and soothed her. It's like finding your car still starts after you've left it for days in the cold—the rush of reassurance that things work the way they should, and sometimes even when they shouldn't. The fact that she'd landed on this particular poem about death wasn't an accident. The news Taylor delivered yesterday brought on a feeling of grief and loss that may be premature but no less paralyzing. It has her sitting, stiff and still, poetry book in her lap, watching the white numbers tick upward on Bessie's dashboard clock. 3:51. 3:52. She will wait until it ticks to exactly 3:55 to enter the bland building where Daisy's grandparents await. She's determined not to be too early, too eager. Her aunt Celia once told her, "Making people wait on you can be an effective power play." Cinnamon wouldn't give the Jacobses the satisfaction of making her wait. But nor would she be late, which would serve to make her feel like she was already behind, already losing. A black mark. *Take the baby from me right now.*

When Taylor told her about the Jacobses coming forward, she assured Cinnamon that CPS would do all the right due diligence. It wasn't just a matter of handing the baby over. "We'll investigate to make sure these people are legitimate and can provide a good home before taking a single additional step. They've already offered to take a DNA test. And they want to come see the baby as soon as possible. They live a few hours away but are going to drive up tomorrow. Can you be at my office at 4 p.m.?"

"That stupid, stupid interview. Why did I do that?" Cinnamon said it to herself more than to Taylor. Her voice was more restrained than the storm raging through her body would suggest, but still she hoped it conveyed the subtext: *You never should have put me in this position.* Taylor had just wanted to parade her on television like a circus act. The nice Black lady with the white baby. *Isn't that something?*

But Taylor wasn't sheepish at all. She was baffled. "Cinnamon, this is what we wanted . . . to find Bluebell's relatives. Reunification is always the goal. We do what's best for the child. And relatives are often best. This is a good thing for her, to have family. To be with family."

Not that family! It took every fiber of her being not to scream this. She muted the phone just in case she couldn't control herself.

Derek Jacobs's mug shot had been popping into Cinnamon's head like he was haunting her—and he was. It was a warning that this was about to happen. That he would get his hands on Bluebell and he would teach her to hate. Because that's how it happens: willfully, intentionally. She pictured a time years hence when Bluebell could pass her on the street and hate her because that was what someone else told her she was supposed to do.

The banging that reverberated throughout the car at that point was not just her heart breaking at that thought but Cinnamon slamming the muted phone against the steering wheel.

"Cinnamon. If it makes you feel better, they seem like decent enough people." But Taylor had no idea. Cinnamon laughed at the notion that the Jacobses were "decent" people. It came out as a hysterical, deranged bark that she freely let loose since she was still on mute.

"Cinnamon? Are you there?"

"I'm here, I'm here . . . Have they been in touch with Daisy? Have the grandparents heard from her?"

It was one thing to give the baby back to Daisy. Despite how she might have felt about Bluebell, she still believed that was probably best for the child if Daisy was willing to step up and raise her. It was another to turn the baby over to those monsters who grew more deplorable in her mind with each passing second. Cinnamon was so distracted simmering in her hate for the Jacobses that it took a second for her to register the confused silence.

"Daisy? Who's Daisy?"

"I meant Amanda. It is Amanda, right? Sorry. I just got the names mixed up."

Taylor seemed to accept this, Cinnamon being a frazzled "new mother" and all.

"Yes—Amanda. We're still unclear on her whereabouts, but that will be the next step. One thing at a time. Let's see where we stand and if we can get more information tomorrow."

"Do I have to bring Bluebell?" Cinnamon's guts twisted like a wrung washcloth at the idea of having to see Derek Jacobs with the baby, of them even being in the same room.

"Not yet. You can come alone. We can then arrange a visitation with the baby if the test proves they are who they say they are."

"Okay. I'm on my way to pick her up now from Jayson's mom, who's watching her while I was here at the class. I'll see if she can look after her again tomorrow."

"You're taking such good care of her. I know that, and look, I know it's hard when you get attached like you have. Last month, I had foster parents that had to reunite a child who'd been in their home for three full years. There weren't enough tissues in the world. So I know it's hard, but I hope it helps to know that whatever happens, you were there for this baby in her time of need. You made a real difference in her life, even if she doesn't stay with you."

The past tense. It was ice water in her face. And she hated Taylor for using it. But she was also frustrated with herself for not being more prepared for this. Bluebell was not hers. The only claim she had to the child was a note left by a desperate teenager who, as far as she could tell, would have done anything to keep her daughter away from the people who raised her.

Cinnamon agreed to all of this to try to do the best by Bluebell, to keep her safe until they could find the best possible home for her. So why did she feel a real flash of pain through her body when she thought about the baby moving on? Not just with the Jacobses, but with anyone. Why did the phrase "even if she doesn't stay with you" leave her with a lump in her throat the size of a lime?

There's no time for her frustration with Taylor right now, or her frustration with herself. She has got to get it together and get into that building the second the clock strikes 3:55, as it does now.

Once inside, Cinnamon is thrown when she gets closer to the designated conference room and hears the sounds of pleasant conversation. Taylor's chipper lilt as she talks about a movie she watched last night, a low laugh from another woman. All that changes the second Cinnamon appears in the doorway—an unwelcome stranger. But why is she the one unwelcome here?

She stumbles, actually trips on her own two feet, when she registers Derek Jacobs's eyes, when they bore into her, the slip costing her both seconds and dignity. They're not just Derek's eyes—they're Bluebell's. The family resemblance is striking all the way around. Cinnamon's sensible flats are filled with lead, making any steps farther into the room feel impossible.

Taylor usually greets Cinnamon with a hug, but this time she only nods to the empty chair to her right, a formality that puts Cinnamon even more on edge. Taylor sits at the head of the table, leaving Cinnamon to slip into the chair opposite the Jacobses. She takes in Derek's broad shoulders—he's still high-school-football-player beefy, though his round head is covered in white fuzz that gives away the fact he must be pushing seventy.

"Hello." Cinnamon's greeting may be short and stiff but she makes sure she looks them both right in the eye. *You will respect me.*

She's planned to muster up as much civility and friendliness as possible, deploying the smile that disarms even the most sullen of the kids she works with. What throws her is that Derek clearly has the same approach, even if he's straining himself with the effort to make nice.

"Good afternoon." He nods at her amiably enough. "This is my wife, Barbara." The frail woman by his side offers a nod and a tight-lipped smile.

Even if she didn't know about Derek's violent and racist past, there's an air about him that's enough to give her chills. Instinct sends her heart thrumming—like in her bones she knows his particular brand of evil. Wisdom of the ancestors passed down in the form of a tingling Spidey sense: *That one's trouble.*

Everyone starts to talk at once as if taking a cue, but it's only Derek who motors on silencing everyone else.

"Our granddaughter, Amanda, is a willful spirit who's turned her back on her family, on God, and now an innocent child. She's 'bout as rebellious as her own mother, who got knocked up at sixteen and then went and got herself killed drinking and swimming."

So much for the grief-stricken father Cinnamon imagined. That sob story, the heartbreak of losing a child, was the only source of empathy she had been drawing on to cut this vile man any sort of slack. Cinnamon sometimes worries she is empathetic to a fault. She bends toward finding the good in people, if not out of generosity, then survival. The way she sees it, you can find the worst in people and keep your distance, or you can do your best to find a way to incline them toward you. Even with Ashley, who ripped up the only picture she had of her mother. Cinnamon kept finding simple ways to endear herself to the broken soul. She'd silently bring her a glass of water when Ashley woke up crying in the middle of the night, or share the Cheetos she bought with her piddly plasma-donation money. Empathizing can only take you so far though. Where is the line? Does a man who committed an actual hate crime deserve her grace? The chill in the air isn't from the overactive AC; it's from the cold liquid steel now pumping through Cinnamon's veins. She's sure it's making the room five degrees cooler.

Derek's agitation rises to the surface when Cinnamon dares to interrupt him mid-rant.

"How do you know this is your granddaughter's baby?" She was careful not to slip up and say Daisy again, or to sound too familiar.

"Come on! You'd have to be blind to see that that child doesn't belong to us. Amanda took off a couple years ago. And then we heard through the grapevine that she went and had a baby and gave it away not too long ago. We also know she was up in this area. Didn't take much to put the pieces together soon as I saw the baby on TV. Those eyes . . . are these eyes right here." He shoves his forefinger into the delicate skin under his right eye. "She's a Jacobs through and through."

"Where is she now?" It feels strange for Cinnamon to vocalize the question that's been haunting her for weeks now.

"Who?" Derek looks genuinely confused.

"Your granddaughter."

"That's none of your business. Doesn't matter no how. She's not fit to raise this child."

Taylor, whose head has been swiveling back and forth between the two parties like she's watching a tennis match, finally speaks.

"We're going to need to get in touch with Amanda. So if you do know her whereabouts, it's in your best interest to tell us."

Derek just crosses his arms and slouches back in his chair, but Barbara looks to her husband as if for permission and speaks softly.

"Last we heard, Amanda might be in Florida. A girl who knew her from school said she was living down there. Orlando or thereabouts. That's all we know."

Daisy's in Florida. It's not much to go on, but it is infinitely more than Cinnamon had known one minute ago. Taylor is scribbling furiously on her notepad, and her demeanor has shifted. She glances at Cinnamon quickly before she leans her elbows on the conference table and addresses the older couple. "Mr. and Mrs. Jacobs, if the DNA test comes back that this child is related to you, is it your intention to raise her?"

"Heck yeah, we're going to raise this child. Third time's a charm. We've recently come into some money. We're well equipped to take this one. And if you think we're gonna leave our kin here with . . . with *that* woman, well then, you've got another think coming."

Here come Derek's true colors. Cinnamon sees it, and so does Barbara. Cinnamon clocks how the woman squeezes his tight fist. "I want that baby now," Derek says.

Taylor slips into her placating social worker voice—the soothing tone adopted whenever bad news is about to be delivered to a hotheaded teenager or frustrated foster parent. "Well, that's not possible. As I said we need a positive DNA test first. For right now the child is in good hands. Cinnamon here completed a background check and home inspection before we approved her to foster. Even if your test comes back positive, we'd have to do the same thing for you to get approved."

"Approved? That child's my flesh and blood. I don't need anyone approving me to raise her!" A ropey red vein starts pulsing in his forehead as if trying to break free and strangle someone.

Cinnamon is pleased by this frenzy of frustration—let him get himself all worked up. He's doing himself no favors judging by the way Taylor's looking at him. That has to earn Cinnamon some points—her relative calmness. Also, the mention of a background check is music to her ears. This man has a felony conviction—surely that will be revealed, and surely it will disqualify them.

Barbara pats Derek again to soothe him but in the tentative manner you might try to soothe a rabid dog, ready to pull your hand back quick. "What my husband is trying to say is that, as God is our witness, Daisy would want us to raise this baby over a stranger."

Abruptly, Taylor drops the pen on her notepad and cocks her head at Barbara. "Daisy?"

"Sorry, I mean Amanda. That's a silly nickname Amanda gave herself a while back."

Cinnamon watches out of the corner of her eye as Taylor shakes her head and brings clenched fists from her lap to the table. All this happens in slow motion, as if time itself were slowing down. "Can I see you outside for a moment please, Cinnamon?"

Derek almost rises out of his chair to object. "You're not allowed to just go and have a side conversation with her. That's not playing fair. You can say whatever you have to say in front of the both of us right here."

"Mr. Jacobs, you need to let me do my job." Taylor sounds much older than her years. But she's not even focused on Derek; she's leveled her gaze right at Cinnamon, who hasn't moved from her chair. She knows what awaits her in that hallway.

When Cinnamon was twelve and living at Momma Jean's, she was desperate to go to a concert with this cute white boy from algebra class. Never mind that he'd made it clear that she'd have to pay for the ticket herself, never mind the queasy sensation she had whenever he called her his "homegirl," never mind the fact that she'd never even heard of Green Day—she crushed on this kid in a way that she now understands was a sick combo of adolescent desperation and hope born of every teen movie she'd ever watched that had made her dumb enough to believe she could be *that* kind of girl for even one night. All she had to do was come up with fifty-four dollars. In desperation, she decided to steal it from the stash Momma Jean kept tucked in a rank, old leather loafer in the back of her closet. It was the sort of pathetic, foolhardy move that only a first crush could make you do, because Cinnamon knew she'd be on the receiving end of a wrath unlike anything she'd ever known if Momma Jean found out. She also knew the likelihood that Momma Jean would find out was high, considering nothing got past the woman. Cinnamon hadn't anticipated being caught red-handed though—right as she was on all fours, digging through the messy pile of shoes. "I know you're not doing what I think you're doing."

The shock of Momma Jean's sharp hiss made Cinnamon feel like she had actual fire running through her body, as did the whacks across her back with the hairbrush Momma Jean grabbed. It's the exact same feeling that hits her now as she follows Taylor into the hallway. The noxious regret that she could believe she could get away with something so stupid.

"You lied to me." The door is barely shut behind them before Taylor makes this pronouncement, arms crossed.

Cinnamon can't look her in the eye, a clear sign of her guilt.

"You know who Daisy is. You mentioned the name yesterday. And that's clearly a name that Amanda goes by. I'm not dumb, Cinnamon."

Cinnamon braces herself against the wall. She's got to tell Taylor the truth and hope the social worker still has some glimmer of faith in her.

"Look, Taylor. I did lie. Only because I didn't want to get Daisy in trouble. Leaving the baby like that was a crime, and I think she was scared. She doesn't deserve to have her entire life ruined for a mistake. I know it's crazy, but I thought I could find her myself, and then things started moving so fast. I never thought someone would come forward. But now . . . now the Jacobses are here . . . and I know for a fact that Daisy would not want these people to have the baby, Taylor."

"How do you know that? And what else do you know about Amanda Jacobs that you've been keeping from us? How do you know her in the first place?"

As usual Cinnamon has no idea how to convey her relationship with Daisy, so she sticks to the basic facts. "I told you that I always took my lunch break on that bench in the park. Well, Daisy—I mean Amanda—she did too, and we would meet there and talk once a week. I've been seeing her in the park for about a year or so."

"So wait, you knew she was pregnant?"

Cinnamon shakes her head as emphatically as she can. "I had no idea; I swear on my life. It was a complete surprise. She hid her pregnancy from me the whole time. The way I found Bluebell is exactly like I told you. Daisy just left her there behind the bench. And I was fully and truly shocked. I should have told you, Taylor. I'm sorry—I am. Like I said, I just didn't want to get Daisy in trouble. I thought I could find her, and then the baby got sick and it all kind of snowballed."

Raised voices waft out of the conference room, Derek calling out they need to "get back in here." He's not going to stand for their "side conversation" much longer. Cinnamon has maybe a minute to convince Taylor that she only lied for the good of the baby.

"You can be mad at me—fine; I get it. But you can't take it out on the baby. Daisy doesn't want her with those people. Trust me. She gave me the strong impression that she had a really hard upbringing and she got away from them as soon as she could. Derek's even been convicted of a crime! He was charged with attempted murder, Taylor. Tammy in our foster certification class said a felony could disqualify you, right?"

The hope in Cinnamon's voice is bald as an eagle.

"Whoa, okay. Well, if all that's true, the judge will take that under consideration. And we'll need the results of that DNA test. So one thing at a time, okay?"

"But what are our options, Taylor?" Cinnamon doesn't even try to hide her desperation. And she had carefully chosen her pronoun. She needs Taylor to feel like they're in this together. She reminds herself that as skeptically as the social worker is looking at her, Taylor knows Cinnamon has taken good care of Bluebell—she'd said it herself. And if Taylor does feel caught between a liar and the unhinged felon in the conference room, Cinnamon has to believe she still has the relative advantage.

"The mother's wishes trump just about any other consideration or factor. So if we can get Daisy to appear and make her wishes known, that would be a starting place."

"What if . . . what if I had a note from Daisy?"

Taylor stands there blinking at her and then speaks very slowly. "Do you have a note from Daisy, Cinnamon?"

Her tone makes it clear that Taylor is slipping away as an ally. Cinnamon takes a step toward her as if she can physically keep Taylor on her side. She doesn't even bother to answer yes, assuming the question is rhetorical.

"A note can't be authenticated. You could have written it yourself."

The look on Taylor's face says she fully believes Cinnamon could have done that, and Cinnamon can't blame her.

"Look, I don't know what to believe right now. This is incredibly messed up. I stuck my neck out for you—I vouched for you! In front of a judge. And you've been lying to me this whole time. I have to talk to my supervisor about this. The Jacobses have a credible claim here, Cinnamon. But I want to respect what the mother wants too. But even if that note is real, we'd have to have Amanda—Daisy, whatever her name is—at the next hearing. We'll get Bluebell a court-appointed advocate too, and I'm guessing the Jacobses will get a lawyer. So I don't know . . . You may want to consult with someone too, just so you have all your options if you're serious about continuing to pursue guardianship."

Throughout Cinnamon's entire life, things have happened to her—things completely out of her control. Where she lived, what she ate, who cared for her—she had no say. Even her relationship with Jayson doesn't feel like so much of a choice sometimes but something she's acquiesced to out of love and desperation. She may not have been able to fight for anything before, but that was about circumstance, not about weakness. She knows one thing to be true in this moment. She is a fighter. She knows this from the strength bubbling up in her. She will fight for Bluebell, for what's best for her, and for the first time Cinnamon is starting to think that maybe she is what is best for this baby, not for now, but for as long as she needs her. Maybe even forever.

And that conviction is the only way she's able to do what she does next. It's going to require a deal with the devil *and* swallowing her pride, and it's a debate as to which one of those is harder to stomach, but she does it anyway. She reaches into her purse and calls the one person who may be able to help her.

CHAPTER THIRTEEN

She'd draped the blanket over Bluebell because she just couldn't take the stares. She's at her wit's end with the people furtively glancing at her, trying to make sense of the situation, why this Black lady has a white baby pressed to her chest.

It took the cake when a middle-aged white woman leaned forward while Cinnamon was sitting at the airport departure gate giving Bluebell her bottle and said, "Your baby's beautiful." Not to Cinnamon, but to the white woman sitting next to Cinnamon. It required slow-motion mental gymnastics for Cinnamon to work out that this woman had the nerve to think Cinnamon was sitting here feeding this other woman's child while said woman relaxed and flipped through *Real Simple*. She knew this sort of thing would happen, but it was still tiresome. It had been enough to make her regret getting this flight at all. But she also couldn't imagine enduring a long drive, trying to focus on the road with a baby crying hysterically in the back seat. And Tammy Thompson had told them in their certification class that foster parents can travel with kids as long as they have their guardianship papers, which Cinnamon has at the ready should anyone demand them.

Cinnamon suddenly can't stop crying on this packed little plane. The soft muslin covering Bluebell's head now serves the dual purpose of protecting Cinnamon from the stares and protecting the sleeping baby from the rebellious tears leaking from Cinnamon's eyes. She can't figure out exactly why she's beset by this sudden fit—crying never made sense to her insofar as it seemed pretty pointless and the sort of thing that, if you gave in to it, might go ahead and happen all the time. So she rarely lets herself, which makes these sobs she tries to swallow both confusing and unwelcome.

She'd read somewhere that people are prone to crying on planes, so she'll chalk this surprising stream of tears up to being thirty thousand feet in the air. There's something about the dim cabin full of strangers and the fact that there is no escape—there's nowhere else but the right here, right now, and for Cinnamon the right here, right now is fraught as hell. Meanwhile, the woman in the seat next to her is already slack-jawed and dangerously close to drooling after promptly drifting to sleep before the plane even took off, which was a level of faith Cinnamon found disconcerting.

She tries to ignore the sad irony that the only other time she's been on a plane in her entire life was when she was headed to the same destination. Atlanta, Georgia. To Aunt Celia's for the first time. It had been a mere forty-eight hours after Sallie the social worker had revealed that she had an aunt that Cinnamon had her things packed in a sad, old gym bag she'd found in Momma Jean's basement and was on the flight south. Sallie dropped her off right at the gate along with a big old tag that said UNACCOMPANIED MINOR. Her counterpart in Fulton County would meet Cinnamon on the other side. That time on the plane, her seatmate was a spritely old Asian woman going to visit her grandkids who was thrilled to jabber on to Cinnamon for the entirety of the two-hour flight. At takeoff she'd grabbed Cinnamon's hand. "You don't mind, do you? I'm a little afraid." Cinnamon didn't mind, not one bit, since she too was afraid as the engines roared so loud she felt it in her chest and the plane rose into the air, defying all common sense. The woman held on to Cinnamon's hand well into the flight, as the aircraft and Cinnamon's hammering heart both leveled out. From then she maintained a steady stream of chatter that included how to make a proper egg-drop soup, and how her granddaughter was four and had two imaginary friends named Kit and Kat, and how she wanted to see the farm she grew up on in Chengdu one more time before she died. The best part was that she didn't ask Cinnamon one question; she was just happy to have an audience for her stories, and Cinnamon was happy to provide one, and it was maybe the most intimate and joyful string of hours of her young life—certainly this woman was the first adult she'd ever interacted with who didn't have an agenda or an obligation to her. Cinnamon was so distracted she didn't have to think about the unknowns that awaited her when the flight landed. She forgot to be terrified of what her "new" life and another houseful of strangers was going to be like, or worried about whether Aunt Celia would like her. All that mattered was Su's cheerful banter.

Now there's nothing more than the roar of the jet engines to distract Cinnamon as she rubs Bluebell's back. She considers getting out the book she'd packed, the memoir about the sex slave she hasn't picked up in weeks, but decides to lean into the melancholy that's enveloped her. She figures it's better to just go ahead and face head-on what awaits her when she lands an hour into the future: her past.

She closes her eyes and there she is, fifteen years old with shabby clothes and scabby legs, showing up at Aunt Celia's doorstep with "Atlanta Sallie," which is how Cinnamon thought of the local social worker who met her at the airport. It didn't seem worth it to learn her name. She knew for sure the woman would never remember hers. The social worker was too bright and eager, pushing her toward the threshold: "This is Cinnamon!" she said like a magician doing a trick. *Would you look at that. A real live girl!*

Cinnamon clocked the look on her aunt's face as she inspected Cinnamon from head to toe—it was disappointment that veered toward dismay. The social worker's initial chipperness deflated a bit when she had to ask, "Uh, can we come in?" Only then did Aunt Celia usher them into the massive two-story marble foyer, a space nearly bigger than Momma Jean's entire house.

"Well, first thing we're going to need to do before you lay on a pillow in this house is take care of that hair."

That greeting told Cinnamon everything she needed to know right then and there, and if she'd been nursing any fantasy that this would be some sort of "I found my family and lived happily ever after" scenario, it was stomped out like the butt of a cigarette underfoot. But that was okay—at least she knew where she stood.

She was shown to her room at the top of the stairs—clearly a home gym that had been hastily repurposed into a bedroom by tucking a brand-new twin bed opposite a treadmill and a rowing machine, both of which looked state-of-the-art and unused. On the way down the hall to the bathroom, she'd passed Corrine's room. Her cousin (she was still getting used to that word) was still at school for the day. She peered in at the ornate princess canopy bed, the mural with Corrine's name spelled out with wildflowers, and a gallery of framed baby pictures, and Cinnamon experienced an emotional vertigo that would take days for her to identify as envy. It was a feeling she was largely unfamiliar with, since she'd never really had anyone or anything to compare her circumstances to—no one she knew had anything she'd ever coveted before . . . beyond a family.

Instead of the stale, recycled air of the plane, Cinnamon smells fresh-cut grass. It somehow always smelled like fresh-cut grass at her aunt's, the result of the twice-weekly visits from the landscapers. Grass and roasted chicken. Her aunt always seemed to be roasting a chicken. All of it—the whole plush-carpet, two-car-garage, family-dinner-every-night suburban ideal—was pleasant enough and should have made her feel safe; it was what she'd always wanted, a fantasy cobbled together from watching TV and reading books. But when she was there, her feet sinking into the thick carpets, sitting at the table with healthy meals before her, new clothes in a closet in her very own bedroom. She found that it all oppressed her in the worst possible way—each whiff of comfort and privilege and pained politeness made her feel constantly out of place, like the interloper you were always surprised to find underfoot. *Oh, you're still here?*

She exhausted herself trying to be the perfect guest, always worried someone would realize she'd overstayed her welcome. It didn't help that that's exactly what happened.

Now, nearly twenty years later, she has the upper hand (or the illusion of it), and that steadies her somewhat. It's Aunt Celia who'd been trying to reach *her* and who had been so relieved when Cinnamon finally called her back five days ago. Cinnamon needs something from Aunt Celia, but the reverse also appears to be true. Though the mystery remains what that is, one that will be solved when she lands. Their conversation had been brief, but when her aunt said, "I was beginning to think I wasn't going to hear from you; thank you for returning my call, Cinnamon," her gratitude seemed genuine. For a split second, Cinnamon almost felt bad that she hadn't even planned to be in touch with her aunt at all—ever—and the only reason she'd done so was so Aunt Celia would connect her with Omar Hardaway, one of the most high-powered family court lawyers in Georgia. He'd done all of the big divorces, representing the who's who of Black Atlanta, including his twin brother, a star tight end for the Falcons. The twins were the stuff of local legend—two boys from Lakewood Heights who'd risen to the upper echelons of Atlanta's Black elite, which is how Omar became an investor in Celia's husband's insurance empire. It was funny how Cinnamon never thought of Uncle Elliot as her uncle but always "Celia's husband." Not that either moniker much mattered, given how he walked out on Aunt Celia. And given he was barely around before that, except for the obligatory weeknight family dinners that Celia demanded of them even if they all sat around eating her dry chicken in a strained silence, plotting how quickly they could escape, Elliot to his man cave in the finished basement, Cinnamon to the study with a book, Corrine to the sixty-inch TV in the living room, and Celia to putter around the kitchen, finishing a bottle of merlot and feeling accomplished that she got to pretend to have a perfect family for forty-five minutes—an hour if she was lucky.

When she'd called her aunt back, Cinnamon got straight to the point as soon as "hello" left her lips. She laid out finding Bluebell, what was happening with the Jacobses, trying to track down Daisy/Amanda all in one breath since she didn't know how to stomach silly pleasantries anyway. Then she humbled herself for the ask.

"Is there any way you could put me in touch with Omar Hardaway? I need legal advice and help." She would have reached out to the big-time lawyer herself if she thought he'd remember the random skinny girl who showed up one day at Aunt Celia's and disappeared just as unceremoniously two years later.

"Omar? You remember him?" Celia seemed surprised, as if Omar and her uncle didn't spend countless evenings locked away in the basement man cave drinking Scotch that cost more than most people made in a week.

"I do," Cinnamon said, fighting to keep her composure. Just talking to her aunt turned her back into a tormented teenager, even after all this time. "And I need to talk to someone of his caliber about helping me with this."

"Okay, I'll reach out to him."

It was almost too easy. Cinnamon didn't know what she was expecting, but it wasn't this, this simple acquiescence. She had to give Aunt Celia some credit for taking this whole surreal story in stride. She was ready to say thank you, and hang up in short order, when Aunt Celia told her the catch. Of course there was a catch.

"I'll connect you to Omar, Cinnamon, but you have to come see me. There are some things I need to say to you face-to-face. And then you can meet face-to-face with Omar while you're here. How's Friday?"

There was a time when Cinnamon would have agreed that there were some things that needed to be said, like, for example, *I'm sorry* and *Can you forgive me?* but she'd long since given up on hearing any such thing from Aunt Celia and had no use for it now. But she needed this favor from Celia, and rare was the quid pro quo in which you were happy with the quid you had to give for the quo. Cinnamon accepted this would be her end of the deal, meeting up with her aunt for a few hours and hoping a little peace came as part of the deal. One saving grace was that the trip was short and she'd get one night in luxurious hotel sheets. The other was that she would get to see the Rev, which would be like the first sip of Diet Coke after the long stretches when she forces herself to give it up, just to prove she can live without it. At one point, she had similar doubts about Reverend Rick, that she couldn't ever live without him.

She'd asked him to pick her up at the airport—she needed to see him before anyone else in Atlanta, and certainly before lunch with her aunt. There was also the fact that she couldn't afford to rent a car after paying for this last-minute flight and was overwhelmed by how she'd manage getting the carrier in and out of Ubers all over town. So being chauffeured around in the church van had a lot of upsides. Especially if it included Reverend Rick plucking the perfect verse from the Bible to buck her up, even though his mere presence would do the trick.

The giant bright-blue van with ALL SOULS HEAVENLY FELLOWSHIP splashed across the side in graffiti paint is impossible to miss in the chaotic passenger pickup lane at Hartsfield. If the sight of the van starts the smile, it's seeing Reverend Rick himself that spreads it to both corners of her face. She has to fight the urge not to run to him so he can lift her up and spin her around, like a father would do. It doesn't matter that the Rev isn't her father, just the closest thing she ever had, or that by the time they met she was already too old for such a thing and would have broken the man's back even at the buck ten she was back then, she still wanted to fling herself in his arms and fly.

"My girl! Get on over here!" he calls out, and she doesn't exactly run, but she does quicken her pace to close the distance between them, eager to lean into a warm embrace, momentarily forgetting they were smooshing the baby between them.

He steps back to look at her, and she does the same to take him in. She wants to run her thumb across the shiny scar that crawls down his cheek from eye to chin. One of his most well-worn stories was how he didn't see Jesus when he almost died, like some people claimed they did, but he saw Satan himself, close enough that the devil breathed fire in his face. When Rev's first words were, "The Lord will rescue me from every evil deed and bring me safely into his heavenly kingdom. To him be the glory forever and ever. Amen." He'd never so much as cracked open a Bible before that, but someone put one in his hand right there in the hospital and showed him that exact verse in the book of 2 Timothy. The only way to make that make sense was Jesus himself. All Souls Heavenly Fellowship was born the next day. His brand wasn't so much people looking for God but those running from the devil.

When he takes in Cinnamon now, he looks as worried as the day he'd found her. "I can't believe it's been this long since I've laid these sore eyes on you, girl. Still a little wisp of a thing, ain't you?"

All the chaos of the last few weeks fades away, along with the bustling crowds around them, and she just fully basks in Reverend Rick and all his glory.

"I've missed you, Rev. More than you know."

"Oh girl, I do know. You bet I know. And right back at you. I'mma save my breath when it comes to reminding how you never should have left in the first place. But you're here now, so let's go."

The van is far from new, but it's newer than the green machine he had been driving around when he first found Cinnamon. This one's just as bright—and just as "loved" as the one of yore. Opening the back passenger door, she confronts the same tufts of fabric worming their way out of ripped leather seats, same amount of crumbs on the floor, same giant wooden cross hanging from the rearview mirror that's big enough to come swinging at you on a sharp turn. The struggle to get the car seat situated is made all the more challenging with the aggressive honks of cars around her and a man in a yellow reflective vest, blowing a whistle and screaming, "You gotta move this vehicle!"

She jumps in the passenger seat and slams the door against another ear-splitting shriek.

"Where am I taking you? You got me up here being your Uber

for the day; you're lucky I miss you, Ms. Thing." He reaches over and affectionately jiggles her thigh.

"I'm meeting Aunt Celia at Park 75 at the Four Seasons."

"Yeah, that sounds about right that your saditty aunt wants to go there. It's even fancier these days. You won't recognize the area with how they've built it up since we used to give out sandwiches by the eighty-five overpass. Chased all those folks out of there. Remember Chuck with his souped-up tent? My man had a speaker system and everything! People sure can make something out of nothing, can't they? Anyway, they're all gone. Just more and more fancy hotels going up every second with rooms that cost a month's rent. Urban renewal my ass. It's some bullshit."

"Dollar in the tip jar!" Cinnamon always teased Reverend Rick about his cursing. She'd once tried to collect a dollar for every bad word, joking that it would be the only way she could put herself through college.

"Oh please," he'd say when she got on him about his foul mouth. "God got much bigger things to worry about than me dropping a few f-bombs."

"Okay, so lunch and then what? You need me to come pick you up?"

"I'm meeting with the lawyer—Omar Hardaway. His office is right near the restaurant, so I'm gonna walk. Or Aunt Celia can drop me."

"Oh Lord, Omar? That shady mofo? You know he's trying to get all into civil rights legislation now, right? He's got his guys coming around the soup kitchen and the streets giving out prepaid phones to people who have a complaint about the police. Word is he's trying to put together a big harassment class-action lawsuit. Thinking he's the next Ben Crump, but Omar don't care about the people from up there in his literal glass tower, just wants to stick it to the city and make a few million more bucks."

"I need him though, Rev. I need to know my options. Like, if I can't find Daisy . . . then what? I don't know what I'm doing."

"I'll tell you what you're doing, Cinnamon. Or what you need to be doing. Following the Lord's plan. You think it was an accident that you found that baby? Your situation has got me thinking all about the story of Solomon. You remember that one, right? When Solomon suggested he cut the baby in half and give one half each to the two women who were claiming the baby. He knew that the real mother would never allow such a thing. She'd let her rival have the baby over her precious offspring being cut in half. That's true mother's love right there. Willing to do whatever you need to do, even give up your child, to keep them safe. When the time comes, you'll know what you need to sacrifice to make sure this child gets the life it deserves. Don't know how many times I have to tell you: you can't deny the Lord's will. And his will put that baby right in your path. And you know as well as I do that it's for a reason."

"But this baby? What right do I have to this baby? Why me? Who am I to raise this child?"

"Who are *you* to raise this child? You're going to have me running off the road with that foolishness. Who is anyone to raise anyone? You're asking the wrong question. Who are you *not* to raise this child?"

"I just never saw it happening this way."

"What did you see happening?"

"I don't know. I didn't think much about having my own kids at all, but the few times I did, it definitely wasn't like this. I sure didn't see myself with this white baby. Or any baby, really. I don't know. I know I shouldn't be all hung up on that, but . . . but . . ."

"Cinnamon Haynes. A child is always a blessing—no matter what color he or she is. The Lord saw fit to bring her to you—for you to be her steward. And frankly, as much as you're hemming and hawing over there, I don't see as how you really have much choice. Trying to defy God's plan never got anyone anywhere, you hear?"

"But the stares. You don't see how people look at me like I'm her nanny or like I might have stolen her from a real or rightful mother. Is this something I could ever get used to?" It was too fresh in her mind, the woman at the airport whose face morphed from confusion to contempt when she realized Bluebell didn't belong to the nice white lady.

"You're worried about some white folks staring at you? Child, please. They've been beating us, hanging us from trees, keeping us from getting jobs and education, and you worry about folks *looking* at you wrong? Do not give them a second thought. Don't give them anything."

Cinnamon looks out the window at the streets passing in a blur. The hustle, the grit, the buildings crammed together, the fact that she smells food and chemicals and not Sibley's ocean air. She can take a deep breath in Atlanta. Isn't that something, escaping to the city to feel like you can breathe?

"Well, the bigger problem is . . . my husband." The one who doesn't even know she's here in Atlanta.

"Let me guess. He ain't on board, nohow, noway."

Her head barely moves up and down.

"Well, you know I was never a big fan of Jayson's—too slick for my taste. One of those cats that thinks he can sell holy water to the devil with the right sweet talk. He sure sweet-talked you, didn't he?"

Reverend Rick, never one to hold back, had not been shy in sharing his reservations about Jayson. When she told him they were getting serious, he'd sat her down and said, "You can spot a brother who wants a woman in his shadow from a mile away. That man will race to keep two steps ahead of you just to make sure you're following." The Rev's wrath intensified when she and Jayson eloped instead of letting him marry them. That Cinnamon allowed him to believe that the elopement was Jayson's idea—and not hers, because she couldn't bear to look at all those empty pews where her family should have been—was enough of a justification, since he wasn't a fan of Jayson's anyway. And now, for the first time in the five years they've been together, she understands what Reverend Rick meant about her walking in Jayson's shadow. She'd never thought about it until it suddenly made so much sense to step into the light. She almost tells the Rev about how her marriage is cracking like a glacier that's about to cleave into the sea, but she bites her tongue. Not because she's worried he'll say, "I told you so," though knowing the Rev, he would do it in the most endearing way possible. Mainly it's because she isn't ready to say the words "My marriage might be over" out loud yet. It will stay a secret she has with herself until she's ready to know what to do with it.

But when the Rev asks if she thinks Jayson's going to come around and Cinnamon slowly shakes her head side to side, the state of their union is as clear as the windshield.

"You gotta do what you gotta do, Cinnamon."

"Amen, Rev. Amen."

The split second of calm she was grabbing for is disrupted when the van suddenly lurches across a few lanes of I-285 and swings off an exit ramp. The carrier shifts across the seat in the back, and Cinnamon chastises herself for not buckling it in tighter, especially at this reminder that Reverend Rick is way better at driving sinners to the word of the Lord than he is at the actual act of driving.

"My bad. My bad. These exits sneak up on you, especially with all the changes they're making 'round here." He shakes his fist at the highway, or the developers, or whoever deserves his wrath besides his own eyes or scattered attention. "But we're almost there, so you know what we got to do." He floats his hand from the steering wheel over to grab hers and bows his head just enough to keep his eyes on the road.

He starts in. "Dear Lord, give Cinnamon here the strength . . ."

From your lips, Reverend Rick. From your lips.

"I'm not hearing you, Cinnamon . . ."

She turns to him and grins and then projects her voice in the small van like it's a pulpit. "Dear Lord, give me strength."

"Now, that's my girl," he says with a familiar smile so bright it can light the way.

CHAPTER FOURTEEN

"You look just like your mother!"

Cinnamon glares at the guy behind the glossy oak maître d' stand like he's got two heads. He's already busying himself gathering menus, so it takes him a second to register her bewilderment.

"Excuse me? I have no idea what you're talking about."

"Oh, I think your mom just came in. She said she was waiting for someone, and then you walked through the door looking like her spitting image. I just . . . I assumed."

"Well, I would be more careful. You know what they say about assumptions." Cinnamon says it quietly, more a piece of advice than an admonishment. "That's not my mother."

The poor guy is utterly helpless to escape the awkwardness he's created. There's no recovery here, for either of them, so he just slumps his shoulders and murmurs "Follow me," as they wind their way through a labyrinth of tables under a long row of massive chandeliers that has the effect of making the whole ceiling look like it's raining glass. Giant pots overflowing with wildflowers and greenery are strewn every which way as if the design cue was "elegant rain forest." Cinnamon feels like she's stepped into another universe even before she reaches the oval booth in the corner where Aunt Celia sits. And then she's even more disoriented, taking in the shrunken, unrecognizable figure.

In the second between the chastened host slinking away and her aunt looking up, Cinnamon is able to give her a good look. Whatever else you could say about Aunt Celia, she'd always had the most beautiful skin, luminous and golden like she was coated in bronze. Now it's gray and ashen. But it's the colorful scarf covering what is clearly a bald head that's the real tell. Cinnamon can almost smell it on her—the cancer. She'd once read a book about a cat who lived in a hospice who could tell when people were going to die—it's like that. And it all makes sense now.

Celia looks up slowly, like she knew Cinnamon was watching and wanted to allow her a moment to collect herself. "I don't look so good, huh?"

"You look . . . great." What else could she possibly say? *You look like you're at death's door?* Cinnamon places Bluebell's carrier on the floor next to her and leans over into an awkward sort of side hug. The ease with which she does these two things, as well as her aunt's unexpected appearance, throws her off-balance, literally. She sort of stumbles into the seat across from Celia.

When her aunt leans down, lifts the blanket to take a peek at the baby, and then smiles up at her, Cinnamon has a fleeting and eerie sensation that it's possible she remembered the past wrong. She knows she hasn't, but it's still easy to imagine a world where she ended up here at this swanky eatery to warmly embrace her wonderful aunt with whom she has a close relationship and is about to enjoy a lovely lunch and visit. In other words, that her life matches up with the one she's pretended to have all these years. In this *Sliding Doors* moment, they both lead to the same place.

Before they can get into much, the waiter appears, and there's the business of hearing a long list of specials, deciding between tap and sparkling, looking at the menu, and settling on their orders: two elaborate salads with beets and poached this and that. All of it buys them five precious minutes of distraction.

As soon as the waiter's back is turned, Aunt Celia dives right in as if she doesn't have any more time to waste.

"The doctors have said I have approximately four months—six if I'm so fortunate. It's my pancreas."

"I'm . . . I'm sorry." Cinnamon has wished this woman so much ill will over the years that she has the sinking sensation that she's caused this somehow, as ridiculous as that is. Seeing her aunt suffering doesn't bring her the satisfaction she once thought it would. Rather than the vindication she'd always thought she'd experience, she truly just feels sorry for Celia, so weak and fragile.

"I appreciate that. The hospital gave me a therapist woman to talk to. She's nice enough but barely out of diapers. She's supposed to be helping me prepare for death, as if there's a way to do that. And with just a few months left . . . it's not enough time to do very much at all anyway, let alone make amends. But I decided it couldn't hurt to try. You see, Cinnamon, everyone has fallen away from me. I say that like it was an accident, like it was something that happened to me. It took death to come knocking to show me a painful truth—I didn't end up all alone by accident."

Celia's self-awareness is as jarring as her appearance.

"What about Corrine? How is she?" Cinnamon has lost track of her cousin, never even been curious enough to find her on Facebook, or rather, never been self-flagellating enough to stomach pictures of Corrine baking bread with two adorable kids or giving a commencement speech at whatever fancy college she'd ended up going to. But she very much assumed that was what was going on in her cousin's life.

"I wouldn't know. My own daughter doesn't talk to me anymore either. We had a falling out a few years back. I wouldn't give her money. For a breast augmentation of all things. I honestly thought I was doing the best thing for her. I didn't want to enable her, you see. I wanted her to realize that she has more to offer the world than her body and pretty face. And to tell you the truth, my pride hurt too—like we only had a relationship if I gave her my money. That's how Elliot always worked out his guilt. Throwing money at the girl. You try so hard to raise decent children and give them what they need—well, we gave her too much. She's spoiled and entitled. It's quite awful to realize that. To realize your own child isn't the person you wanted to raise, especially since you can only blame yourself for that. It wouldn't be as bad if she were actually happy, but she's not. She's chronically miserable and wanting. Living in Miami, working at a job in some kind of marketing that she doesn't care for but sticking with it because it gives her access to fancy parties, celebrities, and whatnot. But she still can't find a husband to save her life. None of it is what I wanted for her. I've tried to call her a few times, and I'm hoping she'll come around. I just don't want to tell her I'm dying over the phone. I don't want that to be the reason she decides to call. Maybe that's naive, but I want her to call me back because she wants to and because I'm her mother. I gave birth to her, and she owes me that at least. To hear me out."

It's good that Aunt Celia doesn't wait for Cinnamon to agree with this sentiment before she moves on. Had her aunt not been so set on continuing with this long speech she'd obviously prepared, Cinnamon might have interjected with, *So you're just now realizing Corrine was the real problem child, huh?* Instead, she bites her tongue and settles in.

"Look, Cinnamon . . . I realize I'm not the easiest person to get along with. Nothing makes your flaws more clear than your impending death—the Grim Reaper might as well be a grotesque mirror staring back at you, saying, *You ruined everything, and it's too late*. But I wanted you to know that I realize I did you wrong, and I wanted to try to explain if you'll let me."

The salads have arrived, and the massive piles of buttery lettuce leaves covered in garish red beets between them feel ridiculous in the weight of the moment. Cinnamon can't possibly do something as basic as eat, when they're finally doing . . . this.

"I was so hard on you. I know that. My parents were never hard on my brother—your dad. They just let him get away with anything. I blamed them. And I resented my brother for it. I wanted he and I to be close, but we just never were. People joked we were oil and vinegar, like it was funny and not sad to have no warmth at all between two people who grew up in the same house. When Daddy died, he left Trevor all of his money. It was only just over seventeen thousand dollars. But still. It ate at me. It broke me. It was the principle—I was the dutiful, loyal daughter, coming home for Sunday dinner every week, and there was nothing for me? It wasn't the money itself—that makes me sound greedy. It was what it represented. What Daddy valued, or should I say, who. I know he'd reasoned I'd be fine—I was engaged to Elliot at the time and he was already making good money in insurance, so no one worried about me. Your dad, he took the inheritance and split. I was surprised to hear that he ended up in the Marines, considering he never took well to authority. I was still cleaning the casserole dishes from the funeral when he left us and never looked back. It was that fast. I'm not trying to talk badly about my own brother—may he rest in peace—especially to his daughter. I'm more trying to explain my feelings on the matter."

"I don't want to be rude, Celia, but this is all hard to hear when I never even got to meet the man." She wishes Celia weren't making her endure this trip down memory lane on the way to her point, which Cinnamon is impatient for her to arrive at. Unless this is all building up to a plea for Cinnamon to come take care of her in her dying days. The thought makes Cinnamon drop her fork to her plate midbite. Imagining having to help Celia to the bathroom or wipe up her drool with a stiff washcloth roils her stomach, but so does the idea of turning her back on this woman completely. Surely the fact that they share some blood doesn't obligate her?

"Well, it's all to say that . . . well, I resented you too, Cinnamon. You arrived at my doorstep, and I'm ashamed to admit it, but I felt like you were another one of my brother's messes to clean up. A teenager that I'd never laid eyes on? Taking you in was a big risk, and I did it. I chose to upend my family."

"I was your family too," Cinnamon interjects. She can't help herself.

"Truth is you weren't. I didn't know you, but I wanted to. I'm not saying I was a saint, but taking in a young girl who had been through God knows what when we already had our own troubles in the house . . . It was a lot. I could have told that social worker no when she called—you realize that, right? And I almost did. But I couldn't have lived with myself, so I agreed to take you in, and maybe that was my mistake. Not for anything you did but because I had enough going on. My marriage was already falling apart—Elliot had already taken up with that . . . woman."

Aunt Celia never says the name of the thirty-two-year-old tennis coach that Elliot had an affair with for ten full years before he finally left Celia.

"When Elliot walked out on me, I blamed you for that too, Cinnamon. He didn't want me to take you in. But I'd calculated—miscalculated, as it turned out—that he'd have to spend more time at home if we had a brand-new teenager in the house. I had this foolish idea that it could actually bring us closer."

Cinnamon doesn't know what it says about her marriage that it didn't even occur to her once that a baby would bring her and Jayson closer together. But she does relate to Celia's marriage woes in a different light. When she was a teenager, she used to think her aunt was pathetic for constantly trying to play happy family, but now, with the turmoil of her own marriage and how hard and how much she wanted to ignore those struggles, Cinnamon can empathize a little more with the notion of trying to fake it until you make it. Though she's loath to give her aunt even an inch.

"That day, I just broke, Cinnamon."

Despite finally feeling a twinge of sympathy, Cinnamon has had about enough of Aunt Celia's pity party. "What you forget, Celia, is I was broken too. And then you made it worse for me. You don't get a medal for taking me in when you just as easily kicked me out. And I didn't do anything to deserve that." She has to fight to keep the panic out of her voice, but she's raised it enough that the balding man next to them who has an eerie resemblance to Judge Harlow looks over disapprovingly.

Celia is unruffled. She's prepared for this, probably practiced it with her therapist.

"There were drugs involved, Cinnamon."

"Not mine! Those weren't my drugs. They were Corrine's! Your perfect daughter's." This time she does yell, such is her outrage that Celia is going to force her to defend the truth again and again. Aunt Celia glances around like she wants Cinnamon to lower her voice, but she knows better than to ask.

They weren't even Corrine's drugs, actually; they were her boyfriend's. The one Corrine kept secret after Celia forbade her to see that "thug." Cinnamon had also kept Corrine's secret. Not for nothing she'd kept Elliot's secret too. She'd been a repository for that whole family's skeletons. She'd seen Uncle Elliot with his mistress one day after school. Elliot had offered her $500 to keep quiet, which was dumb because she'd have done it for free. But she kept the money anyway, not even knowing how badly she'd eventually need it.

"I know they were." Aunt Celia drops her fork on the delicate plate. "I know."

"But did you know then? When we were sitting in the school office? Did you know you were lying? Not just to them but to yourself? Did you know?"

For all the promises she'd made that she wasn't going to show an ounce of emotion, that ship has sailed, so Cinnamon doesn't even try to keep her voice from quaking or to stop the tears that are fast sneaking up on her. It is the same quaking and threat of tears she'd had in Principal Jones's office that day as she offered up her futile denial: "That's not mine."

Aunt Celia and Corrine were already sitting in there, both with their right legs crossed over the left at their ankle, perfectly in sync. A blue backpack sat unzipped on the principal's desk. Cinnamon could clearly see the Ziploc bag filled with weed in the second largest pocket.

"We did a random search during the fire drill today after getting a tip that some students here were selling marijuana. We found this bag in Corrine's locker, but when your aunt got here, she said the bag belongs to you, Cinnamon. Corrine grabbed the wrong one this morning."

That was a lie.

But when Cinnamon finally glanced toward Aunt Celia, the imploring look in her aunt's eyes told Cinnamon this is what she needed to do, and without thinking about the consequences, Cinnamon obeyed her, assuming that this sacrifice might finally ingratiate her with her new family after two years of feeling like the outsider. She would take the fall for Corrine, and she was certain her aunt would smooth things over with the principal and no one would actually suffer. Everyone at the school already assumed Cinnamon was damaged goods despite her good grades. Why fight this when she could possibly earn her aunt's respect by being a good soldier?

So she said yes—yes, it was her backpack. And Principal Jones thanked her for her honesty. Then he announced, emphatically, their zero-tolerance policy and that Cinnamon was expelled, effective immediately. Her locker had already been emptied. No one was surprised when Cinnamon was kicked out of Larchmont Academy, even Cinnamon herself, but she was disappointed—devastated, really. She'd loved the school, as snotty as it was, and the extracurriculars and the neat rows of As stacked on her report card. But the fact that she loved it so much also made it all going wrong feel inevitable. She was doomed like the worst self-fulfilling prophecy, and it was almost a twisted relief when they tossed her out like trash.

When Celia doesn't answer, Cinnamon repeats the question: "Did you know they weren't my drugs? I know that you knew it wasn't my backpack."

"I knew. I knew. But you don't understand, Cinnamon. A mother will do anything to protect her child."

Your real child.

They both glance down at Bluebell, an unspoken new bond passing between them. Cinnamon has come to Celia because she would do anything for this child who isn't her blood, who doesn't even share the color of her skin. That was some irony. It took all of her strength not to point this out to her aunt.

"I couldn't let Corrine get kicked out. She was a poor student and would have been lost at public school. I needed to get her through Larchmont Academy, which would be her ticket to college."

"But that *doesn't* explain why you told me I couldn't live in your house anymore, even though I was barely seventeen and had literally nowhere to go. You watched me pack my bag and walk out the door. No one even said goodbye. Corrine was locked in her room, Elliot was at work, and you were busying yourself in the kitchen while I walked out the door alone and with nothing."

For years after Celia kicked her out, Cinnamon had consoled herself that it was always going to end with her completely on her own, fending for herself regardless of her pit stop at Celia's. She would have aged out of the system no matter what at eighteen, when CPS gives foster kids a piddly stipend and best wishes. But today, sitting across from Aunt Celia, she realizes that as bad as being bounced from home to home was, it was infinitely more painful to have a taste of family and have it snatched away. To be rejected by your own flesh and blood.

Cinnamon doesn't repeat the facts to sound accusatory, though, but simply to set the record straight in case there's any scenario in which her aunt believes it played out any differently than that. She feels bad when Celia winces, whether from pain or from the truth, but it needs to be told. She needs to say it out loud. Like she did with Jayson. And Lucia. It's like she's turned on a spigot within herself and she can't turn it off.

Aunt Celia goes about trying to defend herself, looking visibly weaker from the futile effort. "Not nothing. I gave you the Malibu even though we were going to hold onto it for Corrine to drive when she turned sixteen. And the money."

"A few hundred bucks didn't get me much—a couple nights in a motel, and then you know where I lived? In that car." It's little solace how ashamed Aunt Celia looks.

"You have to understand I was just so angry and overwhelmed. I convinced myself that all of the bad things happening in our house started with your arrival. I blamed you and I thought if I could just get rid of you, it would be better. I could fix everything. Like warding off a curse. And I knew you'd be okay. You had already been through so much and survived, so I convinced myself you would be fine. But I am *sorry*, Cinnamon. So incredibly and deeply sorry. I know what I did was wrong. I am not asking you to forgive me. I am just asking you to hear me."

"You're saying all of this so you can feel better, so you can get this off your chest, lay it on me, and spend the end of your days regret-free. Just put it all on Cinnamon; lay it on her and rest easy for eternity. She's a strong girl; she can take it, right? But I've never had a choice in the matter—I've always *had* to be strong."

"But you were also safe with Reverend Rick."

"Wait—how do you know about that?"

"He tracked me down, called me one day, and tore into me. That man curses a lot, and frankly, it was out of line and inappropriate for him to talk to me the way he did. But I could see he cared. I started sending him a check every month. For you, for his church. He probably didn't tell you that, but I did."

Cinnamon didn't anticipate this curveball, and Celia seizes on what she clearly hopes is a desperate infusion of redemption in this conversation.

"I wanted to help. I figured with your pride you wouldn't want to come home after everything I did, but when I learned you were living on the streets, I wanted to do something."

That is probably true. Cinnamon would have refused any overtures her aunt had made—there was no way she was going to skulk back to that house like a stray dog that doesn't learn a lesson no matter how many times it's kicked. But Celia should have asked. Pride is being able to turn down the offer.

Perhaps sensing the rising tension, Bluebell begins to fuss, and

Cinnamon seamlessly wiggles her out of the buckles and clutches her against her chest to comfort her. To comfort both of them. She doesn't even look around the restaurant to see who's watching. Let them stare.

"You're good with her."

"I know." It's a petty thing to say, but she doesn't need or want her aunt's validation.

"That reminds me . . . I have something for you."

Cinnamon doesn't want whatever her aunt is offering right now either. What she wants is to leave this booth and just go catch her breath somewhere before her meeting with Omar.

But then Celia is waving a cracked four-by-six photo in her face, and even though the two images in the picture are blurry, she knows exactly who they are: her parents. Cinnamon has never laid eyes on her father, only imagined what he looked like all these years. And she'd never seen her parents together, the two of them touching, happy, frozen in time.

"I should have given this to you years ago. The military sent me some of Trevor's belongings when he died and this photograph was in there. I tossed the box in the basement the day it arrived and forgot I had it, but I also had locked the past away. I can't stop going through those boxes now. When there aren't many days ahead of you, you can't stop thinking about the ones that have come and gone."

If she's honest, Cinnamon's not even hearing her aunt's words as she looks down. This photo, this gesture, is a worthy olive branch, and Cinnamon accepts it reverently in that spirit. She wipes her hands carefully before she grabs it. Then she slips it into the diaper bag without examining it. Her aunt doesn't seem to find this odd, as if she too understands that Cinnamon can't look at this picture right now, that she has to wait for the right moment.

Their salads remain largely untouched, but time has run out—or saved her is another way of looking at it. She's going to be late for the appointment with Omar. They ask the waiter for the check, and the busyness of wrapping up their meal and gathering their belongings, especially with how slowly Aunt Celia moves, saves them from having to do the messy work of closure or resolution or digging any deeper than they already have. Their conversation is left unfinished. Or perhaps it's just begun—time will tell.

It's dawning on her, though, that holding onto her anger all these years like a child clutching a ragged, smelly old doll hasn't served her at all. What does she have to show for it but a chronic tension that knotted all the muscles and fibers in her being, a tension that, ironically, has made itself known by loosening just a bit in this moment. As much as she was dreading this sit-down with her aunt, and for as many years as she would have found it unfathomable, maybe it was just what she needed to move past the past, for her own sake. If all those forgiveness books she'd read were any help at all, it was to hit that point home over and over.

"You go now, Cinnamon. Don't be late. Please come see me again. I really want us to talk some more."

What do you say to a dying woman except yes?

As they make their way back to the exit, Cinnamon palms the picture in the pocket of the bag to make sure it's still tucked away, as if it might have disappeared in the last two minutes. It doesn't make sense, how she keeps checking for it again and again. But then it also makes all the sense in the world when you consider how easy it is to lose the things that matter.

Every single surface in the lobby of Omar Hardaway's twenty-fourth-floor office space gleams. The coffee table, the art, the mirrors. Even the fabric on the sofas is shiny and reflective. The long hallway from the elevators back to his corner office suite is lined with photos of Omar and various luminaries: Omar and Barack Obama, Omar and Bill Clinton, Omar and Tyler Perry, Omar and his brother on the sidelines during the 2017 NFC championship game. Cinnamon lingers on a recent picture of Omar and his wife, side by side with a woman Cinnamon recognizes as one of the Real Housewives of Atlanta, along with Uncle Elliot and The Woman, all in golf whites at the country club. God, Cinnamon hated it when they used to make her go to the club—just looking at it in the background of the photo gives her the feeling of all eyes on her, as they seemed to be when she was there. Omar was always bragging, loudly and often, that he was the first Black person ever admitted to Argyle Golf and Tennis (and then he sponsored Celia and Elliot, thereby tripling the number of Black folks overnight). He relished the way some of the white people seethed that they were among them. It made him feel powerful, drawing on their discomfort like fuel. More than once, she'd overheard Omar proudly telling Uncle Elliot what a "trailblazer" he was. Granted, you had to push into places you were unwelcome in the name of progress. Schools and lunch counters were one thing; the opportunity to play golf and eat forty-five-dollar lobster salad didn't seem to be what all the people who bled in Selma had in mind, and yet to Omar, he might as well have been Martin Luther King Jr. himself.

Cinnamon is so absorbed in the photos and these ruminations that she's startled to hear Omar's voice calling out to his secretary from his glass-enclosed lair. She's immediately transported right back to the nights when he came over to the Freeman house for dinner. He had a habit of summoning Cinnamon to bring him and Uncle Elliot fresh ice for their after-dinner Scotches and then holding her hostage while he told increasingly off-color jokes, determined to "get a rise out of this girl." If there ever was a man who treated the sound of his own voice like oxygen, it was Omar Hardaway. She found if she laughed at all the right places and was appropriately fawning, she could escape his bad jokes and his wandering gaze before the next round of ice melted.

The summons from Omar's secretary breaks her reverie. She follows the woman who looks like a supermodel and glides down the hall toward Omar's office like one too.

"Well, look at you, sweet Cinnamon!" he calls out as he stands up from his seat that is more throne than chair and walks around the ping-pong-table-size mahogany desk. He's a full head shorter than Cinnamon, which was always disconcerting to Cinnamon as a teenager, that she could tower over a grown man. It also puts his face right at eye level with her chest. It's no less disconcerting as a grown woman.

"Aren't you as fine as I always knew you would be? What are you—thirty now? No, must be pushing forty. I say that because I'm doing the math, not because you look it, sweetheart. Because you most definitely do not. And you don't look like you just had a baby either. Let alone *that* baby." He lets out a loud guffaw as he nods at the carrier she sets on the plush carpet.

He leans in for a hug that there's no way to wiggle out of, which sort of feels like his intention. "You always were pretty, but a sad thing for being so pretty. I tried to draw you out of your shell. Make you laugh. I missed you when you weren't around anymore. Your aunt said you went to live with another relative back up north?"

Of course that's how Aunt Celia would have explained her away. She'd hardly tell her Jack and Jill friends that she kicked her niece to the curb. Cinnamon's forgiveness for Celia is tentative at best, and it teeters like a house of cards hearing this lie.

"Yeah, I think Celia explained my . . . situation. I was just hoping to get your counsel on my options."

"Oh yes, the situation. White girl left her child with you with a note like she was running out for some milk, and now her racist-ass grandparents want the baby and you maybe want to keep her. But here's a question: You sure about that? I mean, don't get me wrong—I like you with this blue-eyed baby. Just to burn those folks up. But then again, why do you want to do this? That baby is as white as my teeth—you can practically see through her! Reminds me of how my grandma kept praying my color wouldn't come in. She joked I got darker every day I was in the world—it was like watching the sunset. She prayed I would stop at dusk, but here I am, turned out the color of 3 a.m. on a moonless night." He hasn't stopped laughing or talking, and there is no chance she'll get a word in edgewise anytime soon. The conversation is like trying to enter double Dutch. And he isn't even close to being done.

"I can't even imagine what your husband has to say about this, and I don't want to, but I can't think that he'd want to raise this little Miss Anne. If my wife came at me with that nonsense, I'd tell her to kiss my Black ass. We've done enough raising their children. And anyway, if you just want a child, there are enough of our own rug rats out there already that need a home. I say give this baby to those grandparents and get on with your life, focus on you. You know, self-care and all that. You females are big on that. You play golf? That's my self-care."

He stops running his mouth long enough to note Cinnamon's stricken face.

"Okay, look—forget all that. This is about what you want. You do you, sister. She's a cutie-pie. Maybe she'll grow up thinking she's Black and that'll be fun. Have her out here in some blond cornrows and knowing every verse to 'Lift Every Voice and Sing.' Anyway, it's pretty simple. If this kid's great-grandparents have come forward and want the child, the judge is going to give her to them. Those family-reunification laws were invented to keep the white folks from taking our babies from us, and now they'll use it against you. Reunification happens in more than fifty percent of these cases. And anyway, why would the judge give her to you, a stranger? And a Black stranger at that? Come on, Cinnamon." He sounds tickled, like this whole thing is a joke she's playing on him.

"The mother wanted me to have her. That's why. And these grandparents are terrible people—the grandfather has served time. A felony conviction! There's a real case to be made that they shouldn't get custody. For now, I have a thirty-day guardianship, but there's going to be another hearing week after next. I'm trying to figure out my options."

The date looms on her calendar, the same way that her Friday deadline to turn Bluebell in had—these moments where everything could change on a dime. When Taylor had called her to tell her it was scheduled, Cinnamon had asked what she thought the outcome would be. Cinnamon craved statistics, predictions, odds. But Taylor was tight-lipped, not just because she couldn't see the future, but because ever since she'd found out Cinnamon had lied to her, she'd been distant. It was understandable. So Cinnamon had apologized profusely. And not just because she wanted Taylor back in her corner and she found she missed her endless optimism, but because Cinnamon was trying to take responsibility. There was a silver lining to all her lies catching up to her and grabbing her around the ankles. She could finally stop running from her past. For too long lying, bending the truth, and omitting it were her greatest defense mechanisms. But it has to end. She doesn't know about the truth setting her free and all that, but the lies and the lying don't serve her anymore. And that's just what she explained to Taylor in so many words, the girl seemed to appreciate it.

By the end of the call, she'd warmed up. As soon as they disconnected, Cinnamon had gone online and ordered Taylor a Modoc stuffie for her collection to be delivered to her office as a thank-you. Whatever happens from here, she wants Taylor to know she appreciates her, not just for her help with Bluebell, but on behalf of all the Bluebells and Cinnamons out there who need a Taylor in their corner. The little gift was also her way of acknowledging that she'd misjudged her, not that Taylor would ever know that.

She had perhaps misjudged Omar too, and how much he could help her because sitting in his office it's dawning on her this could be a colossal waste of time. With all the money, connections, and power Omar has, he's supposed to be able to fix this problem—that's how the world works; that's why she'd come all the way here—which is now feeling mighty desperate and foolish.

"You don't have many options here, but the one, far as I see it. You have to find the mother. If she severs her parental rights, you could have a chance. The judge will still have discretion as to where they place the child, since she's already a ward of CPS, but if Daisy makes her wishes known to the court, that she wants this baby in your care and that her grandparents are unfit, that could sway things. But bottom line is: she needs to be at this hearing."

"The challenge is I don't know where the mother is. All I know is she might have gone to the Orlando area. And I don't even know how reliable that is. Otherwise, she's just gone."

Omar twists the thick gold ring that encircles his meaty pinky finger. "Believe me, Cinnamon, I've been doing this a long time, and no one's just gone. She may be white as Casper, but she ain't no ghost. You just need to know where to look. And how. I got a great PI on staff. Even consults for Tyler Perry . . . apparently Perry's writing a murder mystery or some such nonsense. Probably another dang Madea . . . *The Madea Murders*—can you even imagine? The man has done a lot for the city, but boy, I can't stand his movies." He throws two hands in the air like he's begging for mercy. "I know I'm going to get smote by the gods for that sacrilege, but those movies are so silly. You like 'em? Tyler Perry movies?"

So much for keeping him on track.

"How much is the private detective?"

"Normally around seven hundred dollars an hour, but you're in luck." He stops and smiles wide. "I got you."

He reaches for a folded piece of white paper sitting on his desk and slides it across the slick glass top toward her.

"What's this?"

"Only one way to find out."

She unfolds it.

Amanda Jacobs, 407-555-6712

"Her phone number? How did you—" The paper shakes in Cinnamon's hands. It was laying right there this whole time.

"Everyone makes a mistake when they're trying to disappear. Your girl logged into her Facebook and sent a message. My PI traced the ISP of the message to a smartphone. Bingo. Told you—he's good. All of this is not strictly legal, so it stays between us."

Cinnamon doesn't have words . . . all of her searching and nada. But you throw some money, or a lot of money, at a problem, and there's nothing you can't solve. How satisfying it is to be right about the world and how it works after all. But even better is the sweet relief that she's gotten what she'd come for. "I can't thank you enough."

"Eh, didn't take nothin' but a few dollars, so you can thank your aunt. She took care of it. Poor woman. Must be hard having your days numbered like that. But hey, ain't all of ours?"

Omar and Cinnamon silently agree that their business has concluded and he grabs her elbow to usher her out of his office. "Say, when your husband, Jayson, lived here, did he have any run-ins with the police? Have him call my office if he did, ya hear? Just something I'm working on."

Cinnamon mumbles, "Sure"—all she can focus on is the paper in her hands. She tucks it into the diaper bag right next to the photo of her parents. The sticky pocket is fast becoming a treasure trove.

As the elevator drops from the twenty-fourth floor of the tower, it's fast enough to send her stomach sinking, or maybe the elevator dropping is not to blame for the sinking sensation. She's built this moment—finally finding Daisy—up in her head for a full month. Until now it's seemed like the answer to everything. But suddenly, all Cinnamon has are questions, and one particularly glaring one: What happens when she finally talks to the girl?

There's only one way to find out.

Dear You,

Hearing from Caleb and watching that video of you over and over again made me think about how Gammy was big on "facing the music"—there was always someone somewhere who needed to do it. She'd grumble it under her breath when she watched a TV show where a character was building to a reckoning, or when she heard gossip in town about people getting what they deserved . . . "Well, what did they expect? You gotta face the music." Funny how little it applied to Gammy, though, or Gamps, for that matter. People who had the most rules in life tended to have the most exceptions for themselves, it seemed to me.

So that's what was in my head—Gammy's voice: face the music, face the music, face the fucking music—as my finger hovered over the button that would play the video.

All the photos they showed of you with the cute headbands and the one of you and that stuffed elephant. I kept waiting to feel miserable and sad each time I rewound and watched and paused on your little face, so much bigger than when I saw you last, more fully formed, like you were made of clay and someone had sculpted your features to be more precise. You were getting to be a real baby. I was surprised when the video didn't make me even more anxious or send me into a spiral of shame. What I felt was like a settling inside me. All the blood that had been racing through my body too fast slowed down some. My insides felt more calm. I suppose maybe that's what they mean by inner peace. I never experienced anything like it before—that feeling like everything was as it should be.

Also, Cinnamon had that cute husband by her side. I'd never seen Jayson—he looked exactly like the guy in *This Is Us* who's such a good father and husband and always wants to do the right thing. Jayson seemed like that type of guy too—and he clearly loved Cinnamon. Sometimes I paused on the moment when he looked over at her in the interview. I'm not going to lie—I ached so bad for someone to look at me like that. Still do. But that's a whole other story. The bottom line is when I saw the video, I was more convinced than ever that you were supposed to be with Cinnamon. I actually felt proud of myself—yes, what I'd done was desperate and bonkers (it's not like I didn't see that—I did; I'm not a total fool, so you know), but it had worked out. I found you a good home. End of story.

It wasn't the end.

I was staring up at the dirty underbelly of a Cessna 172 when the phone rang. There was a tiny airport not far from my apartment, tucked into a neighborhood of run-down houses on my bus route. One of them was all but abandoned, and it had a scruffy yard that butted up to the edge of the razor-wire fence around the runway. I could sit in the postage-stamp-size patch of grass in peace, almost like I lived there, and watch the planes take off. There was a flight school at the airport. Fly Away Pilot Training. I was working myself up to go in and ask questions about how I could go about enrolling one day. For now, I lurked on the school's website, dreaming.

I recognized the number that glowed on the screen immediately. I had memorized it from the time I found it on the SBCC website and dialed it over and over, getting to the last number before I came to my senses. I let it ring and ring as I tried to decide if I was going to answer at all. Even though three rings in, I knew I wouldn't be able to resist. By the fifth I answered.

"Hey, Cinnamon. I'm watching planes take off." That's the absurd thing I said to her, because what else was there?

First thing she said to me: "That's nice, Daisy. I need you to come back."

It was a strange way to start a conversation, but everything about everything was strange. When I'd imagined talking to Cinnamon, all those times I picked up the phone to call, I'd thought I'd be crying a lot and asking a million questions about you. Instead, I thought of the video and told Cinnamon all my random thoughts.

It all came out in a breathless blur, just me going on and on about how I was grateful to her and thanking her for not taking you to the police over and over. Though how could I ever in a million years thank her enough, be grateful enough? It would be as impossible as swimming to Alaska. I told her that I always knew she was the right one to raise you. When she got quiet, I thought it was because I sounded so young and dumb or that she was mad at me. That's when she told me: "Daisy, your grandparents have come forward. They want the baby."

Those words had me scrambling to my feet like I was going to run all the way back to Sibley right then and there. I couldn't breathe on account of getting up too fast and the shock.

She was still talking. "I know you don't want the baby with them, Daisy, but that's what's gonna happen if you don't come home."

There's another expression Gammy loved saying: "Over my dead body." She couldn't just say no to things; she had to be all extra about it.

"Gammy, can I stay up late tonight to see the fireworks?"

"Over my dead body."

"Gammy, I wanna skip church on Sunday."

"Over my dead body."

It started to lose all meaning—but in this moment, the four words never held more weight. I would literally rather be dead than let those people even touch you. Well, that itself would kill me. I didn't know what I would do if that happened.

Cinnamon got to explaining how Gammy and Gamps had seen the news segment just like I had. They must have put two and two together after Heather's blabbermouth mom told the whole town all my business—that I had run away from Sibley to Orlando and that I had had a baby and that I'd given the baby up for adoption.

Cinnamon told me that my grandparents had taken a DNA test and there was a hearing scheduled to determine your best interests and if they could have you. And they likely would get custody because they were family and Cinnamon had no real claim to you. If I came forward and told the judge what I wanted for you, it could make a difference. And the social worker lady said she could help talk to the judge about me not getting into trouble for what I'd done, for leaving you. Cinnamon knew a good lawyer in Atlanta.

Lawyer. Trouble. She said it like it was no big deal to come home, to face them, like I could just show up and wave a magic wand and that would be that.

Cinnamon was barely breathing, like if she didn't get it all out quick enough, I might hang up, and she was not wrong to think that.

I could see why she was trying to make it easy. I just knew better is all. I'd already googled the punishments for leaving your baby. It's a crime. Child abandonment. They can lock you up for a whole year for what I'd done. I was a monster . . . and a fugitive from the law.

I was afraid of going to jail, but I was more terrified of having to confront Gammy and Gamps, having to tell people why I didn't want my baby with them. The way they'd look like they would want to skin me alive if I spoke against them, if I said what Gamps did to me. Either way the fear was taking over—like, no matter how hard I was trying to stare it down, it refused to look away.

I could hear Cinnamon saying my name over and over. "Daisy, Daisy. Are you there? Daisy?" I didn't know what to say or what to do. So I just lay right back down on the hot earth and watched another plane lift off into the sky.

CHAPTER FIFTEEN

The courtroom is too small and too hot. Sitting at this table in a stuffy pantsuit makes Cinnamon feel like a criminal, even though it's not that kind of hearing. Maybe it's being back in front of Judge Harlow, who oozes imperious impatience as he looms over his courtroom like a terrifying god. Those bushy eyebrows are trained down on them—sentinels on alert for any sign of troublemaking. There's a shocking indifference in his affect as he announces that the morning's proceedings will soon begin to decide on custody for "Baby 5370." *Her name is Bluebell!* That's what Cinnamon wants to scream. Bluebell isn't even a "real" name. It's better than a number but still reeks of impermanence, symbolic of this whole enterprise, shaky and tentative.

She feels like a small child, sitting alone at the vast table facing the judge, like a kid waiting for the principal. Cinnamon can't bear to let her eyes stray an inch to the right, over to the table next to her, where the Jacobses sit. They hired a lawyer who's a pasty version of Omar and so out of place and twitchy he might as well have fleas biting his butt. Cinnamon eyed the Rolex encircling his hairy wrist earlier in the hallway, so massive and gleaming that one could spot it a mile away. At odds with the designer watch was the row of tattoos on each of his knuckles.

Aunt Celia had offered to pay Omar's exorbitant fees to come to court with her today, but Cinnamon turned her down. It was a nice offer but she didn't want—or need—any of Celia's ingratiating gestures, and she worried having Omar and all his pomp and ego here might even hurt her. She's rethinking that now that the Jacobses have someone on their side, no doubt bankrolled by the windfall from selling their family land.

Cinnamon cranes her neck to the left, away from the Jacobses, swiveling it all the way to the back of the room for reassurance. Her little posse sits in a row like ducks on one of four oak benches that look remarkably similar to church pews. It's the first time in Cinnamon's life that she feels like she has a team behind her—literally. This must be close to what it feels like to have a family.

The first person she sees is Lucia, and her friend's eyes scream *Stay strong—you got this.* Lucia holds Bluebell up from her lap as if reminding Cinnamon the reason she needs to stay fierce. She maneuvers Bluebell's itty-bitty arm to do a quick baby fist pump in the air, and when Cinnamon laughs, she looks to the judge to see if he notices her trespass, but he's still shuffling papers.

So she turns back around to Reverend Rick, who surprised her by making the trip all the way from Atlanta this morning. She wasn't even awake when he'd called; he just left her a message that she listened to at 6 a.m.: "I'm calling at the butt crack of dawn to tell you I'm on my way. I'm going to have to stop and piss a thousand times with all the coffee I'm gonna need to guzzle, but I'mma be there."

Cinnamon can't make eye contact with him because his head is deeply bowed in prayer, which feels exactly right. She'll take all she can get. His mere presence is a welcome reminder that people as good and kind as the Rev live and walk among us every day, but like the air we breathe, we never notice how they support and nourish us.

The biggest surprise guest sits next to Reverend Rick. It's not Jayson, though that too would have been a surprise. But she knew better than to expect him to come. All she'd gotten was a text this morning that read *I hope this works out the way you want.* She couldn't tell if it was sincere or not, but she'd written back a thank-you and added a smiley face. It was strange to communicate with her husband through emojis, but she also didn't have the energy to hide her disappointment that he was a no-show in her life, not just today but the last few weeks.

The person she didn't expect was Abigail. She didn't expect her last week either when she'd shown up out of the blue with a chicken soup casserole, a bottle of rye, and a whole heap of thoughts about her son.

Cinnamon could no more have foreseen an evening having a heart-to-heart with her mother-in-law than she could have foreseen hearing Abigail say a bad word about her Jayson. So she kept checking the backyard for flying pigs as she and her mother-in-law had the first real talk of their lives, which might have been the most ironic timing in history. Abigail opened the conversation by admitting how she coddled Jayson too much. She wasn't one of those mothers who blamed herself for any of her child's weaknesses, mistakes, or shortcomings, but she knew her son could be stubborn and selfish. And that even as a grown man pushing forty, he had more growing up to do. The true kicker was when Abigail said how she thought Cinnamon had been good for Jayson. Cinnamon couldn't hide her surprise after years of Abigail's aloof indifference and her subsequent conclusion that her mother-in-law found her lacking in just about every respect. Lips loosened by the two sips of whiskey she'd had to be polite, Cinnamon finally confessed this. "I always got the impression that you didn't think I was good *enough* for your son."

"No, no—it wasn't that. I could tell you were a good girl, Cinnamon. Softhearted and kind. If I was standoffish, it's because I wasn't ready to share Jay with any woman, not after he'd finally returned home to me. With Wallace gone, Jayson's all the family I got. I wanted a gaggle of kids, but it wasn't in the cards for Wallace and me. After Jayson, none of the pregnancies took, so I poured everything into him. He became my whole life, and that probably hasn't been good . . . for either of us. I can see that now that he's been living under my roof these last few weeks, leaving his stuff everywhere, knowing I'll clean it up and make whatever meals he requests, even flush the darn toilet for him. Catering to him like that, I set the bar too high for any woman or wife. It's probably why he thinks he can get away with doing whatever he pleases. Probably why he didn't bat an eye when he borrowed every nickel and dime I've saved to keep bailing out his restaurant project, not that I wasn't happy to give it to him. But then he didn't really give me a choice either. He really just doesn't take no for an answer, that boy."

The way Abigail said she thought Cinnamon, Jayson's wife, knew about this, which is a reasonable assumption—but she didn't. She had no idea that Jayson hadn't just drained their own bank accounts, but his mother's retirement too. Cinnamon tried to hide her shock at Abigail's revelation by getting up to get them some ice water. In the process of opening the freezer, she jiggled the picture she'd just put up there, loose from the magnet holding it to the fridge door. She lunged for it before it hit the floor as if it were going to disintegrate if it touched the linoleum.

"Can I see it?" Abigail holds out her hand and takes the photo with a reverence that mirrors Cinnamon's pride. "No surprise you're so good-looking, coming from these two."

Cinnamon was pleased that she didn't have to explain who they were—it was obvious. They were her parents. She didn't have to know them for that to be true.

"You know, we have a lot in common, Cinnamon. My mom left me early on too. When I was a baby, she worked for a white family here in town, cleaning and watching their two kids who were barely younger than me and my sister. When they moved to Chicago, they offered to double her salary if she went with them. They said they'd pay for her to come home on holidays and two weeks in the summer. She couldn't pass up the money. She left us with my grandma Joannie. It used to burn me up that those white kids got to see *my* mother every single day. Damned that it still does, even though I knew she was doing it for us. She moved back when I was thirteen, and maybe it was the timing, me being in the throes of puberty and all, or maybe too much time had passed, but I was so mean to her, so angry. She always sent presents, saved enough to pay for me to go to college, and well, she was able to buy this house you're living in right now. I should have been grateful, but all I could feel was . . . robbed, you know? And I let her know it. I feel bad about that to this day."

Abigail took a big sip of whiskey as if to swallow down her regret. Then she got up and started collecting dirty dishes because that's what you did. Cinnamon recognized the impulse. You got on with things. You didn't have a choice—heartache dies hard.

"I don't know if Jayson and I are going to make it, Abigail."

The only way Cinnamon could say this was to Abigail's back, in a whisper.

"Well, I'd be sorry to see that. Mainly for his sake, if I'm honest. But I get it, honey. I get it. There are no sides here. Well, I'll always be 'Team Jayson,' as the kids say, because I'm his momma. But I'm also a woman, and I was a wife too. I know how hard both can be. I wish I had some better wisdom for you, but what I can tell you is this: sometimes we women have to fight to put ourselves first. It don't come as natural for us, so we have to work harder at it."

"I love him. I want you to know that—I do."

"I know, honey. I know. But I think you think that you *need* him too. Those two things are all too easy to confuse, love and need. And that'll get you in trouble every time."

"But what if I can't do it alone?" Cinnamon's voice was getting smaller and smaller, shrinking right along with the chances that her marriage would survive. Abigail turned from the sink and her bony, veiny hand reached for Cinnamon's. "Oh, honey, you're not alone. You've got people. You've got me."

When Abigail smiles at her now in the courtroom, it's as if she knows this is what Cinnamon is thinking. If Lucia's eyes said, *You got this*, Abigail's remind her, *You've got people*.

Cinnamon's eyes trail to the empty space on the other side of Abigail. A Daisy-size emptiness. She's called a dozen times since they'd spoken once, and she's texted the date and time of this hearing a half dozen more, and Daisy hasn't responded. It's like she's disappeared all over again. Gone without a trace. Along with Cinnamon's optimism about today's outcome.

Judge Harlow looks out at her and the Jacobses like he's already tired, and the hearing hasn't even started yet. He uses the sharp clank of the gavel to bring order, even though the room is already all but silent.

Cinnamon braces herself with a deep breath and a long look at Bluebell. The next part will go fast. There are only two possible outcomes today. The judge decides to give the Jacobses custody, in which case Cinnamon will have to surrender her to them immediately. Or Bluebell continues to be a ward of the state, which can opt to continue to keep her in Cinnamon's care.

"Let's start with hearing from the state. I'd like to hear from the child's advocate first."

Lindsay Holken pops to her feet from a little area for court personnel to the left of the judge. She's Bluebell's representative today, a court-appointed lawyer who will speak to the best interests of the baby. Cinnamon had talked to the woman at length two days ago—a conversation that felt like a cross between a hostile interrogation and a therapy session. Lindsay knew everything Cinnamon knew about Derek Jacobs's record, and it clearly concerned her despite Lindsay repeatedly emphasizing her impartiality.

"Yes, Your Honor." Lindsay holds an impossibly sharp No. 2 pencil in one hand and taps it against her other palm. "I'm representing the interests of Baby 5370, who was taken into state custody after being found abandoned in a county park. She was placed in the care of Cinnamon Haynes as an emergency foster parent in a hearing in Your Honor's court and now we need to make a determination of guardianship based on a claim put forth by the child's biological great-grandparents."

Lindsay starts to talk about the work she's done investigating the issue and what's detailed in the report she'd previously submitted for the judge's review.

Cinnamon is the last to notice. It's not the door opening or closing that tips her off or even the hush in the room like the barometric pressure falling just before a bad storm; it's Derek Jacobs's loud whisper—"You've gotta be kidding me"—that alerts her that someone has entered the courtroom. That someone is Daisy Jacobs.

When all eyes turn to her, you can tell she's fighting not to run right back out the door. So much so that Cinnamon springs to her feet and screams, "Don't go, Daisy. Don't!" Her eyes bore into the girl's like the sheer force of her will will keep her here. And it works. Daisy stands frozen and blinking like a scared deer. Daisy nods at Cinnamon so slightly she wonders if she'd imagined it, before taking a few steps forward in the narrow aisle between the row of benches. If clothes could break your heart, then Daisy's ill-fitting black slacks and white polyester button-up with sweat stains growing at the pits would do it.

"I'm the . . . the mother, Judge." Daisy's head is trained forward as if she's in a neck brace that will not allow her head to move right or left, only straight ahead, at the bench.

Judge Harlow looks less surprised than vindicated, like he just knew today was going to go off the rails and he's happy that his instincts for such things remain so sharp, if not that this melodrama is unfolding in his courtroom.

"The hell you can come back now!" Derek screams, slamming his flat palms on the table. Daisy winces but still doesn't look their way.

The judge bangs his gavel and glares at everyone. Cinnamon sits back down in the face of the judge's withering glare. She still stares at Daisy though, right there in the flesh. She's afraid if she blinks, she'll disappear.

No one seems quite sure what to do, so Cinnamon steps into the vacuum by standing back up. "Your Honor, can we have a . . . recess?" She mumbles lines she's seen on every legal show she's watched, even as she doesn't have any actual authority or place asking for this. But the judge surprises her by agreeing to a fifteen-minute break, and she wastes no time jumping up and shepherding Daisy by the elbow past the confused onlookers toward an empty conference room she saw down the hall.

As soon as she closes the door behind her, Cinnamon grabs Daisy's hand. She has to touch her skin to prove to herself that she's really here. There are a dozen things Cinnamon wants to say to Daisy. She wants to hug her and shake her . . . or give her a sharp slap. All of the above. She's anticipated this conversation ever since she found Bluebell behind that bench, but now that it's actually happening, she finds she's at a loss for where to even begin. She reaches for the basics.

"Are you okay?"

She regrets the silly question as soon as it leaves her lips; of course this sweaty, shuddering girl in front of her is not okay.

Daisy shakes her head.

"I understand. This is a lot. But you did it. You made it." She squeezes her hand hard, but Daisy's remains limp. "I would have sent you a ticket, Daisy. How did you even get here?"

Daisy stands there so still and silent it's not clear if she even hears Cinnamon speaking.

Cinnamon squeezes again. "Daisy?"

The squeeze is enough to trigger whatever Daisy has been holding inside her. Tears spring from her eyes. She barely makes it to the closest chair as her shoulders heave with the effort of containing all the emotions she's clearly bottled up for so long. "I'm sorry. I'm sorry," she repeats over and over. Cinnamon squeezes her hand again and Daisy clutches it like a vise.

"You don't need to apologize. You did the right thing by coming. Thank you. I know it was hard." Cinnamon repeats the question. "How did you get here?"

"I didn't have enough for a bus ticket, but I finally called Caleb. I . . . He was the guy I was living with. I know you guys have been in touch, and he wanted to be here today when I told him about the hearing. He sent the money for a bus ticket. And he called me last night and said he was going to call in sick today and come here, come be with me. He's on his way. It's like a six-hour drive, but he's coming. He's coming. He's coming to be with me." She repeats it as if to reassure herself. *Help is on the way.*

"I'm glad to hear that." Cinnamon brushes Daisy's hair away from her tear-soaked cheeks. "Caleb's a good friend. And we can get this all sorted now, okay?"

But what does "sorted" even mean? Daisy may have showed up today, and it's clear she didn't do it to make a claim to be Bluebell's mother, but Cinnamon still has to ask. She'd promised herself that she would.

"Daisy, is this what you really want? Do you truly want to give up your child? Because it isn't too late. I can go in there with you and we can talk to the judge and the social workers, and you can explain why you did what you did."

Daisy is already shaking her head, but Cinnamon needs to keep going.

"I've been doing all this, keeping her from the police, getting certified to foster, coming to court like this, so that I could find you, so I could find you and talk to you and try to convince you to be her mother. Are you sure you want to give her up?"

"I'm sure." Daisy says it with more conviction than Cinnamon's ever heard from the girl. "I know it seems like I didn't think it through, but I've never thought about anything harder. I know what I want. Cinnamon, please. Will you do it? Will you keep her?"

Cinnamon knew her answer even before she heard the desperation in Daisy's voice. She knew her answer weeks ago. She knew her answer maybe from the first moment she heard the soft mewling in the woods. She just hasn't said it out loud, only in her heart. Four words to change her life.

"Yes, Daisy. I will."

Daisy's shoulders collapse in relief, and Cinnamon hugs the girl, though neither of them really know what to do with the weight of the agreement they've made other than hold on to each other for dear life for a full minute.

"But if I'm going to be able to do this, Daisy, you're going to have to make it clear to the judge that's what you want. It's the only way. When we go back in there, the judge is going to want you to get on the witness stand and explain why you want me to have the baby. Why you don't want your grandparents to have the baby. And I'm assuming you have good reasons for that?"

Daisy's eyes dart around the room like a caged animal. "I do; I do have . . . reasons. But I don't know if I can get up there, Cinnamon. I guess I didn't think they'd be here . . . in real life . . . I don't know if I can." She crosses her arms and starts rocking herself.

She looks much younger than her nineteen years. Cinnamon has a flash to that first night she spent with Reverend Rick at the church when she was only slightly younger than Daisy. How he made her soup and grilled cheese that she swallowed down in minutes, how he asked her how she ended up living behind the Laundromat in Bessie, and she just didn't know where to start or who to blame. All she'd felt was shame that she ended up where she did. It's the same confusion and shame she sees all over Daisy. *How did I end up here?*

"It's just seeing them. Seeing him. After so long. It brings it all back." That the "it" is traumatizing is made clear by the way Daisy is completely shutting down, burrowing within herself to a place no one can reach her.

"I know how that feels." And she does. She felt it when she went to see Aunt Celia in Atlanta and revisited all the demons from her own past, but she also knows without asking that what haunts Daisy is far beyond that—the kind of trauma that can never be erased, the kind that will hold you in its grip for all your days.

"I don't know how I can talk about the things my grandfather did to me in front of this whole courtroom. Cinnamon, he hurt me. He . . ."

She stops midsentence and looks out the window, almost as if she's looking for an escape. Cinnamon expects her to pick back up, but Daisy goes silent, unable to continue. If she can't talk about what Derek did here, alone with Cinnamon in this tiny room, how will she do it in front of so many people, including the man who abused her?

"Your baby needs you right now, Daisy. I need you. I'm here and I'm fighting because I'm going to do what you asked me. I want to raise her. But in order for me to do that, you have to help me. You have to help her. I know this will be a terrible, terrible moment for you, but this is what it's gonna take to create the life you want for her. I know you can do it. You do your part up there, and I'll do mine. I promise you that."

Cinnamon can vow to do her part, but she can't guarantee much else. And she feels like part of the vow is empty because how can she protect Daisy from what revisiting her past in front of all these people will do to her? She's racking her brain for a better solution—maybe Daisy can talk privately to Lindsay Holken—but there's something else they need to know.

"Do you know who the father is, Daisy?"

"I don't. I mean, I do—it's not like I slept with a bunch of guys and don't know. What I mean is, all I know is the guy's name. Zach."

"Okay, okay. We can worry about that later." Cinnamon takes in a deep breath and thinks about calling Omar to get his take as another round of shudders overtakes Daisy's body. Cinnamon is quickly losing faith that she'll get Daisy out of this room, let alone to speak in front of the judge.

She's hoping the knock on the door when it comes is reinforcement—maybe Lucia could help her support Daisy. But when Cinnamon opens the door, there's no ally on the other side. Standing there, stiff as a statue, and so close to the door that she could have been listening to everything, is Barbara Jacobs.

"Can I talk to Amanda?"

This is not Cinnamon's question to answer, but she looks over at Daisy, who doesn't agree to talk to her grandmother but doesn't object either, so Cinnamon allows Barbara in.

"Gam?" Daisy's voice trembles.

"I'm so sorry, Amanda." Barbara makes no move to comfort her granddaughter, or to walk any farther into the room than she has to. It's clear she came here to say something, and once she gets it out, she'll be on her way.

"I didn't know you would show up today, but you're here and you clearly do not want your grandfather and me to raise your daughter. You have your reasons—I know that. I told him we won't fight you. I won't fight you. I'll get him out of here. You can make your wishes known to the court."

Daisy stands on legs as shaky as a newborn foal's. She stares hard at her grandmother but remains silent.

Barbara nods once at her granddaughter and once at Cinnamon before pivoting on her heel and exiting the room.

"I can't believe it," Daisy whispers.

"You can't believe she backed down?"

"No, I can't believe she stood up to him. She's never done it. Not once—never in her life."

Cinnamon chooses her next words carefully. "Did she know that he hurt you?"

Daisy just shakes her head. "I'll never know."

The silence that follows reminds Cinnamon of their time together on the bench, all those Fridays. How as much as they'd enjoyed gabbing away, how they were also perfectly content passing the quiet between them.

After a moment Daisy speaks, and Cinnamon knows exactly what's coming.

"She's here, right?"

Cinnamon doesn't have to be told that Daisy means Bluebell.

"Yeah. She's with my friend Lucia . . . in the courtroom."

"Can I . . . can I see her if I wanted?"

"Of course you can."

"Okay. I'm not sure if I want to though." The words rush out of her like if she doesn't stop her, Cinnamon is going to dash down the hall and run back thrusting the baby at her.

"You don't have to decide now." Cinnamon says this in the same soothing voice she uses on Bluebell to calm her down after bath time—the slightest drop of water on her skin almost always sends the baby into fits.

Daisy walks over to the window, rests her head against the cool glass.

"What did you name her?"

"I've been calling her Bluebell."

"That's nice; I like that. Like the ice cream."

"Well, it's been a nickname, sort of like Daisy for you."

"Yeah, it was weird to even hear Amanda today. I haven't been Amanda in forever. It kinda felt like I left her back in Leesville, even like she died or something. But I guess you can't just go and leave the bad parts of you behind. They always come and find you."

Ain't that the truth? It's impossible to hide from yourself. If there's one thing Cinnamon has learned this past month or so, it was that.

"When I talked to Caleb," Cinnamon says, "he told me you started calling yourself Daisy after your mom's favorite flowers . . . What's your favorite flower?"

"I don't know . . . I've always liked lilies, I suppose. Caleb's dad used to get them for his mom all the time, and he always stole one for me. I'd put it in an empty Coke bottle next to my bed so I could see it every morning when I woke up."

Cinnamon walks to Daisy and drapes her arm around the girl's shoulders. The moment washes over her like the long hot showers she misses—finally something that feels exactly right and in both of their control. The one thing they can choose together for this beautiful baby's future.

"I think that's it, don't you?" Cinnamon says. "Lily."

"Lily?"

"It's perfect. She's a Lily."

So much else remains uncertain, and the journey ahead is long. Yet naming the child feels like an accomplishment completely out of proportion with the simplicity of the task. This one big little thing that makes everything else, everything to come, feel possible.

And it is indeed perfect.

EPILOGUE

Dear Lily,

The years pile up, whether you want them to or not, until you can scramble up to the top of them and look down at what you've built at the end. I'm being too dramatic—it's not the end; that's not the way to look at it. It's also a beginning. Always a fine line between the two.

You'll be eighteen years old tomorrow. I can hardly believe it. I won't write "time flies," because the other day my writing class professor had us make a list of the biggest clichés so we could avoid them. Right up there at the top was "time flies," just before "you can't judge a book by its cover" and "ignorance is bliss."

For the record, though, those are true too.

You know, it's funny how I spent so much of my life trying to forget, and then after you came along, all I wanted was to remember. Every single detail. It's why I started writing these letters to you on your birthday every year—it wasn't just for you, to give them to you one day in the future (at your birthday party tomorrow). It was a way for me to document who you were as you grew into yourself. I could capture all the memories, a lifetime of them, like fireflies in a jar.

I was going to try to reread all of them last night, but I got as far as the first one, the one I wrote the day after your first birthday, and the nostalgia was too much to bear, like the way too-sweet lemonade makes your tongue pucker—that's how it was with my heart. I'm getting sentimental in my old age.

We went all out with a zoo theme for that birthday—even though you could have cared less about themes and decorations and colors schemes. But you know who cares about that sort of thing? Tia Luce. She even decided we had to have an actual live llama who cowered in the backyard for two hours before some pimple-faced teenager picked her up and took her back to the farm where she belonged. Tia Luce was always one to go all out, especially for birthdays, even though I told her you wouldn't even remember. She said, "That's not the point. We're creating a vibe—one that she'll carry with her her whole life as a feeling, even if she doesn't remember the details." She's not wrong. She's not wrong about most things. Because it's true. Most of the people who were at that party may have drifted from our lives one way or another, but they imprinted you with love.

Like Jayson. He brought you a too-big shirt with "The Ruins" printed on it—that was the name of a restaurant he had for a few years before he agreed to sell the space to a national chain that billed itself to him as the "Olive Garden of Seafood." Cashed out and followed a lady friend to Tampa where they've been flipping houses and offering seminars about how other people can get rich doing it too. You never knew Jayson, but everything about that is exactly right.

You were so surprised when you learned I had even been married before. That's the way with kids—they find it shocking that their mothers had a whole other life before them. But sometimes, I'm surprised I was married too. I lost too much time being preoccupied with one question: Would that marriage last? Looking back, all those tears and sleepless nights, all that agonizing, was a waste and only served to drag out the inevitable. Because I knew it wouldn't. Not that we didn't try, did some counseling and all that, but ultimately, it was just so clear that we had completely different ideas about how to live in the world. I craved stability and security, and he wanted to dream and act big. He also couldn't find a way to share me with you. Jayson always needed to be the star, and that can never be the case when there's a baby in the house. It's no surprise he's never had any kids.

I chose you, but I also chose me, because for once it was my time, my chance to get something I wanted—and you were it. Even if it took some time to be able to listen to myself and understand that. It took some time to stop reaching and let go. I think you'll find in this life that you always have a pretty good sense of what's going to happen before it does—the gut is a powerful thing. You just have to be prepared to listen to it and to face things, to be clear on what you want. My wish for you is that you learn that lesson faster than I did.

Sometimes I miss Jayson, his lopsided grin and the way he could always find a way or a reason to employ it. The best thing Jayson did for me is help me learn to love myself when I wasn't sure how to go about that. Experiencing his love for me, flawed as it may have been, made me believe I deserved it, his love and my own. It's pleasant to think he's out there, probably dreaming up some new scheme. The world is dotted with people you cross paths with, whether for a few minutes or days or years, and they change you. Jayson brought me to Sibley Bay, which brought me to you—the true love of my life. And you got an amazing grandma out of the deal, even if she came without the father.

I miss Reverend Rick too. I imagine him raising hell in heaven, all the hand-tailored neon-colored suits of his dreams in an endless closet. Back at your first birthday party, he looked at you sleeping in my lap, wiped out from the sugar crash after the gigantic elephant-shaped cake Susie made for you in honor of your favorite stuffie. I asked him what he was smiling so big about, and he said, "Don't the Lord work in mysterious ways?"

And I have to trust that's true, even if my relationship with God has always been sorta shaky. I need all the help I can get sending you out into the world. I was crazy to agree that you could spend this summer before college in London being a big-time intern with that tech start-up with the funny name. I can't wait to come visit you. My very first passport came in the mail yesterday, all shiny and blue, the empty pages like a book that hasn't been written just yet, one I get to write all by myself. But still, I can't believe you'll be so far away. Then—a college girl. An Emory girl! And another prayer answered: that your entire education was paid for by my aunt Celia, a woman you never even met. She created the account for you right before she passed on. God sure does work in mysterious ways.

It goes without saying that Ruby and I are going to miss you like crazy. She keeps pretending she's glad to finally have your bedroom all to herself and has already made me promise to move your twin bed out so she has room for her "recording studio." To be fair that girl's got a set of pipes on her.

When we moved to Atlanta, two bedrooms seemed

plenty for us. You were so fiercely protective of your space and had spent the full year getting your bedroom exactly how you wanted it. I still can't believe I let you paint your walls black, but it grew on me, your cozy cave. So I was pretty nervous to tell you that you were getting a foster sister. Reverend Rick called me in the middle of the night. "You're still certified to be a foster parent, right?" I was, but I'd never thought about doing it again, truth be told. But I'd also do anything for the Rev, and he'd found another child—our dear Ruby—who needed me. "She reminds me of you, Cinnamon. Always got her nose in a book. Mom's been coming to my fellowship for years and got herself hooked on that H. I'm trying to help the woman get herself together. But in the meantime, will you take her?" There was only one answer. But for ten years, it had been just me and you, like the Gilmore Girls, with more melanin. You didn't bat an eye though. All you said was, "I'll have a sister, and I didn't even have to wait nine months. And she already knows how to play dolls and soccer, so it's perfect."

I'm tearing up thinking about our little weird family. People love to say families come in all shapes and sizes but then get all judgmental when it's not a mom and a dad and three kids who all match perfectly and came from the woman's womb as a result of nice missionary sex. Oh, don't be so scandalized that your mom said "sex"; you're too grown for that now. (Even if I was too scandalized myself when it came time to have that talk and made Tia Lucia do it for me.)

But all the looks and judgments and questions about how a woman like me had a daughter like you and maybe there was a nice white daddy somewhere, a white daddy with real strong genes . . . all of that made us stronger. When you were little and stamped your foot and said,

"That's my momma!" when anyone was doubtful or confused . . . nothing could make my day more.

They were—and still are—the most delightful words in the whole world. "That's my momma."

Which brings me to what I've really been wanting to get to in this letter, and I've been procrastinating. Your birth mother. I know you've heard the story of how I found you and fell in love with you. It was like putting on a pair of glasses you didn't know you needed. Getting to see the world through your eyes made it all seem brand-new and more interesting. You gave me a purpose I didn't know I was looking for and a love I couldn't even comprehend. You made all the colors brighter, my Lily.

Okay, okay—let me stop with all that. I know you hate it when I get so mushy. Your birth mother—Daisy—asked me to give you a series of letters she wrote to you over the years (that's something, huh? Both of us writing you letters—you'll be able to publish a whole book between them) when you got to be eighteen. She also told me to give you her contact information in case you wanted to reach out, which is entirely up to you. She said waiting for you to be eighteen was as much for her as for you. "I want to make something of myself. I want to show her that I didn't give her up for nothing," she told me. And she didn't. She really did make something of herself, putting herself through school and becoming an air traffic controller. Granted, it wasn't the same dream she had when I met her. Back then she wanted to be a pilot. But it's close. She gets to watch the planes take off and keep everyone safe. I'll feel better about you flying around here and there, knowing she's on the case. I'm giving you her letters here, along with this one. I think it'll be clear from them how much she loved you, still loves you. I've sent her some pictures through the years, and she always wrote back, "Please make sure she knows how much I love her."

I hope these letters answer some of the questions you've had about her for all these years. I suspect you'll feel one way reading these letters now, if you're ready, and feel differently reading them again in five years and in ten. That's okay; that's what life is all about—experience and perspective changing the shape of what you know or think to be true about yourself and others. Don't be afraid of that messiness, because in it is the beauty, like when we would dig for oysters at Bailey Beach—all the wet marshy muck under your fingernails was worth it to pull out the best one. Made you squeal every time.

It's hard to see that now. Being a middle-school guidance counselor and raising you two girls has taught me that no one is more hardheaded than a teenager. (But that's fine because I like a challenge!) You think you're more grown than you are, and you roll your eyes at me just about every chance you get, and you have no patience for the very good advice I try to give you, but I'm going to end this letter with some anyway. What kind of mother would I be without sending you off with at least a few nuggets of wisdom?

When you're feeling low, step into a hot shower. It solves 80 percent of your problems. Snacks and naps help too. If you're looking for an answer, it can usually be found in a book. The world is not always going to make sense, so it's important to make your own sense, to create your own beliefs and order and reality. Don't let anyone ever tell you it's too late for anything. Because that's a lie—it's never too late for the life you want. I'm living proof, having become a "college girl" myself at the ripe age of forty-two. I'm going to be screaming just as loudly when you graduate from high school in a few weeks as you did when your momma walked across the stage in my cap and gown. And finally, you can always come home. I didn't have that luxury, and it is the one thing I want to give to you. I will always be your home, and you can always come back to me.

The world is soon going to be yours, baby girl. But remember this: you may have been carried by someone else, you may not look a lick like me, we may not share the same blood, DNA, or color, but none of that mattered when it came to what was meant to be. There's so little I know for sure in life except this: you were always mine.

ACKNOWLEDGMENTS

We have to start with our publishing family, as we think of them as exactly that. We love you, Atria Books! You're a mighty force and your passion and enthusiasm, hard work, and publishing vision make us feel like the luckiest two authors on earth. The same holds true for our agents, Byrd Leavell and Pilar Queen, who we just think of as the Dazzling Duo, like a superhero team, which they are. Their magical power is unwavering support. We also endlessly adore our UK publisher, HQ Books. And we are lucky to have Susan Armstrong on our side. To the entire teams on both sides of the pond: we appreciate you.

No book comes out of the womb fully formed. We're indebted to many early readers who were generous in their feedback and suggestions, among them Casey Scieszka, Brenda Copeland, Lesley Grossberg, and Kara Logan Berlin.

We had the opportunity to interview many incredible people involved in foster care in various capacities to make sure our depiction of Bluebell's care and Cinnamon's journey are accurate. Many thanks to all of you, especially to Sarah Sentilles, whose book *Stranger Care* was an eye-opening and heartrending glimpse into the humans impacted by this system.

Christine: I am beyond grateful for the incredible and deep tribe of women in my life. The one thing they all have in common—besides being brilliant, hilarious, and kind—is that they're all mothers. Seeing them raise adorable little humans brings me more joy than I could have imagined when we were all young and childless. And insofar as motherhood involves offering unconditional support and guidance and love, I'm also grateful to them for mothering *me*—including, at times, helping me pick out clothes and reminding me to go to the bathroom before long trips. I love you all. Your inspiration, I hope, shines in the pages. And given that love makes all things feel more possible, even writing, I'm also grateful for you, Cricket. You're a marvel.

Jo: There is no playbook for how to become a mother. If I have learned anything over the past six years of breeding it's that no one knows exactly how to do this. But I have had some stellar guides throughout my journey, both men and women from so many different generations. My own tribe of mama friends has helped me navigate this stage of life while also being a creative human in the world, and I couldn't be more grateful. I also want to thank my husband for making it possible for me to have the space and time to do the work that I do, as well as my mother, Tracey Piazza, who takes our children for entire weekends at a time, and our caregiver, Tshiamo Monnakgotla, who did all the things while I wrote this book.

Lastly, we both have buckets of gratitude for all the readers who open their hearts to our stories and debate, discuss, support, and share. If it wasn't for you, there wouldn't be any point to any of this—so thank you.

you were always mine

CHRISTINE PRIDE & JO PIAZZA

This reading group guide for **You Were Always Mine** *includes an introduction, discussion questions, ideas for enhancing your book club, and a Q&A with authors* **Christine Pride** *and* **Jo Piazza***. The suggested questions are intended to help your reading group find new and interesting angles and topics for your discussion. We hope that these ideas will enrich your conversation and increase your enjoyment of the book.*

Introduction

The acclaimed authors of the "emotional literary roller coaster" (*The Washington Post*) and *Good Morning America* Book Club pick *We Are Not Like Them* return with this moving and provocative novel about a Black woman who finds an abandoned white baby, sending her on a collision course with her past, her family, and a birth mother who doesn't want to be found.

Topics & Questions for Discussion

1. In the beginning of the novel (page 30), Mother's Day brings up a flurry of emotions for Cinnamon and Daisy. Daisy's mother died when she was young and Cinnamon's mother abandoned her as a baby, leaving them both to grieve a similar loss under different circumstances. How do you think these losses affect their individual views of motherhood?
2. Do you feel Cinnamon's experience of being abandoned as a baby and spending her childhood in the foster care system was a major factor in why she chose to bring Bluebell into her home rather than involving the authorities right away? Why or why not?
3. In addition to themes of motherhood, *You Were Always Mine* has many frank conversations about race. In chapter four, Cinnamon recounts a personal experience being in foster care when a white woman took her to the local art museum to see a collection of nineteenth-century photographs of Black caretakers. Cinnamon has flashbacks of one photograph she saw that day of a young Black child caring for an infant white baby. Why do you think after all these years Cinnamon is remembering this photograph and how do the feelings it brings up influence her thinking about the possibility of raising Bluebell?
4. Along those lines, Cinnamon's husband, Jayson, says that it would be impossible for him as a Black man to raise a white little girl, to even take her to the park. How do you think his fears impact Cinnamon's decision-making about both Bluebell and their marriage?
5. Throughout the novel, readers experience every step of Cinnamon caring for Bluebell in real time, whereas we mostly hear from Daisy through a series of letters, recounting her reasons for leaving Bluebell,

her journey, and her reflections about her past and future. Do Cinnamon and Daisy's alternating voices highlight any important similarities or differences about their experiences and decisions during the novel? Did you relate to one character in particular?

6. In Cinnamon and Lucia's quest to track down Daisy, the pair of friends learn of unsettling information about Daisy's grandfather having ties to a white supremacist group (page 122). How do you think this might initially impact Cinnamon's feelings toward Daisy? Bluebell?

7. Much of this story focuses on the characters grappling with, revisiting, and coming to terms with their pasts. Why do you think Cinnamon decided to keep her time in foster care a secret from those closest to her, especially Jayson?

8. Daisy grew up never knowing her mother or father, just like Cinnamon. Do you think this influenced the connection the two women made?

9. Daisy was raised in an openly racist household, having never known anyone who wasn't white for a majority of her life. Daisy's friendship with Cinnamon is one she recognized would anger her grandfather, but she kept this grim satisfaction to herself (pages 173–174). Do you think that factored into her decision to leave Bluebell with Cinnamon one way or another?

10. How does Lucia's open judgment impact Cinnamon and her decision to temporarily care for Bluebell? Is Lucia right to share her opinion on Cinnamon's choices? Why or why not?

11. Do you believe Cinnamon should have consulted Jayson before agreeing to foster Bluebell? What if he'd refused; should she then have left Bluebell to the foster system?

12. Cinnamon's experience with family, outside of her grandma Thelma, was very traumatic. She experienced abandonment, unstable living conditions, and felt disposed of by family members who agreed to care for her in place of her birth parents. When Celia tries to re-enter Cinnamon's life, she is forced to work through her past. What do you think Cinnamon should have done? Did Aunt Celia deserve forgiveness?

13. One of the important themes of this book is the idea of chosen family

and Cinnamon finds that in her first best friend, Lucia. How does this friendship affect Cinnamon? When Lucia says "I've got you" (page 203), how do you think these three simple words make Cinnamon feel? Supported? Relieved? What might this mean to Cinnamon in the long term?

14. Is Jayson's response to learning about Cinnamon's time in foster care and homelessness warranted? Does the fact that she kept so much from him make Cinnamon a stranger or were you sympathetic to her reasoning? Why or why not?

15. Knowing what she knows about them, what do you think Cinnamon was feeling when Taylor informed her that Daisy's grandparents were coming forward to claim the baby? Is reunification the right solution given the history? Was Cinnamon wrong to knowingly lie to Taylor at CPS? Can you understand her motivations?

Enhance Your Book Club

1. "Lucia doesn't—can't—truly get what it's like to read about a person being attacked or brutalized solely because they are Black" (page 123) and "That's the thing: she and Lucia can both be outraged at whatever injustices, but the danger just isn't the same" (page 124). In these pages, Lucia, who is Puerto Rican, vocally defends herself in a moment of racism. How are Cinnamon and Lucia's circumstances similar? How are they different? And why?

2. Daisy's decision to leave Bluebell with Cinnamon was a very personal one, and one met with little support. "That's when it hit me, the gravity of the mistake I had made. Not in having you. Not even in leaving you with Cinnamon. No, it was telling Heather . . ." (page 167). In this moment, we see why Daisy built walls around her decision, similar to how Cinnamon had a guard up around her past. How do you think Heather's reaction and condescending remarks impacted Daisy's decision-making as Bluebell's mother?

3. "I can't help but think a baby like this will have many potential families stepping forward to care for her and adopt her in the event we cannot locate the biological relatives, which I very much hope the local police are working to do as we speak" (page 212). What do you think the

judge meant by saying "a baby like this"? How do you think Cinnamon felt in hearing these words, having never been adopted out of foster care, and rather left to live out of her car after losing all support?

4. In Cinnamon's certification class for becoming a foster parent, the teacher asks if it's true that "*All you need is love*" (page 232). Is this true? What if you are raising a child in an interracial household, how might your answer change? What steps do you need to take in ensuring all of the child's needs are met, including talking with your children about where they come from?

A Conversation with Christine Pride and Jo Piazza

Q: Where did your inspiration for *You Were Always Mine* come from?

A: We love a premise that involves an enticing "what if," so it started with that nugget: *What if a Black woman found a white baby . . . and kept it?* We came up with this idea back in 2018. So, well before the world was put in a state of upheaval when it comes to reproductive choice in the wake of the repeal of *Roe V. Wade*. But now the themes feel even that much more urgent, important, and fraught to be thinking about and discussing. What does motherhood mean in America? How and why do you choose to become a mother or not? And who gets to make that choice?

Q: Christine, you are childless by choice and Jo, you gave birth to your third child during the editing process of *You Were Always Mine*. How did your decisions on and experiences with motherhood influence your novel?

A: This book is a lot like *We Are Not Like Them* in terms of our wanting to leverage a "she said/she said" perspective. We wanted to reflect the ranges of choices and thought processes and decisions women are presented with, through the lens of relatable characters and by drawing on our own personal experiences and observations, which are very different. There's no one right way to become a mother and there's no one right way not to be a mother, right? There's so much judgment in our society about those decisions, so many preconceptions about that, especially for women who are child-free by choice. There's no shortage of opinions, spoken, some unspoken, some one-on-one, some societal: *You're going to regret this* or, *it's selfish,* or, *are you really child-free by choice or you just couldn't become a mother?* Christine has heard it all!

We want to convey just how much more complicated the decision to become a mother (or not) is than typically gets presented. Because it does become such a binary choice: You become a mother, you don't become a mother. But we wanted to lean into all the nuance and the shades of gray and in doing so challenge our stereotypes and biases.

Q: Are there other parts of the story that were personal to you or drawn from your own lives as inspiration?

A. Christine's parents were foster parents and that was a significant inspiration. They went through the process to be certified as emergency foster parents when she was in middle school. Shortly thereafter, they took in two girls—one infant, one toddler—from two different families. The initial placements were supposed to be for up to seventy-two hours, but her parents ended up adopting the infant and raising her. The toddler was eventually reunited with her birth mom, but continued to spend weekends at their house through adulthood. Christine has had a front-row seat to the rewards, challenges, and complexities of foster care and the CPS system, of blending families, and of the sense of both belonging and displacement that goes hand in hand with these circumstances. That vantage point infused the story.

Q: Can you tell us a bit about your writing process and the research you did for *You Were Always Mine?*

A: We had so much trial and error getting into the collaborative groove with our first book together—there were much fewer logistical hiccups (and tears) in the process for this second go around of our partnership. As always, we outlined extensively so we would have a road map of where the story was going to go and then took turns taking the first stab at writing draft chapters, which we would then go back and forth to revise. As with *We Are Not Like Them,* much of our research involved talking to people who have experience with the foster care system; we also read a lot of first-hand accounts. The direction of the book was also driven by the deep conversations we had while writing, which is a big part of our process and a big advantage to writing as a team.

Q: Riley Wilson was a main character in your last novel, *We Are Not Like Them*. Why did you make the decision to carry her over into your newest novel, and do you plan to intertwine past voices into future works?

A: We just thought an easter egg and cameo would be so fun for readers of *We Are Not Like Them*. We're so attached to Riley and Jen as characters, it was nice to think of them living on and crossing paths with future characters. It would be fun to keep up this tradition in future books if we can find a way.

Q: Cinnamon and Daisy share similar histories. Why did you decide to have their stories align so much?

A: Daisy and Cinnamon are in a lot of ways kindred spirits given that they've both experienced a lot of family trauma and loss—it gives them an understanding of each other that underscores their instant connection and bond. Daisy and Cinnamon's stories align a lot, in the same way so many other people's stories align, which is to say it's not uncommon (sadly) that people have to navigate hard childhoods and we wanted to look at how these two characters found their respective paths as survivors.

Q: You tackle race in this book, but also class in a sense. How important was it to you to create characters that were wrestling in one way or another with these issues?

A: Very! We're very intrigued by this idea of how race plays out in intimate relationships—here a friendship and a caretaking scenario. A lot of people wouldn't think twice of a white woman taking in a Black baby, but the reverse has very different implications and we wanted the reader to be able to wrestle with those. We also have two characters who are decidedly *not* privileged in any sense of the word and that informs their choices and their options.

Our culture focuses on a model of motherhood that is affluent, white, and idealized, a version where you get to the ideal age for procreation—not too young, not too old, then sit down and look at the calendar and decide you're having a baby in spring and then order all the beautiful things from the Internet with your loving partner who is totally on board.

The fact of the matter is the vast majority of women in the world do not find themselves in that idealized scenario. Their pregnancies may be a surprise; they may not have any money to either have an abortion *or* to raise a child; they may want to have a child but not have the resources for fertility treatments or be candidates for adoption, etc., etc. And so it is for all the mothers in this story, they find themselves in more complicated—and realistic—circumstances that we don't talk about nearly enough and that we rarely see in commercial fiction.

Q: What do you hope *You Were Always Mine* will add to the conversation, and what do you hope readers will take away from your novel?

A: We hope that this book inspires people to think critically about who gets to be a mother and why and to whom? We also want people to celebrate the idea of family—especially chosen family, which most of us have in some way or another.

Q: What's next for you both?

A: We're working on another book together! It's called *I Never Knew You At All,* about a Black woman whose life is turned upside down when the grandfather of her white husband is implicated in a decades-old hate crime, exploring questions of justice, forgiveness, and what we can and cannot forgive. We're excited for you to read it in 2025!

Discover more fantastic novels from Christine Pride and Jo Piazza!

Not every story is black and white.

Riley and Jen have been best friends since they were children, and they thought their bond was unbreakable. It never mattered to them that Riley is black and Jen is white. And then Jen's husband, a Philadelphia police officer, is involved in the shooting of an unarmed black teenager and everything changes in an instant.

This one act could destroy more than just Riley and Jen's friendship. As their community takes sides, so must Jen and Riley, and for the first time in their lives the lifelong friends find themselves on opposing sides.

But can anyone win a fight like this?